THE KEEPER

NATHAN BURROWS

BLURB

When an elite team of thieves stage an audacious robbery at the Vatican in Rome, they discover something unusual about the item they are attempting to steal. Someone has beaten them to it.

Elsewhere in Rome, a wandering preacher called Caleb has what they seek in his cloth bag. His travel companion is Anita, a woman burdened by her own secrets and misfortunes, who has just escaped from a fanatical religious cult. The same cult who sponsored the robbery and are now determined to track them down. He knows he is traveling with one of the most precious artifacts known to man. But he doesn't know that it's something the cult will kill to recover.

Unwittingly entangled in Caleb's theft of the coveted relic, Anita becomes an reluctant accomplice. With danger lurking around every corner, the pair embark on a harrowing journey across the storied landscapes of Europe to return the relic to its rightful resting place. Jerusalem.

The cult members are driven by a sinister agenda and

have power and resources on their side. Their intentions for the artifact are far more malevolent than anyone could imagine. For they seek not only power but the ultimate power.

The power to bring about the cataclysmic end of days.

Blurb 2

In the heart of Rome, an elite team of thieves hatches a daring plan to steal a priceless relic from the Vatican. Little do they know, they're not the only ones with their sights set on this mysterious artifact.

Meanwhile, in the bustling streets of Rome, a wandering preacher named Caleb carries a seemingly ordinary cloth bag with a very precious cargo. His enigmatic companion, Anita, carries her own burdens and secrets, having escaped a fanatical religious cult. Unknown to them, this cult is now hunting them relentlessly, desperate to reclaim what they believe is rightfully theirs—a relic of unimaginable importance.

Caleb and Anita find themselves pursued by a relentless enemy, willing to stop at nothing to seize what they seek. Little do they realize that the artifact holds a power beyond their wildest imagination. A power the cult will kill to obtain.

With danger lurking at every turn, Caleb and Anita embark on a treacherous journey across the historic landscapes of Europe, their destination clear: Jerusalem, the relic's rightful resting place. But the cult's members are not ordinary foes; they wield sinister intentions and possess formidable resources. Their true aim reaches far beyond mere earthly power—it's a power that could trigger the cataclysmic end of days.

In this thrilling tale of adventure and intrigue, the fate of the world hangs in the balance as Caleb and Anita race against time, battling forces that seek to unleash ultimate chaos. Will they succeed in returning the relic to its sacred sanctuary, or will the cult's apocalyptic vision become a horrifying reality?

Version 2

In a world where the lines between faith and science blur, a sinister conspiracy threatens to plunge humanity into an age of darkness.

When Anita Delgado, a young woman desperate to escape the clutches of a fanatical religious cult known as the Adelphoi, steals vital information that could expose their terrifying plot, she becomes a target for powerful and ruthless enemies.

On the run and fearing for her life, Anita crosses paths with Caleb, a mysterious wandering preacher with a hidden past. Together, they must navigate a treacherous landscape of deception, betrayal, and dark forces to unravel the truth behind the Adelphoi's plan and the enigmatic Weizmann Institute's true intentions.

As they delve deeper into the conspiracy, Anita and Caleb discover that the key to stopping the impending apocalypse lies in the hands of a vulnerable young woman named Maddy, chosen by the Adelphoi for a terrifying purpose. With time running out and danger closing in from every side, Anita and Caleb must risk everything to protect Maddy and prevent the world from plunging into an abyss of suffering and despair.

From the streets of Rome to the foothills of the Alps, The Keeper is a gripping thriller that explores the consequences of blind faith, the abuse of power, and the eternal battle between good and evil. With richly drawn characters, heart-pounding action, and thought-provoking themes, this novel will keep you on the edge of your seat until the final, jaw-dropping revelation.

In a race against time, can Anita and Caleb outmaneuver the forces of darkness and save humanity from an unthinkable fate? Or will they succumb to the malevolent entities that threaten to engulf them all?

The fate of the world hangs in the balance in this electrifying tale of courage, redemption, and the ultimate fight for survival.

Version 3

Where the lines between faith and science blur, a sinister conspiracy threatens to plunge humanity into an age of darkness.

When Anita Delgado, a young woman desperate to escape the clutches of a fanatical religious cult known as the Adelphoi, steals vital information that could expose their terrifying plot, she becomes a target for powerful and ruthless enemies.

On the run and fearing for her life, Anita crosses paths with Caleb, a mysterious wandering preacher with a hidden past.

As they delve deeper into the conspiracy, Anita and Caleb discover that the key to stopping the impending apocalypse lies in the hands of a vulnerable young woman named Maddy, chosen by the Adelphoi for a terrifying purpose. With time running out and danger closing in from every side, Anita and Caleb must risk everything to protect Maddy and prevent the world from plunging into an abyss of suffering and despair.

In a race against time, can Anita and Caleb outmaneuver the forces of darkness and save humanity from an unthinkable fate?

Or will they succumb to the malevolent entities that threaten to engulf them all?

1

The earthquake during the night had been a small one, but large enough to wake Itamar and his family. Na'ama, his daughter, had come running into Itamar's bedroom in tears. She wasn't old enough to remember the last earthquake that had damaged the buildings in their small farmstead back in 1995, but the tremors the previous evening had almost destroyed the shed they used for their sheep. Itamar had to wait until sunrise to survey the damage, but the shed had needed replacing for several years and it had taken several hours to round up the sheep.

Itamar looked down at Daisy, his faithful Canaan dog whose ancestors had been herding animals in the small corner of Israel they called home for well over two thousand years, and sighed. Daisy was about five hundred yards away from the farm and pawing at a hole that was almost a foot in diameter. Itamar looked at the hole, located half-way up a small incline, and heard a plaintive bleating coming from it. One of his sheep had found its way into the hole which hadn't been there prior to the earthquake, otherwise he would have known of its existence and covered the opening to avoid exactly this situation. The land he owned was small enough for Itamar to know every inch, and he couldn't afford to lose a single sheep. Times were hard enough as it was, more so since the simmering pot that was Gaza and the occupied territories had bubbled over in the last few months.

When Itamar returned later that day with Na'ama, a flashlight, and a shovel, he widened the hole so that he could slip into it. His original plan had been to send Na'ama into the hole as she was much smaller, but his daughter had flatly refused. As he wriggled his way into the hole, Itamar realized his daughter had made the right decision. The hole gave way to a small passageway that led down into the ground at an angle. The passage was obviously hand crafted, as he could still see tool marks on the soft limestone walls. It led to a small square chamber perhaps three yards across, where he could just see his missing sheep cowering in the gloom. The chamber was musty and cloying. As Itamar shone his flashlight around, he noticed dust motes reflecting off the beam of light.

"Have you got him, Papa?" Itamar heard Na'ama calling out from above his head.

"Yes," Itamar replied, reaching forward for the lost sheep. He bent over and grabbed the animal, hoisting it onto his shoulder so he could carry it back up the passage. Then he pushed the sheep through the hole to the outside world with a grunt, feeling its weight fall away as Na'ama pulled the animal through. Itamar turned to explore the small chamber while he was there, knowing that in a short while, the entrance would be covered back over. That would be his next job for the day.

The area where Itamar and his family lived was strewn

with similar chambers. They were near to Jerusalem, a city known for being the center of three of the Abrahamic religions. Islam, Christianity, and Judaism had all vied for control over thousands of years, as had many foreign forces, with varying degrees of success. The city and the land surrounding it had been invaded, fought over, ceded, and recaptured many times. Itamar, and his father and grandfather before him, had little time for such disputes. They lived on and worked the land, but it was becoming an increasingly tough existence.

Itamar took a couple of steps into the chamber and looked around. There was little to see, and he wondered if it was just a chamber that had been made but never used. Then he saw a dark patch in the corner. When he approached, he saw it was a slab of rock, split almost perfectly down the middle. Itamar dropped to his knees and shone the flashlight into the hole, gasping when he saw what was inside. There were several large clay jars, the lids several inches thick, that looked to be covered in some sort of plaster. Shards of pottery surrounded the jars, which all had some sort of inscription on the side in a language Itamar didn't recognize.

"Papa?" Na'ama called out. "What are you doing?"

Itamar ignored his daughter as he approached the jars carefully. He needed to see what was in them. Working slowly, he pried the lid from the jar closest to him, using the knife he carried on his belt to loosen the plaster. When he peered inside, he could see what he thought was an old scroll, wrapped in linen and blackened with age.

He got to his feet, his mind racing. Itamar had heard of such discoveries. The jars and their contents could be ancient, and therefore worth a lot of money to some people. He knew he should report it to the authorities, but he also knew that the Civil Administration's Archaeology Unit was not generous with their compensation. He knew of at least one sheep farmer to the north, in Samaria, that had uncovered an archaeological site and ended up losing his land to the authorities. The compensation offered to the farmer had been a pittance, and his experience was still talked of to this day in the coffee shops Itamar frequented with his friends.

It had been in such a coffee shop that Itamar had first heard the talk of a man referred to as حارس المرمى, or *haris almarmaa* in Arabic. The equivalent in Hebrew was أَمِين or *'amīn*. Regardless of the language, the rumors talked of the same thing. An Englishman known as *The Keeper* with an interest in antiquities, and one with deep pockets. He was also, if the chatter was to be believed, a man of discretion.

Itamar took one last look at the jars before getting to his feet, wincing as one of his knees cracked. He made his way back to the surface, where Na'ama giggled at his disheveled appearance.

"Papa, you're covered in dust," his daughter said, laughing as she brushed at his clothes. Itamar looked at his only child. What he would give to secure her future, even if it meant risking his own? He stooped down and rearranged some rocks to cover the hole in the ground. "Are we going back to the farm now?"

"Yes, my child," Itamar replied as he ruffled her hair. "But after lunch, I need to go into the village." He glanced back at the hole in the ground, now small enough to prevent any more sheep from getting into it. "There're some people I need to speak with."

2

No one in the small cafe in the town square of San Pietro In Cariano was paying much attention to the man dressed in a gray robe who was sitting in the corner, which was just the way Caleb liked it. Men and women in religious clothing were pretty common in rural Italy, especially in an area with so many monasteries and other religious establishments. He'd had one or two curious glances when he had walked into the cafe, but Caleb was well used to that. He'd been able to get a coffee and a pastry using a crude sign language and pointing at what other customers had in front of them, and had taken the last table in the establishment.

The cafe was identical to hundreds, if not thousands, of other cafes in Italy. It was a mixture of retro styling combined with modern comfort. The walls were pastel colored and decorated with artificially aged photographs that appeared to show many years of satisfied customers and the floor was tiled in a checkered black-and-white pattern that reminded Caleb of diners back in his home state of Texas. He glanced around at his fellow customers, realizing that he was the youngest by some years, except for a young couple engrossed in each other in one corner. As he watched, the man fed his partner a fork full of cream cake. Some of the cream spilled onto the tip of her nose, which caused them both to laugh in only the way the young and in love could laugh. She wiped it off her nose with a finger before sucking the cream from it, raising her eyes seductively at her partner as she did so.

From the way they were dressed, most of the cafe's occupants were tourists, no doubt drawn by the many walking trails throughout the area. Lake Garda, the largest lake in Italy, was around twelve kilometers away as the crow flies and Caleb could see more than one set of hiking sticks leaning against the cafe wall.

He took a sip of his fragrant coffee and nodded in appreciation. It was good. Very good. Just the right amount of bitterness for his taste. Then, with no one to share it with, Caleb took a bite of his own cream pastry. As he chewed, he regarded the road outside with curiosity. Before he had entered the cafe, Caleb had spent some moments watching a small roundabout just down from the cafe, convinced that at any moment, there was going to be a horrible car accident. Scooters, driven by young men who obviously thought themselves immortal, fought with cars, SUVs, and small trucks for the right of way. A cacophony of horns filled the air, but Caleb wasn't sure whether they were warnings or greetings. There appeared to be some sort of rules for the roundabout though, although they weren't rules Caleb understood, and the imminent accident he feared never happened.

The bell above the cafe door tinkled and Caleb, along with most of the occupants of the cafe, glanced up at the new arrival. It was a woman, perhaps in her mid to late twenties, with striking red hair. She was shorter than Caleb at five foot six or seven, and was wearing a flowing pale green dress. Caleb watched as she glanced around the cafe, her eyes resting on him but only for a few seconds, before she approached the counter. There was something about the way she held herself as she walked that piqued Caleb's attention. It wasn't because she was very attractive, although in his estimation she was. It was the way she was walking. Her gait was almost stilted, and she was grasping the small handbag she was carrying as if it contained a winning lotto ticket.

Caleb watched out of the corner of his eye as the woman purchased a bottle of water. Then she looked around the cafe again before her eyes rested on the only available chair, the one directly opposite Caleb. He concentrated on his pastry as she approached. The woman said something in Italian, her voice high-pitched and full of tension even though he couldn't understand what she had just said.

"I'm sorry. Do you speak English?" Caleb replied hopefully, looking at the woman. She had pale green eyes that matched her dress perfectly, but they were distracted. Her skin was very pale, as if she'd not seen the sun for some time, but as it was March and the weather glorious, maybe this was by design. Freckles across the bridge of her nose hinted at some time in the early spring sunshine at least.

"You're American?" the woman asked, her brief smile revealing a flash of perfectly aligned teeth. Caleb caught what he thought was a mid-western accent. Minnesota perhaps, or maybe one of the Dakotas.

"Sure am," Caleb replied with a smile. "Texan, born and bred. You?"

"I'm from Iowa," the woman said. "Sioux City." Caleb's

smile turned into a grin. He'd been close. "I was just asking if I could sit down?"

"Of course," Caleb replied, getting to his feet to pull the chair out for his unexpected guest. He watched her as she sat down, her eyes darting around the cafe. She was definitely nervous about something, and Caleb wondered if the dark gray SUV parked over the road from the cafe had anything to do with that. The driver's attention was fixed firmly on the exterior of the cafe as he spoke into a cell phone. "I'm Caleb, by the way."

"Anita," the woman replied, but she didn't offer a hand for him to shake. Both of them were firmly holding onto her handbag and he could see her knuckles had whitened.

"Is everything okay, Anita?" Caleb asked as he took a sip of his coffee. "You look very worked up about something?" Over her shoulder, the man in the SUV was now listening to his phone call, nodding his head every few seconds.

"Not really, Caleb," Anita replied with a small sigh, flashing him another brief smile. "But thank you for your concern."

3

Anita stared at the strange man in the gray robe as he sipped his coffee. He looked back at her with piercing eyes that almost matched the color of his robe before he blinked and looked away, seemingly content with her scrutiny. But could she trust him? He'd picked up on the fact she was in trouble, despite her only saying a couple of sentences, but now seemed to be fixated on something behind her.

All she wanted to do was to get somewhere safe. Somewhere she could relax and sleep. It felt like days since she had last slept properly. As she thought about it, she realized it had been almost a week since she'd had a full night's sleep. One that hadn't been interrupted by a nightmare.

Anita's hands tightened on her handbag and the precious contents that were within it. She saw Caleb glance down at her hands as she did so before he returned to looking over her shoulder. She wanted to reach out and open the bottle of water, but she didn't trust her hands to remain steady and the last thing she wanted to do was to spill water all down herself.

"So, you're a monk?" Anita asked Caleb, nodding at his gray robe. It was a simple garment with no pockets or other adornments that she could see.

"I'm a preacher, not a monk," he replied with an amiable smile.

"There's a difference?"

"Oh, yes." Caleb's smile broadened. "Preachers have way more fun than monks." Despite her nerves, there was something about the way he was looking at her that was reassuring.

"What denomination are you?"

"Christian."

"But what type? Catholic presumably?" They were, after all, only about two hundred and fifty kilometers from Rome and the Vatican.

"No, just Christian," Caleb replied with another sip of his coffee. "I'm not really the church-going type. Are you here on vacation?" It was an abrupt change in subject, and she had the impression that he didn't want to talk about himself anymore. Anita paused for a few seconds before replying. She wasn't sure how to answer that question.

"I was visiting some friends," she said eventually. Caleb's eyes flickered, and she knew he had seen straight through the lie.

Anita let go of her handbag and clenched her right fist twice before she reached out for her bottle of water. Her mouth was parched and she could feel her tongue sticking to the roof of her mouth. To her relief, barring a slight tremble as she unscrewed the lid, her hand did as it was told without incident. The relief when the cold water trickled into her mouth was instant.

"Who are they, Anita?" Caleb asked, his eyes staring back over her shoulder.

"Who are who?" she replied as she replaced the lid on the bottle.

"The people who are watching you?"

Anita felt her heartbeat speeding up at Caleb's words. How had they found her so quickly? She was sure that she'd shaken her pursuers in Verona over an hour ago. They should be at the airport, searching for her among the holiday-makers waiting to board the flight she had a ticket for in her bag. She couldn't understand how they had followed her to this tiny village.

"They're some people I'm really keen to avoid," Anita said. She wanted to look over her shoulder at whatever Caleb was looking at, but she couldn't bring herself to move.

"Why?" Caleb asked. His tone was neutral and nonaccusatory. Anita thought for a moment about making something up, but he had seen straight through her earlier lie.

"I took something from them," she replied, her voice almost a whisper. "They want it back."

"You're a thief?" Again, his tone was neutral.

"Not in that sense, no. I've taken some information that they don't want anyone else to see." Anita stared at Caleb, her fear building. It didn't matter that she was in a public place. She knew the people who were after her wouldn't care about that. Anita reached out her hand for the water bottle, her eyes darting around, looking for an escape route.

Caleb reached out his hand and placed his fingers around her wrist, making her jump. She saw him close his eyes for a couple of seconds. When he reopened them, they were full of purpose. He kept his hand on her wrist as he got to his feet, gesturing to her to do the same thing.

"Come with me," Caleb said as he pulled her toward a door she'd not noticed in the cafe's corner. "We need to go. Now!"

4

As Caleb gently but urgently pulled Anita to her feet, he kept his eyes focused on the two men who had exited the SUV and were now standing by the vehicle. He couldn't see their eyes as they were both wearing sunglasses, but they stood out in the gray suits they wore. While they would have blended into the background in a city, in a small village close to the Alps, they both looked totally out of place. As Caleb watched, the driver said something to the man who had been in the passenger seat. The second man nodded in response, and they started walking toward the cafe.

There had been two factors in Caleb's split-second decision to help Anita. The first, and the most important, had been the intuition he had felt when he had placed his hand on her wrist. Anita was fundamentally a good person, that much was obvious. There were other issues there, but his gut instinct told him her moral compass was pointing in the right direction. The second factor had come to light when the driver of the SUV had got out of his vehicle. His suit wasn't hanging quite right just under his left armpit. The bulge from a weapon was subtle, but was there.

"This way, quickly," Caleb said, pulling on Anita's wrist. He ignored the curious looks it generated from some of the other customers as they made their way to the door. Caleb opened it, hearing the elderly man behind the counter shouting something in Italian, and they hurried through.

On the other side of the door was a narrow corridor. To the left was another door, probably to a storeroom, while to the right it led to a fire door. Against the wall of the corridor was an extensive set of metal shelves with boxes of produce on them. Caleb let go of Anita's hand and pulled the shelving toward him, spilling the boxes on the ground where one of them split open. Then he leaned the shelving against the door they had just come through, wedging it shut while tins of plum tomatoes rolled across the corridor floor. He didn't think the shelving would deter the two men for long, but it should buy them precious seconds.

"Come on," Caleb barked, grabbing Anita's wrist. "Let's go."

The two of them ran down the corridor to the fire exit. As they approached, Caleb raised his leg and drove his sandaled foot into the bar, causing the door to fly open with a resounding crash. They emerged into the sunlight. Caleb glanced left and right, his instincts telling him to turn left. They were in a small service alleyway behind the cafe, lined on one side by garbage dumpsters. If Caleb's geography was correct, and it generally was, to the right would lead to the street, while turning to the left would lead them deeper into the alleys separating the buildings. The risk was that going left could trap them in a dead end, but it was a risk he was willing to take.

"This way!" Caleb said, breaking into a run as his gray robe swirled about his legs.

As well as the dumpsters that lined the sides of the alleyway, there was rubbish strewn across the ground and more than once, Anita stumbled on some of it. Caleb gripped her wrist to stop her from falling as they ran toward the end of the alley where, to Caleb's relief, there was a T junction. They were just approaching the junction when Caleb heard a man's voice shout something in Italian. A split second later, there was a metallic zinging noise as something ricocheted off one of the metal dumpsters only a meter away from them. Caleb ducked instinctively, pulling Anita down with him. She screamed, and he wondered for a few seconds whether she had been hit, but the scream was one of fear, not of pain. There were a couple of puffs of brick dust from the wall in front of them, but then they were round the corner and in relative safety.

The fact the rounds had landed so close to them gave Caleb pause for thought. There had been no accompanying gunshot, which meant the man who had just shot at them was using a silencer. In Caleb's estimation, the gunman was at least a hundred meters away from them, but had almost managed to hit them from that distance with a pistol. That meant whoever the men chasing Anita were, they were good.

Caleb and Anita continued through the labyrinthine alleys, turning into new ones as Caleb tried to keep a mental map of their route. After they had made several turns at junctions, he thought there would be enough uncertainty over their route for them to slow down a little. He was out of shape and had a painful stitch in his side. Anita, by contrast, was barely out of breath.

"Are you okay?" she asked him as they took yet another turn.

"I've not been well," Caleb replied, placing his hand on his side. The stitch was directly underneath a recently repaired wound, and he hoped it was just a stitch and nothing more insidious.

They ran to the end of the alleyway and rounded the corner to see a dark-haired, tanned man in what appeared to be a white chef's uniform. He was leaning against a door, smoking a cigarette. He watched as they ran toward him and, as they approached, Anita stopped running and said something to him in rapid-fire Italian. Caleb saw the man look at him and start laughing hard. Then he flicked the cigarette away and beckoned them through the door, closing it behind them and securing the restraining bar. They followed the man through a corridor and he led them into what looked to be a staff room. There were several cupboards with clothes hanging in them, and a half-open window through which Caleb could smell the chef's residual cigarette smoke. Then the man said something else to Anita, looked at Caleb again with an amused expression, and left, still laughing as he did so.

"What did you say to him?" Caleb asked, sitting down gratefully in a threadbare chair.

"I told him we were running from my husband," she replied, "because he wants to kill you."

Despite their situation, Caleb started laughing as well. But it didn't last for long. He could hear men shouting in the alleyway outside.

"Anita," Caleb said, lowering his voice. He paused and fixed her with an intense glare before continuing. "I need you to take off all your clothes."

5

Brother Giovanni, whose real name was Thomas Gavazzi, considered himself to be as Italian-American as it was possible to be. Although he was from Pittsburgh, he clung to his roots jealously. When he could, he cooked with his grandmother, sung her *Tanti Auguri a Te* on her birthday, and always ate lasagna at Easter dinner. An important part of that heritage was, in his opinion at least, a legendary temper which was currently focused on the man on the other end of the phone line.

"What do you mean, you've lost her?" he shouted down the phone, earning a reproachful stare from the woman in his office. Giovanni listened as the man tried to explain away his incompetence, but he cut him off, telling him not to call back until he'd found her. "Guido," he shouted at the handset, but only when he was sure the line was dead. Giovanni wasn't stupid.

"Giovanni, would you just relax," the woman, Eva, said. She was wearing her customary tunic, a loose dress made of black serge fabric that was pleated at the neck and draped to the ground. It was secured around her waist with a thin leather belt. If the tunic had been accompanied by a scapular and a veil, she would have born a close resemblance to a Catholic nun, which was exactly why she wore it. But Eva, or Sister Eva as she was known to everyone outside this room, was about as Catholic as the Dalai Lama.

"How can I relax when that slut is running around with what is mine?" Giovanni said, trying to calm his voice as he spoke.

"Hush," Eva said, crossing the room to join him. She put her hands on his shoulders and pressed down to indicate that he should sit. Giovanni took the hint and sat heavily in the office chair behind his opulent desk. Like the rest of his office furnishings, the desk was antique and expensive. On the paneled dark wooden walls were a series of tiny oil paintings that were purported to be by Gian Lorenzo Bernini, the seventeenth century inventor of the Baroque style of sculpture, while the twin armchairs were apparently rescued from the monastery of Monte Cassino just before Eisenhower reduced the medieval buildings that housed it in 1944 to rubble. Like Giovanni's backstory, neither history was genuine. The paintings were faithful reproductions by an art student Giovanni had hired back in Pittsburgh, and the armchairs were from an antique store Eva had found near Naples, but Giovanni never let the truth get in the way of a good story. "Do you want a drink, Giovanni?" Eva asked.

"No, Eva," Giovanni replied through gritted teeth. "What I want is for those idiots to locate the woman."

"What did they say?"

"They said they just missed her at a cafe," Giovanni said. "She was with a man in some sort of a robe. They've got the general area they're in, but not the exact location. Something to do with the walls being too thick."

"They're good, Giovanni." Eva stood behind Giovanni's

chair and started massaging his shoulders. "Would you want ex-GIS men on your tail?" She was referring to the *Gruppo di Intervento Speciale*, a tier 1 special force from the Carabinieri.

Giovanni sighed, knowing Eva was right. He had personally reviewed the conduct records of both the men, including the reasons for their dishonorable discharges. Their combat records were impressive, and as for their discharges, all men had needs. Of that, Giovanni knew only too well. Where the two men had gone wrong was that they hadn't tidied up properly after themselves, which is exactly what he was trying to do with the woman.

"Maybe I will have that drink after all," Giovanni said a moment later. He needed something to calm him down, and Eva's usual way of doing that wasn't possible in their office. He watched as she crossed the room to his drinks cabinet, a gothic-looking affair with elaborate carvings on the doors. The cabinet was younger than Giovanni although, if asked, he was quick to mention its apparent previous owner, Padre Pio, whom Giovanni stated had drunk from it when he was still a mere padre and not the saint he had become since his death.

"You need to be relaxed for your sermon later on," Eva said as she passed a crystal tumbler with a generous measure of whisky to him. "So only the one. Okay?" She had a playful smile on her face. It wasn't the same smile she wore when they were live streaming on the internet, but one reserved just for him. Eva leaned in to whisper in his ear. "But later? Once Sister Eva is satisfied, Brother Giovanni can have as much to drink as he wants."

6

"Please excuse me for a moment, Ruth," Hugo said to the woman who had just brought him coffee. He glanced at his cell phone vibrating on the desk in front of him. Ruth, his personal assistant, just nodded in reply. She wasn't the talkative type, but Hugo wasn't paying her for her conversational ability. "Yes?" he said when he answered the call, noticing as he did so it was from a withheld number.

"Mr. Forrester?" a male voice replied in heavily accented English. "It's Nasim. Nasim al-Qassab?"

"Yes, Nasim," Hugo replied, his attention instantly piqued by the call. Nasim was a Syrian man who had been loosely employed for many years now by the corporation Hugo was in charge of. Before working for Hugo, Nasim had worked briefly for the Egyptian Museum in Cairo before a misunderstanding over who owned some artifacts had led to his termination and a brief spell in a local prison. Hugo, who was now the proud but not legal owner of the artifacts, had secured both Nasim's release and his expertise.

"I'm in Giv'at ha-Mivtar in East Jerusalem," Nasim

replied. "There was an earthquake close to here a few days ago?" Hugo nodded, remembering seeing something on the news, but if he remembered correctly, it had been a fairly minor one.

"Yes, I saw," Hugo said, watching as his personal assistant walked to the door of his office, her slim hips swaying as she did so. She was, like most of the women Hugo had working for him, jaw-droppingly attractive and would be the perfect companion for the performance at the Burgtheater—Europe's second-oldest theater—he was looking forward to that evening. The box he had arranged to watch a performance of Ein Sommernachtstraum, or A Midsummer Night's Dream, had cost a small fortune, but Hugo never mixed business with pleasure. It wouldn't be his assistant with him at the theater, but a different companion who was just as attractive and, more importantly, morally dubious. Her agency's cost was all-inclusive, however, and would cover more than just her company. "What of it?"

"The earthquake uncovered a cave on a hill to the northeast of the settlement," Nasim said. "A small one. Only one loculus."

Hugo frowned, running his spare hand through his silver hair as he did so. Most of the tombs in the area had more than one loculi or burial niche.

"Does it contain many ossuaries?" he asked Nasim. Hugo already had several of the small boxes that had been used for the secondary burial of bones and had no particular desire to acquire any more. They were hardly unique, and thousands of them had been discovered around Jerusalem over the years.

"None, just a large earthenware jar. The farmer opened it to find a roll of parchment, still wrapped in linen."

"Time period?" Hugo's attention was instantly attracted by the mention of scrolls.

"Early Empire, I think. The inscriptions on the jars look too new to be Late Republic."

Nasim's words caused Hugo to lean forward on his seat and press the cell phone tighter against his ear. The very early years of the Roman Empire were Hugo's primary area of interest, and the fall of the Roman Republic in 27 B.C. and the subsequent creation of the empire by Augustus was well documented.

"Describe the jar," Hugo said, taking a sip of his coffee. It was, as always, perfect and just to his taste. He listened intently as Nasim did just that, telling him it was in remarkably good condition and still appeared to be sealed with the original plaster coating. "And the inscriptions?" He didn't bother asking Nasim to describe the scroll, as he knew the man would have resealed the jar to protect it.

"I can't be one hundred percent certain, but I think there's a name. Gaius Cassius. There's also a military heraldic symbol with a reference to the Cohors Sebaste." Hugo heard Nasim take a deep breath. "They were the local Samaritan bully-boys in the area after the fall of the empire."

Hugo sat back in his seat and thought for a moment, looking out of the window of his office at the Austrian alps in the distance. Although it was spring, there were still a couple of the higher peaks with a cap of snow and he idly wondered if Nasim had ever been to Austria. Then Hugo nodded his head. The Syrian's knowledge was excellent, as usual, but what he was describing was unusual and very interesting. The discovery of some jars was nothing earth-shattering, but to have a name and a military symbol on them was most unusual. Hugo had a particular penchant for unusual things, particularly when they were from that time period.

"There're pottery remains as well," Nasim told him. "Some spindle bottles and globular juglets." Hugo nodded enthusiastically. Such pottery wasn't in use in the area until after the rise of the Herodian dynasty in 37 B.C., which gave more credence to Nasim's estimate of the era the jars belonged to.

"Is the scroll secure?" Hugo asked, knowing that it would be or Nasim wouldn't have called him.

"Yes, of course. The loculus is on a sheep farmer's land. He has enough money to ensure his discretion." Nasim was speaking slowly, and Hugo knew he was trying to impress him with his use of English. "And of course, he wants some more. I take it you are interested?"

"Oh yes," Hugo replied, a smile playing across his face. "Very much so. Have it sent to Professor Greenford at the Diamond Light Source in Oxfordshire. I'll have Ruth e-mail you the address. He can use their synchrotron to analyze the scrolls without even having to unwrap them." Hugo had a standing arrangement with the Professor back in England for just such eventualities. He had access to the national synchrotron, a device that harnessed the power of electrons to produce bright light that could study anything from jet engines to viruses. Hugo had heard the Professor say, on more than one occasion, that the device was ten thousand times more powerful than a traditional microscope and produced light beams that were ten billion times brighter than the sun. An ancient scroll would be child's play for the professor, and Hugo paid him more than enough to ensure his discretion.

"I will make the necessary arrangements, Mr. Forrester."

Hugo ended the call and turned his attention back to the

mountains in the distance. He got to his feet and walked to the window to fully appreciate the view, as he always did when he was thinking.

Inscribed jars containing scrolls, from exactly the right era, seemingly undisturbed. Hugo had many artifacts in the secure warehouse beneath his feet, but these could take pride of place. Apart from his most prized possession, of course.

It would take a few days, perhaps longer, for them to be in his warehouse. There were palms to be crossed with plenty of silver to make that happen, but for Hugo's organization, it was a well-trodden route. Although his collection was more of a hobby than a business venture like the rest of his organization, occasionally the two elements came together.

Hugo smoothed his hands down the front of his three-piece suit, making a mental note to speak to his tailor to get the waistcoat let out by an inch. If Nasim's estimation of the jars' era was correct, and they were as undisturbed as he had said, then this could well be a most valuable discovery.

He couldn't wait to see what was written on those scrolls.

"What did you say?" Anita asked Caleb, unsure if she'd heard him correctly.

"I said, take off all your clothes. Now!" He was staring at her intently as he spoke. "They're looking for a woman in a green dress." He pointed at the cupboard and the clothes hanging inside. "Put those on."

Anita paused for a moment before replying. What he had said made sense, but she was still uncomfortable.

"Turn around then," she replied.

Caleb laughed, but did as instructed. Anita slipped the dress from her shoulders, struggling for a few seconds with the zipper, but she wasn't about to ask Caleb to help her with it. Shivering, although it wasn't cold, she crossed to the cupboard with her arms over her chest in case he turned round.

"What's in your handbag?" Caleb asked as she pulled out a hanger with a man's shirt and a pair of jeans on it.

"My purse, a memory stick, some other bits and pieces." Anita was just buttoning the shirt when she heard her handbag being upended onto the table. "Hey! What are you doing?" she said, turning to see Caleb rifling through the contents. "That's my stuff!"

"Just get dressed, Anita," Caleb replied, his voice terse as he examined the now empty handbag. Anita was mortified as she watched a sanitary pad drop onto the table, but Caleb didn't seem to notice it. If he did, he paid it no mind. Her hand shot out to grab it and she stuffed it into the pocket of the jeans she was holding, along with a small white thumb drive.

"I think you stand out more than I do, Caleb," Anita said. "You're wearing a robe."

"I'll change in a moment," Caleb replied, still fixated on Anita's handbag.

She turned away from him and returned her attention to the jeans. When she put them on, she realized they were several sizes too large for her. Fortunately, they had a belt which she fastened around her waist. They were still loose, but at least they wouldn't fall down now. Then she slipped her feet back into her shoes before turning to see Caleb. Anita gasped, and her hand flew up to her mouth. He was as naked as the day he was born and facing away from her, the robe he had been wearing in a heap on the floor. She turned away quickly, but not before she had seen the myriad scars that criss-crossed his back.

"Okay, let's go," Caleb said a moment later. When she turned back to face him, he was wearing an outfit similar to hers, but with a t-shirt instead of a shirt. The jeans he was wearing were too small and looked uncomfortably tight, and with his sandaled feet, he looked almost comical.

"Maybe we should swap trousers?" Anita said as the door opened. They both looked up to see the man who had been smoking in the alley looking at them with a confused expression.

"What's going on?" he asked her in Italian. "Those are my clothes!"

"I'm sorry," Anita replied as she reached for her purse on the table. She opened it and pulled out a hundred euro note from a roll of cash in the purse, handing it to the chef with the biggest smile she could muster under the circumstance. "My husband, he's a horrible man. We have to get away." She saw the chef eyeing the roll of notes greedily.

"Do you need transport?" he asked her, his eyes still on the money. "I have a moped. It's old, but it runs just fine."

"How much?"

"A thousand would cover it," the chef replied with a hopeful face. "It's got a full tank of gas."

Anita peeled off some more notes, ten in total. Then she snapped her purse shut to indicate there was no room for negotiation. The money didn't bother her. There was plenty more where that came from, but the principal bothered her even if they were desperate. She handed the chef the cash, receiving a key ring with a single key in return.

"It's parked just outside the restaurant," the man said as he counted the money. "It's the yellow one."

"We've got wheels, Caleb," Anita said, switching back to English and jangling the key in front of him. "Andiamo!"

"What does that mean?" Caleb replied, a half-smile on her face as he looked at the key.

"Let's go!"

Caleb had been surprised by Anita's unexpected purchase of a vehicle, and as they followed the chef through the kitchen of the restaurant, he found himself smiling at her resourcefulness. There was a lot he wanted to know about her, such as the information she had stolen and who she had stolen it from. He had assumed that the information was on the thumb drive, now buried deep within a pocket of her jeans. But whoever was after her meant business. The bullet holes in the wall of the alley were testament to that.

After walking through a deserted dining area, they reached the door to the restaurant. Caleb heard Anita talking to the chef. Unable to understand their conversation, he ignored them and opened the door, peering out into the street. He was half expecting a bullet, but there was hardly anyone on the street and there was no sign of the two men who had been chasing them or their gray SUV. The only people he could see were a young couple walking hand in hand and an elderly woman wearing a tired apron on the doorstep of a building on the other side of the street. She was leaning on a broom, watching the world go by. Not that there was much for her to watch, which was fine by Caleb.

"Coast is clear," Caleb said as he turned to see Anita walking toward him carrying two crash helmets. His gaze flicked back to where the young couple was walking, and he saw there was a row of mopeds. "Seriously? You bought one of them?"

"Yes," Anita replied, handing him a silver crash helmet. Then she reached up and pulled her hair into a loose bun before sliding her own helmet over the top of it. "Can you help me hide my hair?"

He took a couple of steps toward her and helped her tuck a few errant strands of her red hair inside the helmet, conscious of how close they were to each other. He could smell lavender, mixed in with something else. Chamomile, perhaps? He could also smell fear, but she was doing a superb job of keeping that emotion from her expression.

"We can go to the place I'm staying at," Caleb said as he examined Anita to make sure all her hair was hidden. "We should be safe enough there."

"I guess you're driving then?" Anita replied, handing him the chef's key. Caleb thought back to the confusion he'd observed at the junction earlier on that day and grimaced.

"I guess so," he said.

Caleb opened the door to the restaurant fully and stepped out into the sunshine, slipping his own crash helmet over his head. At least he had no hair to worry about.

"It's the yellow one," Anita said. Caleb looked at the line of mopeds to see a filthy yellow Honda at the end of the row. Compared to the others, it looked to be about three times as old. Even from this distance, he could see the rust on the engine.

They made their way over the road and walked past the line of mopeds toward theirs, Caleb running his hand over the newer ones. When they reached the one Anita had bought, he could see it was in even worse condition than he'd thought. But to his surprise it roared into life at the first turn of the key.

Caleb sat on the seat and placed his hands on the handlebars as he waited for Anita to get on the back. He thought back to the last time he had ridden a motorcycle. It had been a long time ago, back in California, and he smiled at the memory of riding a large Harley Davidson through the foothills of the white mountains. Then he felt the moped dip and Anita's hands on his hips.

"Do you read the scriptures, Anita?" Caleb asked over the noise of the engine.

"Not really," she replied. "Why?"

"Just wondering," Caleb said as he pushed the moped off its stand and twisted the gas handle.

9

Eva watched as Giovanni swirled his tumbler, staring at the brown liquid as he did so. He looked tired and older than his claimed age of forty-three years, although she suspected that was an optimistic estimate, anyway. His hair was jet black, helped by the packets of *Just For Men* hair dye he tried to hide in the garbage, and swept back from his head in his customary style, and the navy blue three-piece suit he was wearing suited his slim frame well.

The majority of his congregation was female, with his ideal target demographic being older ones. But Eva knew he had a large following of younger women as well, drawn to his charisma, which he could turn on and off like a tap. She had seen women eating out of the palm of his hand at the live events they occasionally undertook to augment the virtual prayer sessions, only for him to dismiss the ones Eva knew he didn't want to sleep with. Giovanni had a type, and fortunately for Eva, she was within that bracket. The clothes she wore no doubt helped with that. The first time they had gone to bed together, Giovanni had insisted she keep as many of them on as she could.

Eva knew she wasn't particularly intellectual. Nor was she gullible, like so many of their congregation were. She knew, even if Giovanni didn't, that this was purely a business relationship. One with benefits for sure, but still a business relationship. They were a team. It was Giovanni's role to maintain and grow the congregation and thus their coffers, and it was hers to ensure he was operating in an environment that facilitated that. She worked in the background, organizing and manipulating their assets to the best effect, and it was something she was very good at. It was wildly different from her background, working in banks as a software engineer, but a lot more fun.

Giovanni opened his mouth and was about to say something when he was interrupted by a ringing noise from the large Mac computer on his desk. Eva saw him wiggle the mouse and swear under his breath.

"It's Hugo," Giovanni muttered.

"Well, answer it then," Eva replied, smoothing the material of her habit over her chest. "You know he doesn't like to be kept waiting." She crossed the room and took up a position behind Giovanni. A few seconds later, a familiar face appeared on the screen.

"Mr. Forrester," Giovanni said as Eva smiled at the white-haired man who had appeared. Hugo Forrester was one of the most, if not the most, important members of their congregation.

"Brother Giovanni," Hugo replied, his eyes flicking to Eva's. He smiled, the skin around his mouth wrinkling. "And the lovely Sister Eva. How blessed am I this day?"

Eva returned Hugo's smile, nodding her head in deference to their benefactor. She knew at some point she was going to have to sleep with him, but that day hadn't arrived yet. She had thought it would be the last time they met, but Hugo hadn't quite plucked up the courage, although she sensed he'd been close to it. Eva knew it was only a matter of time, and had even purchased some blue pills from the pharmacy for when that day arrived. Giovanni would have been fine with that, as long as Hugo kept putting his hands in his pockets to donate to the Adelphoi's coffers.

"How can we be of assistance, Hugo?" Giovanni asked.

"I'm afraid I'm going to miss your sermon today," Hugo replied. His voice was deep and still retained the last vestiges of an English accent, although it had been many years since he'd left the country. "I have an important meeting in the laboratory, but I was rather hoping Sister Eva might oblige me with a recording of your words."

"Of course, Hugo," Eva said with what she hoped was a disarming smile. "I'd be only too happy to oblige." She flinched as she felt Giovanni's hand on the back of her calf, hidden from the webcam by the desk and she had to make a concerted effort not to laugh as it started creeping up her leg.

"How is the research coming along, Hugo?" Giovanni asked as his hand stopped at the bottom of her thigh. Eva knew he wouldn't be able to get any further without Hugo noticing, and her smile broadened.

"Yes, yes," Hugo replied, waving his hand dismissively. "It's progressing, as we discussed."

"And when is your next trip over the border to Italy?"

"A couple of week's time, I think."

"Excellent," Giovanni said. "Excellent. I'll ensure the suite's ready for you."

"Thank you, Brother Giovanni. That would be most kind."

Eva kept the smile on her face as Giovanni ended the call. Then she reached down and slapped his hand away from her leg.

"I've told you, Giovanni, not here," she said, keeping her voice playful but with an edge at the same time. "What do you think the old fool is coming over for this time?"

"I don't care, as long as he keeps the funding coming," Giovanni said, rubbing his hand. "But I think he'd quite like to know what Sister Eva's hiding under her habit."

"Enough, Giovanni," Eva replied, walking toward the door. "I need to go and prepare the chairs and check the equipment for the sermon." There was a conference room in the center of the building they were in, which had started life as a budget hotel before they had bought it and converted it into their home, if it could be called that. It was a fairly run-down collection of buildings that they were renovating one at a time, starting of course with their own accommodation.

"I bet I know what Hugo's doing now, sitting in that Austrian mansion of his," Giovanni said, making an obscene gesture with his hand. "He's imagining just how obliging Sister Eva actually is when she gets going."

Eva stopped with her hand on the door handle and turned to face Giovanni. She smirked at him before she spoke.

"All he's got to do is ask nicely and he'll find out."

10

It was obvious to Anita that she wasn't going to be able to hold on with just her hands on Caleb's hips, so she reluctantly slid them around his abdomen. She felt him tense up, and when he stopped the moped at a stop sign at the end of the road, he reached down and readjusted her hands slightly. Anita remembered him saying he'd been unwell, and she wondered what had happened to him.

Caleb moved away from the junction and she saw his head darting from side to side. She knew he wasn't looking for traffic, but for the two men who had been chasing them.

As Caleb drove through the ancient buildings that made up San Pietro in Cariano, Anita thought back over the events of the previous few hours. She had been on her way to Verona airport when she realized she had someone on her tail. It was, in fact, her taxi driver who had realized it, an ex-police officer called Lorenzo.

"You know you have someone following you?" he had said as he glanced in the rear-view mirror. "In a dark silver SUV?" When Anita had turned to look out of the rear window, she saw the vehicle a few cars back. There were two men, both wearing sunglasses and suits. "They've been on our tail since the hotel. Is everything okay?"

"They work for my ex-partner," Anita had said, not able to think of anything else to say. "Can you lose them?"

Lorenzo had smiled in response, saying that he doubted anyone knew the streets of Verona better than he did. He slowed as he approached a set of traffic lights, almost stopping in front of them even though they were still green. The action earned him a cacophony of horn blasts from behind, but the moment the lights changed to amber, he accelerated through them and took a hard left turn. He then drove seemingly randomly for several moments until he said he was sure they had lost their followers.

"Where to now?" Lorenzo had asked Anita. "I'm guessing the airport's out of the question. Where are you headed?"

"Naples," Anita had replied. She had the money for the fare, even though it was seven hundred kilometers, but Lorenzo had explained that he was due off shift shortly. He also explained that there would be few taxi drivers wanting such a long trip, as shorter trips paid so much better. A few moments later, he had dropped her off at a bus station.

Anita had decided against heading straight for Naples. If the men in the SUV had tracked her to the hotel, and knew she had been heading for the airport, they might know her ultimate destination. She would need to go via a more circuitous route. She'd decided on a bus to a random location. If she didn't know where she was going, then neither would they. But a few moments after arriving in the small village of Pastrengo, near Verona, she had been running for her life.

The old buildings of the village gave way to open countryside, full of maize and durum wheat fields. They passed swathes of land full of dairy cows, some of whom regarded them with curiosity as they drove past.

"Where are we going?" Anita shouted over the noise of the engine and the wind. The chef had been right about the moped being an excellent runner. The engine had struggled slightly with a low incline a few kilometers back, but had been otherwise fine.

"A place called Spiazzi," Caleb shouted back. "It's not far."

They rode past a fort of some sort, perched on a low hill. Anita looked at it, wondering what it was for. Whatever it was, it looked pretty old. Then the fort and the cows were behind them.

Anita rested her head on Caleb's shoulder. She was exhausted and needed to sleep. Anita knew it was the adrenaline from being chased through the alleys, and the horror of being shot at, but it was a deeper exhaustion than just that. She needed to rest properly and plan what she was going to do next. Even though the men who had chased them seemed to have disappeared, she knew they could be around the next corner, and they would happily kill her for what she had in her pocket.

Caleb had already saved her life once. Could she ask him to help her again? At least until she got the thumb drive to her contact in Naples?

11

Giovanni navigated the Mac's cursor to his secure banking app and clicked on the icon. A screen appeared, the first of three different login screens. The first was Apple's own Touch ID, which scanned his fingerprint even though he'd had to use it to unlock the Mac when Hugo had called. The second was a security question that only he knew the answer to, and the third was a random twelve-digit code that he had written on a slip of paper in the small safe under his desk.

Their bank account was with Credit Suisse, one of the larger banks in Switzerland, and he banked with them purely for anonymity. He wasn't trying to evade taxes. As a religious organization, they were tax exempt in the eyes of the IRS anyway, and Giovanni had the paperwork to prove it, but he wanted his money as far away from American bankers as possible. An additional bonus was the anonymity the Swiss bank offered, which was worth ten times what they charged him for the privilege.

There was another reason for banking with the Swiss than just privacy. One thing they were very good at was international transfers of funds. His main financial advisor, who he met with every six months in Zurich, was very adept at moving money to other countries. Giovanni had established branches of his organization in Malaysia, the Dominican Republic, and Singapore—all countries who treated foreign earned income as tax-exempt. His newest branch was about to open in Belize for the same reason. They existed only on paper, or the digital equivalent of paper, but it meant his money was safe.

There was a constant stream of cash from the branches, all perfectly legal money, into his private bank account in St. Kitts and Nevis in the Caribbean, where he held dual citizenship thanks to a generous donation to their hurricane relief fund several years ago. Not for the first time, he realized how much Eva and her financial background had brought to the organization. Although the accounts belonged to him, she had set them all up.

Giovanni waited for the digital handshaking to complete, staring out through the office window as he did so. The most impressive thing about the ex-hotel he was in was the view from every room, including the one he was in. It overlooked a large lake, Lake Iseo, with a small island in the center, and the location was the reason a hotel had been built there in the first place. But as the roads in the area got better and the access to much larger, more attractive locations like the well-known lakes Garda and Como became easier, the establishment had slowly faded away. What that had meant was that Giovanni had bought the place for a song.

Even though he was a foreigner, the Italian authorities had been only too happy to get rid of the building before the local arsonists got to it. At some point, Giovanni was going to buy a small row boat and explore the island which had a now uninhabited fishing village on it, maybe with Eva and a small picnic, but he was far too busy for that just now.

When the banking app finally opened the main screen, Giovanni's eyes lit up as they generally did. The number of zeroes after the digits in the primary account was very healthy, and he clicked into the balance to ensure the automatic siphoning of funds into his other branches was working as he knew it would be. Giovanni nodded in appreciation of Eva's system. If he had been a religious man, he would probably have offered a prayer to the heavens in thanks, but he didn't.

Giovanni glanced at his watch, which was—on anything other than a very close inspection—a Rolex Oyster Perpetual with a tiffany blue dial. He had thirty minutes before the sermon was due to begin. It was time to get into character to ensure that, following the sermon, there were more funds coming into Switzerland. He sat back in his chair and started doing the warm-up exercises his speech coach had prescribed for him. Placing his hands on the sides of his face, Giovanni slowly massaged his jaw and cheek muscles with slow, small circular motions.

"Ma ma ma ma ma ma," he said, his lips barely touching each other as he did so. Then he changed the shape of his lips into a tight circle. "Wa wa wa wa wa."

Giovanni was just blowing raspberries at his screensaver when he realized his cell phone was ringing. Irritated at being disturbed, he picked it up from the desk and swiped at the screen without even looking to see who it was. Very few people had this number, and he gave it only to people that he wanted to speak to.

"What?" Giovanni said in English. "I'm busy."

"It's the team from Verona," a male voice replied in Italian.

"Go on," Giovanni said, switching languages. "What have you got for me?"

"We've located your package."

"Excellent news," Giovanni replied, a smile spreading across his face. "Where?"

"It's on a moped heading out of Verona. We're tracking them now. I thought you'd appreciate the update." The man's voice was clipped, and Giovanni was reminded of how dangerous the two of them were.

"Retrieve what belongs to me and dispose of what's left. I'm going to be busy for the next few hours, so just message me on this phone when it's done. I'll let Mr. Forrester know."

"Understood," the man replied, ending the call without another word. Giovanni wasn't offended, though. He knew Hugo wasn't paying them for their manners, although whatever they cost would be deducted from the man's next donation. It was, Hugo had said as he had explained this, only right.

Giovanni placed the phone back on the desk, still smiling. Then he restarted his voice exercises from the beginning.

He had an audience to impress, after all, and the more impressed they were, the more generous they became.

12

I t was, Caleb thought as he leaned the moped into a bend in the road, turning out to be a strange day indeed. He had gone from enjoying a simple cup of coffee in a cafe to riding a small motorcycle through the Italian countryside with a very attractive woman clinging to him. Caleb tried to ignore the way her body was pressed up against his back, meaning he could feel the contours of her body in a unique way, but it was difficult to do. As he often said, he wasn't a monk and there was no denying Anita was beautiful. He was grateful for the small cloth bag on his lap that his robe was stuffed into. Were her hands to move from where they were, it would save any potential embarrassment on his part.

Around the bend, the road opened up into a long straight that ran alongside an equally straight river. It was too straight to be natural, and the road looked to be Roman in origin. Caleb imagined legions of Roman soldiers doing what soldiers did so well, which was to march from one location to another. It had been many years since Caleb had marched anywhere, which was fine by him. There were much better ways of getting from point A to point B than on foot.

A few hundred meters ahead of them on the road was a tractor, crawling along the road with a large trailer behind it that was covered with a tarpaulin. Caleb glanced in one of the moped's mirrors, preparing to pull out, but there was nothing behind them. Apart from a few cars and now a tractor, once they had left the village behind, they'd had the road pretty much to themselves.

Caleb's intent was to get Anita to a place of safety near the village they were heading toward. He had been staying in a local monastery for the last couple of weeks, partly while he recovered from his injuries, and partly for a sabbatical of sorts. But it seemed God had other ideas. Caleb had long believed that what he did, and where he did it, was God's work and He had a habit of putting him right where he was needed. Like in the cafe where Anita had needed his help.

They passed the tractor, Caleb looking at the driver to see a dour-faced man at the wheel. The farmer, if that was what he was, didn't so much as glance in their direction. His gaze was fixed straight ahead, and Caleb wondered what he was thinking about. The tractor was in the same state of repair as the moped he was riding, but like the motorcycle, there didn't seem to be much wrong with the engine. Perhaps, Caleb thought, mechanical function was more important than cosmetics in this part of Italy?

Caleb rode on for a few moments, the road stretching in front of him. He needed a rest stop, but there were no buildings in sight. There wasn't even a tree he could disappear behind to relieve his discomfort, and he wasn't going to just stand by the side of the road and urinate with Anita watching. He resolved to carry on until they reached Spiazzi, where there was a public bathroom in the piazza he could use instead.

He glanced in the mirror again to see the tractor was now several hundred meters behind him. As he watched, he saw a small blue car pull out to overtake it. The car was moving quickly, much faster than the moped was traveling, and Caleb knew it would only be a moment or two before it overtook them as well. But as the car approached, it slowed down and remained behind them. Caleb couldn't see through the windshield because of the angle of the sun which was reflecting off the glass. He couldn't even tell how many people were in the vehicle, much less what they were wearing. Caleb eased up on the accelerator slightly, but the car remained around thirty meters behind them, matching their speed. Although the two men in San Pietro In Cariano had been in an SUV, there could be more than one team chasing Anita, and now him.

Caleb thought through his options, but soon realized he didn't really have any. He could continue, or he could stop. There were no other courses of action he could take. On either side of the road was a shallow irrigation ditch with occasional access points for the fields. But the moped they were riding wouldn't be able to cope with the freshly plowed ground beyond the ditch to his right, or the river to his left.

He sped up again, encouraging a slight increase in speed from the moped. Caleb glanced in the mirror again to see that the car had pulled out onto the other side of the road, but was slowly catching up with them as opposed to accelerating past them. The car being on the other side of the road gave him the option of slamming the brakes on and turning the moped around, assuming, of course, the action didn't throw Anita off the motorcycle. There was no time to warn her, and even if he did this, all it would buy them would be a few seconds of time as the car also turned around. The glare on the car's windshield shifted and he could see the silhouettes of two people in the car.

Caleb's heart rate increased as he saw the passenger side window descend.

13

Hugo pushed open the door to the meeting room and noticed with pleasure the effect his arrival had on the people already in the room. He had heard excited conversations taking place inside the room from outside the door, but they faded away as he entered. There was still an air of underlying tension in the room, and he saw several of the researchers giving each other enthusiastic looks.

The meeting room, like the rest of the complex it formed a part of, had had many uses over the years. In the sixteenth and seventeenth centuries, it had been the dining hall for the monks that had lived in the monastery. After a period of disuse following the departure of the monks and several fires in the complex buildings, it had been bought by a wealthy landowner and redeveloped into a country retreat. The landowner, Wilhelm Forrester, had passed it onto his son, who had passed it to his son, and so on. It briefly fell out of the hands of the Forrester family when the Gestapo had taken a shine to it, using the simple cells the monks had lived in as torture chambers. Hugo's great grandfather had returned to it from exile when the war ended, his fortune dented but not wiped out by his efforts to prove he owned it. Finally, on the death of Hugo's father, it had passed to him. Apart from the installation of a modern heating and electrical system, and the upwards extension of the monastery to make space for his laboratories and offices, Hugo had left the original monastery buildings as they were.

"Good evening, ladies and gentlemen," Hugo said as he walked into the room, taking his customary seat at the head of the long oval table. The wall he was facing had a large screen on which the logo of his company, *Forrester Akadmie der Wissenschaften*, was projected via a laptop. Literally meaning the Forrester Academy of Sciences, the logo represented a little known but enormously powerful organization that operated mostly within the law, even if it stretched ethics to the limit. There were only a few people in the room who knew Hugo's true intentions for the research they undertook. Hugo was very cautious with his trust.

"Good evening, Herr Forrester," a woman in a white coat replied. Claudia was Hugo's Head of Research at the academy's Human Genetics Unit, the principal research facility at the academy. She was one of the finest minds that money could buy. Her husband, a permanently miserable man called Albert, ran the supercomputer that supported his wife's unit, and their combined IQ was off the scale, as were their salaries. Neither of them had ever published their projects in the academic press. Nor would they. They weren't the sort of projects that would be universally acclaimed by the scientific community.

Claudia's voice was filled with trepidation. "Thank you for attending at such short notice." Hugo could see that her fingers were trembling slightly. This was unusual for Claudia, who was one of the most emotionless people Hugo knew.

"You said you had some news, Claudia," Hugo said.

"I think we've done it, Hugo," Claudia said with a short, high-pitched laugh. It startled Hugo, who couldn't remember ever hearing her laugh before. He watched, incredulous, as the other researchers in the room broke into a spontaneous round of applause. It died away as Hugo put his hand in the air.

"Claudia, please explain what you have done," he said. "Or what you think you have done?"

Claudia pointed at the screen and pressed the button on a small remote control. The logo on the screen disappeared and Hugo was looking at what he presumed was a view through a microscope. Hugo could see an amorphous blob on the screen that made no sense to him at all. The scientist pressed another button on the remote control and a small green dot appeared on the projection.

"This is the very edge of the lateral plate of the folding neural tube," Claudia said as she maneuvered the green dot on the screen. "They're neural crest cells which will migrate to become a variety of crucial cells." The green dot jumped to another part of the screen. "Surrounding the notochord at the side, just here, is the paraxial mesoderm." Her voice went up a notch, but the rest of the room remained silent. It was almost as if the researchers were all holding their breath. "This will develop into somites."

"Somites?" Hugo asked. He remembered the term from a previous briefing, but couldn't remember what it meant.

"Bilateral paired blocks of mesoderm that form in the embryonic stage of somitogenesis," another male researcher said, his voice almost as high as Claudia's.

"Which means what, exactly?"

"They will develop into muscles, bones, limbs," Claudia replied, clicking the button again. The image changed, but again, Hugo was at a loss to understand what he was looking at.

"This is the primitive streak, Hugo," Claudia said. "It's the early body plan emerging at three weeks post genesis. There're already organs forming." The green dot circled one particular area. "This is a fledgling heart. No one has ever done this before."

Hugo said nothing, but stared at the screen for several seconds. He knew no one had ever done this before as it was against the law almost universally to experiment on embryos past the fourteen day point.

"Is it viable?" he asked Claudia. An excited hubbub of conversation arose from the researchers, and he had to raise his hand again.

"That's the next step, Hugo," Claudia replied. "But yes, we believe it is."

"And this has been created with no egg or sperm cells?"

"That's correct. It's been created from your stem cells. Nothing more."

Hugo steepled his hands in front of his face and regarded the image on the screen, thinking as he did so. His focus was on Claudia's progress, which had surpassed Hugo's expectations and was months in the making. It was just a shame the world wasn't watching as they made history. But Hugo knew it wasn't a part of history that much of the world would be thrilled about.

A hush fell across the room as Hugo continued staring at the image. If it was a viable human embryo they were looking at, it had been conceived asexually. This was no longer science fiction. This was now science fact.

In some circles, this type of conception could almost be considered immaculate.

14

E va looked at the chairs in the conference room, ensuring that they were all lined up in perfectly straight rows. There were twenty of them altogether, although they currently had only nineteen guests staying in the compound. Four rows of five chairs, the front few with *Reserved* signs on them for Giovanni's current favorite followers. Front and center was reserved for a woman called Madeline, or Maddy for short. Eva sighed when she saw Giovanni had added Maddy's name on the sign. Calling her a woman was a bit of a stretch of the imagination, in Eva's opinion. She was perhaps late-teens, early twenties at best, and had flown over from Iowa to join them after only a couple of hours in Giovanni's company during their last trip state-side. Eva knew Maddy would sit in rapture as Giovanni spoke later, as if she was the only person in the entire room who he was speaking to. Which, in Maddy's mind at least, she would be.

At the front of the room, which when the building had been a hotel was optimistically called the business suite, was a single barstool with a small table next to it. Giovanni didn't need a microphone for such a small audience, but he wore a wireless one anyway for the recording of the sermon. All he needed was a chair to perch on, and a space to prowl around as he spoke. The last addition, which wouldn't be in place until the last moment, was an ice-cold bottle of water.

Eva paced around the room, touching the back of some chairs where a few of their longer term followers would be sitting. Then she paused at the end of the front row with her fingertips on the back of what would be an empty chair. It was where Anita should have been sitting if she hadn't betrayed Giovanni.

Eva bore Anita no real ill-will, reasoning that the woman had done what she thought was the right thing. Their followers were all there of their own free will and volition, although Giovanni had a knack for persuading them what that free will was telling them to do. What concerned Eva was that she doubted Anita had acted alone. Someone, somehow, had got to her and undone what Giovanni had done. That was what bothered Eva more than the sudden disappearance of a follower. The fact there were others out there who knew what they were doing, and from the theft of Giovanni's information, appeared to want to stop them in their ultimate mission.

Something must have happened during their last trip to the United States, although Eva wasn't sure how. They'd spent a week over there. Eva, Giovanni, Anita, and another follower called Aaron, who had joined them for the last couple of days. For the entire time, Anita wasn't out of either Eva or Giovanni's sight for more than a few moments at a time. It had been a successful trip, gaining them several hundred new on-line followers and two new guests, including Maddy. Each night had been a new location, and each had followed the same format. Eva had been at the door, welcoming people as they entered wherever Giovanni was speaking. Her religious-like robes helped to filter out attendees who may not have realized this was a faith-based event, or at least appeared to be. Then Anita had opened the evening's entertainment by welcoming the guests and telling them that only a few months before, she had been sitting in such an audience. She had told them her story, and every evening, the attendees had lapped it up. How she had gone from being desperately unhappy working in a bank staring at lines of code to living each day in the glory of God. And in the glory of Giovanni, although she didn't actually say that.

By the time Giovanni had taken to the stage, the audience was already halfway to where they wanted to be. He preached in a charismatic way, almost but not quite evangelical, and peppered his sermon with scientific notions to support his theory that the end of days wasn't coming, but had arrived. By the time he got to the middle section, where he asked them in a stage whisper who wanted to be saved, the first few cries started ringing out from the audiences. His principal theme was that the Messiah was returning, and He was returning soon. This was the audience's opportunity to prepare, preferably with a healthy donation to Giovanni, although this was only hinted at with a vague reference to investing in the bank of heaven. He was sowing seeds in their minds, and this was only one of many.

Eva sat in Anita's chair and considered the view she would have had. The front row was reserved for those Giovanni referred to as the true followers. Eva laughed at the thought. To become a true follower, you had to meet one of two criteria. You had to be a major benefactor to the cause, or you had to be the current object of Giovanni's attention, as Maddy was at the present time. Anita had been both, but not for as long as Giovanni had wanted. After she had vanished, and Giovanni had found out what she had done, he was angrier than Eva had ever seen him.

If the information Anita had stolen got into the wrong hands, it could derail their entire operation. Eva shook her head in sadness. There was no way on earth that could be allowed to happen. There was far too much at stake for that.

15

Anita looked around as she noticed the blue car pulling up alongside them, the passenger window descending as it did so. In the passenger seat was a young woman, perhaps the same age as she was, who was gesturing at them with her hands to pull over. The driver of the small Fiat was also looking through the window, his eyes flicking between her and Caleb and the road ahead. Anita tapped Caleb on the shoulder.

"They want us to stop," Anita shouted.

Caleb eased his hand up on the accelerator and brought the moped to a stop as the Fiat pulled in front of the moped and parked a few meters in front of it. Both doors opened and the car's occupants climbed out. As the two young people approached, Anita saw a cell phone in the man's hand. She could also see they were well dressed, both with expensive but casual clothes. The woman was wearing a figure-hugging black dress with a high neckline that Anita instantly liked, while her companion was dressed in white chinos and an unpadded linen blazer over a white t-shirt.

He was the epitome of sprezzatura, or Italian studied care-lessness.

"Che succede?" Anita asked the young man. *What's up?* He ignored her and addressed Caleb while the woman took in Anita's ill-fitting clothes, a half-smile on her face as she did so.

"That moped belongs to my brother," the man said, the anger in his voice obvious. He must think they had stolen it.

"My friend doesn't speak Italian," Anita replied, "but we bought the moped from your brother." Finally, the young man turned to look at her. "He's a chef, right?"

"Yes," the man said, his voice softening slightly.

"So, call him and ask him." Anita pointed at the cell phone in the man's hand.

"If I could get a signal, I would."

"What are you talking about, Anita?" Caleb asked her in English.

"His brother's the chef," Anita replied. "I think they thought we stole the moped."

"Get him to call him," Caleb said. Anita fixed him with a withering look.

"I already did, Caleb, but thanks for the advice." She waved her hands in the air. "There's no signal."

"How about they follow us until they get a signal? It's not as if we can outrun them, is it?"

Anita suggested this to the man, who nodded in reply, regarding Caleb with a curious expression as he did so.

"You're American?" he asked Caleb in heavily accented English.

"Sure am," Caleb replied with a smile. "Texan born and bred. You ever been?"

"No," the man replied, not returning Caleb's smile. Then

he turned and walked back to the car. Anita saw him glancing at his cell phone in frustration.

"Just ignore him," the young woman said in Italian, smiling and looking again at what Anita was wearing. "He doesn't really get on with his brother."

"But he gets on well enough with him to look out for his moped?" Anita replied. The woman shrugged her shoulders before replying.

"They're still brothers," she said with a smile. "There's a village a few kilometers away where we're going for lunch. We should be able to get a signal there." She glanced at Anita's clothes again. "There're also a couple of boutiques there if you're interested?" Her smile broadened as she turned to walk away.

"Everything okay?" Caleb asked.

"Yeah," Anita replied, switching back to English as she watched the woman get into the car. "Just a bit of fashion advice, that's all."

16

Caleb followed the blue Fiat as it made its way along the road. The encounter with the young couple had unsettled him, although he'd been careful not to reveal this to Anita. His first thought when he'd seen the passenger window going down had been that a gun was about to be pointed out of it, and there would have been nothing he could have done. When he'd seen it was a young couple, he had breathed a sigh of relief although, a few minutes into the conversation, he would have happily punched the young man in the face. Even though Caleb couldn't understand what he was saying, the way he walked, spoke, and held himself was just irritating. Caleb pressed his lips together into a thin smile. Perhaps he was getting old?

Ahead of them, he could see some buildings in the distance and, a few hundred meters later, they passed a sign announcing they had arrived in Ceraino. The area had become more mountainous and the road now had a steep foothill on Caleb's right with mesh netting to stop any rocks falling onto the road. The town of Ceraino was nestled in a small valley to the left and Caleb saw the blue Fiat peeling off toward the Centrum. He noticed the female passenger was waving her cell phone out of the window, so assumed that she had spoken to her companion's brother and verified the sale of the moped.

Caleb rode past several residential buildings, all with red-tiled roofs and painted walls. Most of them were badly in need of a fresh coat of whitewash and weathered wooden shutters seemed to be the de facto covering for the windows, except for a church that looked to be the best maintained building in the area.

As they left the town behind, the rock wall on the right-hand side of the road became almost vertical, and a knee high barrier on the left provided scant protection to what looked to be a sheer drop. With the bends in the road making it even more treacherous, Caleb slowed his speed, not wanting to encounter something coming the other way. Before too long, they were back out in the open countryside, the road gently climbing in front of them.

Almost twenty minutes later, they finally reached their destination, a village called Spiazzi. Like Ceraino, it was next to a mountain, almost as if it was sheltering in its shadow. Caleb parked the moped in the central square and made his way to the public bathrooms after telling Anita that he would only be a couple of minutes. But when he returned to the moped, his bladder empty and wearing his robe again, she was nowhere to be seen, so he took a seat on one of the small benches that looked out over the valleys below. Caleb breathed in a deep breath as he admired the view. The hills he could see were all dark green from the forests and a low layer of mist was obscuring the valley floor.

Caleb had been sitting on the bench for fifteen to

twenty minutes when Anita returned. To his surprise, she was now wearing a very similar dress to the one the woman in the car had been wearing, apart from a narrow pink belt that showed off her hips. In one hand was her handbag, and in the other was a large paper bag with string handles and an Italian name on the side. As she approached, Caleb could see that she had even brushed her hair.

"Wow, you look different," he said as she sat down next to him. "Did you borrow or buy a hairbrush?"

"I bought one," Anita replied, looking at him with a curious expression. "Sharing hairbrushes isn't something women really do." She looked at his shaved head and grinned. "Not that you'd know. Why d'you ask?"

"Because we're not quite at our final destination yet, so you'll be wearing the crash helmet again for a few minutes." When he saw her face fall, he continued. "Or we could walk, I guess. It's maybe twenty minutes?"

"Let's walk," she replied. "My back's still aching from the ride up here."

They got to their feet and set off at a slow pace, approaching the moped, which had their crash helmets hanging from the handlebars.

"What do you want to do about the moped?" Caleb asked her.

"Leave it there, I guess. I can't see anyone stealing it unless they've got a death wish. Did you want to keep it?"

"No, I'm good," he replied with a laugh.

Anita was quite distinctive with her red hair, and she attracted looks from several people of both genders. Some were looks of appreciation, some were envy. By contrast, no one gave Caleb a second look, which was just the way he liked it. There were so many things Caleb wanted to ask

Anita, but there would be time enough for that when they got to their destination.

It wasn't quite twenty minutes when they approached a three-story hotel with faded red painted walls and a walled garden. When they reached it, Caleb led Anita through the grounds.

"This is where you're staying?" Anita asked him. She was looking at the hotel with a smile on her face.

"No, it's not here," Caleb replied. He raised his hand and pointed halfway up the mountain that overlooked the hotel and the village. Anita followed his finger, and he saw her jaw drop when she saw the small church that had been built around halfway up the mountain, perhaps five hundred meters above them. "I'm up there."

"You're staying in a church?" Anita asked, her eyes wide.

"No, there's a small monastery attached to it. I'm staying there."

"I thought you said you weren't a monk?"

"I'm not. They take guests on sabbaticals."

"Will they mind me staying there? I'm not really the religious sort."

"They won't mind at all," Caleb replied, laughing as he did so. "In fact, no one will say a word about it."

"What's so funny?" Anita had a quizzical look on her face as she stared up at the church. It almost looked as if it had been dropped from the sky into its precarious-looking location.

"You'll find out," Caleb said, leading Anita toward a narrow path that snaked up toward the buildings above them. It was cut with steps that were worn in the middle from the passing of time and pilgrims. "Ready for some exercise?"

17

A nita looked at the imposing buildings halfway up the mountain. They didn't look real to her, but more like some sort of model or film set. The more she looked, the more detail she could pick out. As well as the church, with its simple white spire pointing straight up into the sky, there were also smaller buildings congregated around the church. Several of them had crenelations and small watchtowers, almost as if they were defensive positions. But considering their elevated position, what could they be defending the buildings from?

At the start of the path, there had been a small wooden hut with an elderly monk sitting inside. Anita had watched as Caleb walked over to say something to him. It didn't look as if the monk had said anything back to Caleb, but she saw him nodding his head in response to whatever Caleb had just said. When he returned, Caleb had a couple of plastic bottles in his hands.

"Is he the security guard?" Anita had said, hoping for a smile from Caleb, but he'd remained silent.

In front of her, Caleb had set off on the path that wound

its way around the sheer mountain face. Anita followed, wishing she were wearing some more comfortable shoes. It was warm, and although the path was currently in shadow, she could see that after a few hundred meters, it was bathed in sunlight.

"So, what is this place, then?" Anita asked Caleb a few moments later. He paused, and she realized he was out of breath and had one hand pressed to his abdomen.

"It's called the Sanctuary of the Madonna della Corona," Caleb said, his discomfort obvious. "It was built in fifteen hundred and something, but it's been a religious site for far longer."

"Any reason?" Anita asked.

Caleb smiled in response. "Is one needed?"

"It's just that it looks rather, well, rather inaccessible?"

"I think that's kind of the point," Caleb replied, turning to take a few more steps. "You know, many people climb this staircase on their knees, praying for forgiveness as they do so."

"That seems a bit extreme," Anita said.

"I guess it depends on your sins," Caleb replied with a sideways glance at her.

They stopped again a few hundred meters later, just before the path emerged into the sunshine. When Anita looked at Caleb, he looked to be in a lot of discomfort.

"Are you okay?" Anita asked him. "You look like you're struggling."

"I've done this journey many times, Anita," Caleb replied, sipping from his bottle of water. "As long as I take it slow, I'll be fine." He pointed at a small bench that was hewn directly out of the rock of the mountain, still in shade. "Why don't we sit for a while?"

Anita sat on the bench next to him, grateful for the

respite. Her calves were aching from the steps, and the next part of the path was going to be punishing in the sun. Above them, the sky was an azure blue with not a cloud in sight, and below them, Anita could see the shores of Lake Garda. On the surface of the lake, several boats could be seen moving about at a leisurely pace.

"So why are you here, Caleb?" Anita asked him a few moments later. "It seems a bit out of the way for a preacher from the Deep South."

"I usually reply that I have to be somewhere when someone asks me that," Caleb replied, a half-smile on his face. "But I think in this case, I'm here because He needed me to be here." He glanced up at the sky as he spoke.

"He as in God?"

"If that's how you want to refer to Him, yes."

"Why would He need you to be here?" Anita asked. "That makes little sense to me."

Caleb turned to look at Anita, his gray eyes boring into her with an intensity that bordered on uncomfortable.

"I was in a cafe at the exact moment you needed some help, Anita. Does that not tell you something?"

"Not really, no," Anita replied. "I could have been anywhere. As could you."

"But I wasn't. I was there at exactly the same time you were."

"Don't take this the wrong way, Caleb," Anita replied, wishing he would look at something else. "I appreciate the help and everything, but you're just a preacher."

"I have other skills," Caleb said, the faintest of smiles appearing on his face. "May I take your hand?"

Anita hesitated for a moment before extending her hand for him to take. When he did so, his skin was cool and surprisingly smooth. She watched as he closed his eyes. A few seconds later, she noticed a peculiar sensation in her fingers that slowly spread up her forearm. It wasn't uncomfortable, but it was definitely a strange feeling, almost heavy. She opened her mouth to say something, but when she saw the look of intense concentration on Caleb's face, she closed it again.

Perhaps thirty seconds later, Caleb let go of her hand. His eyes, when he reopened them, were still intense, but they had changed somehow. Anita wouldn't be able to articulate how if she were asked, but there was something about their intensity that had shifted.

"Well?" Anita said with a nervous laugh as she rubbed at her arm. "What was that all about?"

"I was just confirming what I thought I knew," Caleb replied, "as well as finding out a few more things."

"Is that one of your other skills, preacher?" Anita was becoming uncomfortable at Caleb's demeanor. "You read minds?"

Caleb didn't reply, but got to his feet. "We should go," he said, looking at the church and buildings that were still a few hundred meters above them. "We'll get to the monastery, settle in, and then we need to talk."

"Talk about what, Caleb?" Anita asked.

"You need to tell me everything, Anita," Caleb said, looking at her as a frigid chill ran down her spine.

"Why?" she replied, trying not to shiver.

"There are dark forces around you, Anita." He looked away as he said this, staring out over the lake below them with an inscrutable expression on his face.

"Do you mean the men who were chasing us?" Anita asked, her voice almost a whisper.

"No," Caleb replied. "I'm talking about something much darker than that."

18

Giovanni watched from the side of the room as his congregation entered the conference room. As they entered, each one greeted Eva, standing by the door, before wrapping their arms around her. Then they milled about, also hugging the others in the room. Giovanni smiled at the sight. The embraces were an important part of their regime and he encouraged it, but he didn't take part. Not that he didn't want to, it was that he needed to keep an element of physical separation between them. That way, when he did touch one of them, it meant more to the person he was hugging.

He watched his congregation for a few moments, a soft smile on his face. Each and every one of them was carefully chosen from their on-line community, thousands of whom would be streaming the live broadcast. Giovanni didn't want the broken and dispossessed in his inner sanctum. They could remain on-line, where they could be as broken and dispossessed as they wanted as long as they still paid their subscription. Giovanni wanted bright, ambitious people from society. Those with a genuine hunger for connection and growth. That was the tribe he wanted. People who wanted to create a world that was more egalitarian, kinder, or more sustainable. At least, that was what he preached.

One of the last members to enter the room was Maddy. She was nineteen and had been studying anthropology at a university in central Iowa when she had attended a special presentation by Giovanni. The presentation had been titled *Anthropology and Armageddon,* a carefully constructed title designed to draw people just like her in. In the presentation, Giovanni had argued strongly for the concept of a human being as a totality of being, not a combination of various parts and impulses. As he had delivered this element, he was studying his audience carefully to see who among them was nibbling at the hook. Maddy had been one of these, sitting intently, listening to every word Giovanni said. When he got to the part about human flesh not being able to exist alone, but only able to exist with the breath of God, he had seen her nodding enthusiastically. That was when he knew she had swallowed not just the hook, but the line and sinker as well. The rest of the presentation, where Giovanni started drawing links between human society's inevitable descent toward the end of days, perhaps half his audience was still with him. Those, he hoped, would become subscribers. They usually did. But Maddy? Giovanni had a much different path he wanted her to take.

The congregation sat and the low hubbub of conversation died down. Giovanni waited for silence before he spoke. As the conversation faded away, he saw Maddy look at him and his eyes met hers. A smile appeared on her face before she looked away, pretending to be embarrassed by his gaze, and she swept her hand up to return a stray lock of blonde hair behind her ear.

Dirty little slut, Giovanni thought as he looked at her. She could play the innocent all she wanted, but he knew she was far from the pious little girl she was pretending to be.

Walking around the margins of the room was a cameraman with a digital camera on a body harness. None of the congregation looked at the camera by prior arrangement. Giovanni waited as the cameraman swept the room before the man returned to his position at the back of the room. Giovanni glanced at Eva, still by the door, who gave him a thumbs up to show he could start.

"Adelphoi," Giovanni said a moment later. Giovanni swallowed back a lump in his throat as he said this, but gender inclusivity was all the rage. When he had started out, it was just brethren. Then, he'd had to add sistren to include female members. Finally, a few months previously and on the advice of a Professor of Linguistics from a college in Cambridge in England, he had changed to adelphoi because it was a gender-neutral term. According to the professor, at least. "Welcome to my church."

"Thank you, Brother Giovanni," they replied, almost in unison.

Giovanni paused for a few seconds, just to build the atmosphere. Then he began his sermon.

The message was a variant of the same message he had been preaching since he had started. The end times were approaching, and they needed to be prepared. When the reckoning finally came, they would need an army to protect themselves, and to protect the returning Son of God. There had been an earthquake in Jerusalem a few days previously, and when he'd seen it reported on the news, Giovanni had punched the air in triumph. That small seismic event had to be worth thousands of dollars in donations from the frightened. It wasn't a large enough event for a tenth of the city to collapse, nor were seven thousand people killed, but it was close enough to what was written in Revelation to be a very dramatic hook.

"Does it not say, in the book of Revelation, that bodies will lie in the street of the great city where the Lord was crucified?" Giovanni asked his audience, lowering his voice to cause them to pay attention to what he was saying. Then he raised it again, shouting this time and causing several of the congregation to jump. "Do you watch the news? Have you seen the bodies lying in Jerusalem?" Several heads nodded, which was just as well as Giovanni hadn't been able to find any footage of this or he would have projected it behind him. The audience members jumping as he shouted would make fantastic television, though, as would the few replies to his question of *Yes, Brother*. "God is preparing us for His return, and we must prepare ourselves for when the trumpets sound." There were more shouts of *Yes, Brother*, these louder and more confident.

Giovanni continued in a similar vein for several minutes, eventually reaching the final stage of his sermon. He lowered his voice again, slowing the pace to appear more reflective.

"The time of horror and judgment upon the earth is approaching," he said. "I look at the television and I see worldwide hardship. I see persecution, disasters, pain and suffering." A slight raise in his tone. "And I am scared, adelphoi. I fear what is to come. I fear what He will see when He returns." Giovanni half-closed his eyes, but he could see several people nodding through his eyelids, including Maddy, who was staring at him wide-eyed as she always did during this part of his sermon. He snapped his eyes back open and raised his voice, looking directly at the camera as he did so. "But we can prepare for the great tribulation. We can get ready for His return." Giovanni's voice increased in volume again. "If you stand with me, He will stand with you!"

Giovanni let his hands fall to his sides and his head bow, seemingly exhausted by his efforts. As if they were one person, the entire congregation rose to their feet, as they always did, and broke into rapturous applause.

He let a smile play across his face as he kept his head lowered. He knew it was an outstanding performance because it always was. All across the world, people would reach for their phones to open the Adelphoi app. There was a button in the app clearly marked *Stand with Him* which led directly to a payment page where the faithful could purchase a bit more reassurance.

It wasn't Giovanni's fault they were so gullible.

19

Hugo sat in silence in his office, deep in thought. Claudia's words about the artificial embryo they had created were still ringing around his ears.

"Yes," she had said when asked if it was viable. "We believe it is."

He knew if the international scientific community found out they were cultivating an embryo in this way, there would be uproar and widespread condemnation. But Hugo wasn't paying the scientists to work for the community. He was paying them to work for him. Other researchers had created similar models, but they were only models designed to provide an ethical way for scientists to understand the earliest moments of human existence. Hugo wasn't interested in understanding those early moments of existence. He was interested in creating life itself.

Hugo eased himself from his chair and sank to his knees on the plush carpet in his office. He raised his hands and placed them palms together before praying for a few moments, knowing that the research wouldn't have got as far as it had done without divine assistance.

"So God created mankind in his own image," Hugo mumbled, trying not to sneer as he spoke. "In the image of God, He created them. Male and female, He created them." He stood a few moments later, wincing as one of his knees popped. Getting old was no fun at all, but perhaps now he would leave a legacy?

Hugo had no children, partly by design, partly by a lack of opportunity. It wasn't that he didn't want children. He had nothing against them from a philosophical perspective, apart from perhaps the cost of raising them, but money had never been an issue for any generation of the Forresters. If he had met the right woman when he was younger, then perhaps it would be different. Hugo's thoughts drifted to the clump of cells he had seen on the screen. Those cells could become his son or daughter if Claudia was right about the embryo being viable. The embryo would never develop, though. This phase of the project was simply to get as far as they could within a laboratory.

There had been some research done in Israel by a team at the Weizmann Institute, which had paved the way for Claudia and the rest of her team. The Israelis had taken some stem cells from a traditional embryo and chemically altered them to coax them into becoming the four types of cells found in the earliest stages of the human embryo. These cells had gone on to develop into a synthetic embryo-like structure, but the team hadn't allowed it to develop beyond the fourteen-day point. The embryo Claudia had shown him earlier was three weeks old, and already forming a heart. Not only that, but the stem cells that it had been created from were from Hugo himself.

When the Israelis had written up their project, they had stressed that their synthetic embryo wouldn't be able to be used to achieve a pregnancy. Apart from the ethical and legal considerations, neither of which Hugo considered applied to him and his team, the Weizmann Institute claimed it would be impossible to implant it into the lining of a womb. When Hugo had discussed this with Claudia, she had just laughed.

"What rubbish," she had said at the time. "They're only saying it to appease the masses and make sure their funding doesn't dry up. The Chinese have done it with monkey embryos and the Brits have done it with mice. Neither project was successful beyond a few weeks, though."

"Why not?" Hugo had asked.

"Because they were in a laboratory," had been Claudia's reply, "instead of a womb."

Hugo sat back in the chair in his office and reached for the telephone. He picked up the handset, and a few seconds later, his aide answered.

"Mr. Forrester?" the young man said. "How may I help?"

"Is there any update from Nasim?" Hugo asked.

"The team is on their way to recover the jars now," the aide replied. "They should be here in a few days. God will be with them."

"Good," Hugo said, nodding his head at his aide's words. He was perhaps Hugo's most trusted companion, and shared his vision for the new world implicitly, no matter how apocalyptic it might be. "When the items arrive, have them sent straight to the laboratory, not the warehouse. Directly to the laboratory."

"Yes, Mr. Forrester, I understand."

"Excellent. Now, I need to go to Italy. To the Adelphoi."

"I have you scheduled for a visit there in a couple of week's time, Mr. Forrester," his aide replied.

"Bring it forward. I need to go as soon as I can."

"Of course, Mr. Forrester," the aide said. "I'll speak to the pilot now."

Hugo looked out of his office window where a white Leonardo AW109 E helicopter sat waiting on a helipad not a hundred meters away from his office. It was a decadent luxury, especially with so many VIP firms operating out of Geneva Airport only a few miles away, but what was the point of having money if you didn't spend it?

"Can you speak to the Adelphoi and let them know I'm coming?" Hugo asked. "If there's not enough time for them to prepare the suite, I'll stay in my usual hotel. If you could make the necessary arrangements, I would be most grateful."

"And if the Adelphoi ask the purpose of your visit, Mr. Forrester?"

"Just tell them I have some very exciting news," Hugo replied with a broad smile.

20

Eva watched with a smile as Maddy started lifting the chairs to stack them together. She was only strong enough to lift a single chair at a time, but this didn't dent her enthusiasm. When Eva had asked her to help rearrange the conference room after the sermon, the girl's face had lit up at being chosen.

"They're heavy, aren't they?" Eva said as she picked up a chair herself, placing it on top of another chair against the wall. "Let's take our time. No point getting all hot and bothered, is there?"

"Okay," Maddy replied, huffing as she moved the chair to the wall.

"So, you've settled in okay?" Eva asked when Maddy had finished moving the chair. The young girl turned to look at her with a smile.

"Oh, yes," Maddy replied. "I love it here. Everyone's so friendly."

"No regrets about leaving Iowa?"

"None at all," Maddy said.

Eva looked at her for a few seconds, realizing that

they'd not really spoken much, and never without Giovanni in attendance. Maddy was, in Eva's opinion, a rather strange looking young woman. Her most striking feature was without doubt her eyes, which were dark brown and doe-like. She had an oval face framed by blonde hair that fell to just past her shoulders, a nose that was ever so slightly too large for the rest of her face, and a full mouth that looked as if it belonged to a much older woman. Even her clothes were slightly odd, with the knee-high denim skirt and baggy hoody hiding her figure almost completely.

"That's good to hear," Eva replied with a smile. "Some people find it a bit disquieting leaving home and going somewhere so far away."

"The university's been great," Maddy said, mirroring Eva's smile. "They said I can just re-enroll at the start of next year's summer semester if I want to."

"Excellent. And your family?"

Maddy grimaced at Eva's question.

"They're not too thrilled about me taking a year off, if I'm honest," she said. "But coming here is so exciting. I'm sure they'll come round."

"How about friends?" Eva saw Maddy's face fall slightly at the question, but she recovered it well.

"All good."

"Boyfriend?" Eva asked carefully before smiling. Maddy's face fell again, and this time it took her longer to recover. Her expression was hard to read, and Eva wasn't sure if it was disappointment or something else. Shame, perhaps? Eva was just wondering if she should change the subject when Maddy answered.

"No," she said, looking at Eva with almost doe-like eyes. "Not a boyfriend." She was chewing her lip as she looked at

Eva. Then she pressed them together before taking a breath. "I, um, I had a partner, but we split up a month or so ago."

"A partner?" Eva asked. "But not a boyfriend?"

Maddy said nothing, but just nodded her head. She almost looked as if she was on the verge of tears.

"Yes," she replied a few seconds later. "She didn't approve of the Adelphoi."

"You're gay?" Eva asked with what she hoped was a maternal look. From the look on Maddy's face, this wasn't something she told many people about.

"Yes," Maddy replied. "It's another reason for coming here. My family doesn't approve. It's okay, isn't it? I mean, me being here?"

"It doesn't make any difference here, Maddy," Eva replied, slipping back into character as Sister Eva. "The God I know doesn't judge us for who we love." She took Maddy's hands in hers and smiled at the girl. "Whoever they are." To Eva's relief, a broad smile appeared on Maddy's face.

"Thank you," she said, her relief obvious to Eva.

"I'm sorry to hear you broke up with your partner. What was her name?" Eva turned to fetch another chair, followed by Maddy.

"It was Annabella, but I don't really want to talk about it, if that's okay?" Maddy replied. Eva just nodded her head in response. Giovanni would be furious at the news. After the sermon, when he had finished basking in the adoration of his congregation, he had instructed Eva to invite Maddy to lunch. It was, Eva was well aware, the start of his process that would usually end up with the young girl in his bed. Not that Maddy being gay would make a blind bit of difference. Eva knew he would probably try to get Maddy into bed anyway, regardless of her sexual orientation. All roads led to Rome, in Giovanni's opinion.

A few moments later, all the chairs were stacked in neat piles against the wall. The conference room was due to be used for a yoga session that afternoon, but it wasn't something that Eva would be attending. She preferred a different type of exercise, one which also involved different positions, but it wasn't yoga. As they worked, Eva considered whether to invite Maddy to lunch, given what the girl had just revealed. In the end, she decided she would invite her, even if it was only to wind Giovanni up.

"Brother Giovanni and I were wondering, Maddy," Eva said as they crossed the room to the door. "Would you like to join us for lunch?"

"Me?" the girl replied, her mouth remaining half open in surprise.

"Yes, Maddy," Eva said with a laugh. "You. Giovanni and I have a proposition for you." She paused before continuing, wondering how best to approach the clothes Maddy was wearing. "Do you have anything smarter than the hoodie, though?"

Maddy clapped her hands together and Eva thought for a moment she was about to jump in the air.

"A proposition?" she said, her eyes bright and full of enthusiasm. "For me? My goodness."

Eva knew, or at least strongly suspected, that Maddy's enthusiasm might wane when she found out exactly what that proposition entailed, but she also knew that by then it would be too late. Giovanni was a very persuasive man.

"Do you have something else to wear for lunch?" Eva asked again. "If you don't, I can lend you something, but it may be a little large for you."

"No, no, I have a summer dress I can wear and I have a shawl to cover my shoulders."

Eva laughed again. What sort of lunch did the poor child think she'd just been invited to?

"The dress will be fine, Maddy," Eva said. "It's an informal lunch, nothing more. There's no need for a shawl." *Besides*, she thought. *Giovanni will want to see a bit more of you.* "We'll be eating on the terrace at one. Do you have any dietary requirements?"

"I'm allergic to garlic," Maddy replied, "but apart from that, I'll eat anything."

"I'll let the chef know," Eva said with another smile. "Now, if you'll excuse me, I have some chores to be getting on with."

Maddy returned Eva's smile, and Eva almost felt bad for her. The poor girl had no idea what Giovanni's intentions for her were, but she was quite looking forward to seeing him squirm his way out of this one.

Lunch was going to be quite amusing.

21

Caleb's knuckles were white as he gripped the side of the washbasin in his small room. He leaned forward and spat into the basin, looking with disgust at the small puddle of bile he had produced. With a sigh, he turned on the faucet to rinse it away before looking at himself in the mirror. When he saw the heavy bags under his eyes, he sighed again. The last leg of the walk up the path had been punishing, and he knew he'd overdone it, but he had things to do.

When they had finally got to the monastery, Caleb had shown Anita to one of the spare rooms a few doors down from his room. He knew it was empty as he'd said goodbye to its occupant that morning. Then he'd sought the Abate, or Abbot, to let him know there was one more person in his accommodation. The Abbot hadn't even blinked when Caleb told him it was a woman, that she was in trouble, and that Caleb was helping her. The elderly monk had just nodded.

"Tutti sono i benvenuti qui," he had whispered. All are welcome here.

Caleb ran some cold water into his hands and patted his face. He needed to rest, but he needed to speak to Anita before that.

A short time later, he and Anita were sitting at a table and chairs outside the main church, which towered above them. It also provided some shade from the heat of the sun. Caleb had refilled the bottles of water that the monk at the head of the path had given them and he sipped his before turning to Anita.

"So," Caleb said after a momentary pause. "Why not start at the beginning? Tell me about these friends you were visiting."

He watched her as she gazed out over the valley below them for several moments. She looked to be gathering her thoughts, and he let her do so uninterrupted. This was, after all, her story to tell.

"It started with an online Zoom session," Anita said in a quiet voice. "A friend of mine back home recommended it. I was bored, and it was something to do." She turned to look at him, but it was as if she was looking through him, not at him. "Have you heard of the Adelphoi?"

"Brothers and sisters," Caleb replied. "It comes from the Greek word delphys." She looked at him with a curious expression. "It means womb, as in siblings come from the same womb."

"That makes sense, I guess," Anita replied with a half laugh that was devoid of any humor. "Anyway, it was a kind of sermon, I guess. I was hooked right from the start. Everything they said made sense. It was almost as if they were talking directly to me." She took a deep breath before continuing. "There's this man, Brother Giovanni, who's in charge of the Adelphoi. That's what they call themselves. They travel to the States a lot and I went to an in-person session to meet him. Next thing I know, I was on a flight to Italy to join the group."

"What sort of group are they?" Caleb asked, careful to keep his voice non-judgmental.

"I was so lonely, Caleb," Anita replied, ignoring his question. "But they made me feel so welcome. So, I don't know, so loved, I suppose." She turned to look back over the valley. "I've not spoken to my mother in years and my father's idea of being a parent is to throw money at me when I need it."

Caleb watched as a solitary tear made its way down Anita's cheek. She brushed it away before continuing.

"It all started off so brilliantly. Finally, I was somewhere I felt happy and fulfilled. I was part of a community with a common purpose. A goal that actually meant something really important. We were preparing for the most important moment in all of history." She looked at him and he saw the anger building behind her eyes. "Every meeting we had started with hugs, and Brother Giovanni made me feel alive. Not just emotionally, but spiritually as well. He told me he could see the real me."

Caleb said nothing, wondering how long it would be before Anita would tell him when it all started going wrong. They sat in silence for a few moments, Anita seemingly lost in her thoughts.

"I never thought I was that gullible," she said in a small voice. "I'm not a stupid woman, but he pulled me in like a fisherman." Anita took another deep breath and unscrewed the lid of her water before taking a sip. "How am I doing so far?"

"You're doing fine, Anita," Caleb replied, again trying to keep his voice neutral. "Just keep going at your own pace."

"Brother Giovanni made me an ambassador for the Adelphoi," she said. "He said I was perfect for the role. He said it was what God wanted me to do. I had to stand up at the start of his sermons and tell everyone watching how wonderful everything was. How we were all doing God's work, and how they could join us if they were committed enough." He saw her swallow a lump back in her throat before she took another sip of water. "I had to prove my own commitment to the cause as well. To prove to God that I was worthy of joining Brother Giovanni in preparation."

Caleb frowned at her words, unsure where she was going with the story. He was desperate to know more about what this important moment they were preparing for was, but he didn't want to break Anita's flow. He suspected it would all come out in time, but he wasn't sure how much of that they would have. Although they had thrown the men in gray suits off their trail, Caleb knew it was only a matter of time before they picked it up again.

"How did Brother Giovanni make you prove your own commitment to the cause, Anita?" Caleb asked a few moments later when it appeared Anita would not be as forthcoming as he'd thought. She looked at him and he saw the anger had spread from her eyes to her entire face.

"In bed, Caleb," she replied with a short laugh. "Where else? The things he made me do, the things he did to me. I should have seen them for what they were, which was pure gratification. His gratification, and the evil witch who works with him."

Caleb looked down at the table, not wanting to look at Anita as she relived those moments. He sensed that the conversation was ending, at least for the moment, and what Anita said next confirmed this.

"I'm tired, Caleb. I need to sleep. Can we talk about this later?"

"Can I ask you one thing, Anita?" Caleb said. He didn't

wait for Anita to answer before he continued. "This moment in history, this cause you speak of. What is it exactly?"

"It's the end of days, Caleb," Anita replied, and he could hear the exhaustion in her voice. "The Parousia. The Second Coming of the Son of God. Whatever you want to call it."

Caleb said nothing in reply. Humans had been preparing for that event for the last few thousand years, but there was no way of predicting when it would occur. As if she had read his thoughts, Anita continued.

"They're not just preparing for it, Caleb," she said, her voice distant. "They think they can make it happen on their terms."

22

Anita lay back on the bed and closed her eyes, praying for sleep to take her away and give her some respite. But, despite her exhaustion, she remained awake with thoughts streaming through her head. She thought back to her conversation with Caleb and about his expression when she had told him of the Adelphoi's plans. His expression hadn't changed, and all he had said in response were two words.

"They can't."

She knew there were more conversations to be had, and that some of them would be uncomfortable, but just telling him what she had already had lifted a weight from her shoulders. Anita knew there was nothing Caleb could do about the Adelphoi. Brother Giovanni's organization was too powerful, and Caleb was only a simple monk, or preacher, as he would no doubt correct her to say. The ease with which the Adelphoi had tracked her to the village was evidence of that.

Anita had persuaded Lorenzo, the taxi driver who had helped her back in Verona, to check her ticket into the flight she had booked and also her bag. It was an internal flight, so no passport would be required to check in, and it wasn't as if Lorenzo was actually going to board the plane. It was just scanning a barcode, and Anita had hoped that this would be enough to send anyone following her in the wrong direction by making it look as if she had taken the flight.

But the men in gray suits hadn't taken the bait. The contents of the bag were irrelevant. It only contained clothes and toiletries. Anita had what she needed in her handbag. She had money, access to plenty more if she needed it, and —most importantly—the thumb drive.

Anita's thoughts drifted to the other flight, one that she had actually taken from Italy to the United States with Brother Giovanni and Eva. She remembered sitting in her seat, wedged against a window with Giovanni and Eva hemming her in, when a flight attendant had approached.

"Excuse me," the impossibly attractive woman had said. "Are you Brother Giovanni and Sister Eva from Covelo?"

Giovanni had nodded in response, and then listened as the attendant told them they had been upgraded to first class seating before asking them if they would like to follow her. Giovanni and Eva had done so without a single word to Anita. She had relaxed, grateful for the additional room in the cramped economy seat, but a few moments later, a new arrival had slipped into the aisle seat. It had been a woman, probably about Anita's age or perhaps slightly older, and she was dressed in baggy jeans and a loose blouse, comfortable clothes for traveling as opposed to anything fashionable. She was also wearing an oversized pair of dark glasses that she didn't remove until the airplane was taxiing. Then she had removed them and turned to Anita.

"Good morning, Anita," the woman had said. Anita looked at her, surprised. She was much more attractive than she had realized, especially without the sunglasses. Her most notable feature were her dark brown eyes, which were now looking at Anita. "My name is Greta, and I need to speak to you."

"How do you know my name?" Anita had asked, but Greta hadn't answered her question. Instead, she had nodded toward the front of the airplane, toward the first-class compartment. What she had said next had made Anita's jaw drop.

"Giovanni squeals when he comes, doesn't he?" There had been with a faint smile on her face as she spoke. "Squeals like the pig he is."

Over the course of the flight, Greta had literally changed Anita's life. She had explained that she used to be a member of the Adelphoi and had been screwed regularly by Giovanni to prove her commitment to the cause. She too had been made an ambassador for the organization until the day she had been abducted by men sent by her father. It hadn't really been an abduction, though, but a rescue mission.

Anita sighed and rolled over onto her side as she thought back to the conversation, phrases Greta had used ringing around in her head. It had been the other woman who had done most of the talking, with Anita listening intently. Greta's words had peeled away the layers that the Adelphoi had covered her true personality with, effectively giving her a second pseudo-identity. As she had spoken, Greta's eyes had been fixed on the curtain that separated where they had been sitting from the first-class area, no doubt watching for Giovanni or Eva.

Greta had been insistent with her words, but at the same time, was respectful and even curious on occasion. She had given Anita plenty of time to reflect and had offered no facts or tried to persuade Anita that she was wrong. The entire conversation had been reality test after reality test.

"Why do you think Giovanni is sleeping with you?" Greta had asked many times. "Because he loves you or because he wants to control you?"

The last thing Greta had done had been to press a basic cell phone into Anita's hand just as the pilot announced they were beginning their descent. The previous hours had passed by in no time at all, their conversation interrupted only by the flight attendants serving meals.

"Take this. There's only one number in it. When you get back to Italy, call it and I will help you." Greta had looked at Anita, her brown eyes full of compassion. "But ask yourself this. If you knew then what you know now, would you have ever got involved?"

Knowing that she would not get a moment of sleep, Anita sat up on the bed and cricked her neck. She was still exhausted, but she wanted to speak some more to Caleb. He deserved the full story, not just snippets of it. He had, after all, saved her life.

23

G iovanni looked at the image on his computer screen with a growing sense of dread. The photograph he was looking at in full 4.5k resolution was a horrific one. It showed two young people, both lying in a crumpled heap in a ditch by the side of a road. Behind them, he could see a moped lying on its side. Giovanni didn't really need to see the bullet holes in the couple to tell they were both dead.

"What have you done?" he muttered to himself under his breath. Those idiot Italians were supposed to neutralize the threat, not to kill random people. He picked up his burner phone and pressed speed dial one.

"Ciao?" a male voice answered, sounding almost cheerful.

"It's me," Giovanni replied, although as far as he knew, he was the only person to have the number he had dialed. "I'm looking at the photographs now. It's not them." He took a deep breath. "The woman in the photo has dark hair. Anita's is red."

"We found the tracker wedged behind the seat," the man

replied. "The woman, or the man she was with, must have found it and put it there."

"Was there no way of confirming their identity before you killed them?" Giovanni asked, but the resulting silence answered the question. He sighed again, more deeply this time. The attention that this would bring would be unwanted, to say the least. "What happens next?"

"I'll reach out to some contacts I have in the local Carabinieri. It'll go down as an organized crime hit that went wrong." The man on the line sounded confident, almost overly so, and Giovanni wondered just how corrupt the local police were. "Then we'll keep looking for her. She can't have got too far." He paused for a moment. "I don't think Mr. Forrester needs to know about this, um, this mix-up. That wouldn't do any of us any favors."

Giovanni shook his head at the man's optimism. Not only had the two idiots lost track of the woman they were supposed to be following, but they had murdered two presumably innocent people in the process. "Keep me informed," Giovanni said, ending the call before the man had a chance to reply. He'd been right about not involving Hugo, though. He would be even more furious than Giovanni was.

Just as he slipped the burner phone back into his desk drawer, the office door opened and Eva walked in. Giovanni reached out for his mouse to minimize the screen with the photograph, but when he looked at Eva's face, he saw he'd been too slow.

"Giovanni," Eva said, her tone making it obvious she wasn't to be argued with. "Bring that photograph back up."

Giovanni did as she instructed, and to his surprise, he heard Eva swearing under her breath. She rarely swore, at least when she was clothed. When she was naked, she cursed a lot, but Giovanni pushed the thought away. There was a time and a place, and this was neither.

"It's under control," Giovanni said, minimizing the photograph a few seconds later. "It'll be put down as a mob hit gone wrong by the local police. I've already sorted it."

"You've already sorted it?" Eva said, looking at him. "You have, have you?" She stood with her hands on her hips and stared at him, the disdain obvious in her expression. "We're supposed to be a religious organization, Giovanni. Not a bunch of assassins. Or did I miss the memo where our strategy changed?"

"Those two buffoons were your idea, Eva," Giovanni replied. As soon as the words left his lips, he knew he'd made the wrong decision.

"Don't you dare, Thomas Gavazzi," Eva said in a sharp whisper, her use of his real name a warning she rarely used. "Don't you dare try to pin that on me." She pointed at him before jabbing him in the solar plexus with her index finger so hard he winced. "You were the one who wanted the threat neutralized. Those were your words."

"Neutralized, yes. As in retrieving the memory stick. I never told them to kill anyone," Giovanni replied, knowing he sounded petulant, "Anyway, what's done is done. We should move forward." He watched as Eva crossed her arms over her chest and looked at him with an incredulous expression. "Hugo's on his way here. He mustn't know about any of this."

"Oh, God, is he?" Eva replied, her expression softening a little. "What does the old fool want now?"

"Do you mean, apart from a quick roll in the hay with his favorite nun?" At least that brought a smile from Eva. "I'm not sure, to be honest. It was his assistant who called to let us know. Hugo's joining us for lunch."

"Shit," Eva replied with a frown. "Maddy's coming to lunch. I'll tell her we'll do it another time."

"No, let her come," Giovanni replied. "It'll stop him talking business while we're eating. At least then, by the time we sit down to talk about whatever it is he wants to talk about, he'll have had a few glasses of wine." He grinned at Eva. One thing he liked most about her was that she was never irritated for long. "I find he's more generous when he's under the influence. Besides, young Maddy's easy enough on the eye."

"If you say so, Giovanni," Eva said, returning his grin.

"I wonder whether a few glasses of wine would loosen her up a bit?" Giovanni said, more to himself than to Eva. Her grin broadened as she replied.

"I'm sure it would," Eva said, "but I'm not convinced that you're going to get very far with her. She's very young, Giovanni." She had a curious expression on her face that he didn't understand.

"Why do you say that?" Giovanni replied, grateful for the change in conversation, although Eva's words irritated him. "She's a grown woman. You've seen the way she looks at me. She's desperate to be saved." He allowed a smile to play across his face as he imagined what Maddy's expression might look like as he was saving her.

"If you say so, Giovanni," Eva said again, turning her back on him to leave the room, but not before he'd seen her smiling. "If you say so."

24

Hugo sat back in the plush leather of his seat in the helicopter's rear and gazed out of the window at the scenery below. They were cruising at an altitude of ten thousand feet above sea level, but with the height of the mountains, it was low enough for him to make out individual cows grazing on the lush grass of the ski runs that criss-crossed the terrain in the winter. Like most Austrians from the mountains, Hugo had skied almost before he could walk, and although he was a lot more cautious these days, he still enjoyed the thrill of barreling down a mountainside.

He saw a ski lift below them with rugged bicycles attached to the outside, taking thrill seekers to the top of the mountain. Hugo shook his head. Where was the fun in that? If you were going too fast, you just put the brakes on. It wasn't like on skis where, if you needed to slow down, it took a carefully crafted parallel turn or, worse case, a hockey stop.

He started thinking about the conversation he was about

to have with Giovanni and, hopefully, the lovely Eva. Whereas before, they had only spoken in hypothetical terms about the project, this conversation was going to be a very different one. Hugo picked up the folder his aide had handed him as he had left his office. He leafed through the papers inside until he found the report he was looking for, an updated version of an earlier report from Claudia's husband, Albert. Across the top of the first page was the report's title in bold letters.

RESULTS OF AI ENHANCED GENOMIC RECON- STRUCTION OF ANCIENT DNA FROM CELL FREE SAMPLES

Hugo tutted as he leafed through the report, realizing that Albert hadn't highlighted the additional text in a different font as he had been instructed. That meant he would have to read the entire thing, and Albert's academic prose was hardly riveting. To save time, Hugo turned to the summary at the end of the document. He read through it carefully, focusing on the last couple of paragraphs.

Using the petrous bone from the inner ear of the human skeletal sample, identified by enhanced radiocarbon dating as being between two thousand and two thousand one hundred years old, a massively parallel sequencing library of the DNA was constructed. Prior to sequencing, the library was quantified and amplified for both single and double stranded DNA samples. The second stage identified genomic sequences from contemporary stem cells, including sequences, to allow designing primers across the complete gene.

He allowed himself a smile at the reference to contemporary stem cells, knowing that this was a direct reference to him. If he understood the science correctly, the third stage of the process was to examine the ancient DNA and compare it against the DNA sequences of his stem cells. This would be repeated millions, if not billions of times, with the artificial intelligence inserting the ancient DNA segments into his stem cells, replacing his own to build up a living sample of the two thousand year old one. Where the ancient DNA was degraded, the AI would run Albert's proprietary algorithms to fill in the gaps, comparing the results against the entire library.

Hugo traced his hand down the page to the last couple of sentences in the report. He wasn't interested in the science. He was interested in the results.

The ultimate phase, the AI enhanced reconstruction of both single and double strands of the ancient DNA into the contemporary living stem cells, has taken several months to complete with several trillion calculations. Our research indicates that we are able to recreate the ancient DNA sample within the contemporary stem cells with a 95% degree of confidence in the final result. This confidence interval will only increase as more calculations are undertaken and the fidelity of the artificial intelligence models used increases.

He placed the report back in the folder, returning his gaze to the window and the scenery outside. From this altitude, his sense of being in the world was always altered. It reminded him of how small mankind was and how inconsequential humanity could be in the grand scheme of things.

But that was about to change, and it was about to change for the better. Perhaps not for most humans on the planet, but for a chosen few, it was going to be the start of a whole new epoch. One without conquest, wars, famine, or death. Without man's inhumanity to man, this new world would prosper and succeed as its predecessor had failed.

But in order to get to that point, there needed to be a

cataclysm, and only one entity could make that happen. Hugo knew it wasn't him. He was, after all, just a man, but Hugo saw himself as having been chosen to facilitate this future.

He had been chosen by God Himself.

25

Caleb sat on the edge of his bed and looked at the wooden door of his small room, wondering how long it would be before Anita knocked on it to continue their conversation. He knew she wouldn't be able to sleep, to rest properly, until she had completed the story she had to tell. What Anita had told him on the plaza of the monastery hadn't been a surprise. He'd had glimpses of her experiences when he had touched her. None of them had been definitive. They never were. But he'd sensed loneliness, love, and what passed for love but was nothing close. Anita had been deceived by nothing more than words. Vacant words with no true meaning behind them. She wasn't the first, nor would she be the last.

"Let no one deceive you with empty words, for because of such things, God's wrath comes on those who are disobedient," Caleb muttered under his breath. "Therefore, do not be partners with them." Then, because he couldn't help himself, he continued. "Ephesians, chapter five, verses six and seven."

His thoughts turned to the man Anita had told him

about. Brother Giovanni. Although she'd not described him to Caleb, he knew enough to recognize him, if not physically, then at least spiritually. Caleb had met many false prophets before. Men, and on one occasion women, who spoke what people wanted to hear. Wolves in sheep's clothing. History was littered with them and the wreckage they left behind. They weren't always religious in nature, either. There were many parallels between cults, pyramid schemes, and other scams that swept people like Anita into their webs. They promised everything and delivered nothing, but they had one thing in common. A charismatic leader of some sort.

Caleb was just beginning to consider he'd misunderstood Anita and that she was, in fact, sound asleep when there was a soft knock at his door. He got to his feet and opened it to see Anita standing with an apologetic expression on her face.

"Sorry to disturb you," she said. "I wasn't sure if you were asleep or not."

"I wasn't," Caleb replied with a smile. "Let me guess, you tried but couldn't sleep." He saw her nodding in response. "You want to talk some more? You can come in if you want to." He stepped back, opening the door wider.

"Is that allowed?" Anita said. "I mean, won't people talk?"

"People?"

"The monks?"

Caleb laughed, and Anita looked confused. "No, Anita, they won't say anything. But if you'd be more comfortable, we can go back to the plaza?"

A few moments later, they were sitting back at their original table, now bathed in bright sunshine. As before, small groups of monks were wandering around, but this time, they were all heading toward the entrance to the monastery where above their heads, a small bell was tolling.

"Is there a service on or something?" Caleb heard Anita ask.

"They're gathering for Sext," he replied, looking at her carefully. He saw her suppressing a smile, which was what he had been aiming for.

"Oh, really?" Anita asked, managing to keep a straight face. "They don't look very excited about it."

"It means the sixth hour after noon," Caleb explained. "It's the canonical hour of the Divine Office of almost all the traditional Christian liturgies." He lowered his voice to a conspiratorial whisper. "Psalms, mostly. Don't say anything to the monks, but it's a bit dull, in my opinion."

"My lips are sealed," she replied. "I won't say a word. You're not going, then? For Sext?"

"Not today," Caleb said with a wry grin. "So, where were we? You were telling me about the Adelphoi. How did you get away from them?"

He sat back and listened as Anita slowly told him about the strange woman on the plane. Caleb nodded along in encouragement as she spoke. He had heard similar stories before, but extricating people from the situation Anita had been in usually took longer than an airplane journey to accomplish. When Anita told him about the continued contact with Greta, using a mobile phone she had given Anita, it made more sense to Caleb.

"I was terrified they were going to find the cell phone," Anita told him, "but I could speak to Greta almost every day after we got back from the States."

"What did you talk about?" Caleb asked.

"To be honest, it was more me listening than us talking, at least to start off with." He saw Anita take a deep breath.

"She gave me things to do, to think about." Caleb nodded in response, knowing that this Greta woman was effectively deprogramming Anita from a distance. "Mental exercises, you know?" Caleb nodded again.

"She was giving you the tools to escape?" he asked, keeping his voice neutral.

"Exactly, but it got more and more difficult. The more I understood what was going on, the more of an act I had to put on to appear normal." Anita sighed again, more deeply this time. "Giovanni still wanted to sleep with me, and I had to pretend I was enjoying it when every time, it was just more disgusting."

Caleb said nothing for a moment, knowing there was nothing he could say to that. Perhaps he and Brother Giovanni would meet at some point in the future? Caleb made a mental note to discuss it with him then.

"Then what happened?" he asked, partly to move the story on but mostly to get Anita's attention away from what she had been describing.

"Greta gave me a thumb drive," Anita said. "I hid it under a log by the lake near where I used to read. All I had to do was put it into Giovanni's computer and leave it there for a few moments. But it took a week before I was alone in his office. He'd summoned me one evening, and I knew exactly what for. He'd gone to the restroom to freshen up, so I put it in the computer then." Anita paused for a moment before continuing. "Then he came back and we, er, he wanted to do it in his office. When he'd finished, I was able to pull the memory stick back out as I gathered my clothes. He was wiping himself down so didn't notice."

"You left straight away?"

"That night, yes. I waited until just before dawn and ran. Then I met you later that day."

"They were after you very quickly," Caleb said. "They must have known about the memory stick." It wasn't a question, but more Caleb thinking out loud.

"I know how they knew," Anita said. Caleb saw her face hardening as she spoke. "While we were having sex, he kept grabbing my hair and telling me to look at a photo on his wall. The photo was of Eva, the bitch who he works with. He kept telling me to imagine she was watching us."

Caleb lowered his head and examined his fingernails, not wanting to look Anita in the eye when she was describing something so horrific. After a brief pause, Anita continued.

"I think there was a camera behind the photo. He was recording us having sex and when he watched it back, or when the bitch did, they saw what I did."

"That would make sense," Caleb replied, raising his head to look at her. There was no pain in her eyes, though. Only anger.

Over Anita's shoulder, Caleb could see the Abbot of the monastery walking toward their table, his black robes billowing around him as he hurried across the plaza. Caleb started getting to his feet as the man approached. Whatever it was, it must be important for the Abbot to have left in the middle of their prayers.

When he arrived, Caleb almost brought himself to attention like a soldier. It wasn't because he meant to intentionally. It was almost a force of habit. The Abbot glanced at Anita briefly with a baleful expression before leaning forward and whispering in Caleb's ear. Caleb was about to reply, but the Abbot silenced him by putting his finger to his lips and shaking his head. Then the monk turned and walked away as quickly as he had arrived.

"Everything okay?" Caleb heard Anita ask. He shook his head in response. No, everything was not okay.

"Is there anything in your room you need urgently?" Caleb asked, gripping his cloth bag as he did so.

"No," Anita replied, her eyes widening.

"We need to go," Caleb said, injecting a note of immediacy into his voice, although from the way Anita's face had paled, it wasn't needed. "We need to go now."

26

Anita gasped as Caleb grabbed her hand and started pulling her to her feet.

"What?" she asked him. "What's going on?" Anita reached down and grabbed her handbag from where she had placed it on the table. Her purse and the all-important thumb drive were inside. Anything else was replaceable. All she really had in her room were some toiletries that she'd bought earlier in Spiazzi, and most of them were still in their wrappers.

"They're here," Caleb replied, his voice terse. "The men who were chasing us are here." He was making his way across the plaza, Anita's hand firmly in his, and she had to half-run to keep up with him.

"I don't understand," Anita replied. "How?"

"Probably just luck," Caleb said. "They saw a man in a robe and put two and two together to come up with a monastery. I should have thought of that before bringing you here." She looked at his face and saw he was annoyed with himself. "There was a tracker in your bag but I got rid of it before we left San Pietro In Cariano. That was how they knew your location."

Anita swore under her breath. Greta had warned her that the Adelphoi would keep a close eye on her, but she'd not thought they would have gone that far. Anita made a swift mental inventory of her belongings, but her bag and its contents were the only things she'd had at the complex that she still had.

"Hurry, Anita," Caleb said, pulling again on her hand. "We need to get out of sight."

"Will they say anything?" Anita asked him as they made their way down the side of the church. "The monks? Will they tell them we're here?"

"I doubt it," Caleb replied, turning to face her briefly with the briefest of smiles on his face. "It's a silent order. Only the Abbot and whoever's manning the entrance hut at the bottom can speak and even then, only when absolutely necessary. Come on, this way."

To Anita's relief, Caleb slowed his pace as they passed the church. Behind it was a service area of sorts that was full of large dumpsters, reminding her of the alleyway they had been chased through. Anita could see a path behind the dumpsters that snaked around behind the gothic church, but she couldn't see where it led from where they were.

"The path we came up is the only way to the monastery that most people are aware of," Caleb said as they passed the dumpsters. "But there is an alternate way out that the monks have used for emergencies for hundreds of years. It leads to the top of the mountain. If we can get up there, we can find some more transport. It takes hours to get there by car, and they'll have to go back down to the village, so we'll have a head start."

Anita nodded in response. Caleb sounded a lot more

confident than she felt. Her mouth was dry and her heart was thudding in her chest. It wasn't from exertion, but from fear. When they reached the start of the path, Caleb paused and looked behind him.

"Wait here," he said, sprinting back to the dumpsters. Anita watched as he pulled them away from the side of the church and into a rough line, obscuring any view of the path they were about to take. "I doubt they'll find the path, but just in case," he said when he returned. Then he reached out and took Anita's hand again, pulling her toward the path. "Let's go."

Anita followed Caleb as he led her down the path. It was only a yard wide, and disappeared between two vertical slabs of rock which narrowed so much that they both had to turn sideways to walk through the cleft in the mountain. When they emerged on the other side of the short passage-way, Anita could see the path hugging the side of the moun-tain, gradually inclining up. She stopped for a moment, her jaw dropping as she looked at where they were going. On one side of the path was the mountain, a sheer wall rising into the sky. On the other side, there was nothing but a vertical drop that seemed to go all the way to the valley floor.

"Are you serious?" she gasped. "That's the path?"

"Yes," Caleb replied, squeezing her hand. "It's not as bad as it looks from here."

Anita shook her head, knowing he was stretching the truth, to say the least.

"I'm calling bullshit on that, Caleb," she said.

"What's the alternative, Anita?" Caleb replied, looking at her with a stony expression that was reassuring at the same time. She shook his hand, but he refused to let go of her. "It's perfectly safe. Trust me."

Anita laughed, a short bark of a laugh that caught in her throat. But she knew Caleb was right. There was no alternative. With her free hand, she gripped the top of her handbag and took a couple of steps toward the path, not trusting herself to look down. The stone that the path had been hewn from looked solid enough, but the drop at the edge was horrifying.

"Just press yourself against the rock," Caleb said as he took a step onto the path. Then he turned and pressed his back against the mountain, keeping his feet close together. "Like this." He shuffled a yard further until their arms were at full stretch. But he still didn't let go of her hand.

Anita swallowed, or tried to. The inside of her mouth was like sandpaper. In front of them, an enormous bird of prey was soaring on a thermal, lazily rising in the warm air. She focused on the bird as she pressed her own back against the rock. The stone felt warm, reassuring somehow.

Maybe this wouldn't be as bad as she had first thought, Anita told herself as they shuffled onto the main trail. But within a few yards, she knew this wasn't the case at all.

It was far, far worse.

27

C aleb could see from the look on Anita's face that she was terrified, but there was no time to reassure her. Where they currently were on the ledge, they were exposed. If the two men from the village found out about the path, although he couldn't see how they could, and made their way to the start of it, they would be sitting ducks with nowhere to run.

The path wound around the mountain in fifty yards—when they reached that part, they would be out of view of the monastery. It led to a small grotto hacked into the rock, known as the Grotta della Madonna, where a small statue presented an opportunity for the faithful to pray. Caleb had no idea why the grotto was there, nor why someone had gone to such lengths to create such a perilous route to it but as it formed the early part of the only escape route from the monastery, perhaps it had been a double bluff. One thing he did know was that if Anita didn't like the first part of the escape route, she was going to hate the part past the grotto.

"How are you doing?" Caleb asked, looking at Anita. She

was staring straight ahead, her face ashen, and was taking rapid breaths in and out through her nose.

"Not great, Caleb," she replied, not turning her head to face him as she took another sideways step along the ledge. "I'm not really a fan of heights, in case you hadn't noticed."

"Nor am I," Caleb said. He wanted to say that it wasn't the height that killed people, but the sudden stop at the bottom, but he knew it wasn't the time or the place. He took another step just as a gust of warm air tugged at his robe, raising it by a couple of inches. Next to him, Anita's skirt was raised even further by the same gust of wind. To his surprise, Anita laughed.

"That's all I need," she said, finally turning to look at him. "It's not as if I can use my hands to stop my skirt from flying up, is it?"

Caleb grinned at her before replying. "I promise not to look."

"You are such a gentleman," Anita said, taking another step along the ledge. "Is it much further?"

"There's a corner up ahead," Caleb replied. "We need to get round it, and then we'll be out of sight." He leaned forward slightly to look beyond Anita at the monastery buildings, now a hundred yards behind them. The colorful buildings were also now below them, although the path's incline wasn't obvious. He could see no activity at all in the visible part of the monastery. But he knew at any moment, the men pursuing them could appear.

As Caleb continued shuffling along the path, Anita staying within a few inches of him, Caleb reflected on the previous few hours. He was feeling bad about bringing danger to the monastery, although the Abbot had been quick to hush him when he had tried to apologize back at the plaza. Caleb knew the occupants of the monastery had faced down many dangers over the years, most of which were far more threatening, but this was his fault. He resolved to do something in reparation to apologize properly.

It took them fifteen, perhaps twenty, minutes to reach the bend in the path, during which time there were no signs of their pursuers at the monastery. The only thing Caleb had seen had been a single monk who had appeared with a trash bag, which he had placed into a dumpster. Then, after several careful looks around his vicinity, the monk had produced a packet of cigarettes from under his robe and lit a smoke, enjoying it with sinful abandon.

"The spirit is willing," Caleb had muttered to himself when he saw the man smoking, "but the flesh is weak." He allowed himself a smile both at the monk's indiscretion and the fact that his brethren would almost certainly smell the smoke on his robes. "Matthew, chapter twenty-six, verse forty-one."

Once they had rounded the corner, the path opened out to lead to the grotto within a few yards. Caleb heard Anita sighing with relief as she moved onto the wider area and away from the sheer drop. In front of them, a triangular wedge was cut into the rock with some steps leading up to the small shrine. On either side of the steps were several signs in Italian, covered in glass. Caleb wasn't sure what they said, but assumed they were religious tracts of some sort. Next to the steps was a small crate with bottled water, and the thought of one of the monks navigating the path carrying the bottles made Caleb smile. Anita crouched down, causing Caleb to become momentarily distracted by the way the movement showed off her hips, and grabbed a couple of bottles.

"Here you are," she said as she passed him a bottle. "Is lying a sin?"

"Um, well, it depends on the context," Caleb replied, caught off guard by the question. "But generally speaking, yes."

"That makes you a sinner, then."

"What does?"

"You lied. You said you wouldn't look, but I saw your reflection in the glass of that no-smoking sign and you appeared to be staring at my ass." Anita's face was neutral, but he could see the faintest of smiles playing around her mouth.

"I think staring is a strong way of putting it, but I may have noticed you, yes."

"You like what you see, preacher man?" Anita asked, raising her bottle to her lips and taking a long drink.

Caleb paused before replying. This was not how he had been expecting the conversation to go at all, so he stalled for time by taking a drink from his own bottle of water. It was Anita who spared his discomfort in the end by changing the subject.

"Where did the path go?" she asked him. "I thought you said it was an escape route?"

Caleb nodded to the side of the grotto, where the rock wall looked to be sheer and featureless. When he'd first visited the grotto, he'd had to look for what he was now showing Anita.

"It's there," he said, using his bottle to point at the wall. Anita took a few steps toward where he was pointing and turned to look at him with an incredulous expression. Caleb knew she had seen the rusty steel cable, half hidden by moss and vegetation, that snaked its way up the mountain. A couple of yards below the cable was a ledge that made the previous path look like a walk in the park. While the path had been perhaps a yard wide, the ledge looked to be under six inches. "A Via Ferrata," Caleb said. "It means iron path."

"Thank you, Caleb," Anita replied, her voice dripping with sarcasm. "I know what a Via Ferrata is. But you have got to be shitting me?"

"No joke, Anita," Caleb said. He looked at the steel cable, which was supposed to offer a protected climbing route to which climbers could attach themselves with carabiners and harnesses, neither of which they had. As an escape route, it was a treacherous one. Caleb was about to say something else to Anita to try to reassure her when the sound of male voices shouting drifted across the wind from the direction of the monastery.

"Is that them?" Anita asked, her voice trembling as she spoke. She glanced at the metal cable and Caleb saw fear in her eyes. But it wasn't just fear that he could see. To his relief, he could also see the resolve in her expression. It wasn't much, but it was there.

Caleb said nothing, but just nodded. A few seconds later, Anita reached out and grabbed hold of the cable, gingerly putting her foot on the ledge below it.

"Well, what are you waiting for?" she said, and Caleb could tell that she was steeling herself for what lay ahead. "Come on. Andiamo!" Let's go.

28

Eva could see the helicopter before she heard it. It was a speck in the sky that gradually took shape as it approached, and she heard the throbbing of the blades growing louder. She reached her hands down and smoothed out her robe. When Eva had heard Hugo was coming, she had gone back to her accommodation and changed into a robe that was slightly too small for her, knowing that it showed her body off much better than the one she had been wearing.

"Who's the visitor?" Eva heard a female voice ask. She turned to see Maddy was standing just behind her. To Eva's relief, the young woman had also got changed and was now wearing a pale blue light summer dress with her blonde hair tied up in a loose ponytail. The dress revealed Maddy's thin shoulders, which were sprinkled with freckles, and Eva nodded in appreciation. Giovanni would definitely like the way she looked.

"It's one of our benefactors," Eva replied. "A man called Hugo." She had to raise her voice over the sound of the approaching rotors.

The two women watched as the helicopter started hovering over a patch of grass that served as a helipad a hundred yards in front of them. When their compound had been a hotel, the helipad had been the eighteenth green of the golf course, the last challenge for golfers before a well-deserved drink in the hotel bar. Giovanni, who to Eva's knowledge had never played golf in his life, paid a small team of gardeners to keep the grounds looking as perfect as possible and on more than one occasion, visitors had arrived and asked where the first tee was.

The sleek white helicopter slowly descended toward the grass and rocked a couple of times as the pilot leveled the wheels. Then, with the gentlest of descents, it landed perfectly in the center of the round patch of pristine grass. The downdraft from the blades washed over Eva and Maddy, but was only really strong enough to ruffle their hair by the time it reached them.

Eva waited and listened for the whine that told her the engines were shutting down. When she heard it, she set off toward the helicopter where the rotors were slowing.

"Are you coming?" she asked Maddy, who nodded enthusiastically.

"Sure," Maddy replied. "I've never been in a helicopter. Have you?" Her voice was child-like and Eva was reminded of how young she was.

"A couple of times," Eva replied. "I'm sure Hugo would take you for a ride in it if you ask him nicely."

"That would be so cool," Maddy said, her voice going up an octave. "Will you ask him for me?"

When they reached the edge of what used to be the green, Eva stopped and waited for the rotors to come to a complete halt. She could see the pilot through the wind-shield and he nodded at her, even though she'd never spoken a single word to the man. Then, once the rotors had come to a stop, the side door to the helicopter opened and Hugo stepped out, placing his trademark Tyrolean hat on his head as he did so. He was carrying a thin leather briefcase in one hand.

"Sister Eva," he called out as he walked over the grass toward them. "How delightful to see you."

Eva took a couple of steps forward, her arms out to her sides in greeting. As he always did, Hugo pulled her into a hug, air kissing her on both cheeks. Eva made sure that she pressed her breasts against his chest, but if Hugo noticed her doing this, he made no sign of it.

"And who's this?" Hugo said when he let go of Eva. He was staring at Maddy with an expression on his face that Eva didn't particularly like, especially when he had to be three times as old as Maddy was.

"This is young Maddy," Eva replied, making sure to emphasize the word *young*. "She's going to be joining us for lunch, if that's okay with you?"

"Of course it is," Hugo replied, holding out a hand to Maddy. When she took it, to Eva's disgust, Hugo raised his hand to kiss the back of Maddy's. "How absolutely delightful. The more the merrier."

"Are you English, Mr. Hugo?" Maddy asked. Hugo threw back his head and laughed.

"A long time ago, yes," he said when he had finished laughing, "but it's just Hugo. Not Mr. Hugo." He slipped Maddy's hand through the crook of his arm and turned to Eva. "Shall we? I'm famished."

As they made their way across the lush grass, back toward the compound buildings, Eva hung back behind Hugo and Maddy. He seemed to have taken an immediate shine to Maddy, which would no doubt please Giovanni—

especially if Maddy did end up in Giovanni's bed—and Eva wondered how they might best be able to maximize this.

She was still mulling this over in her mind when they walked into what had been the main foyer of the hotel where Giovanni was leaning up against the reception desk. The area still looked like a hotel foyer, which Eva knew Giovanni had done deliberately. There were lush plants dotted around the open space and comfortable chairs with low tables. Although it was currently empty, the foyer was one of the primary communal areas in the compound. She knew Giovanni wanted his visitors to feel as if they were in the hospitality sector, as he thought it helped with what he called their transition. When he saw Hugo approaching, Giovanni leaped into action and crossed the marble floor.

"Hugo," Giovanni said as the two men pumped hands. "This is an unexpected pleasure." Eva saw Giovanni glance at Maddy, who had slipped her hand from the crook of Hugo's arm. "I see you've met Maddy?"

"Indeed, I have," Hugo replied, his voice oozing with pleasure as he turned to smile at the young girl. Eva pressed her lips together to suppress a smile. How would Giovanni cope with some competition from an unexpected rival? That would make things interesting, especially given what Maddy had told her earlier. Eva saw Hugo turn back to Giovanni. "We have much to discuss, Brother Giovanni. But first, let's eat."

Eva led the small group into the dining area, where a spread of food had been laid out on the main table. Although Eva's sole contribution to the lunch was to tell the catering staff from the local village what food to prepare, she took on the role of host.

"Giovanni, would you mind getting our guests an aperitivo?" Eva asked. Giovanni nodded and crossed to a counter, returning a moment later with a tray laden with small glasses of Campari. "So, for our antipasto, we have cheese, sopprasatta, and bread. Primo is, of course, pasta, unless you'd prefer polenta?" When she saw Hugo shaking his head, Eva continued. "Secondo is chicken or fish, with a vegetable platter for the contorno. And of course, dolce and coffee to finish. I thought we could take our digestivo on the terrace if the weather stays fine?"

A broad smile spread over Hugo's face as he regarded the food.

"Goodness, you have been hard at work, Sister Eva. I had no idea you would go to so much trouble for little old me."

Eva returned his smile. They did this dance every time he joined them for food. If Hugo wanted to think it was Eva who had prepared it all, who was she to argue with him? He raised his glass of Campari in a toast, looking at Maddy as he did so.

"I propose a toast," he said, still smiling. "A toast to a new chapter. Not just a new chapter, but a new book."

Eva raised her glass, also still smiling, even though she didn't know what the old fool was talking about.

29

G iovanni led Hugo to the seat at the head of the table, acquiescing his customary position to allow their benefactor to have the best seat. Like the foyer, the dining area was still recognizable as exactly that, the only actual difference being that there were no waiting staff present. Meal times were all self-service, but the spread on the table was of a far higher quality than the food usually served in the room.

He hung back as Hugo pulled out the chair immediately to the left of where he was going to sit. Then Hugo gestured to Maddy.

"Please, Maddy, would you join me?" Hugo said. Giovanni saw Maddy, who was looking very different to how she had when Giovanni had last seen her, looking at Eva uncertainly.

"Um, Sister Eva had asked me to serve lunch to you all," Maddy replied, almost in a whisper.

"I'm sure Sister Eva won't mind doing the honors," Hugo said, beaming at Eva and Giovanni in turn

Giovanni caught the briefest of glimpses of annoyance

on Eva's face at the gesture. That was where she normally sat when they had important guests, but to her credit, she recovered well and hovered by the table. When Hugo, Giovanni, and Maddy were all seated, Eva slipped into the role of host and fussed around them to make sure they had plates full of food.

Only when she was sure everyone had what they needed did she sit down with a sideways glance at Giovanni. It was an expression he recognized—barely hidden annoyance which he knew would surface later when they were alone. Giovanni made a mental note to make sure that the next time they had guests, the caterers remained behind to serve them.

As they ate, picking slowly at their food, Hugo regaled Maddy with various stories, all of which Giovanni had heard before. Much as she did at Giovanni's sermons, Maddy was hanging onto every one of Hugo's words. Her facial expression changed in line with Hugo's narrative, moving between surprise, laughter, and even horror at times. Giovanni watched her carefully, enjoying the way she lapped up even the most outrageous of Hugo's tales.

The older man was a gifted raconteur, but a lot of what he was telling her was embellished beyond belief. Maddy either believed every word, which meant she was even easier to manipulate than Giovanni realized, or she was an excellent actress. Either way, it was amusing to watch.

Over an hour later, their stomachs full, lunch—or at least the eating element—finally drew to a close. Hugo got to his feet, stumbling slightly as he did so. Giovanni smiled at Eva. She had done well to keep his wine glass never less than half empty for the entire meal.

"Please excuse me for a moment," Hugo said, patting his stomach. "I just need to pop to the restroom."

The three of them waited until Hugo had weaved his way across the dining area. As the restroom door closed behind him, Eva also stood.

"I'll just clear these bits away," she said, gathering up the plates. "Then I'll get the coffee going."

"Let me help," Maddy replied, making to stand. Giovanni saw Eva put a hand on her shoulder to keep her in her seat.

"You stay here," Eva said with a meaningful glance at Giovanni. "Brother Giovanni here needs to speak to you."

"I do?" Giovanni asked her with a muffled belch. He'd not had as much wine as Hugo had, but he'd still had too much for the time of day.

"Yes, Brother Giovanni," Eva replied. "About the proposition you have for Maddy. And then we need to speak with Hugo privately."

Giovanni nodded, understanding what Eva meant. He waited until she had left the dining area, plates piled up in both arms, before turning his attention to Maddy. He reached his hands out and took Maddy's in his, hoping that he didn't appear as drunk as he felt. Maddy looked down at his hands with a look of surprise, but didn't remove them. Her skin was soft, and Giovanni imagined her fingers trailing over his chest before he shook the mental image away.

"Maddy," Giovanni said, fixing her with what he hoped was an intense look. "I'd like you to consider something for me." Her eyebrows went up in response. "If you're committed enough, that is?"

"Of course, Brother Giovanni," she said, her voice full of excitement. "I'd do anything for the Adelphoi. You know I would."

Giovanni kept his eyes on hers, deliberately not blinking. All he needed to do before Hugo came back was sow a seed in Maddy's mind.

"Come and see me in my office this evening," Giovanni replied. "Around nine. We can speak then and discuss the proposition in more detail." He smiled at the look of surprise on her face that his suggestion caused. "And talk about how committed you are. Now, please excuse us. Sister Eva and I need to speak to Mr. Forrester."

He let go of her hands and got to his feet, walking around the table to stand next to Maddy, who was already standing by the time he got there. He leaned forward, placing his hand on her flank before sliding it round to the small of her back.

"But don't say anything to the others," Giovanni whispered in her ear as his hand moved down so he could just feel the top of the cleft of her buttocks. Maddy flinched, but only slightly. That was a good sign, in Giovanni's experience. "This has to be just between you and me."

"I understand, Brother Giovanni," Maddy replied. Her discomfort was obvious in her voice, but Giovanni didn't care. The seed had been sown. She would be spending the afternoon wondering about how she could best prove her commitment to the Adelphoi. Whether she would reach the same conclusion as Giovanni intended remained to be seen.

Giovanni removed his hand and took a step back just as the restroom door opened and Hugo walked back into the dining room. His face was flushed, but as he walked over to join them, he was smiling.

"Thank you, Maddy," Giovanni said. "That'll be all." He let a smile play across his own face. "For the moment."

30

Eva balanced the tray carefully as she walked across the dining room, not wanting to spill any coffee. On the tray were three cups, elaborate small demitasses each with a silver spoon, and in the center was a small bowl with mismatched lumps of brown sugar and a set of tongs. She would have preferred a decent sized mug of coffee with milk, but that wasn't the normal way in Italy, especially after lunch. With the delicious aroma of the coffee, a blend from a plantation in Kualapu'u in Hawaii that cost over fifty bucks for a pound, wafting behind her, Eva made her way to where Giovanni and Hugo were sitting by an expansive window that looked out over the grounds.

"That smells delicious, Sister Eva," Hugo said as she placed the tray carefully on the table between them. "Thank you." She watched as he reached forward for one of the demitasses, struggling to get his index finger through the small china handle of the cup. Eva waited for a few seconds just in case he spilled any, but he sipped the coffee without incident. She sat down in the third armchair and looked out of the floor to ceiling window. A hundred yards away, past the outdoor terrace where they had originally planned to sit, she could see Maddy had made her way to the helicopter and was being shown around it by the pilot.

"Are you comfortable here, Hugo?" Giovanni asked. "Or would you prefer to sit on the terrace?"

"Here is fine, Brother Giovanni," Hugo replied, reaching for the briefcase which was leaning against his armchair. He replaced his demitasse on the table and put the briefcase on his knee, flicking the latches and pulling out a manila folder. After he had put the briefcase back on the floor, Hugo handed the folder to Eva. "I think it's time you read these as well, Eva. There's an extra report in there about the veracity of the DNA sample that I'm sourcing as we speak."

She took the folder from him, not mentioning that Giovanni had already shown the electronic versions to her. Hugo turned to Giovanni, the older man's expression hinting this was to be a serious conversation.

"Now, Giovanni, you read the previous reports that I sent you?" Hugo asked.

Eva saw a dark look flash across Giovanni's face, but it only lasted for a split-second. He opened his mouth to say something, and for a moment Eva was sure Giovanni was going to tell Hugo about Anita stealing the files, but he didn't.

"I did, yes," Giovanni replied with a sideways glance at Eva. "They were rather, well, complex."

"I know," Hugo replied, a broad smile on his face. "I keep telling them to dumb it down so that even a Luddite like me can understand them, but they don't. You get the principle of those reports, though?"

"I think so," Giovanni replied. Hugo said nothing, but just looked at him with his eyebrows raised. "You're trying to clone DNA and use it to artificially create an embryo."

"Two corrections there, Brother Giovanni," Hugo said good-naturedly. "We're not cloning DNA, not really. We're recreating it. It's a small but crucial difference and there's going to be a slight delay before we get there. But the embryo element has just had a breakthrough."

"What sort of breakthrough?" Eva asked when it was apparent that Giovanni wasn't going to say anything. Hugo turned to her with an exuberant expression that, in her opinion, bordered on manic.

"We've created an embryo purely from stem cells," he said, "and developed it further than any scientist has ever done before." His eyes widened as he continued. "We're ready to move on to the next stage, which is implantation. The proposal is all in the original reports I sent you, but we're now implementing it."

"A surrogate baby?" Giovanni asked, rejoining the conversation.

"Exactly that," Hugo said. "A surrogate baby built entirely from stem cells. That's where I need your help. There're some services I need to procure and I think you are the best people to provide them."

At Hugo's use of the word procure, Eva saw Giovanni's eyes lighting up. If Hugo wanted to procure something, that meant he wanted to buy something. And Hugo had deep pockets, as they well knew.

"Of course, Hugo," Giovanni said. "You only have to ask."

"I need a sanctuary," Hugo replied, turning to stare out of the windows at the expansive grounds of the compound. "Somewhere safe where a surrogate mother can be looked after. Somewhere that's suitable for creating this baby." He took a breath before continuing. "Of course, as well as a donation to your organization, I will cover the additional requirements for the mother. Medical provision and oversight, pastoral care and, of course, security." Another breath, this one deeper. "There are some who would rather not see this baby come into the world."

"Why would that be, Hugo?" Eva asked, not really understanding why a surrogate mother would need security. Unlike Giovanni, she had read Hugo's various reports, but they hadn't actually stated he was looking to progress the project all the way to a human baby. If Eva had understood them correctly, the project was a proof of concept, nothing more.

"This baby will be carrying reconstructed DNA. Ancient DNA that will be reassembled from a long-lost source using the latest advances in artificial intelligence."

"You have this source?" Giovanni leaned forward, and Eva knew he was calculating how soon Hugo would be paying for the sanctuary he wanted to procure.

"I do," Hugo replied, a sly grin slipping on his face. "I do indeed, and the source of the DNA has an excellent provenance." He turned to look at Giovanni, and Eva saw a dark look on the older man's face. "I thought you'd read the original reports? It's all in there. All apart from the actual source of the DNA."

"I apologize, Hugo," Giovanni replied, at least managing to pull off a decent effort at looking apologetic. "Some of the language was difficult, but I will re-read the reports tonight and concentrate more."

Eva stifled a laugh, knowing full well that the only thing Giovanni would be concentrating on that evening was trying to persuade Maddy to get naked, no matter how unlikely that might be. Unlike Giovanni, she had actually read the reports thoroughly and knew exactly what Hugo was talking about.

"The relic mentioned in the report?" Eva asked. "That's the source of the DNA?"

Hugo turned to Eva with a broad smile. He nodded his head enthusiastically.

"Exactly, my dear," he said with a throaty laugh. "I have everything I need. Well, almost everything." Eva watched as his laugh dissipated and his face darkened. "Then it's a case of keeping the dark forces at bay until the child arrives. After that?" A smile reappeared on his face, but his expression remained dark. "After that, we change the world."

"You're going to clone a human being," Giovanni said slowly, "and this individual is going to change the world?" Eva frowned. Giovanni, for his many qualities, could be incredibly slow.

"I'm not going to clone a human being," Hugo said, his eyes fixed on the gardens outside. When he turned to look back at Giovanni, the intensity behind the older man's eyes sent a shiver down Eva's spine. "I'm going to resurrect one."

31

Anita was holding on to the steel cable so tightly that her knuckles were pure white. The ledge her feet were on wasn't even wide enough to fit her feet on unless she turned them sideways, but she was determined not to buckle. She thought back to when she was younger and had gone rock climbing on a school trip, but that had been a completely different experience.

Back then, she had all the equipment she needed. A harness, ropes, and even a helmet to protect her head. Added to that, the fact that the routes they had climbed had never been more than about twenty yards from the ground. Anita didn't want to look down at the drop below her, but it was significantly higher than twenty yards.

"Just remember," she heard Caleb say, "keep three points of contact with the mountain at all times. Move one hand, then a foot, and bring the others up to meet them."

Anita nodded, not trusting herself to speak. She did as Caleb instructed, pressing the entire length of her body against the rock. As she built up a rhythm of sorts, she realized that, for some reason, this part of their escape was somehow more reassuring than the earlier, wider path. Perhaps it was the security of the steel cable, but she knew any reassurance it was giving her was false. One misstep and she would plummet down the side of the mountain to a certain death.

"How long is it until we reach the end?" she asked Caleb, turning to glance at him briefly. To her surprise, she saw him shrugging his shoulders.

"I don't know," he replied. "I've not been this far before."

Anita paused, her hands gripping the steel wire. "What do you mean, you've not been this far before?"

"Exactly what I said," Caleb replied, looking nonchalant. "I've not been this far."

"How do you know it goes anywhere?" Anita said, her voice an octave higher than it had been a few seconds earlier. "What if the Via Ferrata runs out?"

"It'll be fine, Anita. The monk I spoke to said it goes all the way to the top of the mountain. Just have faith."

"Easy for you to say," Anita mumbled before turning her attention back to the route. She found it easier to count her movements in her head. When she moved her leading hand, she counted one. Then it was two for her leading foot and three and four for her other limbs. Keeping Caleb's advice in the back of her mind, Anita made sure that she only moved one limb at a time so that she had three static points of contact with the mountain.

A few yards further along, they reached the end of the first metal cable and the beginning of the second one. Anita looked down at the bolts driven into the rock and the cable that was secured to them. At the end of the cable was an eye with a carabiner, a D-shaped metal climbing device with a hinged element. To her relief, she saw the hinged part had a locking device to secure it in place. While the bolt in the rock looked rusted, the carabiner itself was still shiny and looked to be reasonably new.

"That's a hundred yards," Caleb said from his position right next to her. He was so close, Anita could feel his body heat, which reassured her somewhat. She had to let go of the cable to grab the next one, and the movement sent a sharp spasm of cramp up her forearm, but it dissipated when she grabbed onto the next section of cable. "The monk told me there're five sections altogether, so we're twenty percent of the way there already."

Anita inched her way along the cable until she had both hands on the new stretch. A breeze rustled her dress, and she had a vision of both of them free-falling down the side of the mountain. Anita screwed her eyes tightly shut to banish the image in her mind's eye.

"You okay?" she heard Caleb asking her. It sounded as if he was now much further away than he had been, but when she opened her eyes, he was still right next to her. He reached out a hand and placed it between her shoulder blades. "Just breathe." Anita felt Caleb's hand sliding up her back until it was on the back of her neck. He used his thumb to stroke the nape of her neck while his fingers squeezed the trapezium muscle of her shoulder. It was a gesture which in any other circumstances would be bordering on sensual, but his touch was comforting instead.

"I'm fine," Anita said through gritted teeth. "What are we going to do when we get to the top of the mountain?"

"Let's just get there first, Anita," Caleb replied. "We can work that part out later."

Anita nodded and opened her eyes to look at the metal cable of the Via Ferrata snaking its way around the mountain. Although she couldn't see the full length of the next section, it looked to her to be a lot longer than a hundred yards. She swallowed, wishing that they'd not left the bottled water back at the start of the climb. Her mouth was as dry as the rock they were both clinging to.

"Just have faith, Anita," she heard Caleb say in a low voice. "That's all you need."

32

Caleb didn't need to touch Anita to feel the fear radiating from her, and he could only imagine the thoughts running through her mind. They were probably not dissimilar to his own. Caleb hated heights and always had. He told himself it wasn't a fear of them as such, but more of a preservation mechanism. He remembered, several years ago, standing on the ramp of a Lockheed C-130 Hercules transport airplane, staring out at the night sky from a thousand yards above Fort Moore in Georgia. A burly master sergeant had helped him overcome his reluctance to jump with a hefty shove to the small of his back.

The incredible sensory overload as Caleb plummeted from the airplane had taken his breath away, but only seconds later, his training kicked in as he extended his arms and legs to stabilize himself in the air before pulling his ripcord. The subsequent descent had been uneventful and the landing ungainly, but he had earned his coveted Parachutist Badge. Having a set of jump wings would not help him today, though. Not without a parachute.

He looked at Anita as she moved along the cable. Caleb

wanted to tell her to hurry, but he knew such a statement would be counterproductive. She was scared enough as it was, and she was making steady progress along the route. Caleb could see her lips moving as she proceeded, and he realized she was counting her steps. He nodded in appreciation at the distraction technique.

As they made their way slowly along the Via Ferrata, Caleb thought about Anita's question. What were they going to do when they reached the end of the route? Caleb had been to the village the route led to before, a small place called Brentino that perched high above the monastery. There was another route to and from the church, a paved road that provided access to the buildings through a tunnel dug into the rock a hundred years ago.

It was the most obvious escape route, and Caleb hoped that the men from the SUV would be following it. There was a risk that they would arrive at Brentino at the same time as Caleb and Anita did, but the road was a slow and winding one that would take them significantly longer than the direct route he and Anita were taking. At least Caleb hoped it would.

Caleb started running through various courses of action in his mind as they moved along the route. They could do nothing, which wasn't an option. Although he doubted the two men would gun them down in broad daylight, they hadn't hesitated to shoot at them back in the alleyways of Pastrengo. Another option would be for Caleb to set up an ambush for the two men somewhere along the paved road, with Anita somewhere safe in the village. That was potentially a viable option. Caleb had taken on more than two men at a time many times, guns or no guns. But with no weapons other than his bare hands, that option was a risky one.

Caleb's last course of action—and the one which he knew they would have to take—was to keep running. There were two prerequisites for that path. The first was that they needed to get to the village before the two men did. The second was that they needed transport, and preferably not another moped. But Caleb had a plan for transport, and hopefully it wouldn't be on two wheels.

"How are you doing?" Caleb asked Anita as they approached the next section of the Via Ferrata. When she turned to look back at him, he saw she was smiling, even though he could still see the terror behind her eyes.

"I'm okay," she said, keeping the smile on her face. "My legs are like jello, though."

"Mine too," Caleb replied with a laugh, "and neither of us is exactly dressed for rock climbing."

"This was your idea, not mine," Anita said, her smile slipping slightly.

"It's not much further, Anita," Caleb said, letting go of the steel cable with one hand so he could place it on her shoulder. "We're almost in the third section, which is halfway from what I've been told. We'll be back on a path before we know it."

Anita nodded in response as she navigated her way past another set of carabiners. Caleb saw her fingers shaking as she took one hand off the cable, but her expression was still resolute.

Caleb thought he heard more shouting behind them somewhere, drifting toward them on the breeze. He turned to look in the direction they had just come from, angling his head to concentrate. He stayed in the same position for a few seconds, but heard nothing. Perhaps it was just his imagination? When he turned to look at Anita again, she had passed the carabiners and was a yard along the new section. He saw her head dipping briefly and realized that she had just looked down at her feet.

Then Caleb heard Anita scream as the narrow ledge beneath her feet gave way, sending fragments of rock into the abyss below.

33

Eva watched as Hugo replaced his coffee on the small table and leaned back in the armchair, closing his eyes as he did so. A moment later, she heard him snoring softly. In the armchair next to the older man, Giovanni was deep in thought.

"Giovanni," she said in a loud whisper. When he looked over at her, she took a few steps away and beckoned him to join her. Giovanni got to his feet, and they crossed the room to stand by what used to be the reception desk so they could talk without disturbing Hugo. Eva opened the manila folder and rifled through it to find the new report that Hugo had mentioned. When she located it, she scanned through the single page quickly, not believing what she was reading.

"Eva?" Giovanni said, but she raised a hand to hush him while she re-read the report again.

"Oh my God," she said a moment later, looking at Giovanni with wide eyes. "He really is quite mad."

"What does it say?" Giovanni asked her. "The report? What does it say?"

"He's got, or he's getting, his hands on an ancient relic

from the Vatican," Eva replied, handing him the sheet of paper. "It's not very clear whether he has it already. Hugo thinks there's DNA on it he can recreate, or resurrect, or whatever he's trying to do."

"A relic was mentioned in one of the other reports, but only in passing," Giovanni said, his eyes fixed on the paper. Eva waited until he got to the last paragraph where the actual artifact was identified.

"Shit!" Giovanni said a moment later, and Eva knew he'd got there. "You have got to be joking!"

"I don't think he's joking, Giovanni," Eva said with a quick glance at Hugo, who still appeared to be asleep. "He's after the Holy Lance. The weapon that is supposed to have been used at Jesus' crucifixion to pierce his side. The person whose DNA he's using is Jesus."

"He's trying to resurrect Jesus?" Giovanni said. "That is absolutely bat shit crazy. It can't be done, can it? Not two thousand years later?"

"I don't think that matters," Eva replied, suddenly feeling light-headed. "What matters is that he thinks it can be." She took a deep breath. "I need a drink."

A few moments later, with a large glass of wine in her hand, Eva and Giovanni were sitting in the foyer. They were far enough away from Hugo to not disturb him. Giovanni was re-reading some of the other reports while Eva was staring out of the window, deep in thought.

"It all makes sense now," Giovanni said a moment later. "Why Hugo has been so interested in the Adelphoi."

"Whether or not we intended to, we've created the perfect community to look after a surrogate mother." Eva fixed Giovanni with a hard stare. "One that's full of devout parishioners, all waiting for the end of days so they can be saved."

"And an army of people on-line who all think the same thing," Giovanni replied with a smirk.

"What's so funny, Giovanni?" Eva said, not bothering to hide her irritation. "Why are you grinning like that?"

"This is probably the largest opportunity we've ever had. Just imagine, we are going to be the custodians of the return of God's child."

Eva looked at him, recognizing his expression as the one he used when calculating. She shook her head in exasperation.

"You need to listen to what you preach, Giovanni."

"What do you mean?"

"The Second Coming. Isn't that what triggers the apocalypse?"

"Oh, please, Eva," Giovanni replied with a wave of his hand. "There isn't about to be a Second Coming, no matter what Hugo does with his test tubes. That's nonsense."

"A lot of people would disagree with you, Giovanni. Jesus' return is a fundamental part of most religions."

"Well, thank you for the theology lesson, Eva," Giovanni said with a wry smile. "But according to these reports, Hugo's a long way from actually resurrecting the Son of God."

"He doesn't seem to think he is." Eva frowned, trying to work out what the implications of Hugo's project would actually be if he were successful. Would a child created from Jesus's DNA actually be Jesus, or some sort of cloned version? Whatever the outcome, the ramifications of it would be world-changing. Which was, she reflected, exactly what Hugo wanted.

"That's my point, Eva," Giovanni replied, leaning forward. "If people think that Jesus is about to return, imagine how generous they'll be to the custodians."

"This is about money for you?"

"Of course it is. Imagine the marketing opportunities." To Eva's horror, Giovanni actually rubbed his hands together as he spoke. "The merch alone will be worth millions."

"I don't think Hugo's that interested in a t-shirt range, Giovanni," Eva said, getting to her feet. She needed some time alone to think, and some time away from Giovanni, who just didn't seem to realize the implications of what Hugo was proposing to do. She picked up her wineglass. "I'm going to my room. You can look after Hugo when he wakes up. Maybe you can work out how you're both going to handle Armageddon?"

Giovanni laughed in response, slightly too loudly. "Sure, Eva, we'll do that. I need to scribble some stuff down." He looked over at Hugo, who was still fast asleep. "That crazy dude's given me some awesome ideas for my next sermon."

Hugo awoke with a start, gasping as he did so. Had he been snoring or had he just choked on something? It took him a few seconds to orientate himself, but when he had done so, he looked up to see Giovanni was striding across the marble floor of the foyer. The younger man had a broad smile on his face.

"Hugo," Giovanni said. "You're awake."

Hugo bit back the response that came to his mind, which was *obviously*, and returned Giovanni's smile.

"Sorry about that," Hugo said. "I blame the lovely Eva's cooking." Then he started laughing. "That, and the wine I drank while eating it." He looked around the foyer, but couldn't see Eva anywhere. "Where is Eva? She must think I'm awfully rude, nodding off like that."

"Not at all, Hugo," Giovanni said as he sat down in the armchair next to Hugo. "She's gone to her room to rest for a while."

"Ah, okay," Hugo replied. "That gives us a chance to talk." He settled back into his armchair. "So, what do you think of my proposal?"

Giovanni paused for a moment before replying, unsure whether Hugo was referring to the project itself, or the Adelphoi being used as a sanctuary for the surrogate mother.

"Well," Giovanni said. "It's certainly an audacious plan."

"A game changer, one might say?"

"Yes, you could say that." Giovanni smiled, thinking back to Eva's prediction that it would bring about the end of days.

"It's been a dream of mine since I was a young man," Hugo said, his gaze drifting to the window. "Since I realized how cruel humanity had become. Humanity has gone too far. It needs to be realigned, and His return will enable that. All it takes is people like us to make that happen."

"People like us?" Giovanni asked, frowning. He was the leader of a religious organization, nothing more.

"Visionaries," Hugo replied, turning to look at Giovanni with rheumy eyes. "People with the belief that we have. Those who are with Him are called, chosen, and faithful."

Giovanni nodded, vaguely recognizing Hugo's last phrase as being in the book of Revelation somewhere. He made a mental note to find the verse for his next sermon. It certainly had a ring to it.

"How long do you envisage this sanctuary will be required for?" Giovanni asked, keen to get to the part he wanted to discuss, which would give him an idea of how much money was likely to come his way.

"Well, at least nine months," Hugo said with a deep laugh. "After that, who knows? It depends on what happens when the child is born and how soon the prophecies begin after that. What are your thoughts? You know scripture well."

Giovanni paused again, racking his brain for something

deep and meaningful to say. In the end, he couldn't think of anything.

"I think that's up to God, Hugo," Giovanni said with as devout an expression as he could manage. "It's not for man to predict that."

Hugo nodded, looking thoughtful as he did so. "Indeed," he said. "But we must be prepared. How many, may I ask, does the Adelphoi number?"

"There are twenty of us here, and many thousands on-line. We can increase the number we have here, though. In the sanctuary."

Hugo nodded again. "That would be wise. As I said, I will provide what is required."

"Our costs will increase," Giovanni said, keen to sow the seed early even though his congregation paid for themselves and then some. They had been thinking about expanding for some time, but had held off to avoid drawing too much attention from the Italian authorities. "There are renovations that will need to be done."

"I will cover that, Giovanni," Hugo said. "Do you have a suite available for the mother?"

Giovanni thought for a moment. They had three suites in the complex. He was occupying one, Eva another, and the third was the guest suite where people like Hugo stayed when they visited.

"Yes, we do," Giovanni replied. Eva would have to move into a room. She certainly would not be moving in with him.

"My most immediate concern is security," Hugo said, stroking his hand over his head. "We'll need a personal detail for the mother and then, nearer the time, something much more robust."

Giovanni's thoughts drifted to the two Italians who were

on Anita's tail. They had certainly proven themselves to be ruthless, and might fit the bill for a personal detail.

"I have some people in mind for a personal detail," he said. "I've used them before, and they're very effective."

"Good," Hugo replied with a nod of his head.

"When are you planning on going public with this project?" Giovanni asked, thinking about how soon he could start whipping people up into a cash-giving frenzy.

"As late as possible," Hugo replied to Giovanni's disappointment. "Satan's armies will need time to prepare for the final battle. I want them to have as little time as possible for that."

"We will also need time to raise an army of the righteous." Giovanni knew the more time he had, the more money he could make.

"The righteous will assemble, Giovanni, when He returns. I have no doubt of that."

The two men sat in a contemplative silence for several moments.

"I need a few days to get everything ready," Hugo said, breaking the silence. "Then a few days for Albert and Christine to work their science. Can you be ready in, let's say, a month? Perhaps sooner if things go well?"

"Of course," Giovanni replied. "That's more than enough time to prepare."

"Excellent," Hugo said. He turned to Giovanni and stared at him. "Now, there's just one more thing that we need."

"What might that be, Hugo?"

"The child will need a mother."

35

Anita's scream was still echoing around the mountain as she scrabbled desperately for something that her feet could grip, but the entire ledge had fallen away. Her feet were sliding down the side of the rock face and within seconds, she was hanging only by her hands, which were gripping the metal cable harder than she'd ever gripped anything in her life.

Her stomach lurched as the metal cable of the Via Ferrata became taut under her weight, and Anita felt the metal cable digging into the soft flesh of her fingers. It felt as if it was ripping the skin from them, and she knew she couldn't hold on for long. Sure enough, within a couple of seconds, Anita's fingers began peeling away from the cable. She screamed again, and it seemed as if it was someone else's voice. The earlier image of her falling through the air came back to her, and Anita closed her eyes tightly, just waiting for the moment when she began plummeting to her death. Her feet were scrabbling against the rock, an involuntary movement she couldn't control, but there was nothing for her feet to get any purchase on. The rock wall was smooth and featureless and her feet were still trying to find something—anything—as her fingers continued peeling away from the cable.

The next thing Anita knew was an excruciating pain in her left wrist. She gasped and looked up to see Caleb, one arm hooked around the cable so it was in the crook of his elbow and his other hand wrapped around her wrist like a vice. It felt as if the bones were being crushed, but she instinctively knew that was the least of her worries.

"I've got you," Caleb said through gritted teeth.

Anita could see his sandaled feet on what was left of the ledge. He shifted them slightly, causing a few small splinters of rock to fall away and tumble into the ether. If the part of the ledge he was standing on gave way as well, they were both doomed.

"Caleb!" Anita screamed. "Please, help me!"

"That's the plan," Caleb replied. He had a peculiar expression on his face that was somewhere between amusement and pain. Anita's body was twisting in the air, sending sharp jolts of pain up her forearm, but Caleb's grip was unyielding. She reached back up with her right arm to grab the cable, desperate to ease some of the pressure on her left wrist. "Can you see the ledge, Anita? To your right?"

Anita glanced to her right-hand side and saw what Caleb was referring to. Where the ledge had fallen away from the rock face, there was a white patch of newly exposed rock that contrasted with the weathered areas, but she could see a small outcrop beyond it where the ledge remained. It was perhaps a yard away.

"Yes, I see it," she replied with a gasp as another jolt of pain shot up her forearm and all the way into her shoulder.

"On three, I'm going to swing you. When you get to the

top of the swing, reach out with your foot and hook it over the ledge."

Anita looked up at Caleb, noticing that the tendons in the arm he was gripping her with were standing out like the cable he was hanging onto. She could see a rivulet of blood trickling down his forearm from the corded steel cable cutting into his other elbow, but his face was resolute. He counted to three before swinging her back, away from the outcrop. Then he took a deep breath and swung her the other way, toward the ledge. As she reached the top of the swing, Anita reached out with her leg, causing her dress to fall away and expose her thigh. For some reason, it made her feel even more vulnerable than she already was.

Anita's heel brushed against the edge of the small outcrop, but Caleb hadn't swung her far enough to hook it over.

"We go again!" he said, swinging her back again.

This time, Anita got her heel onto the ledge, but to her frustration, it slipped straight back off.

"And again!"

Anita heard Caleb grunt with the exertion of swinging her body, but this time, she got her heel all the way onto the ledge. There was a sharp edge digging into her Achilles tendon, but she pushed the pain to the back of her mind. Anita slid her right hand along the cable, managing to take some of her weight and relieve the pressure on her wrist. She felt Caleb lifting her up a few inches until she felt the cable between the fingers of her left hand.

"Okay," Anita said when she had a grasp of the cable with both hands. Moving slowly, with Caleb's hand still gripping her wrist so tightly it crunched the bones against each other, she transferred some of her weight onto her right foot and slid both hands along the cable. A moment later, she was able to bring her left foot up and onto the ledge. It was only then that Caleb released her wrist, but it was only to move his hand to her bicep where he grabbed her again.

"Keep going," Caleb said, his voice determined. "You're almost there."

Anita shuffled for a few seconds until she had both feet firmly on the ledge. She pressed her cheek against the cool rock in relief and when she took it away, saw that she had left tears she'd not known she was crying against the rock face. She turned to look behind her and saw Caleb making his way along the cable toward her, going hand over hand as if he was on an assault course, not hundreds of yards from the ground. A moment later, he was standing beside her.

"Caleb," Anita said, looking at a nasty graze in the crook of his elbow. "You're bleeding." She saw him glance at the wound briefly.

"It's nothing," he replied, looking at her with a grin. He reached up and put his fingers to the side of her neck before sliding them to the back of her neck. She felt his thumb rubbing the skin by her hairline. "Are you okay?"

"I am now," Anita replied, stifling a sob. "You're stronger than you look."

His grin broadened as he spoke. "And you're heavier than you look."

"That's no way to talk to a lady, Caleb," Anita said. A sudden noise made them both look back down the rock face. The section of cable before the one they were on was rattling against the rock face as it curved out of sight around the mountain.

"Looks like we've got company," Caleb said, a sudden note of urgency in his voice. "I guess we'd better hurry."

36

Caleb looked back along the cable to see if he could see anyone pursuing them, but all he could see was the cable knocking against the rock. After shouting at Anita to keep going, he started making his way back to where the cable sections were joined. If he could undo the carabiner that held the previous section to the rock, then it would fall away. The thought of their pursuers falling to their deaths didn't bother Caleb in the slightest.

The moment they had shot at him and Anita back in the village had been the moment they gave up any right to sympathy. He maneuvered his way past the stretch where the ledge had fallen away, discovering a thinner ledge a yard higher up that he could wedge his feet onto. It was awkward, but he managed it.

When he reached the bolts that marked the junction of the cables, Caleb reached out and put his fingers around the previous cable which was still rattling against the rock face. He could tell from the way it moved that there was at least one person making their way along it, but he still couldn't see anyone. He braced himself against the rock face as best

he could and tried to twist the locking sleeve on the carabiner, but it was stuck fast. The device had probably been
there for years and wasn't budging an inch. It looked weathered rather than rusted, and Caleb wondered if the weight
of someone on the cable was preventing it from opening.

Caleb mumbled under his breath before he tried the
other carabiner. The locking sleeve started moving almost
immediately, but the problem with undoing it was that then
he would have to free climb along the rock. Caleb had done
quite a lot of free climbing years previously, but only a few
yards above the ground.

"Anita?" Caleb called out as he studied the locking
mechanism. "How are you doing?" When he heard nothing,
he looked up to see that she had traversed the final cable
and was now standing on what looked to be a path. Caleb
realized that the last cable was shorter than the previous
ones. It was this that made up his mind. He swiveled the
locking sleeve on the carabiner and depressed the hinge,
unhooking the cable from the rock face. When he let go of
the cable, it swung down and away, scraping against the
rock as it did so.

Caleb started making his way along the rock face,
moving slowly and ensuring that his hands and feet had a
good grip. As he moved, he tried to recall verses from the
Bible that spoke of falling, but he couldn't bring any to mind
other than one from Proverbs that talked about a righteous
man falling seven times before getting back up again. Caleb
didn't have to look down to know that if he fell, it would
only be once and he certainly wouldn't be getting up again.
He closed his eyes briefly and tried to imagine there was a
celestial hand keeping him close to the rock, but he felt
nothing.

Except for the section of the route where the ledge had

fallen away, the climb wasn't overly technical. There was an angle to the rock face of seventy-five degrees that meant he could lean into the rock, but the knowledge there was nothing beneath him but hundreds of yards of air was terrifying. He could feel a gentle breeze coming up from the ground way below. It was warm, and he wondered if there were birds soaring on the thermal.

"Caleb?" he heard Anita say when he was halfway along, her voice higher than usual. "What happened to the cable?"

"It came loose," Caleb replied through gritted teeth. He only had twenty-five yards to go until he reached safety. Climbing in rubber-soled boots designed for gripping rock was one thing, but he was wearing sandals. While contemplating this, he almost lost his footing on the ledge, prompting a loud scream from Anita. Caleb looked at her to see she had her hands pressed against her cheeks. Her mouth was wide open, as if she had kept it open when she finished screaming. "Anita, move further along the path!" he shouted. She was standing perilously close to the end of the path, and the rock had already failed in one area. If he needed to launch himself at the path, he didn't want too much weight on the edge of the precipice.

With relief, he saw Anita do as instructed. Ten yards to go. He was almost there when he heard a male voice shouting from behind him. Then, a split second later, there was a metallic whine followed by small shards of rock falling onto his head and shoulders.

Caleb only had five yards left when he felt a white hot pain in his thigh.

37

Eva and Giovanni both raised their hands to wave at Hugo, who was waving at them through the rear window of his helicopter. Above Hugo's head, the rotors were turning slowly. Their speed gradually increased and a high-pitched whine started.

"You were right, Giovanni," Eva said, raising her voice as the noise of the helicopter's engine increased.

"About what?" Giovanni replied.

"He is absolutely bat shit crazy."

"I know." Giovanni turned and beamed at her. "Isn't it fantastic?"

The downdraft from the rotor blades started pulling at Eva's robe, and she put her hands down to keep it in place.

"You should let it lift up, Eva," Giovanni said. "Give the old boy something to think about on his way back to Austria."

"I can't," Eva replied. "I've not got anything on underneath."

Giovanni laughed, but it was more of a cackle than a laugh. "Even more reason to give him a flash. I was kind of hoping he might stay so you can work your magic on him."

They remained where they were as the helicopter slowly rose from the landing site and turned away from them, sending the branches of nearby trees into a frenzy. A short moment later, they could speak normally as the sleek helicopter moved away into the distance, soon becoming a black speck silhouetted against the blue sky.

"So, Giovanni," Eva said. "What next?"

Giovanni turned and started walking back to the complex, followed by Eva.

"We need to prepare some more rooms," Giovanni said. "Hugo has a medical team he wants to bring here for the, er, the impregnation. There'll be some security personnel as well, but we've got time. The mother will need a suite as well, so you'll have to move out of yours."

Eva stopped and waited until Giovanni noticed she was no longer walking beside her.

"What?" he said, turning around.

"I've got to move out of the suite?"

"We've only got three. I'm in one, one is for VIPs, and the third is reserved for the mother of Jesus." He had a smirk on his face as he spoke, and Eva knew from experience that arguing with him was pointless.

"Right, I see," she said, hoping her expression told Giovanni what she thought of the plan.

"Where's the girl gone?" Giovanni asked a moment later as they continued walking. "Mandy?"

"Maddy," Eva replied. Then she cursed under her breath, remembering that she'd promised to ask Hugo if she could have a ride in the helicopter. She would have to ask him next time, perhaps offering him something in return.

"Yes, her," Giovanni said. "Find her, have her washed,

and brought to me." At first, Eva thought he was joking, but his expression was serious. She started laughing. "What's so funny?" Giovanni asked with a frown.

"That's not going to happen, Brother Giovanni," Eva replied, still laughing. "You're really not her type."

"What do you mean, I'm not her type? Of course I'm her type."

"No, you're really not. You've got a penis for a start." Eva was now laughing so much she was almost in tears. When she saw the wounded expression on Giovanni's face, she bent double and almost howled at how ridiculous he looked.

"You have got to be kidding me?" Giovanni asked, promoting another round of laughter from Eva. She just shook her head in reply. Giovanni swore loudly and walked off, leaving Eva where she was.

A few moments later, when she had recovered her composure, Eva made her way alone toward the foyer. He might not see it that way, but Maddy's sexual orientation was a good thing for Giovanni, as it would let him know that he couldn't always have what he wanted. She wouldn't put it past him to try anyway, and at some point she would need to speak to him properly to ensure he didn't. There was a vulnerability about Maddy that concerned Eva, and as she well knew, Giovanni could be a very persuasive man.

As she walked across the lush grass toward the complex building, Eva's thoughts drifted back to what Hugo had told them earlier. What he was proposing wasn't just bat shit crazy, as Giovanni had so eloquently put it. It was, in Eva's opinion, dangerous. She didn't for a moment believe that Hugo's plan would actually work. It was too close to science fiction for that, and even if a child was produced, Eva couldn't see how it would actually be the Second Coming.

The danger would be that there were many people who would believe it to be true. Giovanni had alluded to it already, although he was talking about it in the context of how much money they could make from the faithful.

There had to be something Eva could do about the ridiculous scheme. But the question was what?

38

Giovanni was furious. He stomped across the marble floor of the foyer, Eva's laughter still echoing in his ears, and made his way to his office. Then he locked the door before pouring himself a large measure of a very expensive single malt from the island of Islay to the west of Scotland. According to the grateful parishioner who had sent it to him, the Laphroaig whisky was the only one to carry the Royal Warrant of the Prince of Wales. Not that Giovanni cared a jot for the Prince of Wales or his Royal Warrant. He just wanted a drink.

He took a hefty slug of the whisky, neat and with no ice or water, knowing the gesture would be frowned on by any whisky aficionado. Then he coughed and for a moment thought the amber liquid was coming straight back up again. When the burning in the back of his throat had subsided, he took another, much smaller, sip and sat in the chair behind his desk. He gripped the crystal tumbler, tempted to hurl it across the room, but that would just be petulant.

Instead, he booted up his computer and started scrolling

through the photographs of the members of the Adelphoi who were present in the complex. When he reached Maddy's photograph, he paused for a moment and read the biography she had submitted as part of the application process. There was no mention in it about her sexual preferences, and he pondered for a moment about including something in the demographics section for future applicants. If nothing else, it might save him some time and energy when selecting companionship. Then he spent a moment contemplating whether Maddy might in fact be bisexual, in which case there was potentially some fun to be had there. Eva could even join in, fulfilling a fantasy he'd had for many years. Two women and him in a bed, not because he'd paid them to be there but because they wanted to be there. He made a mental note to mention it to Eva later and see what she thought of the idea.

Giovanni continued clicking through the current crop of faithful who were resident. He paused again on a young woman called Diane from Michigan who apparently loved horses, baking, and wanted to make a tangible difference to the world, but she had a slightly too enthusiastic expression on her face. There was another hopeful a few clicks on who he discounted because of a goofy smile, and another from Massachusetts called Bella who just wanted to serve the Lord in any way He wanted her to. Giovanni narrowed his eyes as he looked at the woman's photograph. Unlike the others, it was a candid photograph taken at a beach. Bella was wearing a swimsuit that, while modest, left little to the imagination in terms of her figure. Like Maddy, she was slightly built, which was just how Giovanni liked them. In the photograph, she was standing in thigh-deep blue water with a vast expanse of ocean behind her and, to Giovanni at least, Bella from Massachusetts bore a passing resemblance to a young Kirsten Dunst.

He tutted when he zoomed in on the photograph as it became pixelated too quickly for his liking, but Giovanni could see enough of the woman to spark a physiological reaction. Grinning, he grabbed a notepad from a drawer and made some notes, scrolling through her biography to pick out some key details. Then he brought up his browser and did a few quick internet searches, adding to his notes as he did so. When he had finished, he tore off the page with his scribblings on it and brought up one of the documents he shared with Eva. A few clicks of the mouse later and Maddy was sitting at the back for the next sermon, and Bella had pride of place at the front. Then he switched documents to bring up the Adelphoi's program of events, which told him who was where for the rest of the day.

"Hmm, Bella," Giovanni mumbled to himself when he saw her name listed as an attendee at the afternoon yoga session. After pinning Bella's picture to his desktop, he checked his watch to see he still had a couple of hours until the yoga class started. He finished his drink and opened up a new Word document. His next sermon was already written, but what Hugo had told him and Eva earlier had sparked a lot of ideas in his mind. He needed to work on preparing his congregation for Hugo's bat shit crazy plan, and begin whipping them up a little. Fervor was good for his bank balance, and the thought of Armageddon just around the corner was bound to increase both. With a wry smile as he thought about Bella in her swimsuit, Giovanni typed out a title.

HOW WILL WE KNOW THE SIGNS OF THE TIMES?

39

Eva lifted her head at the sound of someone knocking on the door of her suite. No doubt it was Giovanni, hopefully with his tail between his legs, coming to apologize for acting like a child. She got off the bed where she had been resting, placing her Kindle on the bedspread, and smoothed out her robe before crossing to the door. But when she opened it, it wasn't Giovanni but Maddy. The young girl was standing in the corridor with an uncertain expression on her face.

"Maddy," Eva said with a smile. "What an unexpected surprise." In all the time Eva had been living at the complex, she didn't think one of the Adelphoi had ever knocked on her door. It wasn't explicitly forbidden, but more of an unwritten rule. "Come in, please."

Eva watched as Maddy's eyes widened when she stepped into the suite. It had two rooms, a bedroom with a kingsize bed and a living area with comfortable chairs and a large screen television that Eva rarely used. The only things that differentiated the suite from any other hotel suite were the religious statues dotted around the rooms, more to keep up appearances than anything else.

"Wow," Maddy said. "This is nice."

"It's only temporary," Eva replied, drifting back in her mind to the conversation she'd had with Giovanni about moving out of the suite. "I'll be moving into one of the regular rooms soon. This is a bit too ostentatious for just me."

Maddy nodded in reply, but her gaze kept drifting around the room. Eventually, her eyes rested on a brightly painted statue of a woman dressed in a purple robe with an embroidered blue shawl. It was a yard high and showed the woman wringing her hands and looking plaintively into the middle distance, tears streaming down her face. The most remarkable thing about the statue was the dagger piercing the woman's heart.

"Oh my," Maddy said as she looked at the wooden statue. "That's a bit morbid."

"It's Our Lady of Sorrows," Eva replied.

"How come she's been stabbed?"

Eva paused before replying, wracking her brains for the reason behind the dagger. "It's, er, representing how sad she is." There was something in the gospels about it, and there was a name bouncing around Eva's head. Was it Simon? She shook her head, knowing that none of the gospels were by a man called Simon.

"I think I'd be sad as well if someone knifed me in the heart," Maddy said, looking at Eva with an almost childish smile. Keen to change the subject, Eva continued.

"How can I help you, Maddy?" she asked the young woman.

"Oh, yes, sorry," Maddy replied. "I wanted to ask you

about the proposition you mentioned. Only nothing was mentioned at lunch?"

"I think there's been a slight change in plan," Eva said, thinking about the best way to approach this. "We couldn't really discuss it with Mr. Forrester being there, though."

"Ah, okay. So it wasn't because of what I told you earlier?"

"No, no," Eva said with a smile. "Nothing at all to do with that."

"Is he a member of the Adelphoi? Mr. Forrester?"

"He's one of our supporters, yes."

"Is he rich?"

"Yes. Very."

"I thought he was," Maddy said. "The helicopter's a bit of a giveaway. Did you ask him if I could go in it?"

"I didn't, Maddy," Eva replied, seeing the young woman's face falling as she said this. "But I will the next time I see him, I promise. We had something very important to talk about, and it wasn't really the time."

"Okay." Maddy's face brightened up again. "Thank you."

The two women stood in silence for a few moments before Eva spoke.

"Was there anything else, Maddy?"

"No, I just wanted to make sure I'd not said the wrong thing."

Eva reassured Maddy she hadn't and gently ushered her toward the door of her suite, bidding her goodbye and promising to sit with her at supper. When the young woman had left, Eva paused for a moment in thought. The conversation had illustrated just how young Maddy really was. She might be in her late teens, but she behaved like a much younger person. That, in Eva's opinion, made her vulnerable. She needed to speak with Giovanni, and there was no time like the present.

A few moments later, Eva opened the door to Giovanni's office. When she realized what he was doing, she wished she'd knocked first. Giovanni's hands flew from his lap and he shuffled his chair under his desk.

"You disgust me, Giovanni," Eva said, looking away from him and out of the window as he adjusted his trousers. "Put it away. We need to talk."

Eva waited until he had closed down the windows on his computer, wondering what, or more specifically, who, he had been looking at.

"What is it, Eva?" Giovanni said. "I was just putting the finishing touches to my sermon."

"I know full well what you were putting the finishing touches to, Giovanni, and it certainly wasn't your sermon," Eva replied with a snicker. She walked back to the office door and snagged the lock. Then she crossed to his desk and pulled his chair out from behind his desk. When she had enough room, she lifted her robe and swung her leg over his lap, straddling him. "Are you listening?" she asked as she felt his hands on her thighs.

"I am now," Giovanni replied, his eyes half closed.

"I need you to promise me something," Eva said as she undid his trousers.

"What might that be?"

Giovanni gasped as Eva found what she was looking for.

"How about I give you a hand?" She smiled as she saw the look on Giovanni's face. "But I need you to leave Maddy alone," Eva said, tightening her grip and making him gasp again. "She's too young and naïve for a man like you."

"And what do I get in return, Sister Eva?" Giovanni

asked, closing his eyes completely as Eva started pumping her arm.

"Whatever you want, Brother Giovanni," Eva replied with a wry smile. Men, especially this one, were so predictable. "Whatever you want."

When Anita saw Caleb stumble for the second time, she was too scared even to scream. The first time, he had just lost his footing. Then, a man had appeared at the end of the Via Ferrata where the cable had become disconnected. Despite the distance, she could tell it was one of the men who had been chasing them through the alleys in the village. As she watched, the man raised his hand with a familiar looking black item in his fingers. A pistol.

She saw the pistol bucking twice in the man's hand. There was a puff of dust a few yards above Caleb's head and then, a split second later, Caleb stumbled again. Had he been shot? Anita watched in horror, expecting Caleb to peel away from the rock and plummet into the abyss at any moment. She saw him pause, only for a second, before he continued climbing toward where she was standing.

"Get back!" Anita heard him shout. She had already moved away from the edge as he had instructed a moment before, but she took another couple of large steps back until the rock face obscured the man with the gun. To her relief, a few seconds later, she heard a scuffling sound as Caleb reached the path where she had been standing. When he rounded the corner to join her, he was limping badly.

"Oh my God, Caleb!" Anita said when she saw blood running down the back of his thigh. "Have you been shot? Let me see!" She dropped to one knee to examine his leg and when he reached her, he put a hand on her shoulder to steady himself.

"I don't think so," Caleb replied. "I've been shot before, and this doesn't feel as bad."

Anita glanced up at his face as he said this, noticing that he had a grimace on it. He'd been shot before? But he was a preacher, wasn't he? Who would shoot a preacher? Ignoring the questions hurtling round inside her head, she stooped to examine the wound on his leg. Despite the blood, it was more of a ragged laceration than a bullet hole. Anita swung her handbag round, so it was in front of her and not slung around her neck, and opened it to rummage for what she needed.

"Anita, we need to move," Caleb said, leaning back to look round the corner of the rock face.

"Are they coming?" Anita asked as she picked out a couple of items from her bag.

"No, not yet," he replied. "I think they're trying to decide what to do, but we need to get going."

"Caleb, you're bleeding," Anita said as she ripped open the spare pair of tights she had in her bag. "This won't take long."

"Have I been shot?" he asked her. She looked up at his face again, realizing that he couldn't really see the wound in his leg. "What can you see?"

"It's more of a deep cut in your thigh," Anita said as she opened the other item she had grabbed. She tore the wrapper off it and, after telling Caleb that it might sting, applied it to the wound before winding the tights around his thigh in a makeshift bandage.

"What have you put on it?" Caleb asked, craning his neck to see her attempt at first aid.

"A sanitary pad," Anita replied, "with some tights to secure it." To her surprise, he started laughing. "What's so funny?"

"Nothing," he replied, removing his hand from her shoulder. "Come on, let's get going."

"Are you okay with walking?"

"I'm fine," Caleb said, still smiling. "It's probably just a ricochet. When we get to safety, I'll get it patched up."

"What's wrong with the sanitary pad?" Anita asked, returning his smile as they made their way farther along the path.

"Nothing at all," Caleb replied. "It's very resourceful. We used to use tampons to plug bullet holes if we had nothing else." In front of them, the path broadened and the sheer drop to the side became more of a steep incline.

"Who's we?" Anita asked.

"What do you mean?"

"You said we used to use tampons. So, who's we? I thought you were a preacher?"

"I am a preacher," Caleb replied, a wry smile appearing on his face. "But I've not always been a preacher. I've done many things, as I'm sure you have." He shook his head as if to show that part of the conversation was over.

"I've never been shot at before," Anita said, taking his prompt, "and I've never patched up a bullet hole."

"There is a time for everything. Or so the Good Book says."

"Are you preaching to me now?"

"Ecclesiastes, chapter three," Caleb replied. "Verse one, if I remember correctly. It's one of my favorite chapters, in fact."

They continued along the path, moving as quickly as Caleb's injured leg would let them. Anita heard him speaking quietly as they walked. If he was reciting the chapter he'd been talking about, Caleb was right. There did seem to be a time for everything.

Including a time to die.

41

Caleb was doing his best to hide it from Anita, but he was hurting. It wasn't the wound in his leg although that was smarting a lot. It was his abdomen that he was most concerned about. When he had grabbed Anita earlier to swing her back onto the ledge, he thought he'd torn something in his midriff and he now had a sharp pain just to the right of his belly button. Every step he took sent a sharp pain radiating through the area, which concerned Caleb, as he'd had some significant injuries in that part of his body in the recent past. Hopefully, it was nothing more than a muscular sprain, but he guessed time would tell, as it usually did.

"Not much further now," Caleb said as he saw a set of rough steps hewn from the rock in front of them. On either side of the route were thick chestnut trees with branches overhanging the steps. Caleb regarded the bark's grayish-purple tone, with oblong leaves and distinctive pointed tips. When he saw a small group of mushrooms at the tree's base, Caleb smiled. Porcini mushrooms. Add them to rice and you had a mouthwatering risotto. In the fall, the trees would be a fantastic source of chestnuts that the monks would use to make castagnaccio, a traditional, plain chestnut flour cake adorned with raisins and pine nuts. An entire meal from a tree.

"Let the earth sprout vegetation, plants yielding seed, and fruit trees bearing fruit," Caleb mumbled in a low voice, too low for Anita to hear. God did indeed provide, and the thought of food made his stomach rumble.

Caleb kept glancing over his shoulder, wary about their pursuers, but he saw or heard nothing. Would the man who had shot at him chance the free climb to continue their chase? Caleb knew it was a possibility. After all, the man had watched him doing it so he knew it would be achievable. Caleb's second concern was the location of the second man, whom he had not seen. The other gunman could have taken the alternative route to the top of the mountain and be waiting for them when they reached their destination. Knowing he could do nothing about either eventuality, he pressed on.

"Are you okay, Caleb?" Anita asked him as they made their way up the steps, pushing the branches aside as they did so. "You're very pale."

"I'm fine, Anita, but I appreciate your concern," Caleb said before gasping as another sharp pain knifed him in the abdomen. He paused and put a hand to his side, waiting for the pain to pass.

"Are you sure?" Anita asked, her concern obvious in her eyes. "Do you want to rest for a while?"

"Honestly, I'm fine," Caleb said. "I think I've pulled a muscle, that's all."

"Is that because I'm heavier than I look?" Anita replied, her smile not hiding her anxiety.

Caleb said nothing, but continued climbing the steps.

He noticed Anita had changed her position to walk behind him, a simple gesture that he appreciated. If he were to stumble or collapse, she could stop him from falling back down the steps. He kept one hand against his flank and used the other to brush the branches aside. They formed a canopy over their heads which provided some relief from the sun, although a sunburned scalp was the least of his worries.

A few moments later, they emerged from the tunnel formed by the trees, and Caleb saw a small village in front of them. The houses were all painted white with red-tiled roofs, and apart from a small dog wandering about, the village appeared to be empty. He paused, glancing around for the second gunman, but he could see nothing of concern. Between the end of the path and the village was a medium-sized red car, an Alpha Romeo 159 with its engine idling. Caleb could see the silhouette of someone behind the wheel, but the rear tinted windows obscured any passengers in the back.

"This way," Caleb said, taking Anita's hand and leading her toward the car. As they approached, the driver's door opened and a man wearing a brown robe and, incongruously, a pair of Wayfarer Aviator sunglasses got out. He walked to the rear of the car and opened the door, gesturing to Caleb and Anita to get inside. With a smile at the look of surprise on Anita's face, Caleb slipped into the car, which was blissfully cool. She slid in next to him and the monk closed the door with a soft thunk before returning to the driver's seat.

"Grazie," Caleb said to the monk, who just nodded in response. *Thank you.* He thought back to the conversation he'd had with the Abbot earlier that day. It had only been a few hours ago, but it felt like days. Caleb remembered the way the Abbot's expression hadn't changed in the slightest when he had been informed of Anita's destination. He had just nodded like the monk had just now.

Caleb watched as the driver leaned forward and stabbed at the sat nav screen in the car. When the man entered Naples as their destination, Caleb heard Anita take a sharp breath.

"Caleb," she said, her voice not much more than a whisper. "That's over seven hundred kilometers away." Caleb said nothing, but just smiled as he closed his eyes. The car moved away slowly with a low purr from the 3.2 liter V6 engine, winding its way through the narrow, winding streets of the mountaintop village.

"God has provided," he whispered just before he fell asleep.

42

Hugo leafed through the color photographs his aide had printed out for him, nodding in approval as he examined each one. The A4 printouts were of the jars in Giv'at ha-Mivtar in East Jerusalem and had been taken by Nasim as it had been quietly excavated and prepared for transit. He paused on one of the images showing the jar with the engravings Nasim had described, holding the paper a yard or so away from his old eyes as he did so.

"A prayer to the Manes," Hugo mumbled, tracing his finger over the ancient inscription the photograph depicted, but he wasn't able to translate any of the remaining text. Above the rune-like words was a symbol, obviously military, just as Nasim had described. He leaned forward and pressed a button on the telephone on his desk to summon his aide.

"Mr. Forrester?" his aide's voice answered within seconds.

"Ruth, have these images been e-mailed to me?"

"Of course, Mr. Forrester," the aide replied, the disapproval in her voice evident. "There are copies on SharePoint as well."

"They're clean?"

"Yes, Mr. Forrester. The EXIF data has been deleted and thoroughly wiped."

"Thank you," Hugo said as he disconnected the call. Deleting the EXIF data from the images meant that there was no metadata attached to them. Much of the data was inconsequential, but some was very important. The GPS location of where the photographs were taken was not something he wanted to share just yet.

A few seconds later, he was looking at the screen of his iMac, the browser open at his ProtonMail account, which, if the marketing hype was to be believed, was absolutely un-hackable. Hugo composed an e-mail to a trusted friend of his, a professor in Cambridge, England, who specialized in early Christian symbology. His friend was, like Hugo, a keeper of antiquities and had quite a collection of them himself that were discretely housed in the basement of a large country house in England. Like Hugo's collection, his friend's wasn't open to the public, and never would be.

Lawrence, what do you think of this?

Then Hugo attached a single image, the one he was looking at with the engravings on the jar, and sent the e-mail. He didn't add any other information, although he was sure his friend's attention would be well and truly piqued if the jars were from the era Hugo thought they were.

Hugo glanced at his watch, trying to remember if England was ahead or behind Austria time-wise, but there was no hurry for Lawrence's opinion. If the jars had been in the ground for the last two millennia, then what was another couple of hours?

The e-mail sent, Hugo closed down his computer and

returned to examine the photographs in more detail. As Nasim had said, the jars were in remarkably good condition, given their apparent age. He could even see handprints in the plaster covering them that looked remarkably similar to ones created by modern-day workmen. He flicked back through the photographs until he found one showing the jars in their entirety before they were excavated. From the footprints in the dusty floor of the cave, Hugo fancied that the shepherd who had discovered it had been the first person inside the hollowed out grave for two thousand years.

Hugo was just contemplating having his aide bring him a nightcap when the telephone on his desk rumbled into life. His eyebrows went up at the noise. Few people, if any, still used landlines. He picked up the handset and pressed it to his ear.

"Yes?" he said.

"Hugo," a familiar and very cultured British voice replied.

"That was quick, Lawrence." Hugo smiled, knowing he would have his friend's opinion sooner that he'd thought. "How are you?"

"Where is that photograph from, Forrester?" Lawrence replied, surprising Hugo. It wasn't because of the use of his last name as a salutation—that was entirely normal in the type of schools they had both attended—it was the lack of any preliminary conversation. Normally, they would spend a few moments on the usual pleasantries between old friends before getting down to business. But Lawrence had jumped right in without even so much as a mention of the weather.

"It's from an item that's come into my possession," Hugo replied with a grin. Lawrence would be itching to know more, but Hugo was currently holding the cards, and he favored he had the better hand. There was a pause at the end of the line before Lawrence replied.

"Was it found in an area that's known to us?" his friend said, causing Hugo's grin to widen.

"Absolutely," Hugo replied. There were many areas that were known to them both, ranging from the Middle East to South America, and many places in between.

"And you have these items with you now?"

"I will, in due course. They're being transported now."

"I see," Lawrence replied. There was another pause on the line, this time extending into a silence that lasted for perhaps a full minute. Hugo kept his grin where it was, knowing that his old friend would fold first, as he usually did.

"Their provenance?" Lawrence asked, still fishing.

"Undisturbed, I believe, so impeccable." Another silence, this one not quite as long.

"I was thinking, Hugo, it's been a while since we met. I'm due some vacation time from the university."

"Well, why don't you come and spend some time in the Alps?" Hugo said with delight. "You know you're always welcome and the weather is superb at this time of year."

"When would be a good time to come?" Lawrence asked. Although he made no mention of when the artifact was due to arrive at Hugo's warehouse, Hugo knew that was what he was asking.

"How about this weekend?" The battery of tests Hugo had lined up for the jars would be completed by then. Lawrence, and his expertise, would be very useful indeed once the results were back. While he waited for Lawrence to reply, Hugo scribbled a note on his blotter to remind himself to tell Ruth to get Nasim over here as well.

"Yes, I can make that work," Lawrence replied. Hugo

grinned again. Of course he could. "I'll make the arrange-ments. But Hugo?"

"Yes, Lawrence?" Hugo said, not liking his friend's sudden change in tone.

"If my interpretation of those symbols is correct, what you have is likely to be coveted by many."

Hugo replaced the handset, his grin subsiding. Most of what was in his collection already was coveted by many, or it would be if anyone knew what his collection contained.

43
_____

Anita settled back into the plush seat of the Alpha Romeo and stared out of the darkened window at the village as it passed them by, the small buildings deserted. Before long, all she could see were trees flashing past. The road gradually straightened and within minutes, they had joined a main route. The monk driving the car moved through the gears, the engine responding with pleasure, and engaged the cruise control before settling back in his seat. She saw him glance at her in the rear-view mirror, although she couldn't see his eyes because of his sunglasses.

"So," Anita said in Italian, leaning forward. Beside her, Caleb was fast asleep. "Are you one of the monks who's taken a vow of silence, or are you one who's allowed to talk?" She was smiling as she spoke, but in response, the monk just shrugged his shoulders. "Ah," she said. "A silent one." She couldn't be sure, but she thought she saw the faintest of smiles on his face.

"It's not a formal vow of silence," the monk said a moment later in a quiet voice. He spoke with a southern

Italian accent, faint but still discernible. "It's a practice to clear our minds. When both our interior and exterior are quiet, God will do the rest."

"Okay," Anita replied, not sure how to respond to his statement. "I'll try not to say too much, but thank you for helping us." She saw him nod his head once in acknowledgment. "I was hoping we might stop somewhere on the way to Naples. Caleb has an injury to his leg, and I need to make a telephone call."

"He's hurt?" the monk asked. "What happened?"

"He's got a wound to the back of his leg," Anita replied. "It's got a temporary bandage, but it needs cleaning and dressing properly." The monk nodded again, his expression inscrutable behind his sunglasses. Anita waited for the inevitable question about how Caleb had been wounded, but the monk said nothing. "What's your name?"

"I go by Antonio," the monk replied, turning to face her properly and extending a hand for her to shake. His skin was warm, and he had a firm handshake. Anita was reminded of something her father used to say about never trusting a man with a limp handshake.

"I'm Anita," she replied.

"Yes," Brother Antonio said. "I know."

Anita turned to look at Caleb, taking advantage of the fact he was asleep to study him properly, something she'd not been able to do before. He looked peaceful as he slept, but at the same time, his brow was furrowed slightly. She glanced down at his leg to check the dressing was secure before thinking back to when she had briefly seen the scars on his back earlier that day. How did a preacher come by injuries that caused scars like the ones she had seen? Knowing that Caleb wouldn't be able to understand her, she leaned forward to ask the monk a question.

"Quanto bene conosci Caleb?" Anita asked. *How well do you know Caleb?*

"I don't," the monk replied, also speaking in Italian. "But the Abbott vouches for him, which is more than enough for me."

Anita sighed. She had hoped that their driver might shed some light on Caleb's past, but it was not to be. She returned her eyes to the window where the countryside had flattened out following their descent from the mountains. The road was smooth and monotonous, and it wasn't long before she felt her eyelids drooping.

SOME TIME LATER, Anita's eyes jolted open as the car drove over a speed bump. She looked out of the window to see they were pulling into a motorway service station. Anita looked at her watch to see she had been asleep for almost two full hours. Beside her, Caleb was also stirring into life.

"Where are we?" he asked, stretching his arms as much as the interior of the car would allow.

"We're just pulling into an Autogrill," Anita replied, noticing that the monk had pulled the car to a stop some distance from the actual service station.

"How do you want to play this, Brother Caleb?" the monk asked, turning to look at Caleb and removing his sunglasses. Anita saw he had incredibly dark brown eyes, so dark they were almost black. She saw Caleb lean forward and stare through the windshield. His eyes flicked rapidly from side to side as he took in the buildings a hundred meters or so away.

"Would you mind getting us some food, Brother Antonio?" Caleb asked him. "I'd prefer to stay away from any cameras, just in case."

"Of course," the monk replied, opening the door to the Alpha Romeo and glancing at Anita. "There's a small pharmacia as well. There're some public phones over there," Antonio said, pointing to the edge of the parking lot. "Next to the restrooms."

"Thank you," Anita replied. She looked at Caleb, who after examining the area Antonio had just pointed at briefly, nodded his head.

When Anita got out of the vehicle, she was surprised how warm it still was. As Brother Antonio made his way toward the restaurant area, she headed in the other direction toward the phones. A moment later, after loading the phone with euros, she punched a familiar number from memory into it.

"Ciao?" a woman's voice said.

"Greta, it's Anita."

"Anita!" Greta replied, her excitement obvious. "Did you get away?"

"Eventually," Anita replied with a furtive look around the parking lot. "I needed some help, though. We've had a few problems."

"Were you able to use the thumb drive?"

Anita paused before replying, noting that Greta's primary interest was the contents of the thumb drive, not what the problems she'd had were. "Yes, I was," she said a few seconds later.

"Excellent," Greta replied. Then she reeled off an address in Naples and asked Anita to repeat it. "How long will you be?"

"A few hours, at least," Anita said, "and I've got someone with me."

"Right." It was clear to Anita from the tone of Greta's

voice that she wasn't happy with this development. "I'd prefer to meet you alone."

"He's injured, so I can't just abandon him," Anita said, glancing at the tinted windows of the car. She could just make out Caleb's outline through the smoked glass.

"Can he be trusted?"

Anita paused again before replying. If it wasn't for Caleb, the chances were she would be dead.

"He's a preacher," Anita said eventually. "If you can't trust a preacher, who can you trust?"

44

C aleb winced as Anita peeled the sanitary pad away from the wound in his thigh. The soft material had become enmeshed with the scab that had formed over the area and, as she eased it away, it peeled the wound back open.

"Sorry," he heard Anita whisper as she reached for some tissues to dab the blood away. They were sitting in the rear of the Alpha Romeo, now parked on the far edge of the parking lot. There was a glorious smell of fresh food coming from a paper bag in the passenger footwell, but Anita had insisted they attend to business before they ate.

"Don't be," Caleb replied, trying to smile despite the pain. At least the pain in his abdomen had subsided, unless it was being eclipsed by the pain in his thigh. He watched as Anita poured some disinfectant into a small square of gauze.

"This might sting a bit," Anita said.

"Can I do anything?" Brother Antonio asked. He was sitting in the driver's seat, craning back to see what was going on in the rear of the car.

"Hold me?" Caleb said, looking at him with an imploring expression. To Caleb's amusement, after a few seconds' hesitation, Antonio reached his hands across the back of the driver's seat. "I'm joking, Antonio." Caleb laughed, more for Anita's benefit than for his own. "I've had worse injuries from shaving my head." Antonio paused before returning his hands to where they had been and giving Caleb a tight smile. Not the jokey type then, Caleb surmised.

"Hilarious, Brother Caleb," Antonio said, his face relaxing as his smile became more genuine.

Caleb managed to suppress any sound as Anita dabbed the disinfectant-soaked gauze to the wound on his thigh, pressing his lips together in an approximation of a smile as she did what she needed to do. He watched her as she worked, appreciating the look of intense concentration on her face.

"You've done this type of thing before?" he asked as she unwrapped a bandage to place over the now clean wound.

"Ambassador First Aid badge," Anita replied. "Girl Scouts of Greater Iowa," she continued when Caleb frowned. "That and two younger brothers. They didn't get shot, though. They were just always falling out of trees and stuff like that."

"I didn't know you had brothers," Caleb said.

"I've not spoken to them in years," she replied, effectively cutting off that avenue of conversation. Anita remained silent as she wound the bandage around Caleb's thigh, securing it with a couple of strips of surgical tape. "How's that?" she asked.

"Perfect," Caleb replied. "Thank you."

A few moments later, once Anita had got rid of the

bloodstained temporary bandage and gauze, Antonio opened the bag of food and the mouth-watering aroma intensified.

"I have two Rustichella, and a Camogli," he said, peering into the bag. "As well as chips, soda, and cookies."

"Rustichella for me, please, Brother Antonio," Anita said with a grin. "How about you, Caleb? What do you fancy?"

Caleb, who did not know what a Rustichella or a Camogli was, just shrugged his shoulders. "I don't mind," he said. "I'm so hungry. My stomach thinks my throat's been cut. Brother Antonio, which would you prefer?"

"They're both cheese and ham sandwiches, Brother Caleb," Antonio said. "Well, kind of. I'll take the Camogli, though."

A moment later, Caleb was holding a half-moon shaped sandwich in front of him. The bread was soft and still warm, and he could see bacon and cheese in between the bread. When he took a bite, the cheese formed strings between his mouth and the sandwich that he had to use a finger to scoop up. Caleb nodded in appreciation. It might be a simple sandwich, but it was delicious. Apart from Anita saying this really wasn't how Italians liked to eat, they completed their meals in silence.

"Let me take the trash to the can," Caleb said when they had all finished, having unanimously decided to save the cookies for later. He picked up the paper bag and, once Anita and Antonio had put their wrappers inside, scrunched the top closed. "I need the bathroom, anyway."

"I'll come too," Brother Antonio said.

They walked in silence to the trash can before making their way to the bathroom. Caleb's eyes darted around to make sure there were no CCTV cameras he'd missed, but there were none. They entered, Caleb wrinkling his nose at the odor of disinfectant and stale urine, and stood next to each other at the urinals. Then, almost as one, they hiked up their robes.

"Is she okay, your friend?" Antonio asked, keeping his gaze fixed firmly forward, as was the unwritten rule in such situations. "Anita?"

"She's fragile," Caleb replied, also not moving his head an inch. "And she's in danger, although I'm yet to ascertain just how much. I sense there are dark forces gathering."

"Aren't there always?"

Caleb glanced over his shoulder as a young man entered the restroom. He obviously wasn't expecting to see what he could see. Two monks, both with their robes hiked up to their thighs, performing a call of nature. The young man's expression was, in Caleb's opinion, priceless.

"Mi scusi," the new arrival muttered before he turned on his heel and fled. Once the young man had left the restroom, both Caleb and Antonio laughed.

As the two of them washed their hands, Antonio turned to Caleb with a serious expression on his face.

"The Abbot speaks highly of you, Brother Caleb," he said. "He says you saved his life in Afghanistan."

"It was many years ago," Caleb replied, considering a comment about how, for a man running an order of mostly silent monks, the Abbot talked too much. But that would achieve nothing other than make him look petulant, so he held his counsel. "In a different life." Caleb adjusted his robe. "In a different uniform."

"Not for him, it wasn't," Antonio said. "He still bears the scars, even though they're not on his flesh."

"We are all scarred, Brother Antonio. Psalm one

hundred and forty-seven." Caleb waited to see if Antonio would complete the quotation, but the monk remained silent. "He heals the brokenhearted and binds up their wounds."

"Let's hope so, Brother Caleb," Antonio said, his voice almost a whisper. "Let's hope so."

45

"No, Giovanni," Eva said, pulling the bedspread up to cover her nakedness. "Definitely not."

Giovanni looked at her from his position by the small desk in his suite. He was wearing a short towel wrapped around his midriff that did nothing to hide a developing paunch. To Eva's disgust, he was preparing to light up a small cheroot as if he had just achieved something extraordinary and wanted to celebrate. Eva had enjoyed what they had just done, but it wasn't an event that required any sort of celebration.

"What do you mean, no?" Giovanni replied as he touched the lighter flame to the end of the cheroot. "I've not even told you what my idea is."

"When you start a sentence with the words, hey, here's an idea," Eva replied, snuggling further under the bedspread. "I know for a fact that you're about to suggest something ridiculous."

Giovanni puffed on the cheroot, sending a blue cloud of smoke into the suite. "Hear me out, Eva," he said as he removed the cheroot from his mouth to examine the end. "It was something that Hugo said that got me thinking, that was all."

"What did Hugo say?"

"This plan of his, he has a few requirements."

"I'm aware of that," Eva replied. "Would you take that cancer stick somewhere else?" She waved her hands in front of her face as the blue cloud began creeping in her direction. Giovanni walked over to the patio doors, pulled the curtain aside, and cracked open the door. Outside, it was almost dark, and Eva heard the calls of cicadas coming through the gap in the door. To her relief, Giovanni's next puff was aimed at the outside world.

"Better?" Giovanni asked.

"Yes. So, which of these requirements has made you actually think?"

"Here's the idea," Giovanni said, causing Eva to groan. "One of the things he needs is a mother for the child."

"No."

"I've not explained it properly yet."

"No," Eva repeated, ignoring the petulant look on his face. "I don't have a maternal bone in my body, so you can forget about that right away. Besides, I'm not a virgin. Even if I was earlier today, which I wasn't, I'm certainly not one now."

"Maybe I wasn't talking about you?" Giovanni replied, but Eva knew he was bluffing and trying to wriggle out of his suggestion. "The whole virgin birth thing is really complicated, anyway."

"How so?"

"It's just not clear, theologically speaking, whether the without sex bit refers to the conception or to the actual act of, er, intercourse."

"Been on Google, have you?" Eva said with a laugh.

"No, Eva," Giovanni replied with a look of irritation. "That's what years of theological study have told me."

Eva opened her mouth to say something, but closed it again. Giovanni was no more of a theologian than she was a nun, and they both knew that. He was a manipulator. A very good one, but nothing more than that. A hundred years ago, he would have been wandering the Wild West selling snake oil, and probably doing very well at it. But Eva was not happy about the way he seemed to have latched on to Hugo's scheme. It was one thing taking money from people for words, but quite another taking money from them by telling them Jesus was returning and they needed to put their hands in their pockets to secure His safety.

"So if not, then who?" Eva said, deciding against antagonizing Giovanni, at least for the moment. There was, in her opinion, no harm in letting things develop to see what happened. Even the worst-case scenario would give them nine months to prepare.

Giovanni puffed on his cheroot another couple of times. Eva knew he was buying time until he thought of another option. She watched him closely, and could see from the way his face changed a moment later that he had come up with something.

"What about Maddy?"

Eva groaned again, this time more deeply. He really was obsessed with the poor girl.

"Really?" she asked with a sigh.

"Yeah," Giovanni replied, turning to her with a triumphant smile. "If she's a lesbian, she'll be a virgin. Technically speaking, at least."

"That is one of the most ridiculous things I've ever heard you say, Giovanni," Eva said, throwing the bedspread back and looking around for her clothes. "Were you born a misogynist, or did they teach you that at the theological college you didn't attend?"

"What are you talking about?"

"The idea that female virginity is something that can only be taken by a man." Eva found her bra on the floor next to the bed and struggled into it. "You are way out of your depth, Giovanni."

"I don't know what you're talking about," Giovanni replied, his exasperation obvious. "Why are you getting upset?"

"Then I rest my case," Eva said as she scooped up her habit from where it lay in a crumpled heap on the floor.

"Will you ask her? Maddy, I mean?"

"What? If she's a virgin? Absolutely not."

"No, okay, listen. Forget about the whole virginity thing. Like I said, that bit's really unclear." Giovanni puffed again on his cheroot, but it had gone out. "Will you ask her if she'd be willing to be the child's mother?"

Eva stood, threw her habit over her head, and smoothed it down over her hips. She looked again at Giovanni and could tell from his face that he was deadly serious.

"You're not joking, are you?" she asked him. Giovanni shook his head as he replied.

"No, I'm not. It would sound better coming from you."

"I'm going to bed, Giovanni," Eva said as she turned to leave. "I'm going back to my suite, while I've still got one. We'll talk tomorrow."

"But will you ask her?" Giovanni asked again. "Please?"

"Let me think about it," Eva replied with a sigh.

Without another word, she opened the door to Giovanni's suite and left.

46

Giovanni flicked the now dead cheroot out of the gap in the patio doors with a sneer as the door to his suite closed behind Eva.

"Stuck up bitch," he mumbled to himself. "Who on earth does she think she is?" He screwed his mouth up and tried to impersonate her voice. "Let me think about it."

He briefly considered having a shower, but couldn't be bothered. Besides, he quite liked the smell of sex on him. It reminded him of his power over women, even women like Eva. She would come round. She would have to come round. This was, possibly, the best opportunity the Adelphoi had ever had. Eva could either get on the bus, or get off it. It was her choice, but Giovanni very much wanted her not only on the bus, but driving it alongside him.

As he crossed his suite to get some pajamas from the closet, he entertained a short daydream in which there was a television with a Breaking News banner. On the screen, an excited anchor was talking about the miraculous return of God's child to Earth while, behind him, video clips were being played. Of course, it was Giovanni's face in the video clips. Perhaps he would be waving to crowds of the faithful? Perhaps he would be solemnly blessing a line of people, all waiting to be saved?

How much should a blessing cost, Giovanni wondered. Was twenty bucks too much? He would need to learn how to bless people, of course, but it couldn't be that difficult. The thought reminded him to clear the cache of his web browser before Eva used the computer in his office later that morning.

He'd spent a couple of hours on the thing the previous afternoon after Hugo had left, trying and failing to get his head around the concept of immaculate conception. It would help if people could actually decide what it meant, rather than proposing a myriad of theories and ideas about the belief. It seemed there were as many opinions on it as there were religious leaders, all with their own slant in it. One thing there definitely wasn't was a consensus.

Giovanni made a mental note to discuss it with Hugo the next time they met. If he could work out what Hugo thought, dressing the question up in a debate to avoid looking stupid, then Giovanni could just follow his lead. Hugo was, after all, the brainchild behind the plan. Giovanni nodded to himself as he put his pajamas on. That was a good plan.

He was just buttoning up his pajama top and thinking about cleaning his teeth when his cell phone started buzzing next to the bed. With a glance at his watch, he crossed the room to answer it. Whoever was calling him at this late hour had better have something good to say.

"Yes?" Giovanni said as he answered the call, not recognizing the number on the screen.

"Ciao, Brother Giovanni," a male voice rasped. Giovanni

sighed and scowled at the same time. It was one of those idiot ex-police officers.

"What is it?" Giovanni asked, trying to inject as much authority into his voice as he could manage. "Do you know what time it is?"

"We've lost them."

"What?"

"I said we've lost them. The woman and the priest. They're gone."

Giovanni paused for a moment before replying. While he was angry that the two buffoons hadn't retrieved his property, at the same time, he was relieved that they hadn't killed Anita. More because of how angry it would make Eva than anything else. He couldn't do anything about the situation, other than re-evaluate just how much damage Anita could do with the information she had stolen.

"There goes half your pay," Giovanni said with a smirk. He had paid them half of what they had agreed, with the remaining half due on successful completion of the mission. Success, in this context, was the retrieval of the thumb drive.

"I know," the man replied, and Giovanni caught the resignation in his voice.

"I may have some more work for you, even though your rates will have just gone down," Giovanni said, thinking back to what Hugo had said earlier about security. "How soon can you be back here at the complex?"

"Tomorrow afternoon?"

"Perfect. We can speak then." Giovanni didn't wait for a reply, but just disconnected the call. When he was sure the line was dead, he continued. "Idiots. Absolute idiots."

Giovanni put the cell phone back on the bedside table and climbed into bed, rearranging the bedding as he did so. A short time earlier, Eva had been writhing around under him on this bed as he had pleasured her. Although, if he was honest with himself, Giovanni was more interested in his own pleasure than hers. But she'd not complained, so he assumed she was satisfied with his ministrations. Perhaps the next woman he would be ministering to in this bed would be Bella from Massachusetts? He had arranged to have breakfast with her tomorrow, where he was planning on asking her to contribute to his next sermon. She would be at the front and center of his afternoon Zoom call with the faithful and, if all went to plan, in the evening she would be where he was now.

He sighed in contentment and rolled onto his side. Closing his eyes, he made another mental note.

He'd better get Eva to change the sheets in the morning.

47

Caleb woke with a start, blinking a couple of times to orientate himself. He sat up, leaning his head to one side to relieve a crick in his neck, and glanced outside the window of the car. In contrast to when he had closed his eyes just after they left the Autogrill, they were now in a much more built up area. He could see buildings, some of them high-rises, speeding past, the lights in the windows almost looking like contrails.

"Hey, sleepyhead," he heard Anita say. "You have any pleasant dreams?"

"No," Caleb replied, leaning his head in the opposite direction. "Where are we?"

"We're on the autostrada just outside Naples."

"How long have I been asleep?"

"Hours," Anita replied. He looked at her and saw she was smiling in the flickering lights of the overhead street lamps. "I've never known anyone to sleep so much."

"Sorry," Caleb said, returning her smile. "Eat when you can, sleep when you can. That's what I was always taught." He saw her expression change slightly, and he knew she wanted to ask him who had taught him that. "I take it your friend, Greta, knows I'm coming as well?"

"I mentioned I had someone with me, yes," Anita replied, "but you don't need to stay with me. You can drop me off there and return to the monastery with Brother Antonio. I'm the one they're looking for, not you."

Caleb saw Antonio's shoulders stiffen at her words, but to his credit, the monk said nothing.

"What are your plans, Anita?" Caleb asked.

"Give the thumb drive to Greta, and then I don't really know. See what happens, I guess?"

"Then let me at least stay with you until you know what happens after that." Caleb said this as more of a statement than a question and he saw Anita nodding in reply.

"Only if you're sure," she said. Her tone of voice made her sound indifferent, but the look of relief on her face told another story.

Caleb also nodded his head and turned to look out of the window. If the thumb drive contained the information that Anita seemed to think it contained, then he wasn't going anywhere. Added to that, if the dark forces he had alluded to in the restrooms with Brother Antonio were indeed gathering, then he was going nowhere in a hurry.

He could see beyond the lights of the buildings a large silhouetted mountain that blocked out the stars in the sky. Caleb recognized it as Mount Vesuvius, the sleeping giant of a volcano that had decimated the ancient cities of Pompeii and Herculaneum. Except Mount Vesuvius wasn't that sleepy, if the media were to be believed. Caleb remembered reading an article a while ago that maintained the enormous volcano was overdue an eruption and, with up to three million people in its sight line, the results would be catastrophic at best, apocalyptic at worst.

"Where does Greta live?" Caleb asked. It was Antonio who answered.

"A place called Terzigno," he said. "It's on the eastern flanks of the mountain."

"The volcano?" Caleb asked. "The mountain is a volcano." He saw Antonio just shrug his shoulders in response. "Anita, how much do you know about Greta? Apart from what you've already told me?" Caleb waited as Anita considered the question.

"Very little," she replied a moment later. "But I owe her massively. I never would have had the courage to escape without her help."

"I think you're doing yourself a disservice, Anita."

"You can think what you want, Caleb, but you don't know what it was like for me there." She sighed, and Caleb wasn't sure if he had offended her. "I will be forever in her debt."

"But once you have delivered the thumb drive," Caleb said, "won't that debt have been repaid?"

"Perhaps, but I don't think I can just walk away." The way Anita said this showed that the conversation was over. "Brother Antonio, would you mind putting the radio on, please?"

Summarily dismissed, Caleb sat back in his seat and returned his gaze to the outside world. He smiled to himself at Anita's words. They ran contrary to his philosophy, to a degree. Caleb had never had a problem with walking away. By contrast, it was what he usually did, once the situation he had been dealing with had been satisfactorily resolved, and he never looked back. He glanced at Anita to see she was sitting upright, her jaw almost thrust forward in defiance. But defiance at what? Caleb understood that, for Anita, delivering the thumb drive might only be the beginning. If he had been through what she had been through, Caleb would certainly look for recompense of some sort.

On the radio, an Italian journalist was speaking in rapid-fire Italian, so quickly that Caleb couldn't even distinguish the individual words she said. Next to him, Anita jolted and leaned forward to speak to Antonio.

"Can you turn that up?" she asked him. The monk leaned forward and did as instructed, and they listened in silence even though Caleb had no idea what the journalist was saying. A moment later, Anita sat back in her seat and let out a large breath.

"What is it?" Caleb asked, not liking the way she looked utterly deflated.

"It was a news report about a shooting on the road between San Pietro In Cariano and Brentino." Anita was on the verge of tears. "Two people, a man and a woman, on a moped." When she turned to look at him, Caleb could see that the terror was back in her eyes. Do you think the gunmen thought it was us on that moped?"

Caleb didn't reply, thinking back to the moped where he had hidden the tracking device he'd found in Anita's handbag. His heart dropped as he realized he had probably caused the deaths of two innocent people. He hadn't pulled the trigger, but by leading the gunmen to the couple who had been shot, he might as well have done. But what should he say to Anita? Should he tell her where he had hidden the tracking device?

"It's a possibility, Anita," Caleb said a moment later, clenching the muscles in his jaw. He knew that whatever happened in Naples, he was going to pay the Adelphoi a visit sooner or later. "But the wicked will not go unpunished."

48

Anita got out of the car as Antonio brought it to a halt on a narrow, dimly lit street. For the last ten minutes, they had been driving uphill through an increasingly down at heel neighborhood, leaving the bright lights of Naples some distance behind them. According to Antonio, they were on the edge of Terzigno, one of many settlements built on the foothills of Mount Vesuvius, despite the protestations of the Italian authorities.

She stood in the warm air and turned in a circle, adjusting her handbag on her waist as she did so. There was a diffuse glow to the west where the lights of Naples were reflecting off low clouds, but the area she was standing in was lit only by a few flickering street lamps. Despite the poor light, it was enough for her to see her surroundings. There was a two-story house in front of her which, according to the sat-nav, was where Greta lived. It was enclosed behind a low, crumbling concrete wall with a rusted fence on top. There were several small bins, brown and blue, attached to the railings, and a squat oil tank in what passed for a front yard, and the air had a peculiar smell that Anita didn't recognize.

"Is this where Greta lives?" Anita heard Caleb ask. He had also gotten out of the car and was standing behind her, looking at the house as he inhaled sharply through his nose. Each story had a balcony, and they were all festooned with laundry and satellite dishes. The house had a light on in a solitary window, so hopefully there was someone home.

"I guess so," Anita replied. "This is the address she gave me."

Anita walked to the gate where a metal box on the wall with a frayed cable attached to it was placed. She pressed the button, half expecting an electric shock, and was rewarded instead with a faint buzzing sound. A few seconds later, the door on the first story balcony opened, and a silhouette appeared.

"Who is it?" a woman's voice called out in Italian.

"I'm looking for Greta," Anita replied.

"Who are you?"

"My name is Anita."

There was another, louder buzz from the gate and Anita pushed it open as the woman on the balcony disappeared. Followed by Caleb, Anita stepped into the front yard as Antonio drove further up the road. They had arranged that he would ensure they were in the right place before returning to the monastery, despite Anita's pleas for him to stay. The Abbot would want his car first thing in the morning, the monk had explained, and if he got tired on the way back, he could pull over and sleep wherever he wanted.

Anita looked around the front yard, which, apart from the oil tank, contained only concrete and ragged grass. When a security light flicked into life, it looked even starker than she had realized. Then a door in the side of the house opened, and a figure stepped out. It was Greta.

"Benvenuta a casa!" she said as she approached them, her arms extended. *Welcome to my house.* She looked exactly how Anita remembered her, except for the fact Greta now had bright blue hair, much shorter than it had been the last and only time they had met. She was wearing a mismatched, ill-fitting pale gray jogging suit, the bottoms a different shade to the top, that was a massive contrast to how Anita remembered her looking on the airplane. Back then, she had looked more like a high-flying business-woman than anything else.

As Anita hugged Greta, she realized she had only addressed her welcome to her, and not to Caleb. If she had been welcoming them both, she would have used the plural *benvenuti*, not the singular form she had just used. They disengaged from the hug and Anita saw Greta giving Caleb an uncertain look.

"Greta, can I introduce you to Caleb?" Anita said, switching to English both for his benefit and to signal to Greta that he didn't speak Italian.

"You said you were bringing someone with you," Greta replied, her accent minimal. "You didn't say he'd be wearing a dress."

"It's a robe," Anita heard Caleb mutter under his breath, and she had to press her lips together to avoid smiling.

Greta paused, her eyes taking in Caleb from head to toe. When her eyes reached his sandals, Anita saw Greta's eyebrows raise by a couple of inches.

"Do you trust him?" Greta asked Anita, switching back to Italian.

"With my life, Greta," Anita replied.

"Welcome, Caleb," Greta said in English, stepping

forward with her hand extended. Anita watched as Caleb took her hand but, instead of shaking it, he just held it.

"Lieto di conoscerla," Caleb said, speaking slowly and enunciating each word carefully. *Pleased to meet you.* Anita noticed he kept his eyes fixed on Greta's as he spoke.

When Caleb had finished speaking, Greta threw her head back and a second later, her peals of laughter rang around the yard.

"Il piacere è tutto mio," she replied. *The pleasure is all mine.* Then she turned to Anita and, still speaking in Italian, asked her where on earth she had found this one.

"He found me," Anita said with a grin. It looked as if Caleb had passed the test, but from the frown on his face, he wasn't sure whether he had or not.

"Where's your transport?" Greta asked Caleb, switching back to English.

"He's heading back," Caleb replied. Anita saw Greta glance at her with a curious expression, but she said nothing.

"Let's go inside, then," Greta said with a smile. "This way, this way." She turned and walked back to the door she had walked through. As Anita set off after her, she leaned toward Caleb.

"Very smooth, Brother Caleb," she whispered in his ear.

"Brother Antonio might have given me a few pointers," Caleb replied.

The interior of Greta's apartment was a contrast to the shabby exterior. It was immaculately decorated but, like her clothes, nothing seemed to quite match. Each room had a different wallpaper, some striped, some plain. Some rooms were carpeted, some were bare boards. As Greta flicked on the lights, Anita saw some bulbs had shades, but most were bare.

Greta led them through to the den, gesturing to a pair of threadbare armchairs that had seen better days. Anita sat down and took in her surroundings. The walls were bare of any decoration and the only things of note in the room were a rickety wooden bookcase laden with paperbacks and a gleaming computer in the corner. There wasn't even a television.

"Do you have the thumb drive?" Greta asked, her impatience obvious. Anita, who had been hoping to be offered a drink at least, was surprised how quickly the woman wanted to get down to business. She nodded her head in reply and rummaged in her handbag. When her hand emerged with the thumb drive, Greta's face lit up. "Excellent," she said, taking the drive from Anita before crossing to the computer.

Anita glanced over at Caleb, who was sitting in the other armchair, his eyes fixed on the bookcase. If he realized Anita was looking at him, he made no sign of it. Even when Greta started hammering away at her computer keyboard, he didn't move an inch, but looked to be completely lost in his own thoughts.

"Anita?" Greta said from her position by the computer. "Come and look at this," she continued, in Italian.

"Did I do okay?" Anita asked as she got to her feet.

"Oh, you did more than okay, Anita," Greta replied. "You are not going to believe this."

49

C aleb watched as Anita got to her feet and joined Greta at the computer desk, but he made no effort to join them. Since he had woken up in Antonio's car when they were on the outskirts of Naples, he had felt horrendous and the feeling was only getting worse. Caleb had no reason for feeling so awful. He had eaten, so he wasn't hungry. He had slept, so he wasn't tired. But he had a feeling of dread that he just couldn't shake. It was such a powerful sensation that it had physical manifestations. His entire body felt leaden, and as he had stepped out of the car when they had arrived at Greta's apartment, he'd had to make a concerted effort to put one foot in front of the other.

The air outside the car felt as heavy as he did, with the familiar scent of pine and oak being outweighed by an odor that was far less welcoming. The unwelcome guest was faint, but recognizable to anyone who had ever smelled rotten eggs. It was sulfur, or more specifically hydrogen sulfide, created by microorganisms dining on Mount Vesuvius's sulfur deposits. Caleb found the smell both unpleasant and intriguing at the same time. It was sharp and suffocating, almost like a mix of burned matches and decaying organic matter, but its presence was a timely reminder of the nature of the land he was walking on, heavy step by heavy step.

He thought he had hidden his disconcerted feelings when Anita had introduced him to Greta, but he had caught a flicker in Greta's eye that said otherwise. Although her attention had been fixed on the computer screen, he had seen her glance over at him a couple of times. Caleb sighed and hauled himself to his feet.

"May I use your bathroom, Greta?" he asked, trying to keep his voice light.

"Sure, sure," Greta replied, without taking her eyes off the screen. She waved a hand toward the rear of the apartment. "Through there."

Caleb walked in the direction she had indicated and into a small corridor with two doors. One was ajar and he could see a bed with crumpled bedclothes strewn across it through the gap, so he opened the door to the other room. The bathroom was small and functional, containing only a shower, a sink, and a toilet. As he relieved himself, his eyes scanned the interior of the room purely from force of habit. The only thing that was out of place was a bottle of male shower gel tucked away in the shower's corner, hinting at a previous guest. From the way the gel was dried on the top of the bottle, he'd not visited for a while.

After he washed his hands, Caleb turned on the faucet to splash some cold water on his face, recoiling at the sudden smell that accompanied the water. The sulfur seemed to be everywhere, even in the water supply. When he had finished, Caleb looked at himself in the mirror with dismay. He looked ten years older than he felt, with bags under his bloodshot eyes.

Caleb returned to the den, stood behind Anita, and looked over her shoulder at the screen of Greta's computer. He tried his best to scan through the documents Greta was scrolling through, but she was moving the text so quickly he could barely make out the Italian words. There were several terms in English that jumped out at him, some of which he understood, most of which he did not. But there was one that featured heavily in the report Greta was scanning. The Weizmann Institute was mentioned several times.

"What do you know about this Weizmann Institute, Greta?" Caleb asked, pointing at the screen as another incidence of the name flashed past.

"It's a research facility in Switzerland," Greta replied, glancing at him with a look of irritation. "They're the report's authors." Her hand hovered over the mouse wheel and the document paused on the screen. "This is a report of embryonic manipulation using DNA derived from stem cells. They're much further along than I'd realized."

"What do you mean?" Anita asked, beating Caleb to the question. "What's embryonic manipulation?"

"They've created an embryo in a laboratory and taken it further than any other scientists have been able to." Greta's voice was low and full of emotion. Caleb watched as she switched windows to bring up another document, this one with diagrams of helix-shaped spirals. "This DNA is essentially artificial. They've taken some samples from stem cells and used artificial intelligence to build a complete DNA sequence. The AI has filled in the gaps in the samples."

"Why not just use the full DNA sequence from the stem cells?" Anita asked with a frown.

"Because they want to be able to recreate DNA from incomplete cells," Greta replied, her face dark.

"When you say they, do you mean the Weizmann Institute or the Adelphoi?" Caleb asked, trying to keep track of what was going on.

"The institute is doing the science, and the Adelphoi will do the marketing, I would imagine. The guy that runs the Weizmann Institute is called Hugo Forrester, and he's one of the most dangerous people I've ever met," Greta replied. "He's rich beyond belief and is so fanatical he would make any of the twelve disciples look like career criminals. He's got to be stopped."

"Stopped from doing what?"

"The next stage of the project is to recreate ancient DNA and use it to create a human being. But it won't be Hugo Forrester's DNA this time. Look at this." Greta pointed at the screen and Caleb saw Anita's brow furrowing even further as she read the text.

"What does it say?" Caleb asked. They had obviously forgotten he couldn't speak or read Italian.

"He's got some sort of ancient artifact," Anita replied, almost in a whisper. "It says here it's two thousand years old, but has recoverable DNA on it. They think they can reconstitute it with artificial intelligence."

"Does it say what the artifact is?" Caleb asked her as he felt the heaviness he'd felt earlier returning.

"No," Anita said. "No, it doesn't."

Caleb looked away from the screen, realizing that it didn't matter if the report wasn't specific about what the artifact was.

There was only one thing that was two thousand years old and with DNA on it that a bunch of religious fanatics would be interested in. But as far as he was aware, that item had been in the keeping of the Catholic church for centuries.

Or had it?

nita tossed and turned in the unfamiliar bed. To say the bedroom Greta had offered her was a guest room was a bit of a stretch of the imagination. It was like the rest of the apartment—tiny and full of random things. Greta had moved a pile of laundry from the single bed before haphazardly throwing a sheet on it, and for some reason, there were several stuffed toys staring at Anita from a shelf on the wall. An owl, a frog, and something that she thought might be an octopus, but with fewer legs than it had started life with. With a sigh, Anita threw back the bedclothes and got out of bed, turning the toys around so they weren't looking at her. As she climbed back into bed, she made a mental note to return them to their original positions in the morning.

Although she was tired, sleep eluded Anita. It wasn't just the unfamiliar surroundings. She was concerned about Caleb. Since they'd arrived at Greta's apartment, he'd seemed to be in a funk about something. Anita hoped it wasn't something she had said or done, but she couldn't think of anything. He seemed tired, withdrawn. She'd not known him for long, but they'd been through enough the previous day that she felt she knew him better than a lot of her so-called friends.

Anita closed her eyes and willed sleep to come, but it was useless. She was wide awake. She sat back up, wondering what to do. After sitting there for a few moments, Anita decided that she could creep into the den and grab a book from Greta's bookcase. She wasn't even concerned what the book was about, but it would give her something to do until she felt tired enough to sleep.

She got to her feet and padded to the door of the guest room. After pausing for a few seconds, she crept to the door to the den, which was open by a few inches. Then she stopped. She could hear Caleb talking. Was he talking to someone? Anita leaned her head close to the door, not to eavesdrop but to see if Greta was also there. If they were both still chatting, then she could join them for a while.

It took Anita a few seconds to realize that Caleb was praying.

"The Lord is my shepherd. I lack nothing," Caleb intoned, his voice monotonous. "He makes me lie down in green pastures. He leads me beside quiet waters. He refreshes my soul. He guides me along the right paths for his name's sake." She heard him take a breath. "Even though I walk through the valley of the shadow of death, I will fear no evil, for you are with me; your rod and your staff, they comfort me."

Anita realized she was holding her breath as she heard Caleb take another breath. She felt bad for listening to a man praying and resolved to return to her room when he continued his prayers. But when Caleb next spoke, he wasn't praying.

"It's from Psalm 23, Anita," he said, speaking more

loudly than before. "The psalm of David. Are you coming in, or are you going to stand there like a statue for the rest of the night?"

She opened the door slowly and looked in the den. Caleb was kneeling on the threadbare carpet between two armchairs, a small side light illuminating the room.

"I, um, I was going to get a book to read," Anita said, pointing at the bookshelf. "I couldn't sleep. Sorry for disturbing you."

"You've not disturbed me at all, Anita," Caleb replied with a smile. He looked more refreshed than he had done the last time she had seen him, and as she watched, he raised his eyes to the ceiling. "He's heard that psalm before, many times."

"Even so, I didn't mean to interrupt."

"You haven't." Caleb got to his feet and sat in one of the armchairs. "I take it you couldn't sleep either?"

"No," Anita replied. "Too much buzzing round in my head." He gestured at the empty armchair and she sat down, suddenly conscious of the fact she was wearing a pair of Greta's pajamas that were at least one size too small and she wasn't wearing a bra. Although Caleb hadn't appeared to notice, she folded her arms over her chest.

"What do you want to talk about?" Caleb asked, throwing Anita for a few seconds.

"Um, I'm not sure," she replied. There were so many things she wanted to talk to Caleb about, but now didn't seem like the best time. "Do you pray a lot?" The moment she asked it, Anita knew it was a dumb question, but it raised a smile from Caleb.

"I'm a preacher," he said. "It kind of goes with the territory."

"I guess so," Anita returned his smile. "It doesn't seem to

have done me much good, though. When I was with the Adelphoi, we prayed all the time and look where it got me."

"Look where it got you?" Caleb replied with a contemplative expression. "It got you here, with the information you brought with you. For every darkness, there is light. Now that the information is out in the open, we can do something about it."

"Like what?"

"I need to go to Rome," Caleb replied. "I think the relic mentioned in the report is the Holy Lance. Do you know of it?"

"Of course I do, Caleb," Anita replied. The legend of the Holy Lance, the weapon that a Roman soldier had used to pierce the side of Jesus during his crucifixion, had fascinated her since she was a child. "But why do you need to go to Rome?"

"If the Catholics let me see the lance they claim to have there, I'll be able to find out whether it's genuine. If it is, then Hugo hasn't got it, and if he doesn't have it, then his plan won't work."

"Will they believe us?"

"Us or me?"

"Us, of course," Anita said. "I'm not letting you go on your own, Caleb. Besides, I've never been to the Vatican City."

"Neither have I," Caleb replied with a smirk. "Too many churches for my liking."

"So when do we go? Tomorrow?"

"I think so, yes. We have the evidence of the plan on the thumb drive. That should be enough to persuade them." Caleb looked at Anita with a dark look in his eyes. "Don't you think?"

"All roads lead to Rome," Anita replied with a smile,

unsure where she'd heard the phrase before. "I think we should go into Naples first thing tomorrow, though." She ran her fingers through her hair before her eyes settled on Caleb's robe. "There're a few things I'd like to change about both of us. We're a bit too conspicuous in terms of appearance."

Anita looked at him to see his eyes had become even darker, if that was possible.

"Appearances can be deceptive, Anita," Caleb said, almost in a whisper. "What you see on the outside isn't always what's on the inside."

Anita got to her feet and reached out her hand, placing it on his cheek. "So what you're saying, Caleb, is never underestimate a man in a dress?"

51

Eva pushed the cereal around her bowl with a spoon before deciding that she'd eaten enough. She sipped her coffee as her eyes wandered around the dining room, which was half full. Some of their guests had formed an early morning running club and would arrive for breakfast soon, all red-faced and smug looking, but the thought of going running so early in the day just made Eva feel nauseated. The thought of running at any time of the day made her feel nauseated.

Her eyes settled on Giovanni, who was sitting on the other side of the room with the latest object of his affection. Eva watched the young woman hanging on every word he was saying, and she wondered what bullshit he was spouting. The woman, Bella, if Eva remembered correctly, was leaning forward as Giovanni spoke. Then she leaned her head back and a peal of laughter rang across the dining room, causing several other guests to look in their direction.

"I hope you're thrilled with her, Giovanni," Eva mumbled to herself. She looked again at Bella, who probably had ten years and ten kilograms on Eva, but what she wouldn't have was experience. None of the women that came to stay with them were particularly knowledgeable about bedroom etiquette, although several had left with an entirely new skill set in that area. Perhaps, Eva mused, that was why Giovanni kept coming back to her once the novelty of being an instructor had worn off. She forced herself to stop looking at the younger woman, and let her eyes rove around the room again.

Maybe she should take a young lover? There were plenty of likely candidates here and, in Eva's experience at least, young men tended to be enthusiastic students. There was one such young man sitting not too far from Giovanni and Bella's table. He looked to be early twenties, had broad shoulders and a mop of blonde hair, and was very easy on Eva's eye. As if he sensed he was being examined, he looked up and met Eva's eyes. She thought his name was Julian, but couldn't be sure. Then he smiled and waved at her. Eva smiled and waved back, resolving to look Julian—or whatever he was called—up on their database a bit later to find out a bit more about him. After all, what was good for the goose was good for the gander.

Eva was day-dreaming about teaching Julian what it would be like to be with a real woman, not some inexperienced fumbling girl his own age, when she realized someone was standing in front of her table.

"Do you mind if I join you?" It was Maddy, holding a plate piled to the brim with pancakes in one hand. In the other was an envelope with a handwritten scrawl on the front.

"Be my guest," Eva replied with a sidelong glance at the young man she had been thinking about. That was a daydream she would be returning to later.

Maddy pulled a chair out and sat opposite Eva, who eyed the pancakes with envy.

"A minute on the lips, a lifetime on the hips," she said with a smile at the younger woman. "Isn't that what they say?"

"I've not heard that saying before," Maddy replied as she cut a thin sliver of pancake and raised it to her mouth. As she ate, she pulled out a letter from the envelope and started reading it. From the way the letter was creased, it had already been read at least once.

"News from home?" Eva asked, vaguely remembering Maddy saying she didn't get on too well with her family.

"It's from my sister," Maddy replied. "She's the only one who bothers to write." Then she looked at Eva with a broad smile on her face. "She's having a baby. I'm going to be an aunt." As she said the word aunt, she grimaced. "That makes me sound really old, doesn't it? Aunt Maddy."

"Congratulations, Maddy," Eva said, also smiling. "That's fantastic news." She took another sip of her coffee and watched as Maddy worked her way through the pancakes with enthusiasm. It was good news, but it also gave Eva an opportunity to work the conversation round to something else. "Do you like children, Maddy?" Eva asked, keeping her tone as conversational as she could.

"Yeah, I guess," Maddy replied, glancing in Eva's direction before returning her attention to the letter.

Eva waited until Maddy had finished the letter before continuing. "Do you think you'll ever have any of your own?"

Maddy looked back at Eva with her fork paused halfway toward her mouth. The young girl had a surprised expression, and Eva wondered if she'd blown it with the question.

"Why do you ask?" Maddy said a few seconds later.

"I'm just curious, Maddy," Eva replied, waving her hand dismissively. "You're still very young. I was just wondering, that was all."

"I think so, yes." Maddy's fork continued its journey to her mouth and her expression softened. "When I'm older, maybe. I mean, I'd have to meet the right person and all that. I don't think I'm cut out to be a single mother." She shoveled a mouthful of pancake into her mouth and continued talking, causing Eva to look away. "There's the whole mechanics of it as well, if you know what I mean?"

"I don't think that's an issue these days," Eva replied, watching Maddy carefully. "Lots of gay couples have children. There're many ways round the mechanics." She lowered her voice to a conspiratorial whisper. "There's adoption for a start. Or there's artificial insemination."

"I don't know about adoption," Maddy replied. "I mean, if I was going to do it, I would want the full experience of being pregnant and giving birth. How about you?"

Eva smiled. What Maddy had just said would answer Giovanni's question, at least in principle.

"Oh, it's not for me," she replied with a laugh. "I don't think I have a biological clock, much less one that's ticking." From the bemused look on Maddy's face, Eva wasn't sure the young woman had understood the phrase. "I'm not very maternal, Maddy, and I can't see many children wanting someone like me for a mother."

Eva watched as Maddy finished the last of her pancakes and replaced the letter from her sister in its envelope.

"Have you got much planned for today?" the young woman asked. Eva wasn't sure if she was just making conversation or was genuinely curious.

"I need to do the accounts at some point today," she

replied with a glance in Giovanni's direction. He was still deep in conversation with Bella. "What are you up to?"

"We're going for a bicycle ride around the lake after morning prayers," Maddy replied, pointing at a small group of young people sitting at one of the other tables. "Why don't you come with us? It'll be fun."

Eva thought for a moment. It would certainly be more fun than doing Giovanni's books for him, as long as she could keep up with the younger riders. But the lake circumference was only a couple of miles, and the terrain was flat as the pancakes Maddy had just finished.

"I think you'd all leave me a long way behind, Maddy," Eva replied, hoping the younger woman would take the bait. "It's a long time since I've been on a bicycle."

"Nonsense," Maddy replied with a dismissive wave of her own. "I'm always at the back, anyway. We can go as slowly as you want to." She glanced across at the group at the other table. "Despite what some of that lot think, it's not a race. Come on, it'll be fun!"

"I might just do that, Maddy," she replied with a smile. If Giovanni was serious about this young woman potentially being a surrogate mother for Hugo, Eva needed to get to know her very well indeed. "I might just do that."

52

Giovanni leaned forward, lowering his voice to encourage Bella to do the same thing as he approached the culmination of his story. He had spent the previous ten minutes building a scenario for the young woman where his congregation had all fasted for forty-eight hours for the glory of God. In the story, the congregation was all gathered at the end of the fast, rapt with attention as he was speaking to them with a table full of loaves and fishes in front of him.

"And then," he said, almost whispering, as her eyes widened in anticipation. "I held my hands over the feast to call them to prayer and the entire congregation started laughing and crying at the same time. They had passed the test that He had given them."

"Oh my," Bella said, her mouth forming a perfect O. "That must have been amazing."

"It was," Giovanni replied, leaning back in his chair and nodding in satisfaction. The story was entirely fictional, but he wasn't about to let the truth get in the way of a good story.

"But how did you know?" Bella asked. "How did you know they all needed to fast for so long? To pass the test?" *Good girl*, Giovanni thought. That was exactly the question he wanted her to ask.

"Because He told me it was the right test for them," Giovanni replied with a glance at the ceiling to emphasize who He was. One of the fluorescent lights was flickering, and he made a mental note to have it replaced before he returned his attention to Bella. He stared at her for a few seconds, aiming for an intense but not overpowering look. Then he lowered his voice again to make it clear that he was talking to her and only to her. "Sometimes, the tests He asks us to perform seem wrong, like not eating or drinking for two full days." Giovanni paused, thinking hard. He was sure there was someone in the Bible who had been asked to kill his son, but he couldn't remember what he was called. It began with an A, but he couldn't recall the actual name. It wasn't Adam. Aaron, perhaps? "Do you think you would pass any tests like that?"

Bella nodded with enthusiasm, her eyes widening slightly. She was a very attractive young woman, and was absolutely circling the hook that he was dangling for her. The next step would be to get that hook into her beautiful little mouth.

"I would," she replied in an enthusiastic whisper. "I'd do anything."

Giovanni nodded in response and smiled at the woman. Whether she would still be as enthusiastic when she realized that the test Giovanni had in mind involved being both naked and receptive to his own nakedness remained to be seen, but as his father had always used to say, slowly slowly catchy monkey. He placed his hands over hers and, at the same time, pressed his knees against hers underneath the table. When he felt her pressing her legs back against his, he had to fight to stop his smile from broadening.

"Perhaps we should continue this conversation later, Bella?" he said. "I think He has some splendid plans for you." Out of the corner of his eye, Giovanni had just seen Eva getting to her feet. She had been talking to Maddy, which he hoped had been a fruitful discussion.

"I'd like that very much, Brother Giovanni," Bella replied with a broad smile of her own. "Thank you."

Giovanni removed his hands from Bella's, but left his knees pressed against her legs as Eva approached. When she was a couple of yards away from them, he scraped his chair back and got to his feet.

"Sister Eva," Giovanni said, extending his hands to Eva for her to take in her own. It was a well-practiced move that they always did when in the company of others. "How delightful to see you."

"And to see you too," Eva replied with an amused glance at Bella, whose gaze was fixed on Giovanni's face.

Giovanni pulled Eva's hands slightly to indicate that they should take a few steps away from the young woman. "I see you breakfasted with young Maddy," he said when they were a couple of yards away from the table.

"I did," Eva replied. "It was a, how shall I put this, most productive conversation?"

"What did she say?"

"I didn't ask her outright, if that's what you mean," Eva replied, subtly shaking her hands free from Giovanni's. "But I don't think she'll be averse to the idea. I'm spending some time with her later."

"Excellent, excellent," Giovanni said.

"I'll be in the main office if you need me," Eva said. "I need to do the accounts."

Giovanni grinned at Eva. That was something he enjoyed reviewing very much indeed. He could look at the numbers all day long, but actually putting them into some sort of meaningful report was something that only Eva could do properly. He was just about to say something to that effect to Eva when his attention was drawn to the main doors to the dining room opening. Giovanni turned to see two men, both wearing suits, standing at the entrance looking around with curious expressions on their faces.

"Oh, for goodness' sake," he said, moderating his language in case any of his congregation heard him. "They're not supposed to be here until this afternoon."

"Are they your pet monkeys?" Eva asked with a look of disgust at the two men.

"No, Eva," Giovanni replied with a sharp look of his own. "They're our security detail. Leave them to me. I'll be sure to keep them out of your hair."

He walked away before Eva could say anything else, and approached the two men, smiling as he did so.

"Gentlemen," Giovanni said as he reached them. "I wasn't expecting you until this afternoon."

"We got bored," the older of the two men said with a glance at his colleague. Despite the suits, they both looked so similar they could have been brothers. Both had short hair cut in an almost military style, and the same hardened expressions on their faces. Giovanni was about to say something sarcastic when he remembered that one of these two goons had killed two people on his behalf.

"Let's go to my private office," Giovanni said. He was keen to get the men away from his young and impressionable congregation.

"Any chance of some breakfast?" the younger of the two

men said. His voice was much higher pitched than Giovanni had expected it to be.

"I'll have some brought to my office," Giovanni replied. "You'll be more comfortable eating there."

"As you wish," the older man said with a nod. "You're the boss."

Giovanni returned the nod and held out a hand to show which direction he wanted them to walk in. It was, he reflected as he followed them out of the dining room into the foyer, the most sensible thing he'd heard the man say. Giovanni pointed down a corridor that led off into the foyer.

"Third door on the right down that corridor," he said. "The door's open."

As the two men walked away, their swagger a little too pronounced to be natural, Giovanni turned and walked back into the dining room. It was time for Bella's first test, but Giovanni was pretty sure she would be able to deliver a couple of plates of food to his office.

After all, even assassins had to eat.

53

Eva walked into the office and crossed to the window. After throwing the curtains back to let the morning light into the room, she opened a couple of the windows to let some fresh air into the room. The atmosphere was musty, and she thought she could detect the faintest hint of smoke. She muttered a curse under her breath, firmly aimed at Giovanni, and returned to the faux antique desk that was set in the center of the room. After leaning down to press the power button on the tower case, Eva sat in the equally fake antique leather chair and leaned back while she waited for the computer to boot up.

"Come on," she said to herself as the blue Microsoft welcome screen eventually changed to the login screen. Working from memory—Eva wasn't the sort of person to scribble her log in details on a post-it note—she entered her password before sitting back again in the chair. When she saw the screen change to let her know it was installing an update, she cursed again and got to her feet to get some coffee from the dining room.

A few moments later, a fresh cup of coffee nestled in her

hand, Eva was looking at the main screen for the Adelphoi's accounts. Several years previously, when she was still working in finance, she had co-authored a business intelligence dashboard with a young banker who was as quick with figures as he was in bed. Their brief relationship had floundered within weeks, but Eva had what she wanted, which was the first version of the software in front of her. She had added several additional features to it since his departure, not all of which he would have approved of.

Eva's eyebrows went up when she saw the operating profit for the Adelphoi. It was at least half a million euros more than the last time she had done the accounts. She navigated to the next screen, which showed the chart of accounts and whistled through her teeth when she saw there had been a deposit a few days previously from the Weizmann Institute for exactly five hundred thousand euros. It seemed Hugo certainly wasn't messing about with his hare-brained plan. According to the entry on Eva's screen, the sum was a down payment to the Adelphoi for what was termed Operation Epiphaneia. When Eva switched tabs to google the word's meaning, she grinned.

"The advent of Christ," Eva murmured at the screen. "Very good, Hugo."

Eva returned her attention to the accounts and spent several minutes going through the operating profit screen, double checking it against the chart of accounts to ensure it was accurate. Even though she knew the software was accurate—after all, she had written it herself—she also knew never to trust a computer. When the screen flickered a couple of times, and even froze at one point for a couple of seconds, she tried her best not to get annoyed. It was the same with every Microsoft update. Eva was about to reboot the computer to see if that would fix whatever the problem was when the speakers burst into life with an incoming Zoom call. According to the flashing icon on the screen, it was the Weizmann Institute. Eva quickly used her hands to smooth down both her hair and her habit. If it was Hugo on the line, she wanted to look her best. But when the call connected, she saw it was his personal assistant.

"Hello, Ruth," Eva said, attempting to look friendly to the cold-faced witch on the line. To say she and Ruth hadn't really hit off was a bit of an understatement.

"Sister Eva," Ruth replied. It might have been Eva's imagination, but she was sure the other woman had emphasized the word *sister* sarcastically. She usually did when they spoke, as if just to remind Eva that she wasn't a real sister, although Eva had no idea how she would have found that out. "Do you have a few moments?"

"For the Weizmann Institute?" Eva replied, pettily. There was no harm in letting Ruth know she was just an employee. "Of course, Ruth. What can I do for you?"

"Mr. Forrester wants to speed things up," Ruth said through thin lips. "He's asked me to check with you to make sure you're making the preparations for the project to begin?"

"Of course, Ruth. Please do let Hugo know that it's all in hand." Eva's thoughts drifted to the two men in suits who had appeared in the dining room earlier. "In fact, the security assessment is being undertaken as we speak." To her delight, Eva saw a look of faint surprise on the other woman's face.

"I see," Ruth replied a second or two later. "Mr. Forrester will be pleased, I'm sure. Now, do you have accommodation available?"

"Accommodation for whom?" For a moment, Eva thought her stay in her suite was to be even more short-lived than she had realized. Perhaps Hugo had found a surrogate from somewhere else?

"Mr. Forrester is sending a medical team to your location to prepare the, er, the mother."

"So soon?" Eva asked, playing for time while she thought this through. They did have rooms available, but they would need to be refurbished before they could be used and they were still some way from finding a mother for the child.

"But you've found a suitable candidate, I understand?" Ruth's face was stern, and Eva thought if she didn't have so much Botox in her forehead, she would be frowning. "According to the email that Brother Giovanni sent to Mr. Forrester a few moments ago, she's ideal. Is that not the case, Sister Eva?"

"We're in the process of arranging a suitable candidate," Eva replied, mentally cursing Giovanni yet again. "But we need to ensure she is the perfect match." Eva lowered her voice and tried for a spot of female bonding. "With all due respect to Brother Giovanni, he is a man. There is much he can't understand about such things."

"I see," Ruth said again. If the statement had appealed to her gender, the woman hid it well. "The medical team is en route to your location, anyway. Perhaps they'll be able to help you with your assessment of the woman?"

"Very well," Eva replied, knowing she had been backed into a corner. "How many people are in the medical team?"

"Just two," Ruth said. "A doctor and a nurse. They will need individual rooms, of course."

"Of course. Will they be staying for long?"

"They will be the judge of that," Ruth replied with a condescending look, or as condescending as she could manage. "But if necessary, they'll stay until the project is completed. They should arrive tomorrow."

Eva opened her mouth to reply when she realized Ruth had ended the call.

"Bitch," she said to the screen as she got to her feet, locking the computer as she did so. It was time to find Giovanni and find out what the hell he was playing at.

54

G iovanni waited as Bella walked into his office, deftly carrying two plates on one forearm. In her other hand, she had a couple of mugs of coffee. As she walked past his position, sitting behind his desk, he realized she had some cutlery in the rear pocket of her jeans.

She crossed the office to where the two Italian men were seated at Giovanni's small conference table, a simple design with metal tubular legs and matching chairs. The set was the most modern furniture he had in the room, but he appreciated the contrast from the older pieces in the office. He had put some placemats and coasters on it to protect the glass surface of the table and was hoping that neither of the idiots would make a mess. Without saying anything, she placed the plates and mugs down in front of the men and reached around for the cutlery. Giovanni watched the two men as they both ran their eyes up and down Bella's body as if she wasn't even able to see them. As Bella turned around, he saw the larger of the men raise his eyebrows at his colleague, who just nodded and smiled. To Giovanni's relief, when he looked at Bella's expression, she either hadn't recognized what they had been doing or just didn't care.

"Thank you, Bella," Giovanni said as she walked past his desk. He was rewarded with a shy smile from the young woman, but she said nothing as she left the office.

"Very tasty," the larger of the Italians said as he took a mouthful of the cooked breakfast on the plate.

"This food's not too bad either," his colleague replied, and they both laughed.

Giovanni just fixed them both with a reproachful look, but neither of the men seemed to notice.

"Right then," he said as they ate. "Let's get down to business, shall we? What are your names?" It was the larger of the men who replied first through a mouthful of bacon.

"You can call me Mario," he said, oblivious to the rivulet of grease that was running down his chin. Then he pointed his fork toward his colleague. "And you can call him Luigi."

"Seriously?" Giovanni replied. He had spent many hours playing Super Mario when he was younger, and these two clowns looked nothing like his one time heroes. "Mario and Luigi?"

"They're our names," the younger man, Luigi, replied before laughing. "We're not plumbers, but we are brothers."

"Okay, whatever," Giovanni replied, already bored with the conversation. "So, Mario, you're in charge, right?"

"Yep," Mario said with a nod. He picked up his mug, took a large slurp from it, and then replaced it directly on the leather of the table.

"Would you mind?" Giovanni said as he got to his feet and crossed to the table. He picked up the mug and placed it on one of the coasters. "That's an original Giuseppe Terragni table you're eating from." It wasn't, but Giovanni doubted either of the men was any sort of expert on Italian minimalist designers, much less the golden age of design the furniture was inspired by.

"My bad," Mario replied with a shrug. "So, what's this work you mentioned on the phone?"

"I need a security detail for a VIP that's going to be living here," Giovanni said, looking at the two men. At some point, he wanted to speak to them about the couple on the moped, but he sensed that now wasn't the time. In an ideal world, he would have nothing more to do with these two idiots, but he needed their discretion. While they had failed to retrieve the thumb drive with the information on it that had been stolen from him, they had at least demonstrated that they could be ruthless when it was required.

"For how long?" Luigi asked with a glance at his brother.

"Months," Giovanni replied. He caught the two men exchanging a glance of approval. "It's a woman, a young woman, and her safety is of paramount importance."

"Okay," Mario replied. "From when?"

"I'm not sure," Giovanni said. "Soon, though. I want a full security report done on the complex we're in as well." If these two goons were going to be hanging around, the least they could do was make the most of their time.

"This is at our normal daily rates, right?" Mario asked him, half-narrowing his eyes as he spoke. "They aren't negotiable. If you want people on performance related pay, you'll have to look elsewhere." His eyes flashed to his brother, who nodded in approval, leading Giovanni to wonder which of them was really in charge.

Giovanni sighed. Their rates weren't cheap, far from it, but he would speak to Eva to see how best to invoice Hugo for their services. With a small cut for him, of course.

"Fine," he said with a grimace. "But I want you both in the background. No mingling with the residents at all."

"You got that, Luigi?" Mario said to his brother with a grin. "We can look, but we can't touch."

"I'd rather you didn't even look, Mario," Giovanni said, keen to establish that he was in charge. The brothers just smirked at each other in response.

"Have you got aerials?" Luigi asked a moment later, spearing his final piece of bacon with a fork.

"We've got cable, if that's what you mean," Giovanni replied, thrown by the question.

"No, I'm not talking about the television. Aerial shots of the complex?"

"Ah, right. There'll be some on Google Earth, but the last time I checked was a few months ago, and they were pretty out of date then."

"No problem," Luigi replied. "We've got a drone in the car, so we'll get that up. Can we use this place as our base?"

"No," Giovanni said quickly. The last thing he wanted were these two hanging around his personal office. They could either double up with Eva in the main office, or he could find them somewhere else, like a disused janitor's closet.

"Are your computers networked?" Mario asked, pointing at Giovanni's monitor on his desk.

"You'll need to speak to Sister Eva about that," Giovanni replied. "I'll take you to her when you've finished."

He looked pointedly at the plates the two men were eating from, hoping they would get the message and hurry. He had things to do, and Giovanni had spent enough time with them already.

More than long enough to know he didn't like them at all.

55

By the time Anita woke up, it was mid-morning. She realized with surprise when she looked at her phone that it was almost ten. Sunlight was streaming in through a chink in the curtains, revealing the dust motes floating in the air. Anita threw back her bedclothes, the book she had fallen asleep reading falling to the floor with a thud. She couldn't even remember what the book was called, much less what it was about.

She made her way into Greta's kitchen by way of the small bathroom, wrapping a thin gown she had found on the back of the bathroom door around her as she did so. There was a glorious smell in the air of freshly baked pastry, and she looked at the table where Caleb and Greta were sitting to see a large plate full of cornettos that were filled with cream or some sort of custard. The moment she saw them, her stomach rumbled.

"Morning, sleepyhead," Caleb said with an affable grin, reminding Anita of what she had said to him in the car the previous day. "Half the day's gone already."

"Sit yourself down and I'll grab you a plate," Greta said,

getting to her feet. As she stood, she placed a hand on Caleb's shoulder briefly and Anita saw the two of them exchange a brief smile. Considering how frosty Greta had been the day before, this surprised Anita for a moment. "You want some coffee?"

"Yes please, Greta," Anita replied. "That would be magic, thank you." She watched as Greta fussed about in the kitchen and a few seconds later, the sound of the coffee pot gurgling filled the small room. Greta was wearing a simple summer dress, light blue, which complemented her hair and showed off her shoulders. Her skin was paler than it should be for someone living in southern Italy, and Anita wondered how much time the woman spent outside.

"There's a slight change of plan, Anita," Caleb said as he helped himself to a cornetto. From the number of pastry crumbs on his plate, it wasn't his first, or perhaps even his second, croissant. "We're not going to Rome until tomorrow now."

"Okay, any particular reason?" Anita asked as Greta placed a plate in front of her.

"Greta has offered to lend us her car," Caleb said.

"It's shabby, but it's an excellent runner and you'll fit in more than in a hire car. No paper trail either." Greta sat back down, again touching Caleb's shoulder as she did so.

"Thank you, Greta," Anita replied. "We'll put some gas in it for you."

"You'd better put some gas in it before you go," Greta said with a laugh. "There's not much in it now and I've got to go to a legal firm on the other side of the city. By the time I get back, it'll be on fumes."

"Have you been up for long, Caleb?" Anita asked, picking up one of the cornettos and eyeing the cream inside it with anticipation.

"A few hours," he replied. "Greta and I walked down to the bakery first thing to get breakfast. It's an interesting area."

"What Caleb means is that it's a dump," Greta said. "He's just too diplomatic to say so. But I like it here, so there." Anita watched as she looked at Caleb with her eyebrows raised, as if daring him to contradict her, but Caleb said nothing.

ALMOST AN HOUR LATER, well-fed and freshly showered, Anita and Caleb said goodbye to Greta. As they left her apartment, Greta had pressed a piece of paper into Anita's hand with the address of a hair stylist in Terzigno and told her it was where she always went. Anita wasn't sure how much of a recommendation that was, given Greta's short blue hair, but she needed to do something about her own distinctive colored hair, and they both needed some new clothes, Caleb especially. She had thought that wearing a robe in a place like the Vatican City would be fine, but according to him, his was the wrong sort of robe. When she'd pressed him on the issue, he'd just smiled and said nothing.

They walked down the pot-holed road in silence for a few moments, Anita realizing that the area was a lot more run down than she'd realized the previous evening. In the day's light, the entire neighborhood looked tired and run down. All the buildings were badly in need of maintenance, and there were many shacks that looked thrown together. Even the few people they saw as they walked were moving with their eyes downcast, as if there was nothing to look at.

"You seem to have grown on Greta, at least," Anita said a moment later, more to break the silence than anything else.

"I have that effect on people," Caleb replied with a grin. "Once they realize there's more to me than a dress."

"I think she likes you." Anita thought back to the way Greta had touched Caleb's shoulder a couple of times in the kitchen. The fact that she had been wearing the slightest hint of makeup, in contrast to the previous evening. It was subtle, but Anita had noticed it. The summer dress that Greta was wearing, just right for showing off her curves.

"What makes you say that?"

"Women's intuition, I guess. Do you like her?"

"I barely know her," Caleb replied, his grin widening. "She's a fascinating woman, though."

Anita was just about to reply when there was a loud squawking noise above their heads. She looked up to see at least twenty geese moving through the air, not in a tradition line or V shape, but more of an amorphous flock. They were flying hard, with several of them knocking their wings into the other birds. Towards the rear of the group, there were three or four smaller geese struggling to keep up with the main pack.

"Something's spooked them," Caleb said as they watched the birds flying overhead. In a few moments, they had almost disappeared, although their squawking could still be heard in the distance. "Eagles, perhaps?" Anita watched as he squinted, looking around the sky before shrugging his shoulders.

"That's one way of changing the subject," Anita said with a giggle. "Summoning a flock of geese to distract me. You didn't answer my question."

"Like I said," Caleb replied with a laugh, "I don't really know Greta, but yes, I do like her. But I didn't summon a flock of geese to distract you."

56

As they walked down the road, Caleb could see the buildings were gradually becoming better looked after than those further up the hill. He guessed that was because of their proximity to the town center, but he didn't know for sure. Beside him, Anita walked in silence, lost in her own thoughts.

Caleb thought back to earlier that morning. He had been sitting on the apartment balcony, watching the sun rising over the distinctive peak of Mount Vesuvius, when the door behind him had opened. It was Greta, carrying a cup of coffee in each hand.

"Do you mind if I join you?" she had asked.

"It's your balcony," Caleb had replied with a smile.

It had taken Greta around ten minutes, but eventually she had worked her way round to an apology for her behavior the previous evening. Caleb had tried to dismiss it, but she had been insistent. Then they had talked for a while about the Adelphoi. When Greta had told him about how the so-called Brother Giovanni had manipulated her into his bed, her voice had become low and full of barely repressed anger. Caleb had said nothing, but just listened, knowing that she had been recounting the same experience Anita had been through. If anything, Greta's story just reinforced his wish to meet up with Brother Giovanni at some point.

When she had completed her story, Greta had changed the subject to a much more positive one. She had some plans to take down the Adelphoi, destroy their credibility and make the entire outfit redundant. They all centered on building a critical mass of social outrage, using various media channels to get the full story out there. Her focus was solely on the Adelphoi, which was unsurprising given what she had been through, and Caleb was amazed she wasn't planning something for the Weizmann Institute. He had listened carefully and had nodded at all the right times. As desperate as Greta's story was, and by extension Anita's, Caleb thought the public simply wouldn't care. In his opinion, something much more terminal was required.

"Can I ask you something, Caleb?" Anita asked as he thought about what Greta had said earlier, breaking his concentration.

"Of course you can, Anita," he replied. "Ask away."

"You might not like the question."

"Then I won't answer it." Caleb glanced at her with a smile. "But ask away."

"Have you always been a man of faith?"

"No, not always." Caleb gestured at his robe. "I had a different life before this one."

"So what happened?"

"How do you mean?"

"Where did your faith come from?"

Caleb paused for a moment before replying.

"By grace you have been saved through faith, and that

not of yourselves. It is the gift of God," he said. "It's from Ephesians, chapter two."

"What were you saved from?"

He paused again. There wasn't an easy way to answer that question.

"Myself, I guess."

They walked on in silence for a few moments. Caleb wasn't sure that he'd answered Anita's question, but she was either content with what he had said or didn't want to ask anything more.

"What's your take on the Weizmann Institute and the Adelphoi?" Anita asked a moment later.

"I think they're two strange beasts," Caleb replied. "The Weizmann Institute and the man who runs it are playing with fire by messing around with creation itself. And the Adelphoi just appear to me to be con artists."

"Well, they certainly suckered me in," Anita said with a wry smile.

"That's not true, Anita, and you know it," Caleb replied, keeping his voice firm but gentle. "What happened to you was not your fault."

"Then whose fault was it?" Anita shot back. "God's?"

"I don't believe God exists in isolation, Anita," Caleb said.

"I don't understand what you mean."

"Just as good exists, so does evil," he replied." It's always been that way. Pretty much every faith has that at its core. They just represent it in different ways." Caleb took a deep breath. "It's my belief that the balance between those two forces governs what happens to us. What the Weizmann Institute and the Adelphoi are doing risks upsetting that balance to an intolerable degree."

"But if they're trying to resurrect Jesus, isn't that balancing things in a good sense?"

"No," Caleb said. "When the word gets out, regardless of their success or otherwise, there will be chaos on a global scale." He stopped walking and turned to face Anita, fixing her with an intense gaze. "Armies will be raised, some to protect the child, other to destroy it. Humankind needs little excuse to go to war at the best of times. But if you add religious fervor to that, the consequences will be catastrophic. I don't believe they can actually resurrect the Son of God, but they don't need to."

"That's a bleak picture you're painting, Caleb," Anita said. "Very dark."

"One of the traits of chaos is darkness," Caleb replied, nodding his head. "There are many passages in the Bible where darkness is a metaphor for the absence of God, just as light is a symbol for His presence. It's my belief that both the Weizmann Institute and the Adelphoi are instruments of evil, whether knowingly or otherwise. They are conjuring dark forces together, and they have to be stopped. The real evil appears to be the institute. These Adelphoi are merely riding on their coattails."

"If we can prevent the institute from doing what they're planning," Anita asked a moment later. "That'll stop them, surely?"

"It'll slow them down, but not stop them," Caleb replied. "It's going to take something a lot more radical to actually stop them."

"Like what?"

"I've not quite worked that out just yet, Anita," Caleb said with a sigh. "But I'm working on it."

57

H ugo knew the moment the white-haired professor's face appeared on the screen of his Mac that his friend back in England had some good news. The smile on the academic's face almost split it in two.

"Professor Greenford," Hugo said. "How are things back at home?"

"Musn't grumble," the professor replied as he always did. Hugo felt himself grinning as he knew exactly what his friend was about to say. "I just wish it didn't rain quite so much."

Hugo nodded in agreement. While he occasionally missed England, he certainly didn't miss the weather.

He looked at Professor Greenford on the screen, taking in the cluttered background behind him. There was a large bookcase, full of academic texts Hugo knew had been mostly written by the professor, and a photograph showing a much younger King Charles being shown around the synchrotron. When he had visited the Diamond Light Source buildings a few years ago, he'd been amazed that the professor was holed up in a tiny, windowless office near the center of the huge circular building that housed the light accelerator required for the synchrotron to operate. Surely, he had asked the professor, as one of the brightest minds in the building, he could ask for a better office? The professor's reply had been that he rather liked it.

"You look happy, David," Hugo said. "I take it you have some news for me?"

"I do, I do," Professor Greenford replied. "I was able to examine the artifact last night, under cover of a test run. A quite remarkable scroll."

"What did it show?" Hugo asked, trying to hide his frustration at the way the man was making him wait. He wouldn't have been surprised if the professor decided to go and make a cup of tea before telling him what he had found.

"So I took some micro-CT scans of the papyri. It took a while, but I worked out that the best resolution was eight microns. I then flattened and mapped the 3D mesh to a 2D image before putting a small sample into our supercomputer here, just to confirm what was on it. I've e-mailed the full images to your laboratory."

"What was on it, David? Please stop teasing me and just tell me what's on it?"

He waited as the professor laughed, knowing that he would have happily gone into minute detail over the process he'd used if Hugo let him.

"It's Aramaic, Hugo. I cross checked it with a colleague, a very discreet man I trust implicitly before you say anything. But definitely Aramaic. I also carbon dated the material for you."

Hugo felt his eyebrows going up in surprise. He'd been about to ask the professor to do just that, but he'd been beaten to it.

"And?"

"My estimate is somewhere between fifty and a hundred AD, depending on which standard deviation model I use."

Hugo clenched his fist in triumph. It was from exactly the time period he was most interested in, and the language of Aramaic was predominantly used to record divine worship and religious study.

"That's fantastic news, David," Hugo said. "There's a plane on its way to Oxford Airport to retrieve the artifact. I'll have Ruth e-mail you the details."

"I'll take it there myself, Hugo," Professor Greenford replied. "I've already repackaged it for transit. If they'll let me, I'll even stow it on the plane myself, so you know it's in excellent hands."

"We must meet soon for dinner," Hugo said, as he always did. He'd not seen the professor in person for some time, and they were far overdue a proper catch up over some fine brandy.

"Indeed we must."

Hugo ended the call and picked up the handset of his telephone. As usual, Ruth answered within a couple of rings.

"Mr. Forrester?" she said.

"Could you ask Albert to come to my office please, Ruth?" Hugo asked her. "I have some urgent work for him to do."

He replaced the handset carefully and thought for a moment about what he was about to ask Albert to do with the institute's own supercomputer.

It might even make the miserable man smile. He would, after all, be reading something that hadn't been read for over two thousand years.

58

Anita pushed open the door to the hair salon, unsure at first if she had got to the right building. From the outside, it looked more like a residential building than a commercial one, but as she had approached the wooden door, Anita had noticed a small brass sign just above the letterbox that read *parrucchiera,* or hairdresser. It was set back slightly from a busy road that led into the center of Terzigno, separated only by an iron fence that needed a coat of paint. As the door opened, it moved a small bell attached to a spring and Anita heard a woman's voice calling out.

"Arrivo subito," the voice said. *I'll be right there.*

As she waited, Anita took in the building's interior. She could tell from the smell in the air that it was definitely a hairdresser—the smell of warm blow-dried hair, products, and shampoos was very distinctive and somehow reassuring —but the hallway she was standing in belonged to a house, not a salon. There were coats hanging from hooks on the wall, a small table with some mail and a set of car keys in a silver dish, and a framed photograph of a family on the wall.

A moment later, a woman appeared in the corridor that led deeper into the house. She was perhaps mid-fifties, and was wearing a matronly looking dress with an apron tied around her ample waist.

"Bongiorno," she said, her Neapolitan accent obvious even in just that single word. Anita was reminded of an elderly aunt who was from Naples who had one of the thickest accents she'd ever heard.

"Good morning," Anita replied with a smile. "My name's Anita. I'm afraid I don't have an appointment, but I was hoping you might be available? A friend recommended you to me."

"Which friend might that be?" the woman said, pushing open one of the doors that led from the hallway.

"Her name's Greta," Anita saw the woman frowning. "She's got blue hair?"

"Ah, yes, I know her. Come through. I'm Mariangela, by the way." The hairdresser smiled broadly at Anita and, for a moment, looked as if she was about to throw her arms around her for a hug.

Mariangela gestured at the door and, when Anita walked through, she saw that what had been a front room had been converted into a salon. There was even a sink in the corner of the room, where most people would place a television, and the smell of hair products was even stronger. Where there should have been curtains, there was a flowered blind covering the window.

"Sit, sit," Mariangela said, pointing at a swivel chair in front of a large mirror.

Anita did as instructed, looking around the room. "This is unexpected," she said a moment later, just as Mariangela started running her fingers through her hair.

"It saves on business rates," Mariangela said with a

smile. "They're extortionate around here. What would you like to have done, Anita?" The hairdresser slowly spun Anita around in the chair so that she could see herself in the mirror.

"I'd like to get it tidied up a little," Anita said, knowing that Mariangela would know exactly what she meant by that. "I'd also like to get it colored." When she looked at Mariangela's reflection in the mirror, the woman had a look of astonishment on her face.

"Why on earth would you want to change this beautiful color?" Mariangela said, holding up a few strands of Anita's red hair. "Most of my clients would die to have hair like this."

"It's too distinctive," Anita replied without thinking. When she saw the expression on Mariangela's face change to one of concern, she tried to backtrack. "I mean, I stand out too much in a crowd." But she could see it was too late and all she was doing was digging herself into a deeper hole.

"Are you in trouble?" Mariangela asked when Anita had finished speaking. "Are you trying to hide from someone?"

To her surprise, Anita felt tears springing to her eyes. "Yes," she replied. "It's, um, it's an ex-partner."

"Men can be such pigs," Mariangela said, making Anita laugh at her unintended reference to Giovanni.

"This one certainly was," she replied, dabbing at her eye with a tissue that the hairdresser had pressed into her hand.

Mariangela was just about to say something when there was a deep rumbling sound. Anita glanced over at the blind covering the window to see it was quivering slightly. As she had been walking to the house from the center of Terzigno, Anita had been passed by several articulated lorries. If that was what they did to the house every time they rumbled past, Anita wouldn't be able to live there.

"I think blonde would suit you best," Mariangela said as the noise faded away and the blind returned to normal. "I think it would suit the shape of your face well, and match your eyebrows." She stroked the side of Anita's face gently. "You have such a pretty face, my dear." Then she called her a principessa, or a princess, just like Anita's mother had when she was younger. "When did you last wash your hair?"

Anita had to think for a moment to recall when she had last been able to do this. "Two days ago," she said a moment later.

"Good. Did you use conditioner?"

"Not that time, no."

"Good, good," Mariangela replied with a warm smile.

Anita remained silent as Mariangela started working, first combing through her hair and then separating it into sections.

"This is a semi-permanent dye," the hairdresser said as she started applying the dye. "It should last for about twenty-five washes. Hopefully by that time, your pezzo di merda will be a long way away." Hearing Mariangela refer to Giovanni as a piece of shit made Anita laugh.

Just under an hour later, Mariangela had finished. She had also trimmed Anita's hair, not so much that it looked as if it had been cut, and with the new color, she looked completely different. As she had worked, Mariangela had kept up a near a constant series of tales about her family, some funny and some sad, but still tinged with humor.

"At the end of the day," Mariangela had said at one point, "they all come home from time to time for their mama's cooking. Even my dead-beat ex-husband." Both women had laughed so much at this, they had to take a short break.

"Thank you so much," Anita said, reaching for her purse. "How much do I owe you?"

"Just give me twenty euros for the dye," Mariangela replied with a warm smile. "At least it's not bright blue like your friend's."

"Nonsense," Anita said, opening her purse and pulling out three fifty euro notes. That was what she had paid the last time she had been to a salon. "Please, take this."

"It's too much." Mariangela shook her head.

"Please, Mariangela," Anita replied. "I insist."

After several further protests, all of which Anita had waved away, Mariangela took the money. Just before Anita left the house, both women had hugged in the hallway. Mariangela whispered something in Anita's ear in Neapolitan that she didn't understand.

"It's a blessing, principessa," Mariana said, the skin around her eyes wrinkling as she did so. "A small prayer for good luck to come your way."

As she walked down the street back toward the center of Terzigno, Anita wished·there were more people like Mariangela in the world. And fewer people like Giovanni.

59

Caleb hooked his index finger into the collar of his new shirt, rubbing it around his neck to relieve the irritation from the material. The shirt he was wearing wouldn't have been his first choice, but the young man in the small men's clothing store he had spent the previous thirty minutes in had been insistent on it, as he had the jeans Caleb was also wearing. He still had his sandals on his feet, but in the large paper bag between his legs was a pair of sneakers, complete with a pack of cotton socks nestling against his robe. Caleb was pleased both at the price of the clothes, and at the fact he'd undergone the entire process of buying them without speaking to the shop attendant. The only words Caleb had spoken had been, "Do you speak English?" The young man's reply was just a shake of the head.

He was sitting in the coffee shop where he and Anita had arranged to meet. It was on the corner of a crossroads in the center of Terzigno and was about the best maintained building in the area. Caleb had got a table by the window, and as he sipped his coffee, he watched the world passing by through it. Terzigno was a busy enough place and there was a constant stream of pedestrians and cars passing by.

Caleb wondered how long Anita was going to be. When he'd purchased his new clothes, he'd hurried to the cafe, convinced that he'd taken far too long to complete the transaction. But there was no sign of her. He placed the coffee down on the table and blinked a couple of times. The feeling of dread he had experienced when they had arrived in Naples was hovering in the background, not as bad as it had been, but it was definitely still present. Caleb was just contemplating the unfamiliar sensation when he saw a familiar shock of blue hair through the cafe window. He knocked on the glass more sharply than he'd intended, causing several of the other patrons in the cafe to look at him in alarm. As he raised his hand in apology, he saw Greta pushing the door to the cafe open.

"Oh, wow," she said as she walked in. "You look different. I almost didn't recognize you. Where's Anita?"

"At the hairdressers," Caleb replied. Greta just laughed.

"Yeah, Mariangela likes to talk," she said as a young waitress approached. "She'll be there for a while."

Caleb waited as the two women had a rapid conversation in Italian, not a single word of which he understood apart from *Ciao*. At one point, the waitress glanced at Caleb and broke into peals of laughter, joined by Greta, although she looked reluctant to be joining in. A moment later, the waitress disappeared and Greta slipped into the chair opposite him.

"What was so funny?" Caleb asked, making sure he had a gentle smile on his face as he spoke.

"She was just saying that this was a strange place for you to bring a date to," Greta replied.

"You told her this wasn't a date, didn't you?" Caleb saw

Greta's eyes flicker at the question, and he realized that she hadn't. "What do you think of my new wardrobe?" he asked, deciding to spare her any embarrassment, if that was what the flicker denoted.

"I like it," she replied, glancing at his shirt. "It's better than a dress, anyway."

"You know some people would be offended at that comment?" Caleb said, maintaining his smile.

"Are you offended, preacher man?" Greta asked, twirling a strand of blue hair around her finger.

"Not in the slightest," Caleb replied. "You know what they say. Sticks and stones may break my bones and all that."

As they waited for the waitress to bring over whatever Greta had just ordered, Caleb took the opportunity to examine Greta in more detail than he'd been able to when they had been talking earlier. She was very pretty, but not in a conventional way. Caleb noticed that her eyes were very slightly different shades of blue. The left one was slightly darker than the right one, which was the color of a robin's egg. She smiled at him, and he noticed that two of her front teeth overlapped by a tiny amount. It was the type of thing an orthodontist in the United States would have fixed in a heartbeat, but perhaps they weren't as bothered about such minor imperfections in Europe.

"What is it?" Greta said, her smile widening. "You're looking at me with a really weird expression."

"Am I?" Caleb replied, looking away from her. "Sorry, I didn't realize,"

"Have I got a bit of lettuce stuck between my teeth or something?"

"No, you haven't," Caleb said with a laugh.

"You've got very kind eyes, Caleb. You can look at me for as long as you want to."

Caleb said nothing, but just nodded his head, partly in thanks and partly in acknowledgment of what she had just said. He was only too aware that any kindness in his eyes depended entirely on the situation. He was just wondering what to say when the waitress arrived with a small espresso for Greta and a couple of plates with what looked like lemon drizzle cake on them. She and Greta said something in Italian, and Greta reached for her purse, only to be waved away by the waitress.

"This is a new recipe," Greta explained as the waitress walked away. "She wants to know what we think about it."

"Certainly looks the part," Caleb replied, reaching for one of the slices. The cake was lemon flavored, as he'd thought, and it was perfect. If he hadn't been in a coffee shop, Caleb would have devoured it in a couple of mouthfuls. Instead, he matched Greta's tiny bite for tiny bite, enjoying the way she dabbed at the corner of her mouth every few bites to check for errant crumbs. When she had finished, Greta turned to look at the waitress, calling something out to her. He took the opportunity to look at her again. When she had turned, her dress had ridden up on her thighs by a few inches, and the material was stretched against her body in a way he appreciated a lot. It left little to Caleb's imagination, vivid as it already was.

Then he realized that Greta was watching him in a mirror behind the waitress's head. He tore his eyes away from her. It was his turn to be embarrassed. Greta turned slowly to face him. As she did so, a slow smile appeared on her face.

"You are so busted, preacher man," she said in a hushed voice.

60

"What the hell are you playing at, Giovanni?"

Giovanni looked up as Eva came storming through his personal office door, not even knocking before she did so.

"What do you mean?" he asked, grateful that the two Italian monkeys had left a few moments before. It would have been annoying if they had witnessed her lack of respect.

"What exactly have you told Hugo?" Eva shouted after she had slammed the office door closed. "I've just had his PA on the phone letting me know there's a medical team coming here to look after the mother. Who, in case you hadn't noticed, we haven't actually identified yet."

"I thought you said you'd spoken to Maddy?" Giovanni replied. Eva was angrier than he'd seen her in months, and he knew he was going to have his work cut out for him. He was about to tell her to calm down, but he stopped himself at the last minute, knowing that would only inflame things.

"I spoke to her in general terms, yes, but I didn't ask her if she wanted to be a surrogate mother for Hugo Forrester."

"Well, she won't technically be a surrogate mother for him, will she?" Giovanni tried a pious glance at the ceiling. "She'll be a surrogate mother for God."

"Don't give me that bull crap, Thomas Gavazzi," Eva barked. Her eyes were wild, and she had twin spots of red on her cheeks. "We need to get two rooms ready for these medics. This is actually happening. You realize that, don't you?"

"Yes, I do," Giovanni replied, not rising to the way she had baited him by using his real name. He got to his feet and approached her, wary about being slapped in the face. He held his hands out in front of him, partly in a placatory gesture, but predominantly so he could grab her wrists if she took a swing at him. "Eva, please, listen to me for a moment."

He watched as Eva paused, her mouth half open. Then she closed it and folded her arms across her chest. What was he going to say next, though? He probably should have worked that out before asking her to listen to him.

"Let me talk to Maddy and ask her. If she says no, then we'll just tell Hugo that she's had second thoughts, or we found her to be unsuitable in some way. That'll buy us some time to come up with someone else."

"You're not talking to her on your own," Eva said. "And if she says no, don't you dare tell Hugo I'll do it."

"I won't," Giovanni said with a soft smile. He placed his hands on Eva's upper arms and rubbed them. "Of course I won't."

"Let me get one of the others to find her," Eva replied a moment later, her anger appearing to dissipate somewhat. That was one thing Giovanni liked about the woman. She had a fiery temper, but the explosive element of it was short-lived and the sex after they had argued was normally pretty memorable. Giovanni knew that was going to have to wait, though. He had another companion planned for the evening. Bella was going to be joining him for a private reflection session, and he'd not told Eva yet. Giovanni knew she didn't mind what he did with other people, as long as she knew about it in advance.

"I'M SORRY, can you say that again?" Maddy said. Her face was as white as a sheet. The three of them were sitting in Giovanni's office in armchairs that he had carefully arranged while Maddy was being found by one of the other Adelphoi. To his relief, while they were waiting for the young woman, Eva had calmed down. He knew she was still angry, but in the twenty minutes or so it had taken Maddy to come to the office, Eva had gone from a ten down to a two or three on Giovanni's private scale for how pissed she was.

"The Adelphoi has been chosen as the guardians of the Second Coming," Giovanni repeated, keeping his voice low, conspiratorial even. "And we want you to be the mother of the child."

"But why me?" Maddy whispered. "Why me instead of one of the others?" As she asked this, Maddy's gaze darted between Giovanni and Eva, as if she wasn't sure which of them to speak to.

"I have a feeling about you, Maddy," Giovanni said, leaning forward as he spoke. "I can't explain it, but I feel as if it's just meant to be and that you have been chosen for the role." He risked another glance at the ceiling, as if the inspiration was, in fact, divine.

"Was that what the conversation was about this morning?" Maddy asked, looking at Eva. "At breakfast?"

Eva didn't reply, but just nodded her head. Considering

she'd insisted on being part of this conversation, Giovanni thought she would at least join in.

"It's meant to be you, Maddy," Giovanni said. "I've thought that since the moment we first met."

In the chair next to Maddy, Eva made a coughing sound before raising her hand to her mouth. Giovanni looked at her and could tell from the way the skin around her eyes was crinkled that she was trying not to laugh.

"Maddy?" Giovanni said, speaking more loudly to get her attention before she realized what Eva was doing. "We completely understand if you need some time to think about it, but there would be a medical team looking after you the entire time. You and the baby will have the best possible care. This is history in the making." He lowered his voice back down and put as much fervor into it as he could. "You'll be a part of history, exalted by the entire world for the rest of your life."

Maddy's expression changed, and he wondered if he'd overdone it.

"I don't need any time to think about it," she said a few excruciating seconds later. Maddy looked at Giovanni, her eyes wide. "Of course I'll do it."

Eva looked at Maddy, the laughter that had threatened to erupt a moment earlier disappearing in a split second. Had Maddy really just said that? Without even blinking?

"Maddy," Eva said. "This is an enormous decision. Why don't you at least think about it for a day or two?"

"I don't need to," the young girl replied, a look of newfound determination in her eyes. "It would be a privilege above all others." Her voice was almost breathy as she spoke, as if she was already slipping into the role of the mother of the child.

"That's fantastic, Maddy," Giovanni said with a look of barely disguised irritation at Eva, which she completely ignored. She knew all he was interested in was the money he would be able to get out of Hugo for confirming that they had a candidate. Eva wanted to get Maddy on her own to talk about it without Giovanni listening in. She didn't want to dissuade the young woman from volunteering, not that she'd had much actual choice in the matter, but to make sure that she fully understood what she was letting herself in for. It wasn't just the pregnancy that Eva was worried about. If anything, that was the straightforward part. After all, every single day thousands upon thousands of babies were being born, the vast majority of them without the benefit of an on-site medical team. It was more about what life would be like for Maddy following the birth of a child that would be considered to be the son, or perhaps daughter, of God.

"When will it happen?" Maddy asked, her voice firmer. "The insemination? When will that take place?"

"We'll need to check with, er, with our sponsor," Giovanni replied. Eva realized that when he had been telling Maddy about the project, he'd not mentioned Hugo's name, or the Weizmann Institute. She made a mental note to speak to him later to see if there was a specific reason for that. Giovanni was about to say something else when there was a soft knock on his office door.

"Enter," Giovanni called out, using an authoritative tone. The door opened and Eva looked across the room to see Bella, the latest target of his affections, peering in.

"I'm sorry to disturb you, Brother Giovanni," Bella said, not even glancing at either Eva or Maddy. "Some of the female Adelphoi say there's a drone flying outside their bedroom windows."

"Okay, thank you Bella," Giovanni replied. He smiled at Bella, but he couldn't hide the anger in his eyes. "I'll deal with it."

"Your Italian friends?" Eva asked as Bella eased the door closed and Giovanni started getting to his feet. She tried not to smirk as she spoke, but she couldn't help it. He gave her a furious look once he had turned his face away from Maddy so that she couldn't see it.

"This shouldn't take long," he said. By the time he

turned back to face Maddy, his face was all sweetness and light, which only made Eva want to smirk even more.

At least that would give Eva an opportunity to speak to Maddy. Her only other option would have been to speak to her when they went out on the bicycle ride later, but Eva wanted to avoid that if she could. She knew she might need to concentrate on breathing, rather than talking, when they did go out.

Eva waited until Giovanni had made his excuses, notably only to Maddy and not to Eva, and left the office.

"Maddy, why don't we talk about this before you make any firm decisions?" Eva said a few seconds later.

"What's there to talk about?" Maddy replied. Her eyes were almost sparkling. "Brother Giovanni said it himself. He said it's meant to be. He said I've been chosen."

Eva paused for a moment to consider her options. Giovanni was right, technically speaking. Maddy had been chosen, but by Giovanni. She looked at the young woman in front of her, wondering what the best thing to say was.

"Well, there's a long way to go yet," Eva said eventually, not able to think of anything else to say. She wanted to re-read the material that Hugo had sent them. Perhaps there would be something in there that could help her get Maddy out of the predicament she was in. Eva was concerned that she was too vulnerable, too easily manipulated for this to continue any further. She knew also that she should have spoken up sooner. Tempting as it was to blame Giovanni, she was just as responsible. "Are you still up for that bicycle ride later?"

"Of course," Maddy said, clapping her hands like an excited child. "I'm really looking forward to it."

"So am I," Eva said with a forced smile. "Now, if you'll excuse me, I have some errands to run."

. . .

THIRTY MINUTES LATER, having dispatched a small working party to prepare a couple of additional rooms in the complex for the medical team, Eva was sitting back in the general office, scrolling through some of the material from the Weizmann Institute. She'd seen something earlier about failure rates in one of the reports, and she wanted to find it again to understand it properly. Every few seconds, the screen froze for a split second, much to her irritation. Eva had even changed the batteries in the mouse, but it had made no difference.

Finally, she found the passage she was looking for. According to the report, there was a statistically significant chance that the insemination process would not be successful. Eva tutted under her breath as the loose interpretation of what that rate actually was, especially when the rest of the report was so precise. She guessed the author didn't want to build in a key performance indicator in case they didn't meet it.

"Oh, for pity's sake," Eva said as the screen flickered again. In frustration, she slapped at the side of the monitor, but all she succeeded in doing was breaking a nail.

"You okay in here?" she heard Giovanni's voice saying as she inspected the damage to her cuticle. "What's the computer done to irritate you?" He was standing in the doorway to the office, a half-grin on his face.

"No more than you have, Giovanni," Eva muttered. "Did you sort the drone problem out?"

"Yes, I did," Giovanni replied, taking a couple of steps into the office. "They weren't looking in the windows at all. It was just a misunderstanding."

"Sure it was, Giovanni," Eva said, sucking her index

finger. "Why can't we get a different security firm? I don't like those two at all. Especially after what happened to the couple on the moped. How do know we can trust them?"

"We have to, Eva. They're recommended by Hugo. He wants us to use them so we don't have a choice."

"Of course he does," Eva replied. "And whatever Hugo wants, Hugo gets."

62

"You sent for me, Mr. Forrester?" Albert said as he peered around the door.

"Yes, come in, Albert," Hugo replied. When the computer scientist entered, Hugo gestured to a chair for him to sit. "Would you like a drink? Coffee or tea, perhaps?"

"I'm fine, thank you."

Hugo watched for a moment as the man looked around the interior of his office. He'd been in here before, hadn't he? But when Hugo thought about it, he realized that he probably hadn't. It wasn't as if he invited his staff in for social calls.

"I've been very impressed with the work that you've done on the DNA reconstruction," Hugo said. There was no harm in buttering the man up a little and he had achieved something which, to their knowledge, had not been done before.

"It's all about the modeling," Albert replied with a shrug of his shoulders. "It's the AI that's doing the hard work, not me."

"You're doing yourself a disservice, Albert," Hugo replied. "Now, how familiar are you with ancient scrolls?"

"In what context?" Albert replied, leaning forward.

"I have acquired a scroll that's two thousand years old and I'd like to be able to read what's on it."

"What sort of condition is it in?" If Albert had been surprised at Hugo's revelation, it didn't show on his face. But the computer scientist and his wife, Claudia, were among a small group of people in the building who knew of Hugo's collection in the basement.

"Very good, as far as I understand. I've had a colleague in Britain do some work on it, and he's produced a 2D scan of the scroll. He tells me there's Aramaic text on it. I'd like it to be analyzed and translated for my collection."

"Have you heard of the Vesuvius Challenge, Mr. Forrester?"

"No, I don't believe that I have."

"It was a competition to analyze a carbonized scroll found in the remains of Herculaneum. Some researchers managed to unwrap, virtually speaking, and decipher most of the text on it. What you're describing sounds quite straightforward in comparison."

"I'd quite like to keep the scroll as intact as possible, so if it can be done without physically examining the papyrus, that would be most welcome." For a few seconds, Hugo thought he could detect the faintest of smiles on the usually taciturn man's face.

"Let me start with the 2D scan and see what we can unravel," Albert replied, getting to his feet. Hugo appreciated the fact the man knew when to leave a meeting. He left with a curt nod in Hugo's direction, which he returned.

The door had only been closed for a couple of seconds when there was a knock on it.

"Come in, Ruth," Hugo called out, knowing that she had been outside the door for the entire time. He could have just let her come in—she knew everything there was to know about his pastime—but people needed to be reminded of their place every once in a while.

When she entered the room, Ruth's face was even more pinched than it usually was.

"Is there a problem?" Hugo asked her, motioning for her to sit down in the chair opposite his desk.

"I've heard from the Italians at the Adelphoi," she said, glancing down at her notepad. "They don't like the complex they live in."

"I didn't send them there for their opinion on the decor," Hugo replied, immediately irritated.

"From a security perspective, Mr. Forrester," Ruth said, either not picking up on or just plain ignoring his annoyance. "They say it's far too open for the woman to be properly protected. Apparently, it's surrounded by a golf course."

"I know." Hugo had flown over the top of it enough times. "But I don't accept that it can't be secured. What's the alternative? Bring her here?"

"Perhaps that could be considered as a contingency plan?"

Hugo sighed, knowing what Ruth was saying made sense. To her credit, it usually did.

"Very well," he replied. "How are the rest of the arrangements coming along?"

"The medical team will be in place tomorrow, and your retrieval team is leaving for Rome the day after that to secure the relic."

"Excellent," Hugo said, rubbing his hands together. "Excellent. Is there any more news on the mother?"

"No." Ruth made a clicking sound with her tongue.

"Sister Eva is, shall we say, reluctant to confirm that they have one."

"That's not what Giovanni told me," Hugo replied with a smirk. "If he wants the rest of his money, he'll sort that out. I can't see that being a problem. The place is full of suitable candidates from what I saw the last time I was there." Hugo's smirk turned into a chuckle. "His only problem is going to be to find one he's not slept with."

"Have you changed your mind about the child being nursed once it's arrived?" Ruth asked. Hugo looked at her carefully, knowing her views on this particular subject differed to his.

"Not at all," he said, frowning slightly. The last thing he wanted once the baby had arrived was its mother breast-feeding, or even being anywhere near the child. "She is to be disposed of, preferably before the newborn has even been washed. That is not negotiable."

"Very well, Mr. Forrester," Ruth said with a nod of her head as she got to her feet. "I'll make sure the arrangements are in place when the time comes."

Anita almost hadn't recognized Caleb when she walked into the coffee shop earlier, but even with normal clothes on, he stood out with his shaved head. He had been sitting with Greta, and the way they had both clammed up when she had joined them was odd, but she paid it no heed. After they'd had a coffee, the three of them had left the coffee shop to return to Greta's apartment, their chores all done.

She was sitting in Greta's kitchen, watching her friend preparing supper for them all. Anita had offered to help with the preparation, but Greta had insisted she sit down, telling her she looked exhausted. Although there was no reason for Anita to be so tired, she would quite happily have gone to bed for a nap.

"Here you go, Caleb," Greta said, tossing an onion in his direction. "Make yourself useful and chop that up."

Caleb, who had caught the onion without even looking at it, got to his feet and crossed the kitchen to the knife block. He pulled out the smallest knife and ran his thumb over the blade before frowning. Then he placed both the knife and the onion on the table and left the kitchen.

"Where did he go?" Greta asked when she realized Caleb had disappeared.

"No idea," Anita replied with a yawn.

"Why don't you lie down for an hour?" Greta said. "This is going to take a while and, if you sleep for longer, I can heat it through for you."

"No, it's fine. If I lie down now, I'll be asleep until the morning. I don't know why I'm so tired."

"Did you sleep last night?"

"Not really."

Greta poured some tomato sauce into a pan and set it on a low heat. "It's probably the adrenaline catching up with you."

Anita nodded in agreement just as Caleb returned to the kitchen. In his hand was a small gray stone, rectangular in shape. He placed it on the kitchen table and picked up the knife, balancing it for a moment on his index finger.

"What are you doing?" Greta said as she watched him.

"It's okay," Caleb replied as he started sharpening the knife. "I soaked the whetstone this morning before I did my hair."

Both Anita and Greta watched, fascinated, as Caleb ran the knife back and forth over the stone. He gradually built up the cadence until his hands were almost a blur, and he had a look of intense concentration on his face. A few moments later, he slowed down and stopped, running his thumb over the edge of the knife again. Then, with a broad grin on his face, he used it to shave a few hairs from his forearm.

"There," Caleb said, rising to rinse the knife under the tap. "That's better."

"Thank you, Caleb," Greta replied with a grin. "There're four more in the block, but can you chop that onion first? I need it for this pasta e fagioli." She was about to say something else when there was a soft ping from the den next to the kitchen. Greta wiped her hands on a dishcloth and left the kitchen.

Anita got to her feet and walked to the stove to stir the sauce so it didn't burn.

"Do you actually carry a whetstone around with you all the time?" she said with an impish grin at Caleb. "Just in case you come across a blunt knife?"

Caleb, who was just about to cut into the onion, looked up at her. "I do, yes," he replied, putting the knife down and running his hand over his head. "I need to keep my razor sharp for this dome."

"Anita? Caleb?" Greta's voice called out from the den. "Come and have a look at this."

With a glance at Caleb, Anita turned the sauce down as low as it would go and followed him into the small den. Greta was hunched over the computer, staring at the screen.

"What is it, Greta?" Anita asked as she joined her. There was some sort of a spreadsheet on the screen and, as she watched, Anita saw the cursor moving and some numbers being entered into one of the cells. But Greta's hands were nowhere near the keyboard or mouse.

"Sister Eva's on her computer," Greta replied, whispering, as if Eva might hear her. "These are the financial returns for the Adelphoi." Her index finger pointed at one column. "See the balance there?" Next to her, Caleb let out a soft whistle.

"There's a payment from the Weizmann Institute," he said, pointing at another area of the screen and touching his finger to the glass. "Half a million euros in a single payment." Greta tutted and swiped at his hand playfully.

"Now you've left a fingerprint on my screen, you fool. Go and get a cloth."

As Caleb wandered back into the kitchen, Anita ran her eyes up and down the columns. If she understood what she was seeing, the Adelphoi—or more specifically, Giovanni and Eva—were raking in money.

"How can you see this, Greta?" she asked a moment later as the cursor moved again to another cell.

"The thumb drive." It was Caleb who replied. He was walking back into the den with Greta's dishcloth in his hand. "When you put it into Giovanni's computer, as well as copying the content, it left some software behind." Anita saw Greta look at him with a surprised expression, but he just shrugged his shoulders and smiled. "What?" he said. "It's what I would have done. Although, to be fair, I would have had to get someone else to do it for me. Computers aren't really my thing."

Anita had a sudden thought. If Greta could see Eva's screen, could she see the login details for whatever finance software she was using? If she could, then perhaps there was an easier way to halt Hugo's plan.

"Why don't we steal their money?" Anita said. "That would hold them up a bit." Next to her, Caleb had a broad grin on his face.

"That's just what I was thinking," he said, as his smile broadened.

64

Caleb used a piece of bread to mop up the last of the sauce remaining in his bowl. The pasta e fagioli, or pasta with beans, that Greta had cooked for them all was amazing. She had turned some simple ingredients into an aromatic dish crammed with flavor. Borlotti beans, small ditaloni pasta cooked to perfection, and a spicy tomato sauce with a bunch of herbs. Caleb had laughed as he watched Greta adding the herbs to the vegetable stew. There had been no measuring involved, but if she had been guessing how much of them to add, she had guessed just right.

As they had eaten, Greta had explained to them both that, unfortunately, there was no way to access the funds in the account that Eva had been looking at.

"If I'd thought about it," she had told them, "I would have included a keylogger with the monitoring software."

"That was fantastic, Greta," Caleb said before putting the bread in his mouth. Sitting next to him at the table, Anita nodded in agreement.

"Have you had enough?" Greta asked. "I wasn't sure if I'd made enough."

Caleb waited until he had finished his bread before replying. "Better a small serving of vegetables with love than a fattened calf with hatred," he replied. "Proverbs, chapter fifteen. But that was more than enough for me, Greta. Thank you."

"You're more than welcome," Greta replied with a smile. "But you're doing the washing up while Anita and I have a glass of wine on the balcony."

By the time Caleb had finished tidying away the kitchen, taking a while to locate which items went in which cupboards, the sun was just beginning to set behind the mountain. He joined the two women on the balcony, realizing that while he had been clearing up, they had almost finished a bottle of wine between them.

"It's a beautiful view," Caleb said as he sat on the plastic chair Greta had pulled across for him. He looked at the top of the mountain, which was just beginning to be silhouetted by the sun.

"I'm going to get another bottle," Greta said, getting to her feet. "Caleb? Will you have a glass?"

"Sure," Caleb said, nodding his head. As Greta passed behind him, she trailed her hand briefly over his shoulder, almost making him shiver.

"What time do you think we should leave tomorrow?" Anita asked, looking at him.

"Dawn perhaps?" Caleb replied, watching as a low cloud turned from orange to a deep red. "Or is that too early for you?"

"No, that's fine by me. I'll turn in soon, I think. I've probably had enough wine."

Caleb saw Anita glancing at the doors back into Greta's apartment. When she spoke, she had lowered her voice.

"She likes you, Caleb. She asked me if there was anything between us a few moments ago."

"Did she?" Caleb replied. "What did you tell her?"

Anita didn't reply, but just shook her head from side to side. Caleb sensed a sadness in her eyes, and he cursed the man who had hurt her so much. Men who preyed on other people were the worst sort of men, in his opinion. From what Caleb knew of the way Giovanni had treated both Anita and Greta, and the vast amount of money the false prophet appeared to be extorting from people in the name of his religion, Giovanni had a lot to answer for. Both in this life and the next.

"Everything okay?" Greta said when she returned a moment later, perhaps sensing the feeling of melancholy in the air.

"All good," Anita replied with what sounded to Caleb like false enthusiasm. She got to her feet. "Greta, thank you so much for dinner. I'm going to go to bed. Caleb and I are going to leave early tomorrow."

Caleb watched as the two women shared a brief hug, Anita looking at him over Greta's shoulder. Although her eyes were still sad, she smiled at him.

When Anita had left, closing the balcony doors softly behind her, Greta pulled her chair over so she was sitting next to Caleb. When she had gone inside to get the bottle of wine, she had also fetched a shawl, which she now had draped over her shoulders. Even in the dying light of the sunset, Caleb could see it matched her canary yellow summer dress, and he appreciated her attention to detail.

"Doesn't it bother you? Living here?" Caleb asked as he took the glass of wine Greta had poured for him. He nodded at the mountain, which was now shrouded in darkness. "On the slopes of a volcano?"

"Not really," Greta replied. "We'd have plenty of notice if anything happened. That thing's got more sensors on it than pretty much every other volcano."

"There was a tremor earlier today, wasn't there?"

"There're tremors every day here." He could see Greta smiling at him in the soft orange light from a streetlamp that had just flickered into life. "You can't spend your life worrying about what might happen in the future. It's too uncertain. I'd much rather live in the present."

Calebs smiled back at her. It was a philosophy that had served him well. "Carpe diem," he said, tilting his glass in her direction. *Seize the Day.* "If I was going to have a tattoo, it would be that."

"Amen to that," Greta replied, clinking her glass against his.

They sat in a companionable silence for a few moments before Caleb spoke.

"I'm sorry about earlier, Greta," he said. "In the coffee shop, I mean."

"What are you sorry for?"

"For the way I was looking at you."

"You don't need to apologize, Caleb," Greta said as she sipped her drink. Then a wry grin appeared on her face. "You're not the first so-called man of the cloth who's leered at me. I seem to have a habit of attracting men like that."

"I didn't say I was attracted to you," Caleb replied, mirroring her grin. "I apologized for the way I was looking at you."

"So you're not attracted to me?"

"I didn't say that either." To Caleb's surprise, Greta

swiveled in her chair and lifted her legs, resting her calves on his thighs.

"Not even a little?" she asked, looking at him out of the corner of her eye.

Caleb glanced down at her legs. They were smooth and toned, and he noticed a small scar on her left knee. He could feel the warmth of her legs through his trousers. Caleb closed his eyes and imagined putting his hand on her, how her skin might feel under his fingertips.

"I barely know you, Greta," he said a moment later, opening his eyes and looking at her. She returned his gaze, not blinking.

"But I think you do," she replied in a whisper. "It feels like you know me better than I know myself. When you took my hand yesterday, it felt as if you somehow sensed everything there was to sense about me."

"I barely know you," Caleb said again, but this time with less conviction.

"That can be remedied, preacher man," Greta replied, her grin returning. "Or have you taken a vow of celibacy?" She giggled and took another sip of her wine. "That would make things awkward, wouldn't it?"

"It would, yes." Caleb raised his own glass and took the smallest sip of wine that he could. "But I haven't. I'm not that kind of preacher."

"Do you think I'm wanton, Caleb? For behaving like I am?" Greta moved her legs slightly on his lap, but all she was doing was readjusting her position.

"Not at all," Caleb said, closing his eyes again. He was reminded of another verse in Proverbs that talked of buying a whore for an hour with a loaf of bread before going on to warn that a wanton woman may well eat you alive, but he didn't think it was the time or the place to quote it.

65

Caleb lay in his bed with his hands behind his head, his fingers interlaced. The apartment was silent except for a ticking clock in the hallway, which he could only just hear. He thought back to the previous couple of hours he and Greta had spent on the apartment balcony. When he hadn't responded to her, she had seemed sanguine. It hadn't been that he'd not wanted to respond to her—far from it—but there was something holding him back. Caleb just wasn't sure what. He mulled this over in his mind as he stared at the ceiling, a long crack in the plaster illuminated by the streetlamp close to his window. He could close the curtains, but he liked the light. That, and the gentle ticking sound of the clock, reminded him he was alive.

Greta had been hurt by a man. That much was clear, even though she made light of it. By a man such as Caleb, who professed to be a man of faith. Perhaps that was why he was reticent about responding to her, for fear of hurting her more. But it was Greta who had instigated the conversation, not him. As she had said earlier, as she had topped up her glass of wine, they were both consenting adults. If something were to happen between them, where's the harm? Then, after a pause that threatened to become an uncomfortable silence, she had moved on to talk about her most recent visit to Rome. It was as if the previous conversation had never taken place.

When Greta had finished her wine, she had slowly disengaged her legs from his lap, making his thighs cold for a few seconds. She had stood and placed a hand on his cheek.

"You're a good man, Caleb," Greta had said, rubbing her thumb softly over his cheek. "Sweet dreams." Then she had left.

Caleb had sat alone on the balcony for some moments, wondering what to do. He had looked out over the mountain, now in complete darkness. He could only tell its shape by the stars he couldn't see and he had imagined for a moment the volcano erupting into life, spewing ash and smoke into the air as it enveloped the people on its slopes as it had done so many times in the past. Then, with a heavy sigh, Caleb had gone to his bedroom. He had paused for a moment outside Greta's door. Would she respond if he knocked softly on it?

Caleb closed his eyes, but he knew sleep was some distance away. He started running through what he would say tomorrow when he met the man responsible for the Holy Lance. How much he would tell him of the Adelphoi's plans, and the intent of the Weizmann Institute. Greta had already printed out one report for him and Anita to take to Vatican City. Caleb just hoped it would be enough for them to take action and secure the lance somewhere safe.

His thoughts turned to what he would do after that. Caleb knew he had to stop them, but how? The root of the issue was the institute, not the Adelphoi. They appeared solely to be the enablers of the project, not the instigators. But at the same time, Caleb was very keen to meet with Giovanni. He would take Anita to Rome and the Vatican, but he intended to undertake the next stage of his journey alone. Caleb resolved to speak to her about that in the car in the morning, which was only four hours away.

Caleb was just beginning to empty his mind, not to sleep but to relax, when he heard his bedroom door open and the sound of the clock get louder. He kept his eyes closed and listened, hearing the door close again, muffling the ticking, before footsteps approached his bed. Then he heard the sound of a zipper being unfastened, and the soft rustle of material falling to the floor. When Caleb opened his eyes, Greta was standing a yard from his bed, her summer dress in a wrinkled pile on the floor. She was still wearing her underwear, but as his eyes took in her body, he realized there wasn't much to the garments at all.

Greta raised an index finger to her lips as she took a couple of tentative steps toward his bed. Caleb pulled the sheet aside and wriggled on the bed to make some space for her. Greta paused, looking at him for a moment with a frown, and he realized she was looking at the scars on his chest. Then she slid into the bed and placed a hand on his cheek, just as she had done earlier on the balcony.

"How about now?" she whispered. "Do you think I'm wanton now?" Caleb paused before replying, knowing that the instant he touched her, he would be lost for words. Her body was soft and warm, and he could feel the swell of her chest against his own.

"Very much so," Caleb replied, his mouth dry. "But are you sure this is a good idea?" He watched as she closed her eyes briefly and smiled. When she reopened them, there was nothing in them to suggest it wasn't.

"I think it's a very good idea, preacher man."

"Why?"

"Why not?" Greta whispered. She moved her hand from his cheek to his chest, her fingertip circling the scar from a bullet, but she didn't ask him anything about it. Then her fingertip moved to an almost horizontal scar just below his nipple, courtesy of a man who had died seconds after giving it to Caleb. "You have some interesting decorations."

Caleb wasn't sure what to say, so he chose to say nothing about her comment. "But are you sure this is what you want?"

"This is everything I want, Caleb," she said. Her mouth was so close to his ear that he could feel her breath on his skin. "This is everything I need. To be with a good man for once, but on my terms. And I know you're a good man, Caleb. I wouldn't be here if you weren't."

"You have terms?" Caleb asked with a slight smile. He was reassured by her words, the slim feeling he might have had that he was taking advantage of her disappearing. "Do I have to sign something?"

"My only term is that we're as quiet as mice in a church." She lifted her hand from his chest and hooked it behind her, unclipping her bra. Next in line were her underpants. She slid both garments from between the sheets and onto the floor. Then she curled her body back against his and put her hand back on his chest. "So, shall we?" she asked him.

"I think we should," Caleb replied. There was no sense in prolonging the inevitable. What was going to happen was going to happen. Greta had made that much clear.

She moved slightly, increasing the pressure of her body against his skin. Then Greta moved the hand she wasn't touching him with under the pillow. "There's something for you there, when we get that far." Caleb nodded in response. His body was reacting exactly the way it was designed to, and the sheet covering them wasn't hiding anything in that respect. "Which I think might be quite soon."

Caleb raised his hand and slid it around the back of her neck. Greta's skin was smooth, and the hair at the nape of her neck was soft and downy. She smiled and moved her head to kiss him.

And with that, just as he'd expected, Caleb was lost for words.

66

"Good morning," Anita said to Caleb as she walked into the kitchen. Outside the window, the sky was lightening with the dawn. Caleb was sitting at the kitchen table, waiting for the coffeepot to stop gurgling. Anita had been half expecting him to be in his robe, but he was dressed in a pair of jeans and a polo shirt with a small motif over the breast. "Did you sleep okay?"

"On and off," Caleb said with a wry grin. "But I figured I can sleep in the car."

"Only when you're not driving," Anita replied. She took a deep breath in through her nose. "That coffee smells amazing."

"Yeah, can we talk about the driving?"

Anita looked at Caleb. Was he about to tell her he didn't have a driver's license? "You can drive, can't you?" she asked, putting her hands on her hips.

"I can, yes."

"There's a but?"

"There's a but."

"Go on then, spit it out."

"I can't drive a stick," Caleb said, looking at her with an almost sorrowful expression.

"Are you serious?" Anita said, laughing at the look on his face. "How come?"

"I just never learned, that's all. Do you want a coffee?"

"Don't change the subject. Are you seriously telling me you've never learned to drive a stick shift?" Anita crossed her arms over her chest and giggled at his discomfort. "I think you're the first grown man I've met who can't."

A few moments later, steaming cups of coffee in front of them, Anita and Caleb were looking at the route to Rome on Anita's phone. As he was incapable of driving, she had told him, he was going to have to navigate. According to the screen, Rome was a shade over two hours away and much of the route was on an autostrada. She came out of the maps app on her cell and switched to a parking app. With Caleb watching, she booked a parking space in a garage called Garage San Pietro for the day. According to the app, it was only five minutes from the garage to Vatican City.

"I didn't realize you could do things like that on a cell phone," Caleb said as she placed the phone on the table.

"You can do a lot of things on a cell phone," Anita replied. "You should get one."

"I'm good, thanks." Caleb shrugged his shoulders. "Never really needed one for anything."

"You can call people on them," Anita said with a smile. "You know, stay in touch with friends?" He just shrugged his shoulders again and turned the corners of his mouth down. She looked at him and, just for a few seconds, felt sorry for him. Perhaps he would have been happier back in the middle ages where things like cell phones and stick shifts weren't an issue? But the feeling passed when she saw him smiling. "Shall we get going when Greta's up?" Anita asked him. "Or just head away when we've had our coffee."

"I say let her sleep," Caleb replied. "She knows we're leaving early."

"Did the two of you stay up late last night?"

"Not really, no." Caleb got to his feet and crossed the kitchen to the coffeepot. "You want a refill?" He wasn't looking at her as he spoke, but was studying the coffee pot. Anita felt a smile start to appear on her face. There it was again. A change of subject. Something had obviously happened between Caleb and Greta, and Anita was feeling **mischievous,** so decided to see if she could find out what.

"So, what did you chat about? On the balcony?" she asked, aiming for a nonchalant tone.

"Oh, this and that," Caleb replied, still not meeting her eyes. "Just stuff really. Nothing important." He fell silent, and the only noise Anita could hear was the ticking of the clock in the hallway.

"Did something happen between you, Caleb?"

"No, nothing."

"Did you have an argument?" she asked him. "Only the walls to this apartment are paper thin. I'm sure I would have heard something if you had."

Caleb looked up at her and, for a split second, she saw a look of horror in his eyes, but as soon as it appeared, it was gone. "No, we didn't have an argument."

It took a second or two, but the penny dropped and Anita looked down at her coffee cup, instantly ashamed. Something had happened between Caleb and Greta, and she knew exactly what it was. Caleb was right. It wasn't an argument, but she had no idea what to say.

"I, um, I fell asleep the moment my head hit the pillow," Anita said, knowing she was talking too quickly. "Next thing

I know, it's morning. I was only joking when I said I'd heard you arguing. I didn't hear anything at all."

"Okay," Caleb replied. He looked away from her, but she could see the embarrassment on his face. She felt it too, and she wished she'd thought a bit more before speaking. "Maybe we should get going?"

"I could teach you, you know," Anita said. "To drive a stick shift?"

"Maybe not today, Anita," Caleb replied. To her relief, she saw a grin on his face. "But I appreciate the offer. I'd quite like to get to Rome at some point today, not at some point this week."

"I think that depends on your ability to navigate, Caleb," Anita said as she got to her feet. "Because if we get lost, it's all on you." Caleb also stood and for a moment, Anita wanted to hug him, but it would have been a weird thing to do. "You want to leave Greta a note?"

"Do you think she'll need one?"

Anita paused before replying. It wasn't really a case of Greta needing a note.

"I don't think she'll need one," she replied, turning away from Caleb. "But I think she'd like one."

67

"**A**ccording to your cell, we need to get off at the next exit," Caleb said, squinting at the small screen. They hadn't even made it out of Naples before Anita had to pull over and turn off the robotic voice that was giving them unnecessary directions. Apart from some roadworks close to a town called Valmontone, it had been an easy drive north to the capital of Italy. Anita moved into the right-hand lane to prepare for the exit. As in so many places Caleb had visited, the area close to the autostrada junction was full of industrial units and gas stations, but as they made their way along Via Gregorio VII, it became much more suburban.

Either side of the road were apartment blocks, larger and tidier than Greta's, but none of them were over six or seven stories high. As well as the ubiquitous satellite dishes, many of the balconies were filled with flowers and drying laundry. Along the bottom of the blocks were shops and businesses, and Caleb saw a variety of restaurants and cafes passing by.

"They like their food here," he said as Anita pulled to a

stop at a red light. Caleb was hungry, not having eaten since the previous evening. "I'm surprised they're not bigger. Do you want to stop for some food?"

"Let's grab something when we've parked," Anita said, glancing over at the cell in Caleb's hand. "It's not much further, is it?"

"Ten minutes," Caleb replied, watching as a young man on a moped tried to inch his way through the traffic waiting at the red light. His handlebar clipped one of the tall trees that lined the center of the road, and he wobbled a couple of times, laughing as he did so.

The road they were driving along curved gently round to the left and a few hundred yards further on, Caleb saw the dome of St. Peter's Basilica emerge through the apartment blocks.

"It's the next turn on the right," Caleb said a moment later, pointing for Anita's benefit. "There, just past that cafe with the hanging baskets."

Anita slowed for the turn, narrowly missing another young man on a moped who was trying to undercut her. He shouted something that Caleb didn't understand, but knew it wasn't something complementary. When she had parked the car, they stopped at the cafe for a quick bite to eat. Caleb suggested they get something to go, but was reprimanded by Anita.

"That's not how the Italians eat, Caleb," she had said with an exasperated expression.

"IT'S AN IMPRESSIVE PLACE," Caleb said as they made their way toward St. Peter's Square thirty minutes later. It had been, by Italian standards, an extremely quick breakfast. Ahead of them, the area opened out into a large round shape, the ovato tondo, which was dominated by a large obelisk made of red granite over eighty feet tall. Four cast metal lions guarded the obelisk's base, and it was topped with an elaborate crucifix. Tourists were trying to take photographs with their hands held out at just the right height so that they would look as if they were holding it in their hand. Behind the obelisk, the main facade of the basilica rose into the air, decorated with vast columns and a line of statues along the top. In the center, one statue held a cross in one arm, the other raised in the air in blessing. "Christ the Redeemer," Caleb said as he saw Anita looking up at the statues in awe. "On his left is St. Andrew, and St. John the Baptist is on his right."

"I thought you didn't like churches," Anita said with a grin.

"I don't always like what they represent," Caleb replied as they joined the queue of tourists waiting to enter the main basilica. He watched as several were turned away by the suited men at the door, who looked more like FBI agents than Vatican City employees. One of them, a broad-shouldered man complete with an earpiece and sunglasses, was gesturing at a female tourist's skirt, indicating that it was too short. "That would be a good job," Caleb said. "Fashion police." When they approached the front of the line a few moments later, the surly security guard waved them through without comment.

Inside the basilica, Caleb could sense the reverence in the air. It was much cooler inside the cavernous building. As Anita admired the high ceilings and elaborately painted walls, Caleb looked around. When he saw a middle-aged man wearing a cassock, the black, ankle-length robe that signified he was a member of the clergy, and an identification card attached to a lanyard, Caleb walked over to him.

"Excuse me," he said to the priest. "Do you speak English?" The man looked at Caleb as if he was annoyed at being asked.

"Of course," the priest replied, with barely any trace of an accent. "How may I help you?"

"I'm looking for Monsignor Carrapietti," Caleb said, watching as the man's eyebrows went up. Whether it was the mention of the monsignor's name, or the way he'd pronounced it, Caleb wasn't sure.

"Is he expecting you?"

"I believe so, yes."

"Please, wait here." The priest disappeared into the basilica, his cassock trailing behind him like a cloak.

"How is the monsignor expecting you?" Anita asked, and Caleb remembered he'd not told her the details of this part of his plan. When she had asked him about it in the car earlier that morning, Caleb had just smiled and told her he had a plan.

"I called in a favor from a friend," Caleb replied. "Although I think it's now me who owes him the favors. I even did it without a cell phone."

"The Abbott?" Anita asked. Caleb's smile faltered at her perceptiveness.

"Yes," he said, "although I have other friends."

Anita laughed softly just as a male voice behind them spoke.

"Brother Caleb?"

They both turned to see another man in a cassock, this one with purple piping and buttons. He was older than the previous clergyman by at least ten years, but he had more of an air of authority about him. He stood a few inches shorter than Caleb and had his hands clasped in front of him.

"It's just Caleb," Caleb replied, extending a hand for the

monsignor to shake. When he saw the ecclesiastical ring on the priest's hand, Caleb wondered for a moment if he was supposed to kiss it, but he decided against it. "Thank you for taking the time to see us." He saw Monsignor Carrapietti glance at Anita, as if only just realizing that she was there. Then he smiled, a warm smile that lit up his entire face, and shook her hand as well. He said something in Italian that made Anita laugh out loud, but Caleb did not know what he had said.

"Please, follow me," Monsignor Carrapietti said, turning on his heel and walking away.

"Are they always in a hurry, these priests?" Caleb heard Anita say as they set off behind him.

68

Anita almost had to run to keep up with the monsignor as he led her and Caleb across the ornate marbled floor of the basilica, They passed many statues and carvings that she would have loved to stop to examine, but the priest was walking so fast that they were almost blurred. Tourists parted like the Red Sea as Monsignor Carrapietti, who had told her that his church was rarely graced with such beauty as he had shaken her hand, forged a path through the mostly silent crowd.

The monsignor finally slowed when they reached the north-eastern corner of the central crossing of the basilica. In front of them was a white marble statue at least four yards high, showing a man wearing a robe not unlike Caleb's. The statue had one arm out to the side, and in the other was brandishing a spear.

"The statue is from the seventeenth century," Monsignor Carrapietti said, as he slid his hand into a hidden pocket in his cassock. When it emerged, he had a small ring of keys in his fingers. "It was sculpted by Gian Lorenzo Bernini, considered by many to be the father of the baroque style of sculpture." She watched as he inserted one key into what appeared to be part of the wall of the basilica, but when he placed the palm of his hand against the wall and pushed it, a doorway appeared with a dark passage beyond it. Anita was just expecting him to produce a flaming torch from somewhere when the monsignor reached in and flicked a light switch, revealing a narrow staircase spiraling down into the bowels of the church.

"This leads to an area of the grottoes that isn't open to the public," Monsignor Carrapietti said, stepping back from the doorway and showing with his hand that Caleb and Anita should go first. "Just mind your step. The stairs are rather old and have seen better days."

Anita stepped into the doorway, shivering as a cool waft of musty air flowed over her bare arms. The stairway was lit by a series of low wattage bulbs with a cable strung between them, and she could see what the priest meant about the steps. She chose her steps carefully, and a few moments later, came out into a small room, perhaps ten square yards in total. It was lit by a single bulb dangling from the ceiling. The walls were plain plaster and followed the line of arches that supported the church above their heads, with a simple altar set against one wall. Against the opposite wall was a single wooden chair.

"This is the Capella della Santa Lancia," Monsignor Carrapietti said, as he emerged from the bottom of the staircase. He was speaking in a hushed, reverent tone. "The Chapel of the Holy Lance."

"It's not kept in the basilica itself?" Anita asked. When she had googled it on Greta's computer, the website she had been looking at said the lance was kept in an alcove in the main church above them.

"No," the priest replied. "A replica is kept there. The

genuine relic is down here, and I have the only copy of the key. As I said, this isn't open to the public."

"That might help," Caleb said, looking at Anita.

"What's this about, Caleb?" Monsignor Carrapietti said, his tone suddenly changing to one of authority. Anita saw Caleb looking at her with a hint of trepidation.

TEN MINUTES LATER, perhaps slightly longer, Anita and Caleb were standing in the chapel in an uncomfortable silence. Monsignor Carrapietti had recovered some of the color in his face he had lost when Caleb had outlined what the Weizmann Institute planned to do, and was now sitting in the chair, his hands pressed together in prayer. His lips were moving, but she couldn't hear him talking. Finally, his incantations were complete.

"This really is disturbing," Monsignor Carrapietti said. "Complete madness."

"Monsignor," Caleb said. "The Weizmann Institute either has the original Holy Lance, or they intend to steal it. You must ensure the artifact is kept secure."

"It is secure enough down here. The lance is only taken out once a year during Lent, and there are plenty of security guards when it is."

"Is there somewhere more secure? A proper vault, perhaps?"

"I will need to discuss it with the Archbishop of the basilica, but yes. I will speak to him today." Monsignor Carrapietti got to his feet, his knees making an audible cracking sound. "This will have to go all the way to the Bishop of Rome."

"How does he fit in?" Anita asked, confused by the various titles.

"The Bishop of Rome is the Pope, my dear," the priest replied. "This Weizmann Institute must be stopped."

"I have a plan for that, Monsignor," Caleb said. "Well, an outline of one."

"This needs more than one man, Brother Caleb," Monsignor Carrapietti replied with a kind smile. "Believe me, the Catholic Church has quite a number of resources."

"I can do things the church cannot, monsignor," Caleb replied, glancing at Anita as he spoke. There was a chill behind his eyes as he looked at her. "May we see the lance?"

Monsignor Carrapietti looked at Caleb in surprise. "Really? Why do you want to see it?"

"Just to get a sense of its provenance," Caleb replied. Anita nodded her head. They had come this far. It would be a shame not to be able to see what Caleb had described as such an important relic.

The priest considered Caleb's request for a moment before reaching again for his keyring. He selected a different key and crossed to the altar. Then he pulled the cloth covering it aside to reveal a small safe built into the wooden structure. When he had unlocked the safe, he reached inside and pulled out a pair of purple linen gloves. Once he had put them on his hands, he reached back in and retrieved a small cushion, also purple., with a cloth draped over it. He placed the cushion on the altar and pulled back the cloth.

Anita took a couple of steps forward to look at what was on the cushion. The tip of the lance was not much more than a fragment of metal. It was thin, and the metal was discolored with some areas of rust noticeable. The small room they were in suddenly felt a lot smaller. Was she actually looking at the lance that pierced the side of Jesus two thousand years ago?

She glanced up at Caleb, who was leaning forward, examining the lance with a frown on his face. Then, to her surprise and the monsignor's horror, his hand flashed out, and he picked it up, closing his eyes as he did so.

69

Giovanni watched as the sleek, white helicopter banked into a graceful turn over what used to be the seventeenth green and approached its landing spot. Eva was standing next to him and as the craft came in to land, her robes billowed around her legs. If he hadn't been so uptight, Giovanni would have said something humorous about it.

They had been alerted to Hugo's imminent arrival by Ruth, Hugo's assistant. She had told Giovanni on the phone that Hugo was flying in with the medical team, prompting a rapid response from Eva. Giovanni hoped that the medics didn't mind the smell of fresh paint, not that they had much choice in the matter. She had dispatched a work party to prepare the rooms for the medics. Everything was moving much more quickly than either of them had expected.

The helicopter settled into its landing site and the rotors above slowed. Hugo was obviously staying for a while, even though Ruth had said he was dropping the medical team off. He half hoped the assistant was with Hugo. Giovanni was sure that beneath Ruth's ice-like exterior, there was a salacious woman in there somewhere just waiting to be released, and one thing he did like was a challenge.

When the rotors finally stopped and the whine of the helicopter's engine faded away, the side door opened and a couple of men got out. One of them was carrying a large cylinder with a blue lid which, from the way he was struggling with it, was obviously heavy. They were followed by Hugo, but to Giovanni's mild disappointment, there was no sign of Ruth.

"Are these the medics?" Eva said as the trio walked toward them.

"They must be. I thought one of them was a nurse?"

"Men can be nurses too," Eva replied with a smile. "Believe me, they can be very caring." Her smile widened. "If you know what I mean."

Giovanni stifled a laugh as Hugo approached them.

"Brother Giovanni, Sister Eva," he said before turning to the two men with him. "May I introduce Doctor Turner and Mr. McGarry?"

The older of the two men, a good-looking man in his thirties who was obviously fond of the gym, extended a hand to Eva, barely even glancing at Giovanni.

"Sister Eva," the man said. "I'm Doctor Turner. Tom." They shook hands for longer than necessary, in Giovanni's opinion. As they grinned at each other, Giovanni looked at the container that the nurse had been carrying, which he had placed carefully on the ground with obvious relief. There was a red sticker on the side of the cylinder that read *Warning: Liquid Nitrogen.*

The introductions completed, they made their way slowly toward the complex where Bella was waiting to serve them all coffee. Giovanni had spent several very pleasant hours with the young woman the previous evening in his private suite and, while they had both remained fully clothed, he was very pleased with his progress. As they walked, he felt Hugo's hand on his arm, pulling him away from the others.

"Brother Giovanni," Hugo said when the two of them were some yards behind the rest of the group. "Where is my security detail?"

"They disappeared a couple of hours ago," Giovanni told him, remembering the two idiots' excited departure.

"Where to?" Hugo asked.

"They didn't tell me, but they seemed to be in a hurry."

Hugo frowned and mumbled something about having Ruth track them down. "I'm thinking about getting some additional security personnel on site. I want more of a presence around the perimeter. Their initial report was quite scathing."

"About what?" Giovanni replied, trying to keep the irritation from his voice. They were a religious order, not a prison.

"Relax, Brother Giovanni," Hugo said. "The two that I referred to you are both ex-policemen. The guards I'm thinking of hiring are all ex-military. Much better suited for close protection, don't you think?"

Giovanni nodded in response. He just hoped the additional personnel were more professional than the other two. One of them had irritated the hell out of Eva. It had been something about computers, but Giovanni hadn't paid the incident much heed. He was just pleased someone else was on the end of her temper for once.

"Now, tell me about the woman you have identified for the project," Hugo said. He nodded in Bella's direction. "Is that her?"

"No, that's not her. If fact, Mr. Forrester, you've already met her. She was with us for lunch during your last visit."

"Maddy?" Hugo asked, his face breaking into a broad grin. When Giovanni nodded his head, Hugo clapped his hands together. "How absolutely perfect. She'll be ideal."

"I know." Giovanni plastered a grin onto his own face. "That's exactly why I've selected her."

"She knows everything about the project?"

"Yes, everything. She considers it an honor to have been chosen," Giovanni replied as Hugo nodded his head, seemingly satisfied.

A few moments later, they were all seated in the hotel's foyer, gathered in armchairs. Giovanni had dispatched Bella to go find Maddy, and he was listening to the doctor introduce himself properly. Giovanni was bored with the man already, but Eva sat in rapt attention, hanging on every word. She seemed quite taken with the man. The nurse, by contrast, was a dour man who barely spoke at all other than to introduce himself as Stephen.

Giovanni looked up as the external door to the hotel foyer opened. It was Bella, and a few paces behind her, Maddy. Hugo got to his feet and took a few steps toward the door. Giovanni waved at Bella to show she could make herself scarce, hoping that Maddy had kept her mouth shut about the project and not talked to anyone about it.

"Maddy, my dear," Hugo said, extending his arms out to his sides in greeting. Doctor Turner and the nurse, Stephen, were also standing and Giovanni laughed as he saw Eva wincing as she too got to her feet. She had been out for a bicycle ride the previous afternoon and had been complaining about her legs and backside aching since.

"Mr. Forrester," Maddy said, clasping her hands in front of her as if she was praying. Behind her, the sunlight was shining in through the foyer doors, almost casting a halo around her head. Giovanni nodded in appreciation. He wished he'd thought of engineering that and made a mental note to recreate it in the future. Maddy looked almost angelic with the light behind her.

"She looks good, doesn't she?" Eva whispered. She had sidled up to Giovanni and was watching the scene playing out in front of them.

"She's perfect. Look at that light. It's like she's just descended from heaven." Giovanni heard Eva giggling beside him.

"We need some hallelujahs to sound or something," Eva said. Giovanni made another mental note.

"Eva, my dear," Giovanni said, taking advantage of the fact that everyone's attention was on Maddy to reach down and cup her buttock. She laughed and slapped his hand away. "We are going to make an absolute fortune out of this."

70

Hugo kept the smile fixed on his face even though inside, he was fuming. As they had been talking earlier, he had fired off a text message to Ruth, telling her to find out what the two Italian idiots thought they were doing. They were supposed to be here, protecting the young woman he was looking at, not gallivanting around Italy on some whim or another.

"Maddy, you look radiant," Hugo said, pushing the smile even higher. "Let me introduce you to your medical team. Doctor Turner and er... Nurse Stephen?"

He took a step back to allow the two medics to introduce themselves. There was another thing he wasn't happy about, and that was that the nurse was male. He'd specifically told Ruth to get a female nurse, but his assistant had told him she'd not been able to find one who would be agreeable to the arrangement. Hugo doubted that very much—everyone had a price, after all—but Ruth had been most insistent.

"How is all this going to play out, Mr. Forrester?" Hugo heard Giovanni asking him. "In terms of timelines?"

"The imperative is the impregnation," Hugo replied.

"That has to take place as soon as possible. We have the embryos already. My team has been working 24/7 since our original success, using the original DNA." Giovanni saw a slow smile appear on Hugo's face as he glanced at the container containing liquid nitrogen, but there was almost something sinister about his expression. "Nothing can stop us now."

"Embryos?" Giovanni asked. "There's more than one?"

"As a redundancy, yes. Hopefully, the first one Doctor Turner implants will be successful, but we'll keep some more going in the lab, just in case."

"I see," Giovanni replied. Hugo glanced at him, wondering if he really did. "So when should we start our, er, our campaign? To raise an army of the righteous?"

"We can talk about that later, Brother Giovanni," Hugo replied, hiding his irritation with the man. He hiked the smile further up onto his face. "Let's just enjoy this moment." He turned to look at Maddy, who was in a deep discussion with the doctor. Standing next to her was Sister Eva, listening intently, while the nurse was standing to one side, apparently not included in the conversation.

Hugo knew exactly why Giovanni was so keen to start what he called his campaign. It was simply to fill his coffers with as much cash as he could get. Hugo was no fool and neither, he realized, was Giovanni. They just had different ambitions.

What Giovanni didn't seem to have put together was that the moment Maddy was pregnant, it would cause a schism in the entire universe. Armies would gather for sure, and they wouldn't need to be mustered. The presence of a child of God would summon them from the darkness, of that Hugo was sure, even while the child was still in the womb. The return of the dark ones would be Hugo's reward for his foresight. He closed his eyes and imagined the chaos that would ensue when the Nephilim, the bastard offspring of fallen angels and human women, returned to rule the earth.

"Hugo?" Hugo's eyes snapped open at the sound of his name being called. It was Eva. She was looking at him with a concerned expression. "Are you okay? You kind of zoned out for a moment there."

"I'm fine," Hugo replied, remembering to smile.

"Do you want me to ask Tom, er, Doctor Turner, to have a quick look at you?"

"No, no," Hugo said quickly. The last thing he wanted was that quack examining him. He wasn't even a practicing doctor any more. At least, not since the incident with one of his younger patients that Hugo had paid so much to make go away. "I'm fine. I may go and lie down for a while."

"I'll walk you to your suite," Eva replied, still looking concerned.

"Very kind of you to offer, Sister Eva," Hugo said. "But I'll be absolutely fine. I do have something to ask you, though. If I may?"

"Of course, Hugo."

"Would you mind acting as an advocate for young Maddy? A chaperone, if you will. I was rather hoping for a female nurse, but..." His voice trailed away as he looked at Stephen. "For any of the more intimate procedures?"

"Absolutely, Hugo," Eva replied with a smile and a quick look in Maddy's direction. "I won't let her out of my sight." With Doctor Turner's history, Hugo thought that wasn't a bad idea at all.

He smiled at Maddy, who raised a small hand to wave at him and said he would see Sister Eva later, when he was rested. Then he made his way to his suite, passing several of the Adelphoi's congregation as he did so. They were all very polite, greeting him and standing aside so that he could pass. There seemed to be a type of follower that Giovanni appeared to be keen on. They were all young, well-dressed, and normal. Hardly the makings of an army of righteousness, Hugo thought with a touch of amusement.

Just as he arrived at his suite, he felt his cell phone buzzing in his pocket. He buzzed himself inside and reached into his pocket.

"Yes?" Hugo said, knowing it would be Ruth, hopefully with an update on the two Italians.

"Mr. Forrester," his assistant replied. She sounded flustered, which was most unlike her. "Can you talk?"

"Yes, Ruth," Hugo replied, letting the door to the suite close behind him. "Is everything okay?"

"Not really," Ruth said with a quick sigh. "Monsignor Carrapietti called. We have a problem with the relic at the Vatican City."

71

E va walked back over to the foyer to where Maddy and the doctor were still chatting. She was concerned about Hugo. He really hadn't seemed himself just now, but hopefully a rest would refresh him.

"Sister Eva," Doctor Turner said as she approached them. "I was just telling Maddy here all about the procedure." Eva looked at Maddy, who smiled in response.

"It all sounds pretty straightforward," Maddy said.

"I'll be right at your side throughout," Eva replied, prompting the nurse to finally speak.

"That won't be allowed," he said in a reedy voice. Eva looked at him sharply. What was he called again? Stephen? He was a strange-looking man in a plain shirt and trousers, with a widow's peak accentuated by the way his hair was scraped straight back over his head.

"I think it will," Eva said, forcing herself to smile. "Mr. Forrester is quite insistent that I be her chaperone."

"Of course, Sister Eva," Doctor Turner said, with an equally sharp look at the nurse. "Stephen, why don't you sort out our accommodation?" If the nurse was offended at being so summarily dismissed, he didn't show it. As the man walked off without another word, Maddy asked Eva if she could be excused, as there was a yoga session about to start that she wanted to attend. Then it was just Eva and the doctor in the foyer.

"Would you like a guided tour, Doctor Turner?" Eva said, looking at the man properly for the first time. He was, in her opinion, a very good-looking man and she wouldn't mind at all spending some more time in his company.

"Please, Sister Eva, call me Tom," he replied with an amiable smile.

"And it's just Eva." She lowered her voice to a theatrical whisper. "I'm not really a nun."

Tom laughed, tilting his head back as he did so. "I know," he said a few seconds later. "Hugo told me all about the Adelphoi."

"What's he said?" Eva asked, immediately curious.

"About how you're very good at marketing." He also lowered his voice. "Hugo was quite candid about how Brother Giovanni operates."

"Was he?" Eva was surprised, but relieved at the same time. Perhaps Hugo wasn't as devout as he made himself out to be after all. "So, what do you think of his project? He's told you about that as well, has he?"

"Yes," Tom replied, a look of mild concern appearing on his face. "I can't say I like it, but he is very generous. He's fond of saying that everyone has a price, and he certainly met mine." Eva thought about the deposit Hugo had made to their operating account, and she nodded in response.

"How do you know him?"

"He, uh, he helped me out with a slight issue I had." Tom waved his hand dismissively. "It was nothing, really. Just a misunderstanding. So, how about that tour?"

Realizing that Tom didn't want to discuss how he knew Hugo in any more detail, Eva spread out her hands.

"Well, you've already seen the foyer," she said. Then she pointed to the dining area leading off from it. "That's where we eat, obviously. Let me show you some of the facilities."

As they walked through the complex, Eva told Tom about its history as a hotel before they had acquired it. He seemed genuinely interested, and she found he was an easy man to talk to. As they walked and talked, she found herself wondering about his bedside manner. The more she talked to him, the more she liked the man.

"This used to be a business center," Eva said, as they paused at a set of double doors with portholes in them. She looked through the glass to see Maddy's yoga class under way in a large, airy room with windows looking out over the lush gardens beyond. There were perhaps fifteen people in the room, all attempting what looked to Eva like a stress position. "Do you do yoga?" she asked Tom.

"Not a chance," Tom replied, nodding at the group in the room. "If I tried that, I'd put my back out."

A while later, after Eva had shown Tom around the main parts of the complex, she led him to her office. They sat down, he in an armchair and she behind her desk. Eva glanced at the computer, remembering the argument she'd had with the security man about it. Even though she had insisted it was well protected with the latest anti-virus software, he had insisted on running some more tests on the system. Eva had let him, knowing that as the only place her various passwords existed was in her head, he wouldn't be able to access anything sensitive.

"Thank you so much for the tour," Tom said. "It's a great setup you've got here."

"It's a good center to operate from," Eva replied, wiggling

her mouse to bring the screen to life. "But most of our business is done on-line. We give thousands of people hope with every sermon Giovanni gives."

"You sell people hope," Tom said. "Wouldn't that be more accurate?"

Eva looked at him, her mouth half open. Had he really just said that?

"That's very blunt," she said, not sure what to say. Tom just smiled at her and held his hands out, palm up.

"It's true though, isn't it?" he replied. "We're both just here for the money, and the Adelphoi are going to do very well out of Hugo's little plan, if I understand it correctly. Which means so will you and Brother Giovanni. I'm guessing he's not really a brother either?"

Eva stared at Tom, amazed at how frankly he had just described their business model. Although she should be angry, she couldn't help but admire what he had said. He'd certainly cut right to the core of Giovanni's ambitions, but she wasn't about to answer that question. It was different for her. She never pretended to be a nun, but let people assume she was based on how she dressed. If they asked, she would tell them she wasn't, much like she just had told Tom, although that was for very different reasons. She didn't want him thinking she was chaste, just in case. But for Giovanni, it was totally different.

"We're cut from the same cloth, you and I, Eva," Tom said. She looked at him and the way he was smiling at her. There was no malice in his expression at all.

"How do you mean, Tom?" Eva asked, wondering what he meant.

"You and I are only here for one thing," he said, his smile widening. "It's all about the money."

72

"I just don't understand what you mean, Caleb," Anita said in frustration as they made their way back along Via Gregorio VII toward the autostrada. At least the traffic leaving Rome was better than the traffic entering the city. "How, exactly, do you know?"

"I just do, Anita," he replied with yet another shrug of his shoulders.

In the small room underneath the basilica, Caleb had grabbed the Holy Lance with his bare hand, much to the consternation of the monsignor, who had protested loudly.

"No!" the priest had shouted. "You mustn't touch it!" Anita had the feeling that if he was younger, the monsignor would have physically wrestled the relic back from Caleb. Caleb had complete ignored the priest and closed his eyes, his hand gripped so tightly around the piece of metal that his knuckles had whitened. Then, a couple of seconds later, he had dropped the lance back onto its cushion and turned to Anita.

"We need to go," Caleb had said, his eyes full of consternation. Then, with a hurried thank you to the priest, Caleb had made his way back up the stairs and out into the basilica, closely followed by Anita. It wasn't until they were outside in St. Peter's Square that he had said anything.

"That's not good enough, Caleb," Anita shouted, punching the steering wheel of the car for emphasis. If she hadn't been driving, she probably would have punched Caleb for being so infuriating. "You need to tell me what you're talking about." She glanced across at him to see his mouth opening to say something. "And if you tell me to calm down, I swear, I'll drive this car into the next bridge abutment."

Caleb closed his mouth briefly before opening it again. "I can sense things, Anita," he replied in a voice so low, she struggled to hear him.

"You can sense things?"

"Yes. It's a gift I have. Or perhaps a curse."

"You're going to have to explain that one to me, Caleb, because at the moment, you're not making a whole load of sense to me."

"Have you heard of a man called John Vianney?" Caleb asked her.

"Nope," Anita replied, pressing her lips together. Whatever Caleb was about to tell her had better be good.

"He was a Catholic priest in France in the nineteenth century and was known as the Curé d'Ars. He's a saint now. The patron saint of priests, in fact."

"What's he got to do with the Holy Lance?" Anita asked, exasperated.

"He worked in a town called Ars in France in the Dombes region and became known for many things. Obtaining money and food for his charities and orphans, supernatural knowledge of the past and future, and healing the sick."

"He sounds like a cool guy, but so what?"

Caleb took a breath, seemingly ignoring Anita's question. "After he died, he was entombed in a basilica in Ars, but before they entombed his body, they removed his heart."

"What?" Anita replied as the car swerved by a couple of feet. She'd not been expecting that. "Why on earth did they do that?"

"So that it could be venerated," Caleb said, and Anita could hear the smile in his voice. "I told you I'm not a fan of the church. I was in Nichols, Connecticut, a few years ago when his heart was on tour. The Heart of a Priest tour, they called it, although a lot of people said the Catholic Church only did it to distract from sexual abuse allegations at the time."

"Caleb, this is a fascinating story, but for the third time, so what?" Anita asked as she pulled the car to a stop at a red light. "What's this got to do with the Holy Lance?"

"I'm getting there, don't worry." Caleb paused for a few seconds before continuing. "As the reliquary passed by me, I was able to touch it. When I did..." He paused and she looked across at him to see a distant look in his eyes. "When I did, I felt them."

"Felt who?"

"I felt the thousands of people who had visited him for help." Caleb's voice was strained, tense even, as he spoke. "All those souls seeking something from him. Whether it was knowledge, forgiveness, insight, I don't know. But I could feel every single one of them." He looked back at her and his gray eyes were more intense than she'd ever seen them. "When I shook Monsignor Carrapietti's hand back at the basilica, I could sense the malignancy inside him. He's a sick man. I'm not sure if it's physical or spiritual, but he's carrying a darkness inside him that's as black as the night."

"Are you serious?" Anita asked in a whisper.

"Sometimes, when I turn a door handle, I can sense the soul of the person who last walked through it." He sighed, and the intensity behind his eyes softened slightly. "Like I said, it's both a gift and a curse in equal measure. Sometimes it's so faint it's barely there, other times it's almost too much to bear."

Anita said nothing, letting his words sink in. She had heard of something similar before, and remembered a story from back when she was a child in which people with second sight could see fairies, but what Caleb had just described was quite different.

"That sounds awful," she said, still whispering. Then she jumped as a cacophony of car horns sounded from behind her.

"The light's green," Caleb said with a smirk.

Anita put the car into gear and drove away, still trying to process what he had just said.

"Is it clairvoyance?" she asked a few seconds later. They had only made it twenty yards beyond the lights before the traffic had ground to a halt again.

"No, I don't think so," Caleb replied. "Have you seen the film *The Shining*? Or read the book?" An image of Jack Nicholson with an ax jumped into Anita's head.

"Yes," she said with a shiver. She'd not slept for days after watching that film.

"Stephen King describes it in the book far better than I can. Somewhere between clairvoyance and telepathy is the only way I can describe it."

"So that's how you know? From this sixth sense you have?"

"I wouldn't describe it as a sixth sense."

Anita turned again to Caleb, taking her hand from the steering wheel and placing it on his arm. It was almost a reflex action to see if she could sense anything from him.

"What did you sense when you picked up the Holy Lance, Caleb?" she asked.

Caleb paused before replying. When he looked at her, his eyes were full of something like, but not quite, sorrow.

"Absolutely nothing, Anita."

73

Caleb leaned back in the car and watched the Italian countryside flashing by before closing his eyes. They were finally on the autostrada, heading back at speed toward Naples.

Since his revelation to Anita, she had not asked him any of the questions he'd been expecting her to. Caleb had told a few people of his gift, or curse, in the past and only when absolutely necessary. People's reactions had varied from outright disbelief to amazement and awe. Anita, Caleb thought, was somewhere in the middle. He didn't think she disbelieved him, nor had she seemed that surprised.

From Caleb's perspective, what Anita, or anyone else for that matter, thought wasn't really relevant. Caleb knew with absolute certainty that if the piece of metal he had held in the basilica was indeed the same lance that had pierced the side of Christ, he would have known. Prior to picking it up, he'd had to steel himself for the potential overwhelming sensation that its history would cause. Quite apart from its provenance in terms of the act it was purported to have been used for two thousand years ago, the number of notable people throughout history who were alleged to have owned it was phenomenal.

From the Sasanian general Shahrbaraz who had captured Rome in the seventh century to the Latin Empire, who had sacked Constantinople in the thirteenth century, the lance had changed hands many times, almost always under the dark shadow of war. Napoleon Bonaparte was said to have been desperate to possess it, as was Adolf Hitler. Both wanted the immense power it was reputed to bestow on its owners. It certainly wasn't an exaggeration to say that people had died for it. Yet all Caleb had felt when he picked it up was the cold metal in his hand.

"So what do you think this means?" Anita asked a few moments later. "If I read the report correctly, the Weizmann Institute needs the lance to extract Jesus' DNA. The whole project hinges on that."

"I need to read the report again," Caleb replied. "Perhaps I missed something in the translation?"

"I don't think you did, Caleb," Anita said. "Have they got it already, do you think? They might have substituted the real one for the one in the basilica."

"That's definitely a possibility." Caleb thought back to what he'd sensed in the monsignor. Despite what he'd said to Anita, Caleb's perception of the priest was of a spiritual darkness, not a physical one. "Other lances are considered to be the Holy Lance. There's one in Vienna, one in Krakow. There's even one in Armenia. Perhaps the Catholic Church has been venerating the wrong relic." Caleb felt a smile creeping onto his face. "It wouldn't be the first time."

"So what's the plan?" Anita asked. "Where do we go from here?"

"We'll go back to Greta's, and then I'm going to see the Adelphoi. Maybe this guy Hugo as well."

"And do what?"

"I'll start with good old-fashioned reason and take it from there. I can be quite persuasive when I have to be."

"Caleb, they won't listen to reason," Anita replied. "You've read the reports, and I know these people. They're not going to stop just because a random preacher asks them to."

"Oh, so now I'm random?" Caleb said, grinning at her. He was trying to deflect Anita away from the fact that he had no plan. He'd gone into many situations without a plan, and they had always worked out okay. Most of the plans hadn't survived first contact with the enemy, but he would have preferred to have had something in mind. But with so many unknowns in this situation, he was going to have to do it on the fly.

"I didn't mean it like that. Didn't Greta say that Hugo was a fanatic? She made a joke about it, but he's not going to listen to reason."

"I said I'd start with reason," Caleb replied. "There're plenty of other options."

"Such as what?" Anita asked. "Maybe we should leave it up to the Catholic Church to sort out?"

"Like I said to Monsignor Carrapietti, there're things I can do that the Catholic Church can't."

"Such as what?" Anita asked again, but Caleb said nothing. He was going to stop the Adelphoi and the Weizmann Institute, and if blood was spilled in the process, then so be it.

As he returned his gaze to the countryside, Caleb started trying to put something together in his head, prompted by Anita's words. He usually went with three options when planning something like this. The first option was always to do nothing. That was only included so it could be discounted, but his process had worked in the past and he wasn't going to deviate from it now. The third option was the nuclear option. The absolute maximum response possible. In this case, it could be a tactical airstrike on the Adelphoi's center and the Weizmann Institute's lair. Or perhaps an artillery strike, carefully walked in by a spotter. But Caleb had no access to such things, so that too was discounted. He needed a middle ground, but he lacked enough intelligence to plan properly for one.

"I'll start with reconnaissance," Caleb said to Anita. "Of both locations. Time spent on reconnaissance is seldom wasted. Perhaps you and Greta could tell me about the Adelphoi's hotel complex?"

"I'm sure we can, but what do you need to know?"

"Access points, building weaknesses and flaws, any existing security measures or countermeasures," Caleb replied.

"Maybe we can't if that's what you need to know," Anita said.

"That's the sort of thing I need to know. Maybe Greta could get floor plans of both places on her computer. She seems to know her way around them pretty well." Caleb nodded, effectively agreeing with himself before continuing. "Every building has weak spots and vulnerabilities."

"What? You're going to attack them?" Anita said. To Caleb's irritation, she then started laughing. "Like a one-man army?" She glanced across at him, the skin around her eyes crinkling. "If you grew your hair back, you could pass for Keanu Reeves." Then she looked back at the road before looking at him again. "In the dark, perhaps."

Despite his irritation, Caleb laughed as well.

"One person I've never been mistaken for is Keanu Reeves, with or without the lights on," he said.

"You're kidding me," Anita said, still laughing. Then her smile faded away. "Seriously, Caleb. I don't think there's anything you're going to be able to do."

Caleb returned his gaze to the countryside. "We'll see, Anita."

"W hat sort of problem?" Hugo said, his heart sinking.

"The woman who stole the reports, and the man she picked up in the village, were at St. Peter's basilica demanding to see the Holy Lance," his assistant replied. Hugo let out a sigh of relief. He'd thought for a moment that there had been some sort of problem with procuring the relic. The most likely scenario would have been the monsignor dropping dead before Hugo could take possession of the thing. The priest hadn't looked in the best of health the last time Hugo had spoken to him in person.

"Why is that a problem?" Hugo asked.

"Because the man with the woman knows everything. He was trying to warn the monsignor and persuade him to move the lance somewhere more secure."

"But who is this man? Have we found out yet?"

"All we know is that he's called Caleb, and he's some sort of preacher." Hugo could hear Ruth rustling some papers as she spoke. "He's connected somehow to the abbot at the

Sanctuary of the Madonna della Corona monastery. That was where he and the woman gave our team the slip."

Hugo sighed. He'd thought as much from the earlier descriptions of him, but all he needed was yet another so-called man of God involved. Especially when it was a man of the wrong God as far as Hugo was concerned.

"What else do we know about this preacher?"

"Very little. The data scientists have been looking for him, but without even a last name, he's invisible to them."

"No one is invisible, Ruth," Hugo replied. "Have him found, and have him dealt with. He's in Rome, so that's a start."

"I'll try, Mr. Forrester. I'll speak to our contact at the Agenzia Informazioni e Sicurezza Esterna," Ruth said, referring to the Italian foreign intelligence services. "They might be able to track his passport. If they can get his photograph, they may find him with their facial recognition software."

"Let me know the moment they locate him," Hugo said with an exasperated sigh. "Is he still in Rome?"

"The monsignor didn't know," Ruth replied.

"I'll leave it in your capable hands, Ruth," Hugo said. "Now I need to go. I have the mother here waiting."

"What's she like?" Ruth asked. Hugo paused before replying. It was an unusual question for his assistant to ask.

"She has a womb," he replied grimly, "so she's more than adequate."

His instructions confirmed, Hugo ended the call and tossed the cell phone onto the bed. They were so close to the goal he had imagined for years. If everything went to plan, within the next few days, the embryo would be implanted.

Then the chaos could commence.

75

Anita drove on in silence, mulling over what Caleb had just said. In front of them, the distinctive outline of Mount Vesuvius with another golden sunset behind it told her they were nearly back at Greta's apartment. Once they'd got out of Rome, the rest of the journey had been swift.

Anita knew for certain that one thing Brother Giovanni would never listen to was reason. The only thing he cared about was his own satisfaction and, of course, money. No matter how good Caleb's powers of persuasion were, they wouldn't be good enough. Perhaps they should take what they had to the authorities? Anita didn't know for sure, but it sounded like what the Adelphoi and the Weizmann Institute were doing must be against the law, and they had the evidence to back it up.

"Caleb, why don't we go to the police?" she said a moment later. The more she thought about it, the more it made sense.

"Have they actually broken the law, though?" Caleb

replied after thinking about it for a few seconds. "That's a genuine question, by the way. I honestly don't know."

"They must be breaking some law or another," Anita said.

"But will the police actually do anything about it?" Caleb shrugged his shoulders. "And will they do anything in time? You saw from Greta's computer screen how much money the Adelphoi are banking. If the Italian police are like most police forces, there'll be a few bad apples who can be bought. All it takes is one of them."

Anita held up her hand to silence Caleb. What he had just said about money had triggered a thought in her head. She thought back to when they had been eating the meal that Greta had prepared for them the previous day, and the discussion they'd had about the Adelphoi's bank balance.

"What was it Greta said yesterday about a key logger?" she asked him, a rough outline of a plan forming in her head. "If she'd thought about it, she would have included a keylogger in the software she used to copy Giovanni's hard drive."

"Yes, I remember her talking about that."

"You got all embarrassed because she had to explain what a keylogger was," Anita said with a small grin.

"I wouldn't say I was embarrassed," Caleb replied. "Technology's not really my thing, that's all."

"Caleb, listen. What we could do is go up to the Adelphoi's complex for you to speak to Giovanni and Eva. But not about their plan." She saw Caleb open his mouth to say something, but she held her hand up again. "Hear me out. If you pose as a potential recruit for the Adelphoi, you could distract them long enough for me to get to his office and put the keylogger on his computer. I'll get Greta to show me how to do it."

"You'd be recognized, Anita," Caleb said when she had finished talking.

"Only if they see me," Anita replied. She was starting to get excited. This could work. "Once we've got the keylogger, Greta can get Eva's passwords. If you pretend to be a rich man wanting to make a donation, she'll take you straight to her computer to make it. I've seen her do it before." Anita waited as Caleb thought about it for a few moments. "There was a guy a few months ago. Johann, I think his name was. He turned up at lunchtime, and Giovanni and Eva hosted him for lunch. The moment they had finished, Eva took him to her office for the donation. I remember Giovanni telling me about it that evening." Giovanni had told her in bed, but Anita didn't mention that.

"So when Eva logs in, Greta's watching back in Naples to get the passwords?"

"Exactly," Anita said, her voice quickening. "Then, when you realize you've not got the correct account details with you, she'll log back out again. After that, Greta can empty their accounts." She slapped the steering wheel in excitement. "If we time the visit to coincide with a meal, then there won't be anyone else in the rest of the complex. I can just walk in and out again."

Anita drove on for several minutes, Caleb sitting silently beside her. Eventually, he broke the silence, but it was only to tell her to get off the autostrada at the next exit. When they had passed through the toll at the exit, he finally spoke.

"Okay," he said, to Anita's delight. "It needs a bit of refining, but it could work."

Anita grinned to herself as they made their way through the streets of Naples and back to Greta's apartment. The city was slowly transitioning from day into night, and she saw people making their way home from work as others ventured out for the evening. She envied the younger people she saw, all dressed up for a night out with their faces full of hope for an enjoyable evening. Life had been so much simpler when she had been that age.

As she drove, they discussed various options for what Caleb called the forthcoming operation. She was excited at the prospect of striking back at the Adelphoi. There was a lot they didn't know which could derail their plan. One of these was a potential limit on the size of bank transfers, but Anita was sure the Adelphoi used Swiss banks. Surely, she said to Caleb, they wouldn't have a limit on transfers? They had agreed to see which bank was being used when they got to Greta's apartment and do some more research.

When they finally reached Greta's apartment, Anita parked the car in the allocated parking bay.

"I'll fill it up with gas later," Anita said as she blipped the lock. Then she made her way to Greta's apartment door. When she got there, to her surprise, the door was slightly ajar.

"Hey, Greta?" Anita said as she pushed the door open. Followed by Caleb, she made her way into the hallway of the apartment.

The next thing she knew, Caleb had put his hands on her shoulders, gripping them so tightly it hurt, and shoved her hard into the bathroom door. Anita shouted at him, but he shoved her again, using both hands to send her flying into the room.

"Stay there," Caleb hissed at her through gritted teeth.

76

Caleb ducked down before he scurried out of the bathroom, just as he heard a noise from the kitchen. Moving as stealthily as he could, he made his way toward the kitchen door, seeing it slowly opening as he approached. He looked up to see a black tube emerging through the gap. It was a silencer.

Caleb waited until the tube had been followed by the pistol it was attached to. The moment he saw the hand holding the weapon, he reached up and grabbed the door handle, pulling it toward him as hard as he could. The door caught the wrist of the man holding the weapon, but Caleb hadn't been able to get enough momentum into the move to force the weapon to be dropped, which was his initial intention. Instead, he leaped to his feet and shoulder barged the door to open it in the opposite direction. Caleb felt a satisfying, crumping sensation through his shoulder. Then he grabbed the edge of the door to repeat the same motion, but this time the door flew open, unopposed.

Inside the kitchen, standing a yard behind the door, was a man wearing a gray suit holding the pistol down by his side. He looked dazed, but wasn't so disorientated that he couldn't block the punch Caleb threw at his head with his free arm. The man tried to shove Caleb away from him to get enough space to raise the weapon, but Caleb had used the momentum of the punch to get close to the man. A gun was only any good if you could actually point it, and Caleb used the small size of the kitchen to his advantage. He grabbed the wrist holding the gun and brought his other hand up sharply to slap him in the temple, aiming for the point where four different bones in the skull fused together. When delivered correctly, a blow such as this was incredibly disorientating, but the gunman moved his head a split second before Caleb's palm impacted. Caleb registered he had missed his target, but he wasn't overly concerned. No man likes being slapped around the face in a fight.

With the hand holding the man's wrist, Caleb tried to maneuver his own hand to the front. Then he brought his other hand down, his palm still stinging, in an attempt to fold his wrist inwards, forcing him to drop the weapon. But the man he was fighting was aware of Caleb's intent and pivoted to stop Caleb from grabbing his wrist the way he wanted to. Both men lurched around the kitchen, moving the table and knocking over a chair as they did so. The gun man jabbed Caleb in the lower ribcage with the point of his elbow, causing a sharp exhalation of breath. It also forced Caleb to relax his grip on the man's wrist slightly, and with a roar, the gunman pushed Caleb away, forcing him into the door to the den, which flew open with a crash. Caleb spun around to get out of the doorway as the gunman started to raise the hand holding the silenced pistol.

As Caleb pivoted, time seemed to slow down when he took in the scene in the den. Greta was sitting on her sofa, her head resting on the backrest as if she was sleeping. The hands which had caressed him the previous night were laid in her lap, and he saw several of the fingernails that had dug into his back were broken. In the center of her forehead was a perfectly round black circle. No blood, just tattooing on the skin around the hole. An execution shot from close range.

The sight gave Caleb an instant boost. The outcome of the fight had just been clarified. One of them was going to die, and it wasn't going to be him.

Caleb's hand flashed up and connected with the silencer just as the gunman pulled the trigger. There was a sound like a heavy book being slapped down on a table, and Caleb felt a fiery blast of air rush by his ear. He drove his knee up into the gunman's groin and, when the man doubled over, Caleb brought his hand up to his face. He slid his index finger into the man's mouth, careful to avoid his teeth, and pulled as hard as he could to twist his neck around. Done well, this move could snap the neck, but Caleb didn't have the momentum to do that. When he had pulled the gunman upright, Caleb drew his head back and head-butted him in the nose. There was a crunching sound, and the man took a few steps back, blood starting to pour from both nostrils. The hand holding the gun was wavering by his side.

Caleb took a step forward and raised his right leg, driving his heel forward with all his weight behind it. His foot hit the man just below the diaphragm, a couple of inches below where Caleb would have preferred it to land, but the jeans he was wearing hadn't helped. Regardless, the strike had the desired effect. The man dropped the pistol, which clattered to the floor and took several staggering steps back, butting up against the doors leading to the balcony which flew open, letting a chilly breeze into the kitchen.

The cold air did nothing to dissipate Caleb's rage. His

hand flew out to the knife block, and he whipped out the knife that Greta had watched him sharpen. He flipped it round, so he was holding it point first and he drew his hand back over his shoulder.

"Whoever sheds the blood of man, by man shall his blood be shed," Caleb said through gritted teeth as he threw the knife. It pivoted, end over end, until it hit the man in the throat, almost disappearing into the soft flesh of his neck. The man stumbled back onto the balcony, his eyes wide and uncomprehending. When the back of his thighs reached the balcony railing, Caleb watched as he tumbled over the iron-work and disappeared from sight. A second or two later, there was a muffled thud. "It's from Genesis, chapter five."

He returned to the den to see Greta's body. By her desk, he could see her computer with the side of the case removed. He didn't need to look at it any closer to know that the hard drive was gone, and the thumb drive in the back would also be missing. That was what the man he had just killed had come for. Caleb kneeled in front of Greta and took one of her lifeless hands, but there was nothing there. Greta—and her soul—had gone.

Caleb closed his eyes and offered a prayer that she was at peace. Then he got to his feet and walked back into the kitchen. He approached the balcony doors and leaned over, ducking his head back instantly as a series of shots impacted the wooden frame surrounding the door. He dropped to the floor, inching forward to see into the front yard. A few seconds later, he saw a gray suited figure running from the yard and, a few seconds after that, heard the screech of tires.

77

Anita remained where she was in the bathroom, crouched down and listening to the sounds of a scuffle in Greta's apartment. She flinched when she heard a muffled bang, putting her head in her hands as if it would offer her any protection. Two, perhaps three, minutes later, the bathroom door opened and Caleb looked in. At first glance, he seemed flustered and slightly out of breath, but when she looked at him more closely, she could see there was more to his appearance. Anita wasn't sure what the expression was. He was holding one hand to his flank, had a pistol in the other, and the beginnings of a bruise forming on his forehead.

"Are you okay?" she asked with a gasp. "What's going on?"

"Anita, we need to leave," he said, his tone stern and insistent at the same time. "Now!"

"Why?" Anita got to her feet. "Where's Greta?"

"Greta's dead, Anita," he replied, his voice softening slightly as he spoke. Anita felt her chest constrict at his words.

"What? No!" she gasped. "What happened?"

"Later."

Caleb reached out his hand, and Anita took it, allowing herself to be led from the bathroom. She could feel tears bubbling into her eyes at the thought of Greta being dead. Caleb took her to her bedroom to get her things, and they stopped at his room for him to get the shopping bag from the previous day. Anita could see his cloth bag inside, with his robe neatly folded next to it. As Caleb reached the front door of the apartment, she pulled against his hand.

"Caleb, stop," she said with a sob. "I want to see her." She saw him hesitate for a couple of seconds.

"Quickly," he said. "But we have to go."

They made their way back to the den and Anita put her hands over her mouth as she saw the body of her friend.

"Oh, my God," she said through her fingers as tears streamed down her face. Anita realized this was the first time she'd ever seen a dead body in her life, let alone the body of a friend. But Greta had been more than a friend to Anita. She had saved her life and now, it appeared, given it for her.

"She wouldn't have felt or known anything," Caleb said in a low voice, but Anita knew he couldn't know that. Not for sure. "It would have been painless." She turned and pressed herself against him, thumping his chest with her fists as he pulled her close to him. Then he gently turned her away from the awful sight and led her back to the apartment door.

Outside the apartment, it was as if the air had changed. It felt closer, heavier somehow. They descended the steps to the front yard and when she saw a suited body lying on the ground, a dark bloodstain behind the head, Anita had to stifle a scream. It was one of the men who had been chasing them, and his head was canted at an unnatural angle.

"Oh, my God!" Anita said with a gasp. "What happened to him?"

"He got something stuck in his throat," Caleb replied.

Anita glanced at the man's body lying on the ground and saw the hilt of one of Greta's kitchen knives in the flesh of his neck.

"You killed him," she said. It was a statement, not a question. She shrugged herself away from Caleb, not wanting to be in the arms of a murderer.

"Let's go, Anita," Caleb said, his voice insistent again. "We can talk about this in the car." In the distance, Anita could hear the distinctive rise and fall of a siren. A few seconds later, it was joined by another.

TWENTY MINUTES LATER, when Caleb had determined they were far enough away from Naples, Anita pulled into a roadside cafe. As they had descended the side of the mountain, two police cars with determined-looking officers inside screamed past them and toward Greta's apartment.

Caleb had said very little during the journey, and neither had Anita. She didn't know what to say. The image of Greta sitting on her sofa with a bullet hole in her forehead kept flashing into her mind. When she pushed it away, it was replaced almost immediately by an image of the man in the gray suit whom Caleb had killed. Anita pulled into a spare space in the lot outside the cafe and let out a deep sigh. She had been driving on autopilot, and could remember little of the journey.

"Anita," Caleb said in a soft voice. "We should talk."

"Coffee first," she replied, not even looking at him.

"Then we'll talk." She got out of the car, motioning to him to remain where he was.

Anita used the time buying the coffees to consider her options. There was a bit of her that wanted to tell Caleb to get out of the car and for her to just drive away and leave him. Should she report him to the police? He had, after all, killed a man in cold blood. For a split second, she even considered whether it had been Caleb who had killed Greta, but the instant that thought appeared, it disappeared. But he had been holding the gun that had been used to kill her. If she went to the police, they would surely arrest him for her murder? That wasn't going to help bring whoever had killed Greta to justice. If anything, it would stop justice being done if the police were fixated on Caleb, as they surely would be.

It wasn't until she was sitting back in the car with Caleb that she felt the first vestiges of grief start to prick at her conscience. Greta was dead.

"What do we do, Caleb?" Anita asked, choking back a sob. "What do we do now?"

When he looked at her, Anita could see a steely determination in his gray eyes.

"I'm going to continue as planned and visit the Adelphoi. What I do when I get there might be different, but I'm still going." Caleb continued looking at her, the intensity in his eyes seeming to deepen. "I need a car."

"We're in a car," Anita replied flatly.

"I mean, one I can drive."

"No, I'm coming with you. Greta was my friend, too."

"I want to find whoever it was that sent those men to Greta's apartment," Caleb said. "And when I find them, it won't be pretty."

"I'm coming with you," Anita said again, sipping her coffee. It was bitter and so hot she almost burned her lip.

"We need to eat and sleep," Caleb said, nodding his head, "and I need to make a call or two. Let's find a motel for the night."

78

Giovanni lay back on his bed and listened to the sound of the shower in his suite. In an ideal world, he would have been in there with Bella, helping her soap and lather herself, but perhaps that would come in time. They had spent a very pleasant couple of hours that evening talking until finally she had agreed that if the test she needed to pass for full inclusion in the inner sanctum of the Adelphoi was to offer herself to Giovanni, then so be it. Giovanni grinned when he remembered the solemn expression on her face when she had finally acquiesced. She wouldn't be looking quite so solemn in a short while.

He closed his eyes and imagined the scene in the shower, feeling himself respond at the thought. Bella was no innocent, but a few fumbles with teenagers who didn't know what they were doing was very different to what he had planned for her. Orgasms were, he had told her, a gift from God Himself. Giovanni had also told her that by providing him with that gift, or preferably several of them, Bella would be doing the Lord's work. The way she had nodded in agreement was just sublime.

Giovanni's thoughts were interrupted by a loud knock on the door of his suite. He tutted in annoyance and got to his feet. Giovanni was just rearranging his clothing to hide his anticipation when whoever it was knocked again, louder this time.

"I'm busy," he said, crossing to the door but not opening it. "Who is it?"

"Giovanni, it's me," Eva's voice replied. "I need to speak to you."

"Now's really not the time, Eva," Giovanni said, lowering his voice as he heard the shower being shut off. "Like I said, I'm busy." He saw the door handle moving and realized Eva was trying to get into the suite.

"We need to speak to Hugo," Eva replied. Giovanni could hear the desperation in her voice. "There's a problem."

Giovanni swore under his breath and unlocked the door. When he opened it, he was surprised at the look on Eva's face. She looked more than flustered. If anything, she looked scared. "What sort of problem?"

"It's the woman, Anita," Eva said. "Your goons have found her and retrieved the material she stole."

"So, what's the problem?" Giovanni asked, glancing over his shoulder at the bathroom door. Any moment now, Bella was going to appear and the last person he wanted to be here for that event was Eva.

"One of them died in the process," Eva replied. "And do you remember Greta?" Giovanni nodded in response. Of course he remembered Greta. "Well, she's dead too. There was some sort of struggle, apparently. This has to stop, Giovanni. People are dying." Giovanni could sense the tension coming off her in waves.

Behind him, Giovanni heard the bathroom door open. He turned to see Bella standing in the doorway, wearing an almost see-through negligee he had picked out for her. It was satin with lace trim, was colored a pale mulberry pink color, and suited her perfectly as he'd known it would.

"Bella, I'm so sorry," Eva said before Giovanni could respond. "Brother Giovanni's been called away on urgent business. Why don't you get dressed and go back to your room?"

"But what about the gifts?" Bella asked, looking at Giovanni as she spoke. Yes, he thought. What about my gifts?

"Another time," Eva replied with a sideways look at Giovanni. She grabbed his arm and pulled him out into the corridor. "You still peddling that old line?" Eva whispered as the door closed behind them.

"You're one to talk," Giovanni shot back, knowing he was being petulant. "Have you given Doctor Turner your *I'm not really a nun, but I can pretend to be one if you want* routine yet?"

"Oh, shut up, Giovanni," Eva said.

"You've been inseparable since he got here," Giovanni replied. What he said was true. Giovanni hadn't been so caught up in his preparations for Bella's inauguration that he hadn't noticed Eva and the doctor becoming as thick as thieves over the previous couple of hours as she had moved out of her suite to make room for Maddy.

"No, Giovanni, I haven't," Eva said as she walked along the corridor, pulling Giovanni along with her. "We've been talking while he was helping me move my stuff, that's all. Tom's as concerned about all of this as I am. He doesn't know about the security guard or Greta, or the couple on the moped, though."

"So what's he concerned about? He's being paid, isn't he?"

"Hugo wants to do the procedure with Maddy now," Eva replied, ignoring Giovanni's question. "He says the time is right and it must be done this evening, and he wants you at his side while it's being done."

"What for?" Giovanni asked, finally realizing that he probably wouldn't be receiving any gifts from Bella that evening.

"I don't know. To pray, probably." Eva looked at him, and he could see that she wasn't just scared. She was angry as well. "You think you can manage that?"

79

Eva looked down at Maddy lying on the bed that, until recently, had belonged to her. It could have been the size of the bed, but she looked so small on it, and the hospital gown she was wearing made her look even more vulnerable.

"Are you okay, Maddy?" Eva asked as Doctor Turner turned his back on Maddy so he could prepare a syringe without her seeing. She took Maddy's hand, careful to avoid the small cannula in the back of it. It was just the three of them in the suite. The nurse, Stephen, had been dispatched earlier that evening after Maddy had taken a dislike to him and asked Hugo if Eva could help the doctor with the procedure instead. At first, Hugo hadn't been keen on the idea, but Maddy's perfectly timed tears had sealed the deal.

"I don't trust him," Maddy had said. "I don't think he's a true believer, Mr. Forrester." Eva's role, apart from being the one who had persuaded Maddy to dislike Stephen in the first place, had been to pull Hugo aside and mention the medical training she'd had previously. If Hugo saw through the lie, he didn't show it. There was definitely something creepy about the nurse, and Eva had been pleased to see the back of the man. From the look he'd given her as he'd left the suite, Eva was going to have to watch her back if he remained with them for the next nine months.

"So, Maddy," Doctor Turner said. "I'm going to give you something that'll make you very sleepy through the needle in the back of your hand." Eva squeezed Maddy's hand to reassure her. On the floor beside the bed was the cylinder containing the embryo frozen in liquid nitrogen, as well as a small tray with the implements Tom would need to use. There was a speculum which had made Maddy wince when she had first seen it, as well as a slim catheter that would be used for the actual implantation. "When you wake up, everything will be over."

"Will it hurt?" Maddy asked, and her tone reminded Eva again how young she was.

"No, no," Tom replied with a genial smile. "It won't hurt at all. It's a really simple procedure, and you won't remember anything about it. One of the advantages of the medicine I'm going to give you is that it also wipes your memory."

"How long will I have to wait until I know it's worked?"

"A couple of weeks, generally speaking."

Maddy looked up at Eva and smiled at her. "I think I'll know straight away," Maddy said. "I think I'll be able to tell."

"Perhaps," Eva replied, unsure quite what to say.

As Tom fussed around with his equipment, humming as he did so, Eva thought back to the argument that Hugo and Giovanni had had an hour previously. Giovanni, no doubt spurred on by a bad case of blue balls, had reacted badly to Hugo's assertion that the situation they found themselves in was his fault. He'd gone on the offensive, denying that he'd done anything wrong. Hugo, in contrast, had remained quiet and composed, but Eva could see in his eyes how furious he was. And with good reason, in Eva's opinion. If Giovanni had been more careful about where he sowed his wild oats, Anita wouldn't have had the opportunity to steal the material in the first place. Hugo knew none of this, of course, simply that Anita had stolen from them.

What was really bothering Eva was Giovanni himself, though. The sight of Bella emerging from the bathroom was one contributory factor. Like Maddy, she was an adult but at the same time, a young and arguably impressionable one. To see her there dressed up for Giovanni had affected Eva more than she thought it would. But what really irritated Eva was Giovanni's reaction to the death of Greta. A woman who, like so many others, had shared his bed for a time. It wasn't his reaction to the news, though. It was his complete lack of one. Eva might have just told him that his car had a punctured tire for all he appeared to care.

Eva watched as Tom raised the syringe in his hand, flicking at it with his index finger to dispel an air bubble. Then he turned to Maddy and smiled at her again.

"Are you ready, Maddy?" he said in a soft voice. Eva saw Maddy nodding in agreement, shuffling on the bed to make herself comfortable. Tom connected the syringe to the cannula and started depressing it.

"You'll stay, won't you, Sister Eva?" Maddy said, her voice again like a child's.

"Of course I will," Eva replied as Maddy's eyelids started to flutter and the faint smile on her face began to fade away. A few seconds later, she was out for the count.

"Okay, Sister Eva," Tom said, glancing at the liquid nitrogen cylinder on the floor next to the bed. "It's show-time, I think."

80

Hugo lifted his hand and used the remote control to silence the television in his suite, leaving the news playing in the background. There had just been a soft tap at the suite door, and he'd asked Giovanni to open it. When Giovanni pulled the door open, he saw Doctor Turner standing outside.

"Doctor Turner, do come in," Hugo said with a brief smile, talking across Giovanni as he did so. Hopefully, the doctor was here with some good news. To his relief, Doctor Turner got straight to the point as he walked into the room.

"Everything went well, Mr. Forrester," the medic said with a broad smile.

"Excellent, excellent," Hugo said, returning the smile. "And the patient is doing okay?"

"She's resting with Sister Eva looking after her. Now we just need to be patient."

"Would you like a drink?" Hugo nodded to his desk, where a bottle of single malt and several crystal tumblers were waiting.

"You know, I think I will," Doctor Turner replied. "Thank you. It's been a long day."

"Brother Giovanni?" Hugo didn't want to offer the man a drink, but manners were manners. Giovanni had spent the previous thirty minutes trying to persuade Hugo that everything would be fine now that they had retrieved what had been stolen, but Hugo remained far from convinced. If anything, Giovanni was much stupider than he'd given him credit for if he really believed that.

"Not for me. Thank you, Mr. Forrester," Giovanni replied, obviously desperate to get away from Hugo. "I may go and see Maddy and Sister Eva if that's okay with Doctor Turner?" Hugo said nothing, but just nodded his head in agreement. Without another word, Giovanni left and Hugo felt the mood in the room lighten considerably.

Hugo poured both himself and the doctor a generous measure of malt, more than he would normally pour for a member of staff, but this was a monumental moment. He gestured to the two comfortable armchairs, and they sat down facing each other. Hugo raised his glass in a mock salute.

"What shall we drink to, Mr. Forrester?" Doctor Turner asked.

"To the future, Doctor Turner." Hugo watched as the doctor raised his own tumbler. For a horrible moment, he thought the other man was actually going to chink his glass against his, but to his relief, he didn't. That really would have been most crass.

"Mr. Forrester, do you want me to have Stephen replaced?" Doctor Turner asked a moment later. "It'll be a lot easier now that the procedure has been done. Much more straightforward."

"Yes, I think so," Hugo said, thinking for a moment. He'd

been mulling over his argument with Giovanni earlier in the evening, and the nurse wasn't the only thing he was considering replacing. "I'll make the arrangements."

Hugo realized that because he had offered the other man a drink, he was now going to have to engage him with small talk until he'd finished it. Regretting his generosity, he asked Doctor Turner to remind him what the next steps would be, even though he knew them inside and out. As the doctor talked through the stages of Maddy's forthcoming pregnancy, Hugo's mind drifted to what else would happen next. He closed his eyes briefly, imagining the deep rift that Maddy's pregnancy would cause.

When it would become apparent, Hugo was unsure. A small part of him had thought that perhaps the first sign would be at the moment of conception, but that wasn't what was taught in the scriptures he had read. It would be at the moment of birth that the schism would form properly and all hell would break loose, both figuratively and literally. Hugo allowed himself a small smile at the thought. There would be signs, of course, but no one would recognize them for what they were.

Hugo's smile broadened as he realized that, apart from him, none of the people he was with currently had more than around nine months to live. If anything, they would be among the first to be taken to hell. Would they have all been so keen on the project if they had known that?

"Are you okay, Mr. Forrester?" Hugo heard Doctor Turner ask.

"I'm fine, thank you," Hugo replied, blinking.

"I noticed you seemed a little distracted earlier on, in the foyer. When was your last medical exam, if you don't mind me asking?"

Hugo frowned and took a large sip of his single malt,

hoping the doctor would get the message and do the same thing. He knew Doctor Turner was only doing his job, but the truth was, Hugo did mind him asking.

"I'm fine, Doctor Turner, but thank you for asking. I'm just tired, that's all."

Five, perhaps ten minutes later, to Hugo's relief, Doctor Turner finished his drink and said good night. The two men shook hands and finally, Hugo was alone with his thoughts. He opened up his laptop and browsed to the scripture he was looking for. A moment later, he had found it in the book of Revelation. It described what he had just started by recreating the Son of God. Because before the child was born, something else would happen.

"The great dragon was hurled down—that ancient serpent called the devil, or Satan, who leads the whole world astray. He was hurled to the earth, and his angels with him." Hugo closed his eyes and smiled.

Some of the serpent's angels were already here.

A nita tossed and turned on the uncomfortable bed. She and Caleb were in a cheap motel next to the autostrada just outside Naples. Not for the first time, she regretted stopping at the first place they had come to, but Caleb had been quite insistent. As the first rays of the dawn lightened the curtains, she decided to get up and find some coffee for her and Caleb.

When she reached the foyer of the motel several moments later, the elderly man who had checked them in the previous evening was nowhere to be seen. It wasn't the sort of place that had twenty-four-hour service, and he was probably sleeping behind the blinds that shuttered off the office. Anita walked across the deserted foyer, which was eerily quiet, and pulled open the door to the motel. She shivered as a sharp gust of wind blew through the open door before wrinkling her nose at the sulfurous smell that came with it.

Anita stepped out into the parking lot and then stopped dead in her tracks. Greta's car had disappeared. There were only four cars in the lot, and none of them were hers.

"What the...?" Anita mumbled. Had it been stolen?

She was just trying to work out what to do when the hazard lights of the car closest to her, a nondescript black Audi sedan with local license plates, blipped into life. The flashes were accompanied by two short beeps of the horn. Anita jumped in response, pressing her hand to her sternum as she did so.

"Good morning," she heard Caleb say from behind her. "Sorry, I didn't mean to startle you."

Anita whirled round to face him, her hand still pressed to her chest.

"Oh my, that made me jump," she said, gasping in relief. "Where's Greta's car gone?" She glanced at the key fob in Caleb's hand. "And where did this one come from?"

"Brother Antonio dropped it off last night," Caleb replied, "along with some supplies that are in the trunk. He took Greta's car away with him."

"But why?" Anita asked, momentarily confused. They'd not really talked about what they were going to do with Greta's car, but it wasn't Caleb's to just give away.

"The Italian police will have it on their watch list," Caleb said. "Those police cars we passed will have the license plate on their dash cams. Brother Antonio has taken it to a place where it can be sanitized before being put to good use."

"Right, I guess that makes sense," Anita replied after thinking about what Caleb had just said. "I was going to grab some coffee."

"Excellent idea," Caleb said, taking a few steps toward the car. Anita followed him, peering into the car through the driver's window. When she saw the automatic transmission, she laughed. "So, you're driving, I take it?"

"Why don't we head north?" Caleb replied. "We can grab

some coffee on the way. It's going to take us most of the day to get to the Adelphoi."

A few moments later, Anita was sitting in the plush leather passenger seat as Caleb drove through the almost deserted streets. It hadn't taken them long to retrieve their belongings from the motel, and they had glimpsed the elderly man behind the reception desk. He had just grunted at them when they deposited the keys to the rooms on his desk, and Anita had laughed, telling Caleb that they weren't the only ones that needed coffee.

The car was comfortable with leather seats and a built-in sat-nav that was suggesting the closest coffee shop that was open was only a couple of miles away. Outside the car, the air looked almost dense and the sulfur smell was still apparent. She leaned forward to turn the radio on, navigating to a news channel. It was just before seven in the morning and when she heard the announcement that the news headlines were imminent, she turned up the volume slightly.

"Are there any stations in English?" Caleb asked.

"Nope, sorry," Anita replied. "I'll translate for you, though. Don't worry."

Anita listened to the news headlines. The lead story was from an observatory on the slopes of Mount Vesuvius where scientists were, apparently, becoming increasingly concerned about seismic activity in the area. The female newscaster went on to explain that a vent had opened up in the side of the mountain and was emitting clouds of sulfur. That explained the smell, at least, Anita thought as the woman reassured listeners that the volcano wasn't about to erupt and there was no need to panic. But from the amount of traffic on the roads, quite a few people had decided to do exactly that. Every other car had a roof rack laden with belongings.

"What's going on?" Caleb asked when the news gave way to music.

"Mount Vesuvius is rumbling," Anita replied, pointing at a car with a family in it, the vehicle weighed down with suitcases. "It looks like a lot of people are getting away, just in case."

Caleb nodded in reply, looking at the car. "I don't blame them," he said.

"Caleb, you've still not told me what we're actually going to do when we get to the Adelphoi."

"I have," he replied. "We're going to plant a keylogger in one of their computers, just as you suggested."

"But we don't have a keylogger," Anita said. "We were going to ask Greta to get one." A lump formed in her throat as she mentioned her friend's name. "It's not as if she can get one for us now, is it?"

"There'll be a thumb drive in the trunk with one on it. Brother Antonio said, all you need to do is put it into a USB slot and turn the computer on. The software will do the rest."

"How does a monk get hold of something like that?" Anita asked, her voice incredulous.

Caleb just smiled at her. "Brother Antonio is an extremely resourceful man. He's very well connected." His smile turned into a grin as he glanced across at her. "For a monk." He turned the indicator on and slowed as the coffee shop appeared ahead of them. "Let's get some supplies. We've got a long day ahead of us."

Caleb rolled his head from side to side to ease the ache in his neck. They had been driving for several hours and, apart from a brief stop for lunch and a restroom break, hadn't stopped. They had driven past Verona some time ago and the signs at the side of the autostrada were all for various activities and attractions near Lake Garda. A few hours previously, Anita had offered to swap places so she could take a turn at the wheel, but Caleb had told her he was happy to continue. He didn't drive that much and was enjoying the experience to an extent. As he drove, he rehearsed in his head how he was going to handle the conversation with Brother Giovanni. The most important thing would be for him to keep his cool and not let what the man had done to Anita and Greta before her get under his skin.

"Can I ask you something?" Anita said a moment later.

"Sure," Caleb replied. "Fire away."

"That man back at Greta's apartment?"

"What of him?" Caleb asked, his mood instantly darkening.

"Did you have to kill him?"

Caleb thought for a moment before replying. "Yes," he said. "It was him or me."

Anita was silent for a while, and Caleb knew she was thinking about the best way to ask her next question. He was tempted to continue speaking, but decided to let her lead the conversation for the time being.

"But doesn't it say in the Bible that you shouldn't kill people?" she asked a moment later. "Isn't it one of your ten commandments?"

"Exodus, chapter twenty," Caleb replied, nodding his head. "It's also in Deuteronomy. But it doesn't say you shouldn't kill people. It says you shouldn't murder them."

"There's a difference?"

"To murder is to kill someone intentionally and with malice." Caleb was choosing his words carefully, not wanting to come across as condescending. "Greta was murdered. She didn't have to die. He could have just taken what she had and left without killing her." He kept his eyes firmly on the road ahead of him, thinking about what to say next. "Taking the life of a murderer is not something I'm going to lose any sleep over."

Anita didn't reply, and Caleb wondered if he'd been too glib with his response. He'd wanted to tell her she shouldn't lose any sleep over it either, but decided against it. Eventually, he heard Anita take a deep breath.

"Well, this might be the wrong thing to say, but I'm pleased he's dead."

He glanced across at her to see a single tear making its way down her cheek. If he hadn't been driving, he would have wiped it away.

"That's not the wrong thing to say at all, Anita," Caleb

replied. "He chose the path to go down. I just helped him along it."

"I hope he burns in hell," Anita said with a note of finality in her voice as she brushed the tear away with the back of her hand. She turned to look out of the passenger window, and Caleb knew the conversation was done.

A few moments later, Anita turned the radio back on, mumbling about seeing whether Mount Vesuvius had erupted yet. When the music that had been playing finished, Caleb heard the same newscaster as before, speaking rapid-fire Italian. He heard Anita take a sharp intake of breath, causing him to look over at her in concern.

"What is it?" he asked, but she held up a hand to silence him so she could listen to the newscaster.

"It's the Adelphoi," Anita said quickly as the newscaster drew a hurried breath. "They're on the news." She held her hand up again as the woman on the radio continued. Caleb tried to listen to the report to see if he could discern any words, but she was speaking way too fast.

"What did the report say?" Caleb asked when Anita turned to look at him after turning the radio down. She summarized the story as best she could.

"She said that a law firm in Naples sent some documents to the Agenzia Nazionale Stampa Associata. They're one of the main news agencies in Italy. The documents describe how the Adelphoi are attempting to recreate a human being using reconstituted DNA, and that they're fleecing people of millions of euros. Incontrovertible proof is the phrase she used. Greta was mentioned as well."

"What did they say about Greta?" Caleb asked.

"That she gave the documents to the law firm before she was murdered."

"She must have left copies of the reports you took from

the Adelphoi with the law firm as a fail-safe," Caleb said, remembering Greta's comment about visiting a law firm from the previous day. He glanced down at the sat-nav but couldn't see where their estimated time of arrival was. "Can you look on the sat-nav to see how long it's going to take to get to the Adelphoi? We're going to have to change our plan."

He waited as Anita fiddled with the sat-nav. "Just under an hour," she said a moment later.

Caleb responded by pressing down on the accelerator, the car responding instantly.

"We might not have that long," he said.

"What are we going to do?" Anita asked, the tension in her voice obvious. "The news report said the agency was passing the documents over to the Italian authorities. The police will be on their way soon."

"It'll take the authorities a while to put it all together," Caleb said. "They'll want to be sure they've got everything in order before they act, and then it'll take them a while to put a response together." His mind drifted back to Waco and what happened there. Even though that was back in the United States, Caleb knew that the police would be reluctant to mount a raid on a religious establishment.

"It didn't take the media that long to put it together," Anita replied. "I don't think it'll take the police long at all." Caleb saw her pressing her lips together in a firm line. "They're going to run." His response was to press even further on the accelerator before he replied.

"Then we'll need to stop them."

83

Anita's hand dropped to her seatbelt to make sure it was properly secured as Caleb gunned the engine. She glanced at the speedometer to see they were doing over one hundred and ten miles an hour, but the engine noise had barely increased inside the cabin of the car. Caleb had the car in the fast lane of the autostrada. His hands were gripped tightly on the steering wheel, almost exactly at the ten to two position she remembered from when she was learning to drive, and his gaze was fixed on the road in front of them. She wanted to talk to him and ask him what they were going to do when they got to their destination, but she didn't want to distract him when he was driving so fast.

As the car flashed past a circular sign with a red border and the number one hundred and thirty, she tried to do the math in her head to work out just how far over the speed limit Caleb was driving. One kilometer was zero point six of a mile, which meant that if her sums were correct, they were doing almost one hundred and seventy kilometers an hour. The car sped under several gantries, and she remembered seeing the flashes of speed cameras built into a gantry on the opposite side of the road when they had been driving to Naples with Brother Antonio.

"Caleb, there're speed cameras in some of those gantries, I think," Anita said. "Maybe we should slow down a bit?" She didn't mind traveling at the speed they were going. The car was more than capable of it. If anything, it seemed to prefer being driven harder, and Caleb was a very competent driver. As she watched him, she could see his eyes scrutinizing the road ahead constantly. It was more about Brother Antonio getting into trouble on their account.

"Don't worry, Anita," Caleb replied, not taking his eyes off the road. "This car's currently in the long-term parking lot at the Naples-Capodichino airport." She saw him grinning. "Did I say that right?"

"You did," Anita replied.

"Someone's in for a surprise when they get back from their holiday," Caleb said, but he eased up on the gas a little to bring it back down, anyway. "But I guess there's no point drawing attention to ourselves."

Despite the sat-nav's earlier prediction of just under an hour, it was only forty minutes later when they reached the small town of Pilzone on the shores of Lake Iseo. Caleb was forced to slow down to way under the speed limit because of the traffic. They drove past a hotel called Hotel Araba Fenice with several flags fluttering in the breeze. Anita remembered eating in the restaurant at the hotel one night with Giovanni, one of the few times they had spent any time together away from the Adelphoi's complex. Next to the hotel was an ambulance station with a line of high-sided ambulances with their distinctive orange and white livery outside waiting to be washed by a man in a matching orange jump suit who was more interested in his cigarette than the vehicles waiting for him.

"Where am I going?" Caleb asked as he drove along the main drag running parallel to a train track. On their left was a marina with several boat masts clearly visible.

"We need to loop round on ourselves," Anita replied, pointing at the road ahead. "Just ahead is a place to turn round, and then we're heading down past the marina. The complex is further along the shoreline of the lake."

Caleb nodded in reply and did as instructed. The car rattled over the train tracks and, a few moments later, they were driving along a much smaller road that hugged the shoreline of the lake. The water of the lake was calm, with barely a ripple despite the breeze, and the blue sky and white clouds that were scudding across the sky were reflected on the mirror-like surface.

"Perfect day for sailing," Caleb said with a grin.

"I wouldn't know," Anita replied. She'd never even been in a canoe, much less a sailing boat. Ahead of them, the road started to lead away from the shoreline and up an incline.

"Maybe I'll take you out on the water once all this is over?" Caleb's grin broadened. "Although something with an engine might be safer."

"They're not far from here now, Caleb," Anita said as the car approached the top of the small hill they were climbing.

"Is there somewhere we can pull in to do some reconnaissance?" Caleb asked.

Anita knew there was a small parking lot at the top of the hill that overlooked the Adelphoi complex, as well as providing amazing views over the lake itself.

"Just up here by that small group of trees," she replied. "There's a lot for the tourists in the summer." She pointed down the hill where the Adelphoi's complex was located.

They were perhaps a mile away. It was close enough to make out the buildings and the layout of the old golf course, but too far away to make out much else.

A few moments later, Caleb had parked in the lot. In the summer, it would have been full, but at that time of year, there was only one other car parked. Anita saw a man throwing a ball for a very excitable Dachshund, but the dog didn't seem to have gotten the hang of actually coming back with the ball. She and Caleb got out of the car, and she waited as he fetched something from the trunk. When he returned, he was carrying a green metal case with a black handle. She saw him glance at the dog walker and then at the small group of trees.

"Come on," he said as he started walking toward the copse. "Let's hide ourselves in there."

Anita followed Caleb as he strode toward the trees, almost having to run to keep up with him. When he reached them, he dropped to his haunches and undid the metal case, pulling out what looked to Anita like some sort of video camera that he placed carefully on the ground. The next thing out was a small metal tripod, which he assembled with ease before screwing the camera-like device to the top. The last piece of equipment inside the case was a small tube that looked like a telescope.

"What it that?" Anita asked as she watched him running practiced hands over the device, checking that everything was secure.

"It's an M151," Caleb said, not taking his eyes off the equipment. "Twelve to forty times magnification with a sixty millimeter lens diameter. It's even got a laser filter unit."

"Try that in English?" Anita replied with a nervous laugh. She watched as Caleb sat on the ground, put his legs on either side of the device, and put his eye to the small tube.

"It's a spotting scope, Anita." Caleb twisted at some dials on the machine and adjusted its position by a couple of inches. "Snipers use them for target identification."

It was obvious to Anita that Caleb was familiar with the device, which intrigued her, but the way he had just spoken seemed to indicate he needed to concentrate. She sat down on the ground next to him and peered down at the Adelphoi's complex below them. There was a white helicopter outside the main building, but she was too far away to make out much else.

While she waited for Caleb to finish his assessment of the complex, Anita studied him carefully. He seemed to have slipped into another persona, one that was more determined than before. She'd seen it before, back when they were traversing the Via Ferrata to escape the gunmen.

"What can you see?" Anita asked a moment later, realizing she was whispering.

"What car does Brother Giovanni drive?" Caleb asked, his eye still glued to the scope.

"A BMW, I think," she replied. "Dark blue, if I remember right. Why?"

"Because he's just left the central building and is driving in this direction," Caleb said. She saw him lean back from the scope and look at her, the determination now more pronounced in his eyes. "Looks like he's in a hurry."

84

C aleb scrambled to his feet, almost knocking the M151 sniper scope over in the process. He steadied the device to stop it from tumbling over. At three thousand bucks a pop, Brother Antonio wouldn't be best pleased if Caleb gave it back to him with a crack in the optics. Although, as it was designed for the military, it should be able to take a few knocks.

When he'd looked through the scope at the complex below them, he'd made a rapid assessment of the situation, or at least as much as he could under the circumstances. The first unusual thing he'd noticed was the white helicopter parked close by. A man in a dark suit—the pilot, presumably—was lounging about by a small shed smoking a cigarette. Unsurprisingly, there were no obvious armaments on the aircraft. Caleb didn't think the Italian authorities would take too kindly to a civilian helicopter flying around with a chain gun mounted on it.

His gaze flicked to the main building. It was two stories high and laid out in a U shape. Presumably the accommodation was on the arms and the main communal areas at the base of the U. He could also see a deserted swimming pool and a couple of cars parked behind the complex.

Caleb took his time and examined the complex more methodically, using a grid system to work his way from left to right, up and down. He mentally divided up the area he was looking at into thirty-six squares. A six by six grid, alpha to foxtrot from left to right, and one to six from bottom to top. He had completed perhaps half of the surveillance when his eye was drawn to movement in one of the squares.

"Movement, charlie three," he mumbled to himself as he zoomed the scope to its maximum. Then, when he saw what he thought was a familiar face making its way toward one of the cars to the rear of the property, he continued mumbling. Old habits died hard. "Target acquired."

The face he was looking at, albeit in profile, matched the photographs that Greta had shown him of the so-called Brother Giovanni. Caleb zoomed back out, but could see no other movement through the scope. It looked as if wherever Giovanni was going, he was traveling unaccompanied.

Caleb broke into a run as he made his way toward the parking lot. As he approached, he blipped the locks. Caleb threw open the driver's door and reached down underneath the seat. When his hand emerged, he was clutching the pistol, still with the suppressor attached. Caleb made sure that the weapon was hidden from view of the dog walker, who was still unsuccessfully trying to persuade his sausage dog to return the ball. All Caleb could hear was the dog yapping, and the owner shouting in Italian. Caleb had never owned a dog, but he imagined the man was swearing at his companion.

"Is he running?" Anita asked when Caleb returned to the copse. To his surprise, she was sitting with her legs on either side of the scope, her eye pressed to the eyepiece.

"Sure looks that way," Caleb replied, looking down at the road leading to the Adelphoi's complex. He could see the blue BMW, perhaps halfway between their location and the buildings. Caleb had less than a minute before the car would come speeding past them. "He needs to be stopped."

Around fifty meters in front of them, the road took a sharp bend, which Giovanni would have to slow down for. After the bend, it continued in a straight line toward them. Caleb thought for a few precious seconds. If he could take out a tire when Giovanni slowed for the bend, that would stop him. But fifty meters was a hell of a distance with a pistol, especially one with a suppressor. Caleb had made similar shots on a range, but those had been with the benefit of time and a static target. This time, he had neither.

Caleb kneeled in front of Anita and then laid on his stomach. He canted his legs apart, bending his right leg to an almost ninety-degree angle. Then he shuffled his body to make himself as comfortable as he could. From the angle he was at, he could no longer see Giovanni's car, but he could see the bend in the road. When the car appeared, he would have only seconds to line up and take the shot. Caleb took a deep breath, counting to three and then releasing it slowly as he put his arms out in front of him with the pistol in his hands.

"What are you doing?" he heard Anita ask. She kneeled down next to him and he felt her hand on the small of his back. "Caleb, you can't shoot him. You mustn't!"

"When he slows for the bend, I'm going to take a tire out. He's got to be stopped." To Caleb's relief, she said nothing else.

He closed his eyes for a few seconds and concentrated on his breathing. He would have preferred more time to prepare for the shot, but he knew he would have to forgo his normal preparation for a long distance effort. It was only long distance because of the weapon, though.

As he waited, Caleb focused on the sounds he could hear. The dog was still barking, but was now further away. The distinctive raspy calling of a male mallard duck was floating over the water. And then, the sound he was waiting for. The sound of a car engine approaching.

Caleb closed one eye and aimed down the iron sights of the pistol. He had a much better weapon for the task in the trunk of the car, courtesy of Brother Antonio, but there'd not been enough time to assemble it. He focused his attention on the curve in the road, knowing that at any second, Giovanni's car was going to appear.

Then, quicker than Caleb had been expecting, the car was in his line of sight and slowing down for the bend in the road. He adjusted his aim, bringing the rear driver's tire into his aim. He had no time to adjust his breathing as he squeezed as gently as he could on the trigger.

As the pistol bucked in his hand from the recoil, Caleb saw a plume of earth rise into the air from just behind the tire.

"Damn it," Caleb whispered as he saw the tire itself was still intact.

He had missed.

85

E va stared with horror through her room window at the blue BMW making its way up the hill. She had watched, open-mouthed, as a few moments previously, Giovanni had run to the vehicle with a suitcase in his hand. He had thrown the suitcase into the rear of the car so hard that it had popped open, and she could see clothing spilling out. When he had started the car, he had driven out of the courtyard so fast that he'd left twin tracks in the surface that were so deep, she could see the earth beneath the gravel.

"Where the hell are you going?" Eva whispered to herself. She reached for her cell phone and tried to call him, but it went straight through to Giovanni's answerphone. Eva disconnected the call before the beep, not wanting to leave a message.

Her heart was hammering in her chest as she crossed to her computer. While she waited for it to boot up, she tried calling him again in case he'd been on a call, but the result was the same.

When her computer finally whirred into life, the first

thing she did was check her e-mail. As the software appeared on the screen, a few seconds later she saw a flood of e-mails coming in, all from the same Google Alerts e-mail address. A while ago, she'd set it up so that any mention of the Adelphoi on a web page, newspaper article, or other on-line source triggered an e-mail. It was a useful way of moni-toring what was being said about their organization, but as she read through the alerts on the screen, a knot of fear formed in the pit of her stomach.

The news had broken perhaps forty minutes ago and was now being picked up by both the national and the international press. Eva put her hand over her mouth as she read the headlines. Some of them were lurid, some of them were speculative, but they all had one thing in common. They were utterly devastating.

Religious cult aiming to recreate Jesus!

Thousands fleeced by false prophet!

Police investigation launched into an online Jesus cloning scam and scandal!

Many of the articles had found photographs of her and Giovanni. Not long after they had opened the complex, they had paid a publicity firm to do a photoshoot of them in the grounds. Now, as she looked at her and Giovanni's smiling faces, she started to feel sick.

"Think, Eva, think," she said to herself as she drummed her fingers on the desk. Should she do what Giovanni appeared to have done and just run? She was struggling with the fact he had departed without her. The Adelphoi was their creation. It was something they had worked so hard on for years. And he was just prepared to up and run the moment the shit hit the fan?

Eva's resolve started to harden as she considered these developments. As far as she was aware, they hadn't actually broken any laws. They'd always been very careful to err on the side of caution and not cross any legal boundaries but, at the same time, neither of them were lawyers. She got to her feet and crossed the room to grab a bottle of water from the fridge. The inside of her mouth had turned to sandpaper over the last few moments.

Nodding her head, she returned to the computer. Eva knew what she had to do, which was to hit the kill switch on their affairs. Her fingers flew across the keypad as she brought up a command-line interface and prepared to type in the command that would wipe absolutely everything. Eva paused, her index finger poised over the enter key. She knew once she pressed the button, there was no going back. Everything on their servers would be wiped, and then written over again and again until the computer was turned off and the command stopped. The software would also do some other security related countermeasures that she'd written into it for just such an eventuality, although she never thought she'd need them in a million years.

Eva grinned as she remembered one of the files that would disappear from Giovanni's so-called personal file space was called *Banking Passwords*. He would soon come crawling back to her when he realized he couldn't access the money. He should have done what she had done, which was to store them in her head. With a determined expression on her face, she stabbed the enter key.

The screen turned black and the word *Initializing* appeared, followed by some flashing periods. Eva took a sip of water as the screen started filling up with letters and digits. There was no going back now.

As she watched, Eva considered her next steps. Should she do what Giovanni had done and just flee? What would become of Maddy if she did that? Would Hugo and the

Weizman Institute take care of her? When she thought about Hugo, her heart dropped again. She'd not even considered the impact this would have on him. But as she considered it, he was big enough and rich enough to deal with any fallout.

The same might not be able to be said about the Adelphoi. From what she had read on the internet, the organization's days were numbered and, if Giovanni had indeed run and was never to return as she feared, it couldn't continue, anyway.

Eva was about to grab a suitcase of her own and start filling it with some of her belongings when there was a sharp knock at her door. Whoever it was didn't wait for her to answer, but just opened the door and walked in. It was no surprise to Eva to see Hugo standing there, his face like thunder.

"So, Sister Eva," he said, flecks of spittle flying from his mouth as he spoke. "I think we need to talk. Where's Brother Giovanni? I can't find him anywhere."

"I don't know where he is, Hugo," Eva said in as forlorn a voice as she could muster. She sensed an opportunity here, perhaps not for the future of the Adelphoi, but for her own future. When she next spoke, she even managed a small sob. "I can't believe what he's done."

86

Giovanni pulled through the bend and pressed down on the accelerator, causing the car to skid slightly on the road. He'd only had a few seconds to pack, and didn't really know what he'd thrown in the suitcase. But it didn't matter. He could just buy anything he needed. His immediate priority was to get as far away from the Adelphoi as possible. An entire world of pain was about to descend on them, and he had no plans at all to be in the vicinity.

Deep down, he'd always known a day like this would come. He had a small grab bag in his private office with a couple of alternate identities, all completely legal and aboveboard. There were a few thousand euros in there as well, and Giovanni had enough in the bank to see him through for the rest of his life, if necessary.

He was driving up an incline toward a small group of trees. Giovanni thought for a few seconds, trying to work out where the nearest autostrada was. His immediate plan was put some distance between himself and the Adelphoi's complex before the authorities arrived. From the breathless excitement that he'd heard in the news-reader's voice, he wouldn't be surprised if there was a crack squad of whatever the Italian equivalent of SWAT teams were in a helicopter bearing down on their location. The thought even made him glance at the sky to see if he could see anything, but there was nothing there.

Giovanni felt bad about leaving Eva. He'd panicked when he'd seen the news. It was as simple as that. When he got away from the complex, he could stop and call her. They could arrange to meet somewhere further away and hole up for a while to work out what they were going to do next. He wouldn't have been at all surprised if Eva had her own grab bag and alternate identities, although it was a discussion they'd never had.

He felt less bad about leaving Hugo. It was fair to say that over the previous few days, their relationship had soured. He'd seen the look of contempt in the older man's eyes frequently. It was as if now that Hugo had a mother for the child, Giovanni's role in the plan had ended, even though the project had only just begun.

He slammed his hand on the steering wheel in frustration at the thought of having to start over somewhere new. One thing was for sure—Brother Giovanni was no more. He was going to have to go back to being plain old Thomas for a while, at least until he re-grouped and came up with a new plan. Still, he reflected, despite his frustration, it had been a good run with plenty of benefits. He just needed to make sure that his new plans included easy access to similar benefits, both financial and physical.

As he had come flying out of his private suite only moments ago, he'd barreled into Maddy, knocking her to the floor. Giovanni had stopped to make sure she was okay and, as he helped her to her feet, had heard her asking if he'd seen the news.

"No, I haven't, Maddy," Giovanni had said, probably too quickly. "But I really need to go. I'm very late for a very important appointment." Maddy had frowned and opened her mouth to say something, probably to ask him with whom, but Giovanni had turned on his tail and left her standing alone in the corridor, one hand pressed to her abdomen. Giovanni pressed down on the accelerator. What happened to Maddy now wasn't his problem anymore. As far as he was concerned, he had met his side of the arrangement with Hugo and his institute. Giovanni had provided them with a suitable mother for their plan. A slow smile crept across his face as he recalled what he had called it.

"Bat-shit crazy," he whispered. Giovanni knew he sure had got that right. He accelerated harder, now only twenty yards from the small copse.

Giovanni was just beginning to laugh, both at the bat-shit phrase and the fact that he was pretty much clear of the complex when the steering wheel bucked violently in his hands. The car lurched hard to the right, and he jammed the wheel in the opposite direction. At the same time, he noticed the entire car was juddering.

"What the hell?" Giovanni said as the back of the car started to slide. He turned the wheel back again, trying to correct the slide, but the car wasn't responding as it should. The back end continued to slide out until the car was almost at a ninety-degree angle to the direction it had been traveling in. "Shit!" he shouted as he felt the car starting to roll and he looked out of the driver's window to see the small group of trees approaching fast.

Giovanni screamed as the car launched into a flip, the driver's window he had just been looking through smashing with a loud pop and showering him with fragments of glass. There was a loud bang, and he registered the airbag deploying a split second before something smashed into his face. The next few seconds were so confusing that he was completely disorientated. One second he was upside down, the next his head was slamming off the headrest, and the noise was deafening. It was a combination of metallic screeching, what sounded like explosions going off inside the car, and his own, almost unrecognizable screaming.

Then there was one final detonation, accompanied by a bone crunching sensation through his entire body, and everything went black.

87

"What do you mean, you can't believe what he's done?" Hugo asked Eva. Despite his rage, the way she spoke made him pause for a few seconds. "Apart from allowing that woman to steal the information, Giovanni's done absolutely nothing but spout hot air." He watched as Eva's mouth opened and closed. She looked like a goldfish. "Well? What exactly has he done?"

"Giovanni, er, Giovanni's disappeared," she replied eventually. "I've just seen him driving away like a man possessed."

"Where's he gone?"

"I don't know," Eva said, tears forming in her eyes. "He just left in his car. I've tried phoning him, but he's not picking up."

"The bastard," Hugo replied as he looked at Eva, who was wringing her hands in front of her. "He's just left you to deal with what's happened?" She just nodded her head and sniffed loudly before apologizing. Hugo reached into his pocket and pulled out a handkerchief. He passed it to her and waited as she blew her nose before dabbing at her eyes.

"Just keep it," Hugo said when she tried to pass it back to him. He had a collection of them, all made of jacquard cotton with hand-rolled edges, that he'd had imported from Paris, and didn't particularly want that one back.

Hugo thought for a moment about how best to proceed. None of the news reports had mentioned the involvement of the Weizmann Institute, a fact which had cost him several thousand euros in legal fire extinguishing. If any news outlet so much as mentioned the institute and an association with the Adelphoi, they would be buried with so many lawsuits they wouldn't be able to afford to print a single newspaper in the future. His primary concern was Maddy and her future, because her future was destined to change the world.

His thoughts were interrupted by his cell phone ringing in his pocket. Hugo apologized to Eva and crossed to the other side of the room to take the call. He knew it would be Ruth.

"Yes?" he said as he answered the call.

"Mr. Forrester, I've just been informed that the police are planning to raid the Adelphoi." Her voice was clipped and business-like, just as it always was. Not for the first time, Hugo wondered what it would take to actually rattle the woman. She was, in many ways, like Lot's wife in the Bible. A pillar of salt.

"When?" Hugo shot back.

"Soon. Very soon," she replied. "Hours, not days. I think you should return to the institute immediately. I've taken the liberty of telling Philip to prepare for your departure."

"Who's Philip?"

"He's your pilot, Mr. Forrester."

"Of course," Hugo replied, privately embarrassed at being caught out. "Thank you."

"There are four seats in the helicopter, Mr. Forrester.

Whom will you be bringing back with you?" Ruth asked. "I'll need to make the arrangements for accommodation."

Hugo paused for a moment to think. The helicopter had originally had eight seats, but he'd had four of them removed to give him more space in the rear of the aircraft.

"Well, me and Maddy, obviously," he replied. That left two seats. "And Doctor Turner." There was one seat left— but who should be in it? "I'll call you back in a moment, Ruth."

Hugo disconnected the call and turned to Eva. He looked at her for a moment, trying to work out her role in both the current situation and her potential role as the project moved forward. Was she really as innocent as she claimed to be? Hugo wasn't sure, but at the same time knew that Maddy would need female company at the institute. Even if she was complicit in what had happened, the woman could still be useful to him. Ruth wasn't really the maternal type.

"Sister Eva, what are your plans?" he asked her. Hugo watched as she wrung her hands in front of her again, her face full of uncertainty.

"I don't know, Hugo," she replied.

"The police are on their way," Hugo said.

"The police?" Eva gasped, pressing one hand to her chest. "Why? We've done nothing wrong."

"They'll be looking for evidence of fraud, Sister Eva."

"Brother Giovanni has been defrauding people?" Eva replied. Hugo looked at her in surprise. She had a plaintive expression on her face and her eyes were wide. "But I had no idea. It's Giovanni who does all the finances. I just look after the Adelphoi and make sure they're happy."

"I think you should come with me, Sister Eva." He looked at her with a degree of sympathy before nodding his head, his decision made. If she was lying, and he suspected she was, she was very good at it, but Eva would be useful moving forward—even if that meant there would be one more body to deal with when the time came. "Who knows what else Brother Giovanni has done without your knowledge? Perhaps it was him who leaked the information to the press, instead of the woman they're claiming it was?"

"Oh, my, do you think it could have been him?" Eva replied, a frown appearing on her face. "He seemed so happy last night. He looked like a cat who'd got the cream."

"I'm not surprised," Hugo said, mirroring Eva's expression. "I paid him the rest of the money we'd agreed on yesterday. And now today, the press knows all about the Adelphoi and he's disappeared. Do you have access to the bank accounts?'

"No," Eva said, shaking her head. "Giovanni took care of all that. He said I wouldn't understand them."

"That's why he's run, then. He's got his money and now he's left you to it. Brother Giovanni is nothing more than a fraudster. I've suspected as much for some time." Hugo sighed. "Come with me, Sister Eva. We need to leave."

"No," Eva said, shaking her head harder as a look of determination appeared on her face. "No, Hugo, my place is here with the Adelphoi. We are innocent in all of this. The police will be able to see that."

Hugo paused for a moment, wondering what else he could say to persuade her to come with him.

"Eva, please?" he said. "Please, come with me. I beseech you."

"No, Hugo," she replied. "Not now. But I will come to the institute once everything here is sorted out. I owe our followers that much. They're so young, most of them. I need to be here for them."

"As you wish, Sister Eva. But could you find Maddy for me?"

"Of course." Eva nodded her head and took a couple of steps toward the door. "Will I ask her to come to your helicopter?" As Hugo said yes, he saw a brief smile on Eva's face. "She'll be so thrilled. She told me she'd never been in a helicopter before."

"Thank you, Sister Eva," Hugo replied, fixing her with what he hoped was a friendly smile. "I'll be seeing you soon. Come to the institute as quickly as you can."

88

The moment the door had closed behind Hugo, Eva sat down on her bed with a loud sigh. Then she leaned forward and put her head between her knees for a moment, the conversation she'd just had replaying in her mind. Had Hugo fallen for what she had just said? Eva thought he had, but wasn't a hundred percent sure.

"Jesus, talk about thinking on the fly," she muttered to herself. It hadn't been her intention to blame everything on Giovanni, but as the conversation had progressed, it seemed to be the best thing to do. She could even do what she'd just told Hugo she was going to do, which was to wait at the complex for the police. By making Giovanni the villain of the piece, that would deflect attention away from herself. Whatever was in her future, she could do without the authorities breathing down her neck or looking for her, wherever she ended up. Spending the rest of her life looking over her shoulder wasn't what she had planned at all. Eva nodded as she recalled telling Hugo that only Giovanni had access to the money. That had been a stroke of genius, even though she said so herself. If she could divert all the attention onto Giovanni, then she could melt away.

Eva got to her feet and crossed the room to grab a suitcase, pleased that she hadn't done that before Hugo had walked in as she had been intending to do. It would have looked very different if, when he'd burst into her room, she'd been packing her things. She worked quickly, only packing the essentials for a brief stint on the road. As she threw clothing into the case, not bothering to fold anything, she wondered about where she could go. France was an option. Eva had heard the south of France was very nice, although she'd never been there. Monaco, perhaps? Or St. Tropez? Her French was rudimentary at best, but it wouldn't take her long to get to grips with the language.

"Bonjour," Eva said as she threw some underwear into the case. "Je m'apelle..." *Hello. My name is...* Then she paused for a moment. What was she going to call herself? She was going to have to come up with a completely new identity at some point, and get documentation for the new Eva if she wanted to travel outside the Schengen zone of European countries without border controls. Which she would need to do at some point. A couple of pairs of slacks were added to the case as Eva realized that everything she was packing would need ironing when she reached her destination. She laughed at the banality of the thought.

A few moments later, her case so full she had to sit on it to close it, Eva was done. She grabbed her laptop, even though there was now nothing on it, and its charger and put them into a large rucksack that she had bought the previous year when she and Giovanni had planned on hiking through the Alps. Then she paused for a moment to think. Did she have everything she needed?

When she had decided that she did, Eva slipped her arm

through the rucksack handle and hefted the suitcase from the floor. It was heavier than she'd realized, but as she peered out of the door to her room to make sure no one was about, she knew she would need the contents over the next few days.

Eva made her way through the complex, not encountering anyone on her way. She glanced at her watch and realized that the Adelphoi would be gathering in the main conference room for the afternoon devotional that she or Giovanni usually ran at that time of day. It would be a good opportunity to speak to them all and make sure that Maddy and Hugo were united. She sensed that all Hugo really cared about at that moment was Maddy and her baby. As she made her way through the deserted corridors, she thought about Maddy and what would happen to her. Hugo would take care of the girl, of that Eva was sure. But at the same time, she would effectively be sacrificing her to appease Hugo.

A few moments later, once she had placed the suitcase and rucksack in the trunk of her car, Eva was hurrying back through the corridors to the conference room. As she approached the room, she saw Maddy and Bella standing outside it, deep in conversation.

"Sister Eva," Maddy said as she approached them. She had a look of deep concern on her face. Bella appeared less concerned, but still confused. "What's going on? Where has Brother Giovanni gone?"

"Come into the conference room, Maddy," Eva replied. "Let me tell all of you what's happening."

"He knocked me over," Maddy said, her hand slipping to her abdomen. "He ran straight into me and sent me flying."

"Are you okay?" Eva asked, suddenly concerned. While

Giovanni's actions would help alienate Giovanni against Hugo more, she didn't want any harm to come to the girl.

"I'm fine," Maddy replied as a slight smile appeared on her face. It was one she had been wearing almost constantly since the procedure the previous day.

"Is it true?" Bella asked. Eva turned to her, wondering if Giovanni had done what he'd wanted to do with the young woman. She thought Bella had been spared that indignity, but couldn't be sure. Giovanni had a habit of escalating things slowly with the women he wanted, and Eva wanted to ask how far he'd escalated things with Bella, but it wasn't the time or place to ask. "People are saying he's run away because of the lies that the media are telling about us."

Eva looked at Bella. The young woman's face was full of uncertainty. Eva needed to know what had happened between her and Giovanni. She couldn't help herself.

"Did he touch you, Bella?" Eva asked. "Did he ask you to touch him?"

Bella's face instantly colored, and Eva knew that something had happened between them. Her anger started to rise at the thought of Giovanni manipulating the young woman for his own enjoyment. She just hoped that whatever had happened was at the lower end of Giovanni's scale.

"He said it was what God wanted me to do," Bella said in a whisper, as if she didn't want Maddy to hear.

"Brother Giovanni hasn't run because of the lies the media are telling about him," Eva said, placing her hand on Bella's forearm. "He's run because they're all true."

89

Anita shrieked as she saw the car flip onto its side and roll over. It was heading directly for her and Caleb, and her shriek was as much a warning to Caleb as a cry of horror. She stared at the car, which was only yards away, frozen to the spot. But the car hadn't even completed one full turn in the air before Caleb was on his feet, scrabbling in the dirt for purchase. In one hand was the pistol he had just used to take out the front tire of the car barreling toward them, his second shot a couple of seconds after the first hitting its mark. He used the other hand to grab the scope from the ground. He lurched toward her, using his shoulder to barge into Anita, sending her flying several yards back into the trees.

Caleb's shoulder barge knocked the wind out of Anita in a split second, ending her shriek with a rapid exhalation of air. As she flew backward, her shoulder caught on a tree trunk, sending a spasm of pain down her arm and she spun in the air before landing on her back on the ground. Then, to add insult to injury, Caleb himself landed on top of her. A split second after she hit the ground, the car impacted the tree trunks, showering them both with fragments of glass and drops of fluid. The impact was accompanied by a terrifying metallic crunch as the roof took the brunt of the impact.

"Get off me!" Anita shouted, her voice muffled by Caleb's body. He did as she asked, rolling onto his side so they were lying next to each other, staring up at the trees, which were raining leaves. "I think you just broke my arm," she said, raising her hand to her shoulder, but to her relief, any damage actually seemed minimal. The car rolled back onto its tires, shuddering as it did so. All the windows were broken, and she looked up to see Giovanni's head lolling from side to side as the vehicle settled after the collision.

"That wasn't supposed to happen," Caleb said as he lifted himself to a seated position. "Are you okay?"

"I'm fine, no thanks to you," Anita replied with a groan. She watched as Caleb got up, carefully placing the scope back down on the ground, and started walking to the car. If he hadn't knocked her off her feet, it would have hit her full on. She stood up gingerly, knowing that she owed him at least a thank you, but her diaphragm was already aching where his shoulder had smashed into it. "Is he alive?" she asked, looking at Giovanni's head.

Caleb didn't reply at first, instead reaching into the car to turn the engine off. "I think so."

She watched as Caleb grabbed the rear door handle, wrenching at it.

"What are you doing?" she asked as she lurched toward the car, one hand on her stomach. As she got closer to Giovanni, she could see his chest moving, but his eyes were closed and a rivulet of blood was running down his face from a deep gash in the side of his head. Caleb said nothing, but continued to pull at the door. Finally, with a shriek that matched the one Caleb had so rudely interrupted, it opened. Anita watched him climb inside the rear of the vehicle and place his hands on either side of Giovanni's head.

"Cos'è successo?" a male voice said. *What happened?* Anita turned to see the dog walker they had seen earlier. He had his dog tucked under one arm, and his cell phone in his hand.

"Ha perso il controllo e si è schiantato," she replied. *He lost control and crashed.* It was technically accurate. She'd just not mentioned the reason he'd lost control. Anita saw the man glance at his cell phone and shake his head, muttering about not having a signal.

"Chiamo un'ambulanza," he said as he glanced at Caleb and Giovanni. *I'll call an ambulance.* Then he turned and walked away, staring at the screen of his phone as he did so.

"Anita, listen to me," Caleb said, waiting until the dog walker was out of earshot. Anita leaned toward him so she could hear his words. "This man is a thief. A philanderer. A misogynist." She could see Caleb's knuckles whitening on either side of Giovanni's head. "He's a rapist." Caleb looked at her, his eyes full of menace.

Anita stared at Giovanni's seemingly lifeless features. She remembered how she had tried to rationalize what he did to her as being for the greater good. Looking back, Anita didn't understand how she could have been so naïve. How she had surrendered herself to his degradation, all the time thinking she was doing the right thing. Caleb was right. The man was a rapist, even if the restraint had been psychological and emotional instead of physical. He had manipulated her into a position where she couldn't knowingly consent, as he had many others before her.

"He is," she said, almost under her breath. Then she forced her voice to be stronger. "He is."

"The world would be a better place without him in it," Caleb continued. "One of the most common injuries following a rollover is damage to the cervical spine. You asked me what I was doing?"

"Yes," Anita whispered, looking over at the dog walker. He had put his dog down and was deep in conversation on the phone, complete with hand gestures even though whoever he was talking to couldn't see him.

"I'm either stabilizing his cervical spine while we wait for the ambulance," Caleb replied, his voice full of steel. "Or I'm preparing to break his neck. It would be attributed to the accident. I have a question for you."

Anita gasped, knowing what Caleb was about to ask her. Then she shook her head in disbelief.

"What, Caleb?" she asked him, anyway.

"You decide, Anita." He looked away from her and she saw him readjust his hands on Giovanni's head. "You decide."

90

Caleb closed his eyes in anticipation of Anita's response. He knew she had thought many times about how she would like Giovanni to die because she had told him as such. In her mind, she had murdered him over and over again. No, he told himself as he recalled their earlier conversation. Not murdered. Killed. Now Caleb was offering her that opportunity. It would be at his hands, but her decision.

He thought back over some of the words he had just used. Misogynist. Thief. Rapist. Giovanni was all those, and more. Had he even been complicit in Greta's death? Caleb had no way of knowing for sure, but Greta had died because of the project the Adelphoi was involved in, and the Adelphoi was Giovanni's brainchild. He'd not pulled the trigger, but he was absolutely part of it. But did he deserve to die? Caleb had killed men for lesser offenses than murder and, although they weighed heavily on his mind at times, each and every one was deserved in his opinion.

Caleb flexed his fingers slightly to make sure he had a

good grip on Giovanni's cranium, ignoring the blood that was trickling over his knuckles. Keeping his eyes closed, he offered up a short prayer for Giovanni's soul, but he wasn't to waste more than a couple of seconds of his life on that. Giovanni was still unconscious, which meant that the muscles in his neck would be relaxed and not offer any resistance. He estimated he needed somewhere between eight hundred and fifteen hundred newtons of force to fracture the cervical vertebrae, probably less. A well-thrown punch had about three thousand newtons behind it. But he didn't even need to fracture the vertebrae.

If he got the movement right, the individual discs in Giovanni's neck would criss-cross and damage his phrenic nerve. Its destruction would be followed by respiratory failure within seconds. Or perhaps the movement would induce spinal shock, impairing the nerves that controlled blood pressure and heart rate. That would be slower, but Giovanni's inability to oxygenate key organs would have the same result, albeit more slowly.

Caleb opened his eyes and looked at Anita. She was staring at Giovanni with an expression of absolute hate on her face. He couldn't just see hate, though. He could see loathing, rancor, even venom. But what Caleb couldn't see was revenge.

"No, Caleb," Anita said as she turned her eyes on him. "No. Absolutely not." She shook her head a couple of times. "That won't be my decision, and it won't be yours either."

"As you wish," Caleb replied, easing the pressure on his hands. That was what he'd been expecting Anita to say, but he'd wanted her to have the opportunity. The knowledge that she'd had Giovanni's life in her hands, or more accurately his hands, and chosen to spare it, was powerful and would serve her well. But equally, if she had decided not to spare Giovanni, Caleb wouldn't have lost a moment's sleep over taking his life.

In the distance, Caleb could hear the distinctive two-tone sound of ambulance sirens. He looked over at the dog walker who was standing up in the parking lot, presumably to show the emergency services where the accident was located once they arrived.

"Anita?" Caleb said. "Would you mind putting the scope back in the trunk? I was going to pretend to be a bird-watcher, but they don't normally use that kind of kit." He smiled at her as he spoke and was relieved to see her smiling back at him. She gathered the equipment together and set off to the lot. Caleb was watching her walk away, thinking about the determination in her voice when she'd told him not to kill Giovanni, when he felt the man move and then cough.

"What the hell?" Giovanni said, as he coughed again. "What the hell happened? Who are you?"

Caleb looked in the rear-view mirror, about the only piece of glass still intact in the car, to see Giovanni looking at him with fearful eyes.

"My name is Caleb, Brother Giovanni," Caleb said, hoping the man could hear the hatred in his voice. "And I happened to you. Are you familiar with the writing of the Apostle Paul? I'm guessing as a man of faith, you must be?" Caleb could feel Giovanni trying to move beneath his hands, but he said nothing. "Don't move. You don't want to hurt yourself. So, the Apostle Paul? Yes or no?"

"Not in detail, no," Giovanni replied through gritted teeth. "What happened to me? I need something for the pain."

"I can give you something for the pain," Caleb replied

with a grin. "In the book of Galatians, chapter six, verse seven, there's a phrase that I want you to consider for the rest of your life. It says 'God is not mocked, for whatever one sows, that he will also reap.' Or as the Hindus or Buddhists might say, karma's a bitch."

91

E va walked into the main foyer of the complex where most, if not all, of the Adelphoi were gathered. Some stood alone, some stood in small groups. There had been an excited hubbub of conversation as she entered, but it died away and she was scrutinized by every eye in the room.

"Maddy," Eva whispered, pointing to the doors leading to the garden. "Go and join Mr. Forrestor and Doctor Turner. They're going to be looking after you for a while, just until everything's sorted out here."

"But what about my things?" Maddy replied, also whispering.

"I'll bring them with me," Eva said. "I'll be joining you in a few days." She gave the girl a quick hug, unsure whether she would actually ever see her again. Eva had grown very fond of the young woman over the last few days.

Seemingly satisfied, Maddy made her way through the groups of people. Several of them smiled at her as she passed them, but Eva saw the smiles instantly disappear when they turned back to look at her. As Maddy opened the doors to the garden, Eva could hear sirens in the distance. She wouldn't be able to flee now, not if the police were on their way. That just made what she was about to say to the Adelphoi even more important.

"Fellow Adelphoi," Eva said as the doors closed behind Maddy. Then she cleared her throat and spoke again, louder this time. "My fellow Adelphoi."

Her eyes scanned the room, from one youthful face to another, until she found Bella. The young woman was standing apart from the others, a ball of tissue paper pressed to her mouth. Eva could see the tears on her cheeks.

"What's going on, Sister Eva?" a male voice asked. Eva located the speaker. It was Julian, the young man with a mop of blonde hair whom she'd briefly entertained a fantasy about on more than one occasion.

"Brother Giovanni is not who he says he is," Eva said, injecting as much authority into her voice as she could. For them to be aggrieved, she had to be aggrieved. "He has been lying to us all."

There was a collective gasp in the room that surprised Eva. She had thought that at least some of them would have suspected this from the media coverage. A few cries of *no* could be heard, and Eva's announcement prompted a fresh wave of tears from Bella, although no one went to comfort her. If anything, a few of the females in the room shot her scathing glances. That was something Eva needed to rectify. A victim was needed, and Bella would be perfect. "Who here has seen the media reports?" Almost every hand in the room went up.

Eva wished she'd thought to grab a bottle of water before speaking. "There is much the media doesn't know. They don't know the full depths of Giovanni's—I can't even bring myself to call him by his false title—of Giovanni's crimes. He has not just lied, he has stolen." Another gasp. "He has fornicated." Eva wasn't sure if that was a bit strong, especially when it was her he had been fornicating with, but from the louder gasp the words generated, it had the desired effect. "He has been a wolf in sheep's clothing," she said, sure that was in the Bible somewhere. "All these years, I have worshipped him. We have worshipped him." Tears would be good here, but Eva couldn't summon them on demand. She settled for a sob as she put her hands over her face as if she was mortified by being fooled for so long.

"He made me perform a sexual act on him." To Eva's surprise, she peered through her fingers to see it was Bella speaking. The young woman took a few faltering steps forward and stood next to Eva, turning to face the others. "He told me it was a test. To prove my worthiness to serve." Eva was not expecting what happened next.

"And me," another female voice in the crowd said. Eva looked at who had spoken, recognizing a young woman called Samantha from the bike ride. Then another young woman also spoke up.

"He squeals when he..." Her voice faded slightly. "When he finishes. Like a pig." To Eva's disgust, both Bella and Samantha, as well as a couple of other young women in the audience, nodded in agreement. Giovanni's extra-curricular activities, if that was what they could be called, were more prolific than she'd realized. But the effect on the group, especially the male members of the Adelphoi, was dramatic.

"He's a false prophet," a male voice called out from the rear of the foyer.

"A false teacher in our midst!"

"He's working with the Beast!"

As the calls of indignation got louder, Eva had to suppress a smile. She even heard the word *antichrist* being called out a couple of times. Perhaps this group wouldn't be as difficult to be aggrieved as she had thought? Giovanni's lack of morals seemed to be doing it without much encouragement from her.

"Okay, fellow Adelphoi," Eva said, raising her hands in the air to silence them. "Let's convene in the main conference room in ten minutes. The authorities will be here shortly. We must tell them the truth about Giovanni and how he has wronged each and every one of us." *Especially me*, she thought.

The hubbub of conversation Eva had heard earlier returned, but this time, it was more excitement than anger. There was another sound in the background that Eva recognized as the engine of the helicopter starting up. She breathed a sigh of relief.

Whatever happened to them now, at least Maddy was safe.

92

Giovanni tried to take stock of his situation. He felt groggy and nauseated. The last thing he remembered was getting into the car at the Adelphoi's complex. A woman's face floated into his mind's eye. It was Maddy. He'd run into her, literally, before getting in his car. The next thing he could remember was now. He was sitting in the driver's seat of his ruined car, a man with the coldest eyes he'd ever seen had his hands clasped on either side of his head, and he had the most unimaginable pain in his lower back. The car was ruined and full of broken glass fragments and, bizarrely, leaves. He could smell gasoline and panicked for a few seconds at the thought of it catching fire, but he realized the engine was off. Maybe he'd stalled when he crashed?

He could hear sirens getting louder and louder. Then there was the sound of tires on gravel and doors slamming, followed by people running. More than one, from the sound of it. There was a female voice to his left, and he tried to see who it was, but the strange man holding his head had him in a vise. He could just see a concerned looking young woman peering in the window. She was wearing a red jump-suit and had blonde hair, partially obscured by a white hard hat with a red cross on the front.

"Riesci a sentirmi?" It took Giovanni a second or two to process what she had asked him. *Can you hear me?*

"Yes, I can," he replied in English.

"American?" the woman replied, a smile appearing on her face. "I am Cecilia, a paramedic. We're going to get you out of there."

Giovanni closed his eyes and drifted off for a few seconds to the sound of more sirens approaching. When he came to, the hands were gone from the side of his head, but he had a rigid collar around his neck. There were several voices, all speaking in urgent Italian. He heard a couple of male voices talking about *il tetto*. The roof. But he couldn't concentrate on the conversations.

"We're going to give you something for the pain," the woman, Cecilia said. Giovanni felt a sharp scratch in the crook of his arm. "Then the Vigili del Fuoco—the fire brigade—will need to take the roof of the car off so we can get you out. What's your name?"

Giovanni closed his eyes again and didn't reply. He didn't want to give this woman a name in case he needed to change it.

"His name is Giovanni," another female voice said in Italian. It sounded familiar, but Giovanni couldn't place her. Was it Eva? Perhaps she had followed him and seen the accident?

"Eva? Is that you?" Giovanni called out, but he wasn't able to move his head to look to see if was her.

"Just relax," Cecilia said as Giovanni felt a cold sensation in the crook of his elbow. "This is going to make you a little sleepy."

Giovanni sat in the driver's seat as, around him, a hive of activity bustled. He felt some protective glasses being put over his eyes, and a set of ear defenders on his head. Then there was more metallic screeching, not unlike the noises he thought he'd heard during the accident. A few moments after that, he sensed fresher air around his face. When he opened his eyes, the car's roof was completely gone. In front of him were a couple of burly firemen in full protective gear.

It took the rescue team several moments to actually extract Giovanni from the car, not helped by the fact they'd had to stop to give him some more analgesia. The pain in his back as they'd placed him on a hard board had been excruciating, the worst pain he'd ever suffered in his life. But finally, he was secured to a spinal board, flat on his back and staring at the sky, unable to move.

"Shit," Giovanni muttered when he realized that his grab bag was still in the car somewhere. He needed that bag. When he saw the strange man appear in his peripheral vision, he called out to him. "I have a bag in the car," Giovanni said. "Can you get it for me?" He saw the man talking to someone he couldn't see, their voices almost drowned out by the sound of a helicopter above them somewhere. Giovanni sighed, realizing that he must be badly injured if they were sending an air ambulance to him.

"The Polizia di Stato have your bag," a female voice replied. It was the one from just now. He knew that voice. Giovanni blinked a couple of times as a new face appeared in his line of sight. A very familiar one.

"Anita?" Giovanni said. "Is that you?" In the background, the sound of the helicopter was getting louder. He watched as Anita leaned over to speak to him. For a moment, he thought she was going to kiss him, but instead, she put her mouth next to his ear.

"I hope you burn in hell, Giovanni."

93

As the sleek helicopter banked around, Hugo's attention was drawn to some flashing blue lights on the ground a mile away from the Adelphoi complex. He peered down to see an ambulance, a couple of fire trucks and several police cars, all parked in a small lot. A few hundred yards from the lot, there was a small group of trees with a car next to them. Even from this distance, Hugo could tell the car was totaled. He could make out a small group of people walking up the road to the parked emergency vehicles carrying a stretcher between them while back at the car, there was a couple staring up at his helicopter.

As Hugo looked at the couple, he felt a stabbing pain in his sternum. He winced at the uncomfortable searing sensation, raising his hand to rub the skin. But the sensation wasn't on his skin—it was deeper than that. He'd never had any cardiac problems apart from some mild hypertension and they didn't run in his family, but Hugo imagined this is what a heart attack might feel like. He was just getting concerned about the pain when he realized that as quickly as it had appeared, it had disappeared.

Looking across the cabin, he noticed Maddy's thrilled expression as she peered out of the helicopter window. Hugo smiled at her when she looked over at him, aiming for a friendly grandfather look. She raised a hand and waved at him, even though there was only a yard between them. Hugo was about to wave back when he realized the pilot was trying to get his attention. Hugo picked up a set of headphones attached to the side of the helicopter with a curly wire. After he had put them on his head, he then toggled a small aluminum switch on the cable.

"Mr. Forrester?" the pilot asked a few seconds later. "Your assistant, Ruth, needs to speak with you urgently."

"Hello, er, hello Philip," Hugo said. "Would you mind patching me through?"

"Of course, Mr. Forrester."

A few seconds later, Hugo heard the voice of his personal assistant greeting him.

"Ruth, we're on the way back now," he said. "We've just left, so we'll be about twenty minutes."

"Very good, Mr. Forrester. We may have an issue that I wanted to appraise you of."

"Go on," Hugo said, mentally cursing whatever it was she needed to speak to him about. He had never known Ruth to need to speak to him urgently.

"The material that was leaked to the media by the woman in Naples.?"

"What of it?" Hugo asked, with a sinking feeling in the pit of his stomach.

"It appears that it's also been shared, in its entirety, on a website called Reddit."

"Well, have my legal team take it down, then," Hugo

snapped back, although he knew if it had already been published, it would be too late.

"Reddit's not that sort of website, Mr. Forrestor." There was something he didn't recognize in her tone. She sounded different. Was she concerned? That would, Hugo mused, be a first. "It's more of a community than a website. There's already a lot of talk about the information."

"And this talk includes us?"

"I'm afraid so."

"I see." Hugo thought for a moment, knowing that Ruth would wait on the line for him to continue speaking. "Remind me again of our contingency plan?"

"It was to travel to Sicily before stopping to refuel at the heliport on Isola di Marettimo. Then across the water to Tunisia, where we have a safe house."

Hugo drummed his fingers on his knee as he thought. Everything was tumbling down around him, it seemed, and all because of that damned woman his men had failed to silence.

"Okay, we'll enact the contingency plan."

"We can't, Mr. Forrester. We'll need a new one."

"Why?" Hugo asked, thumping his thigh in frustration. The sudden movement caused Maddy to look over at him in concern, but reassuring her was not his priority.

"The airspace across Southern Italy is closed. Mount Vesuvius is, it would appear, in the process of erupting." Hugo could definitely hear the fear in Ruth's voice now. "I'm working on a new plan now, but it won't be as secure. We don't have any assets in place. We can reconfigure, but it will take time."

"Okay, okay," Hugo replied, trying to calm himself and, by extension, Ruth down. "The Institute is secure enough for the time being. We can just lock it down and remain silent, so send all the personnel home apart from the security. Then, when we have a suitable alternative contingency, we'll enact it then. How long will it take you to come up with something, do you think?"

"Twenty-four hours at the most," Ruth said, and Hugo imagined he could hear relief in her voice. That was the problem with women, he thought. They were too emotional by far. "We have contacts in Eastern Europe. I've put word out that we need assistance."

"Very good, Ruth," Hugo replied, knowing that her words would have doubled or even tripled the price of such assistance. "I'll speak with you soon."

"See you soon, Mr. Forrester."

Hugo heard a click on the line and the next voice he heard was the pilot's.

"Did you hear about Mount Vesuvius?" he asked Hugo.

"I did, just now. Is it bad?"

"It's worse than bad, Mr. Forrester. They're trying to evacuate hundreds of thousands of people, but they don't think they have time. If it goes the way the media seem to think it will, it'll be apocalyptic."

Hugo took the headset off and stared out of the window as they approached the foothills of the Alps. He allowed himself a small smile at Philip's choice of words.

They would prove to be more accurate than the man realized.

94

Caleb held his hand over his eyes to shield them from the sun as the sleek white helicopter receded into the distance. The darkness he'd felt when he had looked at it—the same darkness he'd felt in Naples—subsided as the aircraft faded into the distance. In a matter of minutes, it was nothing more than a black speck on the horizon.

He turned to look at Anita, who was watching the emergency services transport Giovanni to the waiting ambulance. On the back of her blouse was a stain that was partly grass and partly mud, and it extended down her back to her buttocks. Caleb felt bad at the way he'd knocked her off her feet to get her to safety, but it had to be done. He knew only too well how people responded to perceived threats. Fight, flight, or freeze. He'd read somewhere that there was a fourth option which was to flop, or faint, but he'd never experienced that.

Anita had frozen as the car had rolled toward them. It was a natural reaction that prepared people for action and increased their visual perception, but when the threat was a car weighing somewhere around four thousand pounds traveling toward you at speed, it wasn't going to give anyone the best chance of survival. Caleb's instincts had always been to fight or to flee, and always in that order.

"So what next?" Anita asked, turning to face him. "I'm guessing that was Hugo in the helicopter, heading back to his institute."

"I guess so," Caleb replied with a shrug of his shoulders. "Where is the institute located?"

"It's just over the border in Austria," Anita replied, rubbing her stomach. "Close to a mountain called Piz Bernina. Do you ski?"

"Not a chance," Caleb replied with a laugh. "I'm from Texas. There're no mountains near there."

"You should try it," Anita replied, remembering how agile he had been on the Via Ferrata. "Never too old to try something new, my mother always used to say. Anyway, the institute's near St. Moritz in Switzerland. That's why I was asking."

"How far is it from here?"

"It's not far as the crow flies, but it's a good few hours by road, I would imagine."

"Why don't we head down to the Adelphoi?" Caleb said, taking a few steps toward the car. "Get an update on what's going on. We could still plant the keylogger that Brother Antonio gave us."

"Is there much point?" Anita asked as she looked at the police officers accompanying Giovanni to the ambulance. "Looks like the cat's well and truly out of the bag now."

Caleb nodded in agreement after considering what Anita had just said, and the two of them walked in silence to the parking lot. As they approached their car, a diminutive man in a Carabinieri uniform approached them. Caleb then had to wait as the police officer and Anita had a rapid conversation in Italian that he didn't understand. He thought Anita had asked the man if he spoke English at the start of it, but either he didn't or he didn't want to, so Caleb amused himself by watching their body language. The policeman, who had a faintly ridiculous pencil mustache as if to make up for his receding hairline, appeared to be speaking as much with his hands as with his mouth. Every sentence was punctuated with some sort of hand gesture. Anita wasn't so animated, but Caleb saw her describing the moment when the car had rolled over.

Finally, the policeman seemed to run out of steam. He put his hand in his pocket and extracted a leather wallet that he pulled a business card from. Then he handed it to Anita and said something else before turning to Caleb.

"Have a good day, and drive safely," the policeman said in accented English before he turned and walked away. Caleb watched him strutting across the parking lot to his marked car and laughed.

"What's so funny?" Anita asked as they got into their own car.

"Him," Caleb replied, nodding at the policeman. "I never trust a short man in a uniform. They always try to use it to make up for their lack of height."

"That's a bit harsh, Caleb," Anita said, but she was smiling as she spoke. "I'm supposed to contact him to arrange a witness interview at some point, but I think I'm washing my hair whenever he wants to see us."

Caleb maneuvered the car out of the lot and started driving down toward the Adelphoi's complex. He slowed as they passed the copse where Giovanni's car, now a convertible, was sitting low on whatever was left of its suspension. "Do you think he was badly injured, Anita?" he asked.

"I hope so," Anita replied in a firm voice. "And when he's recovered, I hope they lock him up and throw away the key."

"Perhaps they will," Caleb said.

It took less than ten minutes to reach the complex. Caleb examined it as they approached. When he'd been looking at it earlier, he'd not seen much in the way of security. No CCTV cameras, no fences. He remembered Greta telling them it used to be a hotel and, to his eyes, it still looked like one.

He parked in front of the white single-story building and, with Anita a few steps behind him, made his way to the front door. It was open, but as they walked through, there was no one in sight.

"Where is everyone?" Caleb muttered under his breath. The place was deserted, eerie almost. Anita walked past to him to what would have been the reception area and leaned over the counter. A few seconds later, Caleb could hear a bell ringing somewhere deep within the building. A moment after that, the sound of approaching footsteps could be heard. Then a door to the side of the reception desk opened and a woman walked through, wearing a robe not unlike Caleb's own. When she saw Anita, the woman's face turned first to horror, then to shock.

"Anita!" the woman said. "I wasn't expecting to see you again."

"No, Sister Eva," Anita replied, glancing at Caleb as she did so. "I don't imagine you were."

95

E va willed her hands to stop shaking as she poured coffee for Anita and the man she had brought with her, who she now knew was called Caleb. He had said little since arriving, apparently content to take a back seat in the discussion. She found him curious at first, but the way he was looking at her was rattling her.

"Are you okay there, Sister Eva?" Anita asked.

When Eva had seen Anita standing in the foyer, her heart had dropped into her stomach. She was the last person she was expecting, and it had taken Eva a few moments to compose herself. When she approached, Eva was half-expecting Anita to slap her face, but she had done nothing other than introduce Caleb. Then Anita had told Eva about the car wreck.

"I'm fine, Anita, thank you," Eva replied as she focused on not spilling the coffee. "I'm just a bit shaken up about Brother Giovanni's accident, that's all. At some point, I'll need to call the hospital to see how he is."

"You could always go and see him," Anita said. "Take him some grapes, perhaps."

Eva looked at Anita to see her eyes were dark with anger, or perhaps disdain.

"I don't really want to see him, if I'm honest. After everything he's done."

"You really knew nothing about any of it?"

"No, nothing." Eva looked again at Anita, blinking a couple of times as she tried to keep an innocent expression on her face. "I can't believe it went on for so long without me realizing what he was up to. I would have thought there would be something that I would have picked up on." This was another time where tears would be useful. "If I'd known the extent of his, his immorality, I could have done something about it. And as for what happened to poor Greta, well, it's just unfathomable." Eva stopped talking at that point, not wanting to overdo it.

While they had been waiting for the coffeepot to percolate, Eva had told Anita and Caleb about Giovanni's actions, or at least her interpretation of them. Coming directly from her discussion with the Adelphoi, her presentation had been slightly more refined than it might have been otherwise. She had told them of the abuse of the women in the Adelphoi, Giovanni's theft of their money, and his sudden departure. Anita had told her she was one of those women before telling her of Giovanni's accident. The shock on Eva's face at what had happened to Giovanni had been the most genuine expression she'd worn all day.

"And this girl, Maddy?" Anita asked. "You knew nothing of that? And you didn't think it odd that Hugo took her with him in the helicopter?"

Eva shook her head vehemently before replying. "Absolutely not." She fixed Anita with what she hoped was an earnest expression. "I knew she and Giovanni had gotten close the last few weeks, and Hugo has been here more often than usual. I didn't even know Maddy had gone with Hugo until they'd left." She risked a quick glance at Caleb. "But you know what men are like? They would squirrel themselves away in Giovanni's office having conversations that didn't include me." Eva risked another glance. "No offense, Caleb." He just shrugged his shoulders in response, but said nothing.

"It's strange that all this was happening under your nose and you knew nothing of it," Anita said with more than a hint of accusation in her tone.

"I guess I'm not as perceptive as I thought I was," Eva said, aiming for self-deprecation. "Cream and sugar?"

As she poured cream into the coffee, the shake in her hands was less noticeable.

"What are your plans now?" Anita asked a moment later.

"I'm not sure. No doubt the authorities will want to speak to me, but I don't know what I can tell them. I've had the wool pulled over my eyes just like everyone else. After that, I don't know. I might go back to the States and start over somewhere. Everyone else is leaving to go home. They're packing now." Eva was keen to steer the conversation away from herself, and particularly her plans for the future. As the sirens she'd heard earlier were the emergency services responding to Giovanni's accident and not those of the police on their way to the complex, a discreet exit was still a possibility, despite what she had just said about speaking to the authorities. "Can I ask you a question, Anita?"

"Of course, Sister Eva," Anita replied with a slight frown.

"Why did you come back here? After what Giovanni did to you?"

"I came back to give him a message, which has been

delivered," Anita said in a matter-of-fact voice. Eva looked at her, unsure if she was telling the truth.

"And what's next for you?" she asked her. Eva saw Anita look at Caleb, who just shook his head almost imperceptibly.

"I'm not sure, to be honest," Anita said. "Maybe a brief vacation? It's been an intense couple of days."

They drank their coffee in an uncomfortable silence. Eva was reluctant to say anything more. While she thought what she had said had been believed by the two people sitting with her, she wasn't convinced. She watched as Caleb finished his coffee and got to his feet.

"Well, it's been a pleasure, Sister Eva," he said, looking at her with cold eyes. "But Anita and I have somewhere we need to be."

96

"So, what do you think of Sister Eva, Caleb?" Anita asked as they made their way back to the car.

"I think she's lying through her teeth," Caleb replied, not even looking at Anita. "She'd make a crap poker player."

"Does it matter, Caleb?" Anita said, opening the passenger door. "She might be complicit, but she's lost everything."

"So she says." Caleb didn't look convinced. "It's all very convenient, isn't it? Giovanni being the rotten apple, not her?"

"I guess," Anita replied. "I'm just not sure it matters. We're going to the Weizmann Institute, I take it?"

"Yup."

"And what are we going to do when we get there?"

"I'll think of something," Caleb replied. "We need to get the girl away from this Hugo."

"Why?"

"Because I think I know what he is," Caleb said as he buckled his seatbelt. "Or rather, what he represents."

"You're not making sense, Caleb. A few days ago, you'd never even heard of the man."

"If Hugo represents what I think he does, then I have heard of him and his kind." Caleb started the car and reversed it so they could leave the Adelphoi's complex. "He represents darkness. An indescribable darkness. I can feel it."

Anita folded her arms over her chest and sighed, causing Caleb to look over at her.

"Right," she said, looking away from him and out of the passenger window. A few seconds later, she leaned forward and turned the radio on to signify to Caleb that she didn't want to talk anymore. She'd had enough of this woo-woo nonsense about feeling things that simply weren't there.

They drove on in silence for a while, leaving the town of Pilzone and the Adelphoi behind them. Anita's thoughts turned to Giovanni, and how much she had wanted Caleb to kill him back in the car. Wherever Giovanni was now, she hoped he was in pain. A lot of pain. She thought about the girl whom Eva had told them about, Maddy, who was supposedly carrying the son, or perhaps the daughter, of God. She was pondering about the impending eruption of Mount Vesuvius that the radio was talking about when she had a sudden thought.

"Caleb, what exactly does it say in the Bible about the end of the world?" she asked him. He looked over at her, a surprised expression on his face. "Let's say, hypothetically speaking, Maddy is carrying the child of God, then what would actually happen?"

"I don't believe she's carrying the child of God, Anita. My fear is that people will believe that she is."

"As a hypothetical scenario. What would happen?" She saw Caleb taking a deep breath.

"War, violence and lawlessness," he said. "But we have those already. We also have disease and epidemics. There'll be natural disasters."

"Like Mount Vesuvius erupting?" To Anita's surprise, her comment made him laugh.

"I guess, yes. But it's not what's written in the Bible that's important. Have you heard of the New Testament apocrypha?"

"The what?"

"The apocrypha. It's a bunch of books written around the time of Christ and just after that have been pretty much shunned by the major religions. Certainly Judaism and Christianity, although there are some churches that still use them," Caleb said. "Several of them talk about apocalyptic scenarios, particularly the Book of Enoch, which was one of the much older apocrypha." She looked at him and saw a half-smile playing across his face. "I'm guessing if you've not heard of the apocrypha, you've not heard of Methuselah, either?"

"Nope."

"He was a distant descendant of Enoch who apparently wrote his own book, the *Apocalypse of Methuselah*, but it's been lost for centuries. According to the myth, the book contained a passage that spoke of the return of the messiah, but in his book, the baby was killed shortly after being born along with its mother."

"Sounds like a riveting read," Anita said, shivering at the thought of such a thing happening. She looked again at Caleb, who wasn't smiling anymore.

"In the *Apocalypse of Methuselah*, the death of the infant was followed by a thousand years of darkness. Most of the world's population is killed by the return of the Nephilim, condemning their souls to eternal damnation. Only those with pure evil in their hearts are saved, and they rule the world with pain and suffering beyond belief. Apparently, in comparison, Revelation is about as dark as *A Very Hungry Caterpillar*."

"Who are the Nephilim?"

"They're the bastard children of fallen angels and human women and, according to Enoch and Methuselah, they're the epitome of evil."

"Do you believe all that, though?" Anita asked, stifling a laugh. "About the years of darkness and children of fallen angels?"

"No, not a word of it," Caleb replied, his half-smile reappearing. "It's not even clear if the book actually exists or existed. But like I've said before, there are people that believe in that type of prophecy. People like Hugo. There are entire religions dedicated to the *Apocalypse of Methuselah*, clandestine organizations for whom the predictions are very real."

"Let me guess, you can sense that Hugo is one of them?"

"In a way, yes."

"Even though you've never actually met the man?" Anita asked. Caleb just shrugged his shoulders.

They drove on in silence for a few moments, Anita watching out of the window as the foothills to the mountains they were approaching emerged from the flat land. There were several lakes nestled between them, some with sailing boats moving across them. What she would give to be sailing right now, instead of talking about the end of the world. She thought back to what Caleb had just said, and then the penny dropped.

"Shit!" Anita said with a gasp. "If you're right, that means Hugo's going to kill Maddy."

"At some point in the next nine months or so, yes." Caleb

turned to look at Anita and his eyes bored into hers. "I can't let that happen."

97

C aleb steadied the tripod legs on the trunk of the car and leaned down to look through the sniper scope. He and Anita were on the side of a hill that overlooked the Weizmann Institute on another hill opposite them. Between their location and the institute was a deep valley, but it was the best vantage spot, according to the map on Anita's phone. It was also only a couple of hundred yards away as the crow flies, which was well within the range of what he was thinking of.

They had made good time to get to their current location, with Caleb making the distance in just over three hours. As they had got deeper into the mountains, the roads had become narrower and more challenging, winding their way round the rock faces. While they drove, Caleb had given Anita a crash course in the New Testament apocrypha, or as much as he could remember. Despite her scepticism, which he shared, Anita had been surprisingly interested. Or at least, Caleb thought as he adjusted the scope, she had pretended to be fairly convinced. Caleb knew more about the shadowy organizations that used what was known of the lost *Apocalypse of Methuselah* as their own version of the Bible. He knew they existed, and he knew they were close by.

The Weizmann Institute was indeed a formidable place. It was similar in many ways to the monastery he had been staying in. Not as dramatic, perhaps, and nowhere near as high up. It was a curious mixture of old and new architecture, and looked to be just as inaccessible. Caleb could only see one obvious road from the valley floor up to the buildings that nestled in the shadow of the mountain above it. As before, he divided the structure into a grid. At the top of the grid, sitting on the roof of a modern rectangular structure that looked like an office complex of some sort, was the helicopter they had seen flying over their heads back in Pilzone. The office space looked incongruous, as it had effectively been built on top of the older part of the building. Caleb wondered how they had got permission to build it, but if Hugo was as rich as Greta said he was, he probably just bought someone's permission.

The bottom left-hand corner of the grid had what seemed to be the only access point, guarded by a small hut behind some serious-looking fencing which was closed. He could see a guard leaning up against the wall of the hut, a sub-machine gun slung across his chest. As Caleb watched, the man puffed out a cloud of cigarette smoke before crushing the butt under his foot and meandering back to his post inside the hut. Caleb was too far away to determine the make and model of the rifle, but he thought it was either a Beretta PM12S or Heckler and Koch MP5. Both were pretty serious weapons in the right hands and from the way the guard was carrying himself, his were good enough to be a concern.

Caleb scanned the structure, noting the small courtyard

in front of one of the older parts of the institute. It was surrounded by a small wall, only three feet high, and it separated the institute from a sheer drop to the valley floor of perhaps fifty yards. Apart from the guard, Caleb couldn't see any other activity, but the angle of the sun meant he couldn't see through any of the windows, either the small ones in the old parts of the building or the floor to ceiling ones in the upper, newer part.

"Can you see much?" Anita asked. She was leaning up against the hood of the car, watching him.

"Not really," Caleb replied, turning his attention to the rock face below the buildings. "There doesn't seem to be much activity. One guard on the gate, so there'll be more somewhere else. First thing I need to do is to take out that helicopter."

"How are you going to do that?" Anita said, looking over at the buildings. She was using her hand to shield her eyes from the sun. "There's no way to get all the way up there without being noticed."

Caleb didn't reply but walked to the trunk of the car. He opened it and pulled out a long, slim case, which he snapped open. It only took a few seconds to assemble the Barrett M82 sniper rifle inside.

"I'm going to do it from here," Caleb said to Anita.

"I was wondering what was inside that case," she replied, watching as his practiced hands screwed the scope on top of the rifle.

"It's an older version, but it's a reliable weapon. The Provisional IRA used them for years over in Ireland against the Brits. And each other occasionally." Caleb walked to the front of the car, moving quickly. He didn't want a car to come round the corner to see him lying prone, taking aim at something.

"What are you going to do?" Anita asked.

"Shoot the pilot."

"No, Caleb!" Anita said with a gasp. "You can't do that."

"Relax, Anita," Caleb replied, grinning at her. "I'm pulling your leg."

He lay down in the dirt in front of the car, listening intently for any sound of an approaching vehicle. The sniper rifle was carrying 12.7 x 99mm rounds, designed specifically to be anti-materiel. As he settled into position, he started considering the variables he needed to take into account. Wind speed, wind direction, range, mirage, where the sun was, and finally the temperature and barometric pressure.

"Can you look through the spotting scope, Anita?" Caleb asked.

"Of course," she replied, looking pleased to have been asked. "What do I need to look at?"

"The tail rotor," Caleb said. He waited until Anita was looking through the scope, focusing on slowing his breathing rate down. Distance wise, it wasn't particularly challenging, but he only wanted to take one shot. The sound would reverberate around the valley, and the guard would certainly hear it, but as they had been driving into the mountains, they had passed several trucks full of hunters.

"Okay, got it," Anita said a moment later.

Caleb settled into the scope and focused on the tail rotor through the optic. The blades were perhaps half a yard long, eight inches in width, and striped red and white. He wanted to put the round directly into the middle of one blade, shattering it completely. Replacing it was relatively straightforward, once you had the right person and the right equipment, but Caleb was bargaining on Hugo having neither.

There was a pause of almost exactly half a second between the time Caleb squeezed the trigger and the tail rotor blade splitting into pieces, sending shards and fragments of titanium, carbon fiber, fiberglass and stainless steel across the helicopter landing site on top of the building. Caleb instantly switched the rifle sight to the hut to gauge the guard's reaction. To his surprise, the man hadn't reacted in the slightest. When Caleb saw the white earbuds in the guard's ears, he instantly went down in his estimation.

"Okay, Anita," Caleb said as he got to his feet. He disassembled the rifle as quickly as he could, keen to get it out of sight. "Are you ready for the next stage?"

98

Anita looked through the sniper's scope at Caleb, deep below her in the valley. He had just parked the car near to the rock face in front of the institute and was now standing next to it, his head craned upward as he looked at the rock.

"Any movement at the institute?" his tinny voice said in her ear. She pressed a finger to the acoustic earpiece he had given her to wear, along with a quick lesson in how to use it.

"You just speak and I'll hear you," he had said as he'd fitted it to her ear. "There's an inline microphone in the cable."

Anita swiveled the scope, so it was pointing at the institute. She could see the guard still in his hut, and no one else.

"No, I can't see anything," she replied.

Although she'd not said anything to Caleb, she thought his plan was idiotic and not thought through. He was going to ascend the rock face to get into the institute building without having to go past the guard. It would mean, he had told her as he'd explained what his intentions were, that he wouldn't have to kill the guard. But Caleb had no ropes, no climbing equipment. He had nothing and from where Anita was looking, the rock face looked to be sheer.

"But how are you going to get Maddy out?" Anita had asked. Caleb hadn't answered that question, but had mumbled something about he'd work that out when he got there. Then they had argued about her role. Anita didn't want to be where she was. She wanted a more active role. But Caleb had been adamant that he needed what he called eyes on.

Anita returned her attention to Caleb, who was still studying the rock in front of him. She watched, her heart in her mouth, as he started climbing. He moved slowly and deliberately, always keeping three points of contact with the wall as he had told her to do a couple of days previously. That all seemed like a lifetime ago now, though. A couple of times, she could see him double-checking a hand or foothold before putting any weight on it. He had a small rucksack on his back that he'd produced from the trunk of the car. When Anita had asked him what was in it, he had just replied *supplies* with a lop-sided grin.

When Caleb was perhaps half-way up the rock face, he paused for a few moments.

"Are you okay?" Anita asked, nervous that something was wrong.

"I'm all good," Caleb replied, slightly out of breath. "Just taking a break."

It took him almost twenty minutes to reach the top of the rock, and he stopped again just below the small wall that separated the courtyard from the drop below him. Anita's attention was drawn to something at the base of the building. She moved the scope quickly to see what it was.

"Caleb, stay where you are," she said in a whisper, even

though she knew only he could hear her. "A door's just opened and there's a man coming out."

"Okay," Caleb whispered back.

Anita swore under her breath as she saw the man, wearing a gray suit, walking toward where Caleb was dangling. It was one of the men they had escaped from earlier. He stopped a few yards to one side of Caleb's location and scanned the horizon. Anita instinctively pulled away from the sniper's scope. It seemed as if he was staring straight at her. Had he seen a reflection or something? Had he been sitting in one of the rooms in the institute, staring at her through a similar scope? But to her relief, the man turned and started walking toward the hut.

"He's walking toward the hut," Anita said, still whispering. "But they'll see you in the courtyard."

"I'm good where I am for the moment," Caleb replied.

It was ten, maybe fifteen minutes before the man walked back toward the door in the bottom of the building, but to Anita, it felt like hours. She kept looking at Caleb, hoping he was okay, but he barely moved an inch during the entire time. She waited until the guard had disappeared back inside before she said anything.

"Okay, he's gone back inside," she said, her voice back to normal. Anita moved the scope to the hut. "Caleb! The guard's going for a smoke."

"Let me know when he's round the side of the hut." Caleb's voice was strained. This was the moment he'd been waiting for. The area where the guard hid to smoke was around the side of the hut and Caleb could cross the courtyard unseen. Anita just hoped the other guard wasn't looking out of one of the windows, but if he was, there was nothing she could do about it. She paused for a few seconds until the guard was in his smoking hideaway.

"Okay, go!" Anita said. She kept the scope trained on the guard in case he changed his mind about a cigarette, even though she was desperate to see what Caleb was doing. Anita took her eye away from the optic for a few seconds and could just make him out, running across the courtyard. To her relief, the door stayed closed, and she saw Caleb reach out to open it. He was almost inside.

"Where's the guard?" Caleb asked a couple of seconds later. He sounded strained, which wasn't a surprise, given the circumstances. Anita put her eye back to the scope.

"He's still smoking," she said. "Are you inside?"

"No," Caleb replied, and she could hear him breathing hard. "There's a swipe card mechanism for the door."

As Anita watched, she saw the guard crushing his smoke under his heel.

"Caleb!" Anita said. "He's finished. He's going to see you!"

99

Hugo sat patiently in his opulent chair as Ruth finished her phone call. She was wearing, as she always did, a navy-blue business suit and cream blouse, but today, in contrast to her normally immaculate appearance, the jacket was creased and there was a small brown stain on the front of her blouse.

"I see," he heard her say several times, making notes on a pad as she spoke. Eventually, she finished the call and turned to face him.

"Okay, Mr. Forrester. I think we have a plan," she said, taking a breath as if to compose herself.

"I'm all ears," Hugo replied.

"We fly to Geneva and take a commercial flight to Istanbul. From there, we can fly into Diyarbakır Airport."

"Where on earth is that?"

"Southeast Turkey. From there, we can travel by road to Kurdistan. We have friends there."

"Please tell me you're not talking about the Yazidis?" Hugo said. "I'd hardly call them friends."

"Allies, then. They are sympathetic to our cause."

"They're devil worshippers," Hugo retorted.

"Mr. Forrester, we don't have many options. They have a good network and can hide the girl until the time is right. They have plenty of women to look after her. The location they're looking at even has its own hospital. It's small, but perfectly adequate and they have midwives for later on. They've said they'll help us."

"At a price," Hugo said, looking up as the door to his office opened. He didn't bother to hide his irritation as Doctor Turner walked into the room. "I guess they didn't cover basic manners at medical school then?" he said to the man. "It's customary to knock?"

"I thought you'd appreciate an update on Maddy," the medic said. "She's resting just now, and I've given her something to help with that, but she was asking if there's somewhere more comfortable for her to stay. Her room's really quite austere."

"There will be, yes. That accommodation is only temporary," Hugo said. "She's secure, I take it?" Hugo asked. A look of puzzlement appeared on Doctor Turner's face.

"Yes, she's quite secure." He spread his arms out. "We're all quite secure here."

"No, you idiot. I mean, is the room secure? I don't want the stupid child just wandering around."

"I'll see to it, Mr. Forrester," Ruth said, walking toward the door. Hugo waited until she had left before continuing.

"Turner, things have changed a lot over the last few hours," he said. If the doctor was annoyed at losing his professional title, spurious though it was, he had the sense not to show it.

"Yes, they have. I've seen the news. I wanted to discuss the situation with you."

"What did you want to discuss?" Hugo asked.

Doctor Turner glanced across at one of the chairs in the office, but Hugo didn't invite him to sit down. He just wanted the man to say what he wanted to say and go away.

"I sense our position has become more precarious with the girl," Doctor Turner said.

Hugo let a smile play across his face, partly to hide his anger and partly at the doctor's clumsiness. If he wanted more money, he should just spit it out.

"Do go on, Doctor Turner," Hugo said, this time emphasizing the title. "What exactly is it you want? I'm quite tired, so let's stop beating about the bush and just get to the point."

"I'd like to renegotiate my remuneration considering the increased danger," Doctor Turner said after a brief pause.

"Danger from whom? Who, exactly, do you think is after us?"

"The authorities will be. People are saying on the internet they're already building a case against you."

Hugo paused, considering the doctor's use of the word *you*, instead of *us*. Hardly a team player, just like his nurse.

"Let me think about it, Doctor," Hugo said, forcing an affable smile onto his face. "Now, I too must rest. Will that be all?"

Doctor Turner looked at Hugo for a few long seconds, and Hugo wondered if he was going to say anything else. But the man just nodded and turned to leave. As he walked over the office floor, Ruth's words about the Yazidi's facilities came back to Hugo and when the door had closed behind the doctor, Hugo reached out his hand and pressed a small button on his desk. A couple of moments later, the door opened and the surviving member of the Naples team walked in, still wearing his gray suit. Hugo tutted. Some people had no decorum. The least the man could have done was to change his shirt.

"Yes, Mr. Forrester?" the man said, his eyebrows raised.

"Doctor Turner has outlived his usefulness," Hugo said, nodding his head.

"I see. Do you want me to escort him off the premises like I did with the nurse?" There was a faint smile on the man's face that Hugo appreciated. Despite the mishaps in Naples, at least he still had some professional pride. When Hugo had told him to kill the nurse, the man hadn't even blinked.

"If you could," Hugo said with a smile. "Sooner rather than later."

100

Anita focused all her attention on the guard, who was slowly nodding his head in time to the music he was listening to. She wanted to adjust the scope to see where Caleb was, but didn't want to take her eyes off the man she was watching. In her ear, she could hear Caleb breathing hard, as if he was sprinting.

The guard rounded the corner of the hut and looked up. He was going to see Caleb in the courtyard, of that Anita was sure. Sure enough, she saw an expression of alarm appear on his face and his hands started moving toward the weapon slung across his chest. He opened his mouth as if he was about to shout an alarm, and a blur of movement obscured him from Anita's view.

It was Caleb, moving at speed with his head down in front of him. He had covered the ground across the court-yard in no time at all, and Anita watched as he reared his head back just before connecting with the guard. Then he drove it forward, using the momentum he had built up to headbutt the guard in the face. Anita saw the man's face almost implode with a spray of blood erupting from his nostrils before he flew backward, tumbling into a bush. Anita stifled a shout of surprise and watched as Caleb quickly flipped the man onto his front and wrapped his arm around his neck. He then used his other hand to subdue the guard in a headlock. She could see the cords and muscles of Caleb's forearm in sharp relief as they strained with the effort.

"Don't kill him, Caleb," Anita said, using her index finger to make sure her earpiece was in the right place.

"I won't," Caleb replied, hissing as he spoke.

A few seconds later, Caleb released his grip, and the guard fell to the ground in a heap. He was out for the count but, as Anita watched, she could see he was still breathing. Caleb disentangled the weapon from the man's chest and reached down to grab something from his belt. Then he used his foot to roll the man over onto his side.

"There," Caleb said into her earpiece. "Sleeping like a baby."

As Caleb had been explaining his outline plan to Anita in the car as they had been traveling to the institute, Anita had tried to persuade him not to kill anyone. Two people were already dead because of her actions, and that was two too many as far as she was concerned. She wouldn't have stolen the information from the Adelphoi if she had known someone would get hurt, much less killed. Caleb hadn't flat out promised that he wouldn't take any more lives, but he had said he wouldn't unless it was absolutely necessary.

"If it's him or me," he had said to her with a wry smile, "then it's him." It hadn't been what Anita wanted to hear, but she understood why he'd said that and so far, he seemed to be keeping his promise.

Through the optic, Anita tracked Caleb as he made his way back across the courtyard. As he hurried along, she spotted him inspecting the weapon he snagged from the guard. First, he checked the magazine was secure. Then he pulled back the racking handle and peered inside a slot on the side. Finally, he made some sort of change to a small lever on the side of the weapon. Anita moved her view to the door at the base of the building, even though she knew Caleb could see it. If it did open, she might buy him a split second of time to react.

"I've got the swipe card," Caleb said through her earpiece. Anita saw him press it to a small black box to the side of the door. A second later, he pulled the door open. "We might lose comms, Anita," he said, pausing at the door, "but tell me if you see anything. I might hear you."

"Okay," Anita said, suddenly fearful at the thought of not being able to talk to him anymore. "Be careful."

She watched as Caleb turned and looked at her. Even though she knew he wouldn't be able to see her from that distance, he was looking directly at her.

"I will," he replied. "If something happens to me, go directly to the police."

"Okay," Anita whispered as she tried to think of something meaningful to say. But before she could think of anything, he had slipped through the door.

Anita relaxed for a few seconds, taking her eye from the scope as she did so. She realized her heart was pounding in her chest from the adrenaline of the last few moments, even though her role had only been one of an observer. There was nothing more she could do to help Caleb now, other than watch for any movement. But even if she did see anything, she might not be able to warn him.

Caleb was on his own.

101

Caleb paused as the door closed. He put one hand behind him to stop it making any noise as it shut, but the door closed in silence without him needing to.

He was standing in a corridor that led into the interior of the building. The walls were painted a dull ochre color, and the floor was bare stone. Caleb stayed where he was for a moment, listening intently. When he was satisfied he couldn't hear anything, he made his way down the corridor, moving slowly and carefully.

Caleb passed several doors set into the stone walls. They were all old and made of wood that almost looked weathered, despite being inside, and they all had two thick metal bolts on the outside. He placed his hands on one of them as he passed, running his fingers over the rough texture as he wondered how old they were. Towards the end of the corridor, there were two stairwells. The one leading down looked as old as the doors themselves, and he could make out indentations from centuries of feet in the center of the steps. By contrast, the stairs leading upward were modern and made of steel. Caleb looked at them with suspicion, wondering how noisy they would be if he ascended them.

Taking his time, he ascended the stairs as slowly as he could, testing every step as he did so. He inched around a turn in the staircase, using the sub-machine gun to sweep the area. It was an old weapon, a Beretta PM12S and not an MP5, but it appeared to be well cared for. The Italian military had replaced the model with the newer Beretta PMX a few years before, and Brother Antonio had told him the older models had pretty much disappeared before they could be sold. Caleb didn't care how old the gun was, as long as the 9x19mm Parabellum rounds did what they were supposed to do if required.

At the top of the stairs, Caleb paused again to listen. He was now in the new part of the building that he'd seen from the outside. To his left was a glass door with a single word etched into the frosted glass. *Laboratorio*. Next to the handle was a swipe card receiver. He couldn't make out any movement through the glass, so he used the guard's swipe card to open the door.

The interior of the room was exactly as described on the outside. It was a laboratory full of gleaming equipment that Caleb glanced at briefly. He didn't understand what any of it was for. There were test tubes and papers littering the work surfaces, as well as several computers dotted around the room. To one side of the laboratory, a line of cylinders as tall as he was stood like sentries. There were ten of them in total, all linked with tubes and a light blue diamond stenciled on the side. Under the diamond was a single word in the same shade of blue. *Propane*. Next to them, a couple of chairs lay on their sides.

Caleb took a few moments to explore the laboratory, but there was nothing really of note. It has been years since he'd been in a room like this, but there was nothing out-of-place other than it looked as if the people who'd last occupied it had left in a hurry. He left, closing the door behind him, and made his way back to the staircase. His hunch was that the main offices, where he hoped to find Hugo, would be on the top floor of the building.

"Anita, can you hear me?" he said, hoping that the newer building would allow their two-way radios to function. A few seconds later, he was rewarded with the sound of her voice.

"Caleb, where are you? Is everything okay?"

"All good. I'm on the first floor. Can you see through the windows yet?" Caleb asked.

"No, the sun's still at the wrong angle. It's reflecting straight back off the glass."

"Okay," he replied, testing the first step of the stairs to the next level. He heard a slight creak, but just as he was about to put his full weight on the step, he heard another noise from above him. Someone was coming down the stairs. Caleb swore and retraced his steps down the corridor. The footsteps were getting louder. He reached the laboratory door and held the swipe card to the reader, but it flashed a red light at him and emitted a soft beep. "Come on, come on," he muttered under his breath, steadying the Beretta as he did so.

If the door didn't open, he might have to use it.

102

"I can't really give you any information on his condition unless you're a family member," the woman's voice said, "but if you come up to the hospital, we'll be able to tell you a bit more."

Eva cursed under her breath, wishing she'd told the nurse she was talking to she was Giovanni's sister or something like that. Perhaps she could call the hospital back in a few moments and get a different member of staff on the line?

"But he's okay, right?" she asked.

"He's seriously injured and needs surgery," the nurse replied without a hint of sympathy in her voice. "But he's stable. That's all I can tell you."

"Could you tell him Eva called?"

"Sure."

Eva was about to thank the woman but as she did so, she realized she was talking to a dead line. "Bitch," she muttered instead. Eva threw her cell phone on the table as she heard a noise outside. She crossed to her window and peered out to see a yellow taxi had just pulled up in front of the

Adelphoi's complex. The driver, a swarthy-looking man who wouldn't have been out of place in a gangster movie, got out and popped the trunk as Bella, lugging a heavy suitcase behind her, made her way toward the cab. Behind her were another couple of the Adelphoi, also with bags. Eva sighed as she watched the taxi driver maneuver the bags so they all fit into the trunk. Then the three young people all climbed into the cab without so much as a backwards glance at the complex. She sighed again, knowing that things were well and truly over.

Eva looked down at the screen of her cell phone as it vibrated on the table. It wasn't a number she recognized.

"Hello?" she said cautiously as she picked it up, swiping at the screen to answer the call.

"Eva? It's Tom. Tom Turner."

"Tom, are you okay? Where are you?"

"I'm at the institute, but I'm leaving."

"Why? What's wrong?" she asked. He sounded out of breath, and the line wasn't a great one. His voice was crackly and there was a hissing sound in the background.

"I'm not sure, but I don't like it. Hugo's changed somehow, and he's got Maddy locked in her room. It's not just that, though. Stephen's disappeared."

"How d'you mean, disappeared?"

"Disappeared as in I can't find him anywhere. He's not answering his cell. Are you still planning on coming up here?"

Eva paused before replying, looking at the suitcase on her bed. It was full of clothes, and the truthful answer to that question was no. She had been planning to take advantage of the fact that the police hadn't appeared yet to slip away.

"In a few days, yes," she said, hoping the lie wouldn't be

obvious in her voice. "I'm going to take a couple of days just to process everything. Then I'll be up."

"Hugo's going to take Maddy away. To Kurdistan."

"What? Are you sure?"

"One hundred percent. I, er, I overheard them discussing it. They don't know that I know, though."

The hissing sound in the background disappeared, and Tom's voice suddenly became a lot clearer.

"Where are you going to go, Tom?" she asked him.

"I don't know yet. I just want to get away from here."

Eva was about to say something else when she heard a male voice shouting in the background of her cell phone. She heard Tom swearing and, a few seconds later, the unmistakable sound of a gunshot rang out.

"Tom?" Eva screamed down the phone.

A few seconds after that, the line was disconnected.

103

Caleb sensed the urgency in Anita's voice instantly. He was standing in the laboratory, having opened the door seconds before a set of footsteps had hurried past. Perhaps ten seconds after them, there was another set, moving faster, and then he heard a muffled gunshot.

"Caleb? Caleb? Are you there?" Anita asked, talking so quickly all the words ran into one another.

"I am," he replied. "What's happening?"

"Oh, Caleb. A man just got shot in the courtyard. He was running away." She sobbed and let out a small cry. "He was running away, Caleb, and they shot him in the back."

"Did you recognize him, Anita?" Caleb asked.

"No, I've never seen him before."

"Who shot him?"

"It was one of the men who was chasing us back in the village. The ones in gray suits." Anita sobbed again. "This is awful, Caleb. He's dragging him back toward the door."

Caleb paused to think for a moment. What Anita had just told him presented an opportunity to neutralize the man in the gray suit. If he were hauling a body, then he would be preoccupied. Caleb nodded, his promise to Anita coming back to him. "If it's him or me," he muttered, "it's him."

"What did you say, Caleb?" Anita asked.

"I need to take him out, Anita."

"Oh, God, Caleb, no," she replied. "Enough people have died already."

"He just shot a man in the back, Anita."

"I don't care, Caleb. He needs to be handed over to the police. You can't just kill him."

"How many other people are in the building?" Caleb said, looking down at the man on the floor. His gray suit was ripped slightly at the collar, and he had a deep gash on his forehead from where Caleb had slammed his face into a door before apologizing on Anita's behalf. Both the man's hands were zip-tied behind his back, and his ankles were similarly bound. A few yards away were the contents of the man's pockets. A wallet, a car fob, and a cell phone. Caleb had also relieved him of the pistol in a shoulder holster. He said something in Italian that Caleb didn't understand.

"Speak English," Caleb said, but the man just smiled at him, revealing bood-stained teeth. In response, Caleb lifted the Beretta, releasing the safety catch as he did so. He glanced down at the catch to make sure single fire was selected. "If you don't talk, then you're no good to me. If you're no good to me, then I'll kill you." The man just looked at him and it wasn't until Caleb's finger started tightening on the trigger that he spoke.

"If I tell you, then you'll kill me anyway," he said in heavily accented English.

"If you tell me, then I'll let you live," Caleb replied with a smile of his own. "Boy Scout's honor."

"How do I know you're telling the truth?"

"Because I'm a man of my word," Caleb replied, easing the pressure on the trigger. Nothing would have given him greater pleasure than to put a bullet in the man's forehead, but as he'd just told him, Caleb was a man of his word. "Put it this way, either you tell me and live or you tell me and die. If you don't tell me, you die. What have you got to lose other than the chance to live?"

Caleb waited as the man considered his predicament. Neutralizing him had been surprisingly easy. He had been in the middle of dragging the man he had just shot into one of the rooms Caleb had passed by in the older part of the building and hadn't even heard Caleb approaching. In the room he was dragging the body into was another dead man, also with a bullet wound in his back.

"There's a guard at the gate," the man said, causing Caleb to smirk. There was a guard at the gate, and he would be unconscious for a while yet. "Other than me, there's Mr. Forrester and his assistant on the top floor."

"That's it?" Caleb replied, surprised. "Where's everyone else? Where's the girl?"

"Mr. Forrester sent them away. There were a few researchers and lab staff. But a minibus came for them. I don't know anything about a girl."

Caleb regarded the man for a moment, wondering if he was telling the truth about Maddy. He finally decided that he probably was. As Caleb had said, what did he have to lose?

"There's no one else in the building?"

"No one."

"If you're lying..." Caleb let his voice tail away as he gestured at the man with the sub-machine gun.

"Sure, you'll come back and kill me."

Caleb nodded and swept up the man's possessions, placing them in his rucksack. He looked down at the man on the floor, contemplating hitting him in the head with the stock of the gun, but he decided against it. At least he would be conscious when the police arrived. His eyes swept the room to ensure that there was nothing in it that his captive could use to escape his ties, but other than the two dead bodies, there was nothing.

He left the room, securing the bolts behind him. Caleb looked at the other doors and walked to the first one. He loosened the bolts and pulled the heavy door open. Inside the small room was nothing more than a single bed with a bucket underneath it. A small window high on one wall let a sliver of light through. The next door he opened revealed an identical room, except this one had a young woman inside. She leaped off the bed as he opened the door before staring at the Beretta with a look of horror.

"I'm guessing you're Maddy?" Caleb said with a smile as he re-slung the weapon so it was across his back.

"Who are you?" she said, her voice trembling.

"My name is Caleb," he replied, broadening his smile. "Sister Eva sent me."

nita's face broke into a broad smile when she saw the door of the institute open and a young woman walk out, closely followed by Caleb. She vaguely recognized her from her own time at the Adelphoi, but she didn't think their paths had actually crossed. Anita zoomed in on Maddy's face. She looked confused, but happy at the same time. Anita laughed. Having spent the previous few days with Caleb, she knew the feeling well.

She listened through her earpiece as Caleb spoke to the young woman.

"Hugo Forrester is not the man he claims to be, Maddy," he said. "That's why Sister Eva sent me to come and get you."

"I don't understand," Maddy replied, her voice less distinct, but still clear enough for Anita to make out.

"We'll explain everything. Don't worry."

"We?"

Anita saw Caleb pointing in her direction.

"On the other side of the hill is a friend of mine, Anita. You might know her. She used to be one of the Adelphoi."

Even though she knew Maddy wouldn't be able to see her, Anita raised her hand and waved.

"Is she the one who left a few days ago?" Maddy asked with a frown.

"Yes, that's her," Caleb replied.

"Brother Giovanni was ever so angry. He said she stole something from him."

"She stole nothing, Maddy. She took some information from his computer that revealed the truth behind the Adelphoi and the Weizmann Institute. Who they really are. If we leave you here, you'll be in danger."

"But what's going to happen to me now?" Maddy asked, and Anita saw the young woman's hand go to her abdomen. "I'm pregnant."

"I know," Caleb replied, and Anita could hear the ice in his voice. "Let's get you somewhere safe first, then we'll work out what's best for you."

"Okay," Maddy said with a faint smile. Anita thought she came across as very young and trusting, and she wondered if that was one of the reasons Giovanni had chosen her for his abominable program.

Anita watched as Caleb led her to the black car parked in the courtyard. Then he reached into his pocket and pulled out a key fob. A few seconds later, the indicator for the car blinked into life. Caleb pulled open one of the rear doors and ushered Maddy into it. When he had closed the door behind her, he took a few steps away from the car.

"Anita?" he said.

"Yes?" she replied. "I'm here."

"Maddy's safe."

"I know." Anita breathed a sigh of relief. "I can hear you, remember? Through the earpiece you gave me?" She heard Caleb chuckling softly at the end of the line.

"She's very trusting," Caleb said. "All I said to her was that Sister Eva had sent me to get her, and she was like 'okay, cool'."

"What are your plans now?" Anita asked him.

"I'm going to secure the guard at the hut with some zip ties I found in the laboratory, just in case he decides to wake up," Caleb replied, "and then I'm going to go and meet the mysterious Mr. Forrester."

"What about the man in the gray suit?"

"He's taking a nap," Caleb replied with a grin that, despite her distant vantage point, she could see on his face. "Got a bit of a headache, I would expect."

"You didn't kill him, did you?"

"No, Anita, I didn't. But he did run into a door."

"Be careful, Caleb."

"Always."

She watched through the scope as Caleb turned and waved to Maddy before he turned to walk over to the hut. As he made his way across the courtyard, she saw him re-sling the weapon on his chest. He paused briefly inside the hut and then disappeared behind it.

While she waited, Anita thought about the young woman waiting in the car, Maddy. She was pregnant, and not just carrying any child. What would happen to her now?

Anita could hear rustling through the earpiece, followed by the distinctive sound of a zip tie being pulled.

"You stay there, my friend," she heard Caleb mumble, but the guard didn't reply. A moment later, she saw Caleb reappear and make his way toward the building with purpose.

105

C aleb used the guard's swipe card to let himself back into the building. Despite what the man in the gray suit had said, he proceeded as if there could be other armed men in the building, and he swept through the corridor with the Beretta in front of him. When he got to the staircase leading down, he decided to take a quick detour to see what was down there. He descended the stone steps carefully, feeling the temperature drop as he made his way down the narrow staircase. There were perhaps thirty steps, and they led to another small corridor with a thick wooden door at the end. Next to the door was what looked like a swipe card reader, but as he approached, Caleb realized it was some sort of biometric hand reader. He could see the outline of a hand on a glass screen with a flashing red dot underneath it. He shrugged and placed his hand over the glass, but nothing happened.

Leaving the door behind him, he retraced his steps and made his way back up the stairs and continued upward into the modern part of the building. He paused at the entrance to the laboratory, but couldn't discern any movement beyond the frosted glass.

"Any signs of movement, Anita?" Caleb asked as he continued down the corridor to the next set of stairs.

"Nothing," she replied, her voice crackling through his earpiece. "It won't be long before the sun moves off the windows, though. Do you want to wait for a few moments?" Caleb nodded. What she said made sense.

"Okay," he said, turning and making his way back to the laboratory. He could use the time to have a proper look round.

Inside the laboratory, it was exactly the same as when he had left it moments before. Caleb took a few moments to walk around, examining each bench as he did so. On one of them was a computer keyboard covered in some sort of plastic film with a screen above it that showed a spinning logo. He tapped the space bar on the keyboard, but was rewarded with a login box asking him for his credentials. Caleb lifted the keyboard on the off chance the username and password were on a post-it note underneath, but there was nothing.

Next to the computer was a microscope, a complicated-looking piece of equipment with a thick cable running from the back of it to the floor. It was surrounded by glass slides and other smaller pieces of equipment that he didn't recognize. On the next wall of the laboratory were a couple of machines standing next to each other. One was some sort of centrifuge, the other a glass-fronted cabinet with yet more tubes and pipettes inside. Caleb shook his head, not comprehending in the slightest what it was all for. The only thing he recognized the utility of was a filing cabinet near the door of the laboratory. He walked to it, pulling the top drawer open to see a bunch of reports in spiral bound books. Caleb pulled one of them out, but quickly realized he wouldn't be able to read them as they were in German.

Caleb closed the door to the filing cabinet and slowly spun on his heels, taking in the laboratory. He tried to imagine it full of scientists and researchers, but he struggled in the silence. It was almost as if whatever had happened in this room had been completed. There was a peculiar air of finality in the room.

"Caleb?" Anita's voice said in his earpiece. "I can just about see into the rooms on the top floor."

"What can you see?" he asked her, taking a few steps toward the door of the laboratory.

"There're two people. One of them's Hugo. He's standing at the window of an office, staring into the valley."

"Who's the other person?"

"It's a woman. I don't recognize her, though. She's just sitting at a desk." Anita paused before continuing. "It looks like she's crying, Caleb. She's got a wad of tissues in her hand."

Caleb resisted the temptation to make a comment about crocodile tears and walked through the door, leaving the empty laboratory behind him. "I'm going to head up to the top floor, Anita," he said, readjusting the Beretta so it was across his chest. He took a deep breath to ward off the heaviness that was building again in the center of his chest. "It's time for me and Hugo to talk. This all ends today."

106

Hugo looked out over the valley that sprawled below him like a scar between the mountains. He could make out people, tiny from this distance, going about their daily business. There was a farmer in a tractor towing a trailer full of feed into a field. Behind him was a group of cows, jostling against each other as they vied for a good feeding position. Hugo wondered briefly what it would be like to be that farmer, living a simple life governed mostly by the weather. But as he thought about it, he realized that a farmer's life was probably far from simple.

He turned away from the window, still deep in thought. His carefully made plans, formulated over months, years even, had unraveled spectacularly quickly. It had all been because of the actions of a single woman, a stupid woman who had taken something that wasn't hers and shared it with others. If she had kept what she had taken, as he kept what he took from others, then none of this would have happened.

Hugo sighed, feeling a sharp pain in the center of his

chest as he did so. They had been so close to achieving their goals, but he knew they still had a chance to achieve them. He still had the woman and would have her child, albeit briefly. If what Ruth had told him about the Yazidi was true, then it was just a case of adjusting their plans. But Hugo's problem was that he didn't trust the Yazidis as far as he could throw them. There was a reason so many people had tried to wipe them out over the centuries, and Kurdistan wasn't a part of the world he particularly wanted to live in. In fact, Hugo realized, the Yazidis didn't occupy any areas he wanted to live in.

His thoughts turned to Brother Giovanni. He'd trusted the man up to a point, and he'd let him down. Hugo knew that there was more to the theft of the information than Giovanni had told him, and that was what had precipitated the crisis he was now facing. There had to be a reason for someone to want to bring down the Adelphoi. It all seemed far too personal from Hugo's perspective. In his mind, it was the Adelphoi that had been the target, not the Weizmann Institute. They had just been caught in the crossfire.

Hugo walked over to his desk and used his phone to summon Ruth. He wasn't going to live in a tent in Kurdistan. There had to be another way. He had apartments in several of the major capitals of Europe and there was no reason he and Maddy couldn't stay in one of them. As he waited for his assistant, he ran through them in his mind. Paris was an option. He owned an entire townhouse in the 8th Arrondissement, a chic neighborhood defined by the broad Avenue des Champs-Élysées, which linked the iconic Arc de Triomphe and the chaotic traffic circle of Place de la Concorde. Apart from their obsession with cheese and genetic hatred of the English, the French would be better bed fellows than the Yazidi. Or there was the villa in Santa

Teresa di Gallura, a small tourist resort on the northern edge of Sardinia which had sea views to die for. Hugo nodded his head, his mind made up. Ruth would just have to be more creative.

"Yes, Mr. Forrester?" Ruth said a moment later. Hugo jumped at the sound of her voice. He'd been so caught up in his thoughts that he'd not even heard her enter the room.

"Ruth, we need to speak," Hugo said. "I'm not going to Kurdistan."

"But I've already made the arrangements," she replied, her brow furrowing.

"Then unmake them," Hugo shot back, looking at his personal assistant carefully. She looked as if she'd been crying. "We're going to Paris instead. Speak to Philip and have him plan the journey. We'll need at least a couple of fuel stops."

"Philip's not here, Hugo," Ruth replied. "You sent him away with the others."

Hugo cursed under his breath. Sending the institute employees to safety had been his idea, not hers, so he couldn't reprimand her for it.

"Then get him back here." Hugo pointed at the door, noticing his index finger was trembling. "Do it now, Ruth. Go! I don't want to see you again until the rotors are turning." Then he turned to look out of the window again, not wanting to look at his personal assistant any more. He waited until he heard the door close behind her. A few seconds later, he heard her speaking, presumably on her cell phone to the pilot.

When the door reopened a moment later, Hugo didn't turn to face Ruth. Whatever she had to say, it wouldn't be good news.

"I thought I told you I didn't want to see you again?" he

said after a few seconds, not bothering to hide the anger in his voice. Ruth didn't reply, which only angered him more. He took a deep breath, preparing to chew his assistant out for disobeying his orders. But when he turned around, it wasn't Ruth standing in the doorway.

It was a man Hugo had never seen before. That wasn't what bothered Hugo, though. It was the fact that the temperature in the room seemed to have plummeted, and the squat black machine gun that was pointing at his chest.

107

"Last call for flight BA 725 to London Heathrow," the automatic voice said through the public address system. Eva looked up from the book she was reading, the large sunglasses covering her eyes slipping down her nose as she did so. The VIP departure lounge in Geneva Airport she was sitting in was almost empty, the only other occupants a couple of businessmen in the far corner who were engrossed in conversation. "Would all remaining passengers for flight BA 725 to London Heathrow make their way to the gate immediately?"

Eva got to her feet, slipping her book into her carry-on bag. As she made her way to the gate, she glanced around nervously, expecting at any moment that armed police were going to storm the lounge to arrest her. When she reached the desk leading to the gate, Eva handed her boarding pass to the flight attendant.

"Thank you," the flight attendant said with a practiced smile, glancing down at the pass. "First class is just through the door and to the right. I hope you have a great flight with British Airways." The woman had a British accent that sounded like it was straight out of *Downton Abbey*. Eva nodded in reply as the flight attendant handed her back her boarding pass.

Inside the airplane was a hive of quiet efficiency. Another flight attendant, who could have been the previous one's sister, greeted Eva and showed her to her seat. Eva declined the offer of a complimentary glass of champagne but said yes to a glass of orange juice. She needed to keep her wits about her for the next eighteen hours or so. It was only a short hop to London, then an hour and a half layover before another British Airways flight to Miami. From there, the final stage of her journey was another short one.

Eva settled into the comfortable chair and secured her seatbelt, pushing her sunglasses back up her nose as she did so. She knew wearing them made her stand out, but she wanted to keep her face hidden as much as possible. She had even considered wearing a surgical mask after seeing several people wearing them in the airport, but the thought of having her face covered wasn't very appealing.

"Are you traveling for business or pleasure?" the flight attendant asked as she placed a frosted glass of orange juice on Eva's fold-out table. Eva smirked before replying, considering the question.

"Both, hopefully," she said, picking up the glass. The orange juice looked to be freshly pressed, and her smirk turned into a smile at the thought of the other passengers who were slumming it behind her. "One leading to the other, all being well." The flight attendant masked her confusion well at Eva's cryptic reply.

Eva sipped her orange juice slowly, keeping her eyes fixed on the door to the airplane, which was still open. At any moment, the police could arrive. It wouldn't be until they were in the air that she could finally relax. As she saw the door being secured, she let out a breath that she'd not realized she'd been holding. She was almost there.

Eva didn't think that there was anything still linking her to the Adelphoi. She was traveling under her real name, using her genuine passport and a ticket she'd bought under her own name, not Eva's. She wasn't traveling under a false identity, but her real one. Sometimes hiding in plain sight was the best option, and she'd been careful not to reveal her real name to anyone. Even Giovanni didn't know what it was.

As the flight attendant told Eva that she would need to collect her glass in the next couple of minutes, Eva felt the aircraft moving. The pilot said something about doors to automatic and cross-check before the cabin crew started their safety briefing. Eva ignored them and gazed out of the small oval window at the airport beyond, sipping her drink before the flight attendant returned for the glass. A few moments later, she felt the aircraft turning to one side before coming to a halt. Then the engines burst into life and the airplane lurched forward.

Eva smiled as the airplane accelerated down the runway. When the nose lifted into the air, her smile almost turned into a laugh.

She had made it.

108

H ugo stared at the man holding the gun, his mind working quickly. Where was Ruth?

"Who the hell are you?" he said, staring at the barrel of the weapon, which was pointing directly at his chest. He looked up to see the new arrival, who was staring at him with the darkest gray eyes he thought he'd ever seen. Hugo watched as he raised a hand to his ear.

"Sorry about that. I was getting distracted by the voices in my head. I'm going to have to get a name badge at this rate," the man replied with a smile that was far from friendly. "My name is Caleb. I'm a preacher."

"Most preachers I know don't point weapons at people," Hugo replied. "What do you want?"

"You've been hanging around with the wrong preachers, Mr. Forrester," the man called Caleb replied. Hugo was surprised at how politely he was speaking to him, given the weapon and everything. "What I want to do is to kill you, but it's your lucky day." He gestured toward a chair with the barrel of the gun. "Have a seat. We have much to discuss."

"I doubt that very much," Hugo said, but he took a seat,

anyway. As he made himself as comfortable as he could under Caleb's steely gaze, he thought through his options. He recognized the weapon Caleb was holding as belonging to his security guard, but the idiot in the gray suit should be about somewhere. Hugo's problem was he had no way of summoning him. "What did you do with Ruth?"

"If you mean the woman I was talking to a moment ago, she's now an ex-employee. I kind of fired her on your behalf. Sorry about that." Caleb paused and Hugo saw him raise a finger to his ear. When he took it away, Hugo noticed a small earpiece. That meant there were at least two of them, which made Hugo's situation worse. "She's just been seen leaving the building and heading to her car. A small Volkswagen Beetle. Sound familiar?"

"Why do you want to kill me?" Hugo said, deciding to cut straight to it.

"Because of who you are," Caleb replied, settling into another chair and resting the weapon on his knees. He was three yards away from Hugo. Even when he was younger and faster, Hugo wouldn't have been able to cover the distance between them without being shot. "And because of who you represent."

"I've never met you before," Hugo said, "so you can not understand who I am. I'm curious, though. Who exactly do you think I represent?"

"You are a believer, yes?"

"In a sense," Hugo replied, allowing himself a brief smile. "But I'm not a preacher, if that's what you mean."

"Your plan is to recreate the child of God. Why might that be?"

"There are many reasons," Hugo said. Although the media had been vague about the project, Caleb had obviously read the information that had been leaked, which linked him somehow to the woman Hugo had been seeking. "To bring about the rapture. To bring forward our destiny. But mostly to end the current situation on this God forsaken planet."

"That's an interesting turn of phrase for someone like you," Caleb said, narrowing his eyes. "You read scripture, I take it?"

"Yes, I do," Hugo said, his smile returning. He had read scripture that this man had never seen.

"But do you follow its guidance?"

"Some of it, yes."

"A man after my own heart," Caleb said with a wry grin that only lasted for a few seconds. "Why did you have Greta murdered?"

"Who is Greta?"

"Greta was a friend of mine." Caleb's face hardened as Hugo watched him. "You had her murdered, which means her blood is on your hands. Are you familiar with Matthew, chapter five?"

"I said I read scripture, not that I had memorized the entire Bible." Hugo's eyes drifted down to the weapon on Caleb's knees.

"Verse twenty-one says 'you have heard that it was said to the people long ago, you shall not murder,and anyone who murders will be subject to judgment.'" Caleb shifted the weapon a couple of inches. "It also says in Leviticus, as well as in several other books, that anyone who takes the life of a human being is to be put to death."

"You know the Bible well, Caleb," Hugo said, watching nervously as Caleb shifted the weapon again. The barrel was now only a few degrees away from pointing directly at him. "But I didn't murder this, this Greta woman. That wasn't supposed to happen."

"But it did happen, Hugo," Caleb replied with a sneer. "Why did Greta have to die?"

Hugo thought for a few seconds about the best way to answer that question. In the end, he decided to be honest, or almost honest at least.

"She wasn't supposed to die," he said, his voice soft and, hopefully, contrite. "That was never my intent. I was trying to recover something, and I didn't realize they were going to kill her to get it."

"Her blood is on your hands as much as if you'd pulled the trigger yourself. Judgement is upon you, and you have been found wanting."

To Hugo's horror, the sub-machine gun was now pointing directly at him and Caleb's index finger was tightening on the trigger.

"Do not judge," Hugo whispered, trying to keep the terror out of his voice, "or you too will be judged." To his surprise, Caleb threw back his head and laughed.

"Very good," he said, looking at Hugo intently when he had finished laughing. "Also Matthew, but chapter seven. So you do know your scripture after all."

Then Caleb pulled the trigger.

109

"Caleb?" Anita screamed as she saw Caleb through the sniper scope, raising the weapon. "Caleb? Can you hear me?"

There was no response, and she realized that he'd taken the earpiece out. A split-second later, she screamed again as she saw the floor to ceiling glass window shattering into a million pieces, the glass fragments tumbling down the side of the building to the courtyard three stories below. The sudden movement caused her to jerk away from the scope, which almost fell to the ground. When she returned her eye to the rubber eyepiece, it took her a moment to reorientate her view of the institute. Where the window had been was now a gaping hole in the building's side. She looked through it into the office beyond and saw a chair with its back to her, Hugo's white hair clearly visible. Caleb was standing a few yards further back inside the office, staring at the occupant of the chair. Anita zoomed in on his face to see a look of grim determination.

"Caleb?" she said again, more softly this time. "What have you done?" As if he'd heard her, she saw him glance away from Hugo and toward her. Then he raised his hand back to his ear and a moment after that, he spoke.

"Anita," Caleb said, his tone even and measured. "Hugo and I just needed to have a little chat about a few things."

"What have you done, Caleb?" Anita asked him. "Did you kill him?"

Caleb didn't reply, but returned his gaze to Hugo. Anita frowned, not understanding what was going on. Had Caleb shot Hugo with the bullet continuing on to shatter the window? She scanned the room through the scope, but couldn't see any blood. Why wasn't he talking to her? She was about to say something else when her attention was distracted by an unfamiliar noise in the distance somewhere. Anita took her eye away from the scope and angled her head to focus on it. It was sirens, she was sure, and from the sound of it, lots of them. The sound faded away, carried perhaps by the wind.

Anita picked up the scope and repositioned it so it was pointing in the general direction of where the noises were coming from. She put her eye back to the rubber eyepiece and started scanning the town below her, moving the scope from side to side as she had seen Caleb doing when he was looking at the institute earlier. It took her several moments, but eventually she located the source of the sirens.

Around a mile beyond the village was a convoy of cars, all with flashing blue lights on their roofs. The convoy wasn't moving quickly and, as she scanned the length of it, Anita saw why. At the rear of the group of perhaps ten vehicles, apparently struggling to keep up, were two squat vans. The navy-blue vehicles had metal mesh covering the windscreen, and she could make out the bulky armor that covered the bodywork. The vans lumbered around a corner and Anita could make out the while lettering stenciled on the side. *Einsatzkommando Cobra.* It was the Task Force Cobra, the closest thing that the Austrians had to a SWAT function. Anita had read several articles about them and their tactics, which were said to be heavy-handed and trigger-happy at best, lethal at worst.

"Caleb?" Anita said, dropping her voice to a whisper as if the approaching police units might hear her. "There's a police convoy approaching."

"How far away?" Caleb asked instantly, his voice urgent.

"A few miles. There're two tactical units from the look of it, and a whole bunch of cars." Anita kept her gaze focused on the front vehicle in the convoy. In the passenger seat of the car, she could see a dark-haired woman in a navy-blue uniform barking orders into a handheld radio. "They're moving pretty slowly, but they have to be coming here." She heard a rustling noise through her earpiece before she continued. "Where else would they be going?"

When Caleb didn't reply, Anita swiveled the scope back round to focus on the institute. "Caleb?" she said as she focused in on the hole in the building's side. "Caleb? Are you there?" But she heard nothing but silence.

Anita swore under her breath. He must have disconnected his earpiece again.

"For God's sake, Caleb," she muttered under her breath. How could she help him if he wouldn't even talk to her?

110

Caleb turned his attention to Hugo, who was sitting slumped in the chair in front of him. There was a breeze blowing in through the hole where the window had been, and he could hear birds calling to each other outside. Caleb angled his head to one side. It was, he thought, a pair of redshanks calling to each other. Caleb closed his eyes and imagined the small birds, their distinctive orange legs tucked underneath them, as they circled in the air looking for a suitable spot below them to forage for food. He smiled, envying their much simpler lives.

"What did you do that for?"

At the sound of Hugo's voice, Caleb opened his eyes to see Hugo rubbing the palms of his hands over his ears. "Damned near deafened me."

"I was going to blow your head off, Hugo," Caleb replied tersely, "but I changed my mind at the last second. I gave her my word."

"Gave who your word?" Hugo asked. "Greta?"

"No," Caleb replied, irritated at the way Hugo had asked

that question. He didn't deserve to have Greta's name on his lips. "No, it wasn't Greta."

"So what happens next, Caleb?"

"You have a choice, Hugo," Caleb said, taking a few steps toward Hugo. He knew that if he touched the man, he would be able to sense how depraved he was. "I know you worship a different entity. I know you follow the so-called teachings of Methuselah and what people have said was written in his book. And I know you must be stopped."

To Caleb's surprise, a slow smile was spreading over Hugo's face.

"What people have said was written?" Hugo said, starting to laugh. "And what would you know of that, preacher?"

"I know what I have read," Caleb replied. "About the second coming of the child of God. About the child's murder, and the thousand years of darkness that will apparently follow."

"Apparently?" Hugo said, his laugh deepening. "Have you read the *Apocalypse of Methuselah*?"

"Of course not." Caleb frowned. "No one has."

"Would you like to?" Hugo replied as Caleb felt the temperature in the room plummet. "I have it downstairs. I am a keeper of such things."

"You have the actual book of Methuselah? The apocalypse apocrypha?" Caleb looked at Hugo, wanting nothing more than to put a bullet in his brain.

"Among many other fine treasures, yes." Hugo was still smiling, but there was no warmth in his face. On the contrary, all Caleb could feel was evil emanating from him. "They're all here, in the basement."

"The Spear of Destiny?" Caleb shivered as he saw Hugo nodding his head. "What else?"

He saw Hugo steepling his hands in his lap as he considered the question.

"An early draft of Paradise Lost, complete with Milton's hand-written notes in the margins," he said. "Alistair Crowley's dress uniform, complete with his medals. A chalice used by Anton LaVey in his first ever Black Mass. And of course, the Spear of Destiny, complete with the DNA of Jesus himself."

It was Caleb's turn to laugh. Paradise Lost was a poem about the allure of Satan, written in the seventeenth century. It had long been held in high regard by those who worshipped the darkness. But that wasn't why Caleb was laughing.

"John Milton was blind," he said, watching Hugo carefully. "The poem was dictated."

"I said an early draft," Hugo replied with a smile. "Written before God made him blind to silence him. I have quite the collection of such things, but probably not of that much interest to someone like you. All procured quite illegally, of course, but at least they're in the hands of someone who truly appreciates their qualities."

"Enough talking, Hugo," Caleb said, raising a hand to silence the man. He needed a moment to think about the most appropriate course of action to take. What Hugo had just told him had changed things if he was telling the truth. Hugo was describing a collection of items that epitomized evil, except for the spear. But that was an item that many had died for and, apart from its provenance, Caleb didn't think the world would miss it too much.

"So, what is this choice?" Hugo asked a moment later.

Caleb looked at him, his alternative course of action decided.

"You can live, or you can die," he said in a monotone.

"You can leave here, in which case the police will arrest you. They are on their way as we speak. Or you can stay here, and you can die."

"How, exactly?" Hugo asked, a trace of mirth in his voice. "I have no fear of death."

"On the wicked he will rain fiery coals and burning sulfur; a scorching wind will be their lot," Caleb replied. "It's from Psalm six, and it's what I'm bringing down upon you."

"You've been watching the news too much," Hugo said, his face creasing into a smile. "We're miles away from Mount Vesuvius."

"If the Mountain won't go to Mohammed, then Mohammed must come to the Mountain," Caleb replied, mirroring Hugo's smile. "If I may borrow a phrase from my Muslim brothers."

"How very pluralistic of you." Hugo's smile started to slip.

Caleb took another step toward Hugo, his face hardening as he did so.

"As I said, you can live or you can die," Caleb said. "But for the sake of everything that's good in the world, I hope you choose the latter."

Giovanni rested his head back on the fresh pillowcase and sighed as he watched the nurse fussing around him. She was in her mid-twenties, wearing a set of unflattering mauve scrubs with matching Crocs and—at least in Giovanni's imagination—would be utterly filthy in bed. She would take the concept of a bed bath to the next level, but when he had been washed earlier, it hadn't been by her but by a muscular male nurse called Hans.

"You have some visitors, Brother Giovanni," the nurse said in heavily accented English, which only added to her allure. A few seconds later, the door to his hospital room opened and two men entered. One of them was familiar to him, the other not. The first man who entered was the doctor who had been treating him, a sour medic called Doctor Werner Klüber. The man with him was wearing a pale blue suit, shirt and hideously patterned tie and, bravely, light red shoes. Giovanni looked at the new arrival with curiosity as the nurse finished her duties and left the room.

"Giovanni," Doctor Werner said. "How are you feeling?" Unlike the nurse, he had barely a trace of an accent.

"Like I've been run over by a train," Giovanni replied. Neither of his visitors' expressions changed. "What's going on?"

"I have the results of your MRI scan," Doctor Werner said as his brow creased into a frown that instantly concerned Giovanni. "It's not good news, I'm afraid." He paused for a few seconds before continuing, not looking at Giovanni as he did so. "You have an extensive spinal cord injury in your lower back. The lumbar region, to be exact. It's worse than I realized when I examined you in the emergency room."

"How much worse?" Giovanni asked, trying to concentrate on the doctor's words but becoming distracted by the second man examining his cuticles. Who was he? Giovanni thought he could be some sort of specialist, but he didn't look like a doctor.

"The spinal cord has been completely transected by a bony fragment," Doctor Werner said in a low voice. "It is, I believe the word is, unrepairable." A painful silence filled the room as Giovanni took the information in.

"What does that mean?" he asked a moment later.

"We'll need to do some more tests, but it's unlikely, if not impossible, that you'll ever walk again. You may also have other issues such as problems with continence, sexual function, that sort of thing."

Giovanni stared at the man, barely able to comprehend what he had just said. He was never going to walk again? And what were the issues he was talking about?

"Issues?" Giovanni said as he grasped the sheet covering him. "What sort of issues?"

"The likelihood is you'll be doubly incontinent." Doctor

Werner glanced at him but quickly looked away. "And impotent." The next silence in the room wasn't painful. It was agonizing. "I'll come back later when you've thought about this news. I expect you'll have many questions."

With a look of relief on his face, Doctor Werner turned to leave, his white coat billowing behind him. The second man turned his attention from his fingernails to Giovanni and put his hand in his pocket as he introduced himself. To Giovanni's surprise, he spoke with an American accent.

"My name is Jonathan Barnes," he said as he pulled out a leather wallet from his pocket. Giovanni looked at it as he flipped it open to reveal a gold shield. "Special Agent Jonathan Barnes from the FBI section based in Rome. May I call you Thomas Gavazzi?"

"What the hell?" Giovanni said. "Why is the FBI here?"

"It's just a courtesy call," Special Agent Barnes replied. "To introduce ourselves. The Italian authorities are very interested in you, Mr. Gavazzi. Multiple counts of fraud, embezzlement, sexual assault. It's likely you'll be spending a long time in Italy before we're able to extradite you. But I hear the penitentiaries here are fairly comfortable compared to what's waiting for you back home."

"I want a lawyer," Giovanni said, trying in vain to inject some authority into his voice. "I'm due to be transferred to a private clinic later. Have the lawyer visit me when I get there." He waved a hand to dismiss the special agent, but this just made the man smile.

"Sure, sure," Special Agent Barnes said. "But you'll be staying here for the time being. I would post a policeman outside your room, but it's not as if you can run away, is it? Then you'll be transferred to a prison hospital wing." The FBI agent had a faint smile on his face. "You're not going to be able to afford a private clinic."

"I have plenty of funds," Giovanni replied. "I've already given the details of my bank account to the hospital administrators here."

"Are you sure you have plenty of funds?" the agent asked. "Only we can't find them, and we've been looking pretty hard."

"This is nonsense," Giovanni said. He had plenty of money, and even considered offering some to this man to make him go away before dismissing the idea.

"You have some powerful enemies, it would seem," Special Agent Barnes replied. "Enemies who are quite keen to ensure you remain incarcerated while due process is followed."

"What are you talking about, powerful enemies? That's nonsense. I don't have any enemies."

"You have at least one with plenty of clout. Do you know Senator Patrick Williamson?"

"No, I've never heard of him."

"He's a powerful senator who's widely thought of having a good chance of being the next occupant of the Oval Office. A very influential man who really doesn't like you."

"Why?" Giovanni protested. "What have I ever done to him?"

"It's not what you've done to him," Special Agent Barnes replied. "It's more what you've done to his daughter." The FBI agent fixed Giovanni with a look that he really didn't like. It was somewhere between contempt and hatred. "She's given us a very convincing account of how you forced her to give you oral sex under false pretenses, and her father's most unhappy about it. I have other agents getting statements from the rest of the young women who you've abused. It may take them a while as there're plenty of them who've come forward. I hope you like prison food, Mr. Gavazzi. You're going to be eating it for some time."

"This is nonsense," Giovanni said with much less conviction than a moment before.

"I can quote you on that, can I?" Special Agent Barnes said. "The next time I speak to Bella Williamson?"

112

Even though she knew Caleb had turned his ear piece off, Anita swore at him several times as she watched him talking to Hugo who, to her relief, appeared to be unharmed. She tried to zoom in on Caleb's mouth but wasn't able to make out anything he was saying. He looked furious, though, and he gestured toward the older man with the weapon several times. Anita held her breath every time he did this, concerned that Caleb would shoot Hugo, but a few short seconds later, she saw Caleb turn and leave the room. Anita watched as Hugo got to his feet and walked toward the window, peering down at the courtyard below.

"How much time do I have?" Caleb asked her a moment later, his voice crackling in her earpiece.

"Nice of you to join me," Anita replied frostily. She moved the scope away from Hugo and to the area where she'd seen the convoy. It took her a few seconds to locate the vehicles, which were now winding their way through the village streets. "They're in the village, so a few minutes at best. There's only one road to the institute, though. Once they're on that, you won't be able to get away."

"There's a dirt road about half a mile from the gate. It'll be on my left as I'm coming down the main road," he replied, his voice fading in and out a couple of times. "I can duck into that, even if it's only to hide while they pass by."

Anita located the end of the road and worked her way along it. Sure enough, Caleb was right. There was a narrow dirt road, just as he had said. She followed its route, using the scope to see it led to a small clearing where there was a stack of logs piled up against each other.

"Yes, I have it," Anita said. "It leads to a clearing. Some sort of logging area." Caleb said something, but Anita couldn't make out what he said. "You're breaking up, Caleb." She waited and listened, not able to do anything else. There was the occasional rustle through the earpiece, but she didn't hear him speaking at all. "Hurry, Caleb," Anita whispered as she returned her attention to the convoy which was now leaving the village. Caleb didn't have long at all.

Anita waited for what seemed like ages but was in reality only a few moments. Then she saw the door to the institute open and Caleb came running out with a bunch of files in his hands. He sprinted to the car and threw them into the trunk before running back to the door.

"Caleb?" Anita said, her voice a mixture of frustration and annoyance. The convoy had increased its speed, having left the village and wasn't far from the turnoff to the institute. "What the hell are you doing?"

"Keeping my word," Caleb replied as he disappeared through the door. When he returned a moment later, he was dragging a man behind him. Anita recognized him as one of the men who had been chasing her and had, in all probability, murdered Greta. Even if it hadn't been he who had pulled the trigger, he was just as responsible in Anita's opinion. She watched as Caleb dragged the man unceremoniously across the courtyard, his zip-tied legs leaving dark tracks in the gravel. Caleb pulled him behind the hut and threw him to the ground. For a moment, it looked as if Caleb was about to kick the man, which wouldn't have bothered Anita in the slightest, but he didn't.

"You need to hurry, Caleb," Anita said, switching her view to the road where the convoy was just slowing down to enter the turnoff leading to the institute. When she looked back at the courtyard, she saw Caleb opening the driver's door to the large black car and getting in. What he said next made her laugh out loud, despite the circumstances.

"Maddy?" Caleb said. "Can you drive a stick shift?"

113

Eva looked down at her phone, waiting for the Wi-Fi screen to refresh. Above her head, there was a gentle chime followed by the sound of her fellow passengers undoing their seatbelts. At the same time, the air stewards bustled into life almost as one and Eva heard the chink of glasses from the galley at the rear of the first-class compartment.

When the text *BAWi-Fi* appeared on her phone, Eva tapped it and, after a few seconds, started entering her information to connect to the internet. As she did so, she marveled at the fact that you could now get connected to the internet, even when cruising at whatever altitude they were at. She glanced out of the window briefly at the mountains below, some of which still had white peaks despite the time of year.

The first thing she did when her phone connected was to check the secure e-mail account she had set up as part of her departure strategy. There were three e-mails waiting for her. She recognized that one of them was an auto-response to the hotel booking she had made for this trip. When she opened it up to see confirmation from the Kimpton Hotel and Spa for her booking of the Presidential Suite, the most expensive suite in the most luxurious hotel in the Cayman Islands. she couldn't help but smile at the photographs. They showed the bright white sand contrasting against the azure sea only yards from the hotel and were full of smiling, beautiful people enjoying the Caribbean lifestyle. Eva closed her eyes for a few seconds and imagined the feel of the fine sand between her toes. She only had the suite for a week, but the second e-mail from a high end real estate agent had a schedule of viewings lined up for apartments and houses across George Town during that week.

The third e-mail, and the one which she was most excited to read, was from a man called Connor Henderson. It included a photograph of him, showing him to be a smug-looking young man in a sharp suit standing in front of a row of luxury yachts. He was a so-called wealth management specialist whose expertise lay in tax reduction, smart investments and, most importantly, global citizenship. The e-mail confirmed that the accounts she had set up in the Cayman Islands months ago were all of good standing and now contained more than enough money to start the citizenship process.

When Eva had entered the code to start the process of wiping the computer network at the Adelphoi, it had also started a piece of software she had written and refined over many years. The code started a series of micro-transactions that took debits from the Adelphoi's accounts, all small enough to be almost unnoticeable. The power lay in the number of them. Each transaction started a new one, and the funds in the accounts decreased tiny amount by tiny amount almost like the individual sands on the beach she was so looking forward to walking along being moved by the waves. The money bounced, a few dollars at a time, from account to account and country to country, via shell companies that were closed and erased after the last transaction. The money moved along a complicated and untraceable journey that ended up in one place. One of her bank accounts in the Cayman Islands, to which only she had access.

The best part of the plan, which Eva had nicknamed the kaleidoscope, was that it was all one hundred percent legitimate and legal. Eva started laughing when she thought about Giovanni's likely reaction to finding out he'd been so completely and utterly fleeced. Even if he reported the procurement—Eva much preferred that term to theft—to the authorities, it would take an infinite number of forensic accountants to trace the funds and they would have more chance of writing the complete works of William Shakespeare by accident.

"Would you like to see the lunch menu?" a male voice said. Eva looked up to see a man wearing immaculately pressed full chef's whites standing next to her. He had a crew cut hairstyle with small patches of gray by his ears and an almost seductive smile on his face.

"Thank you," Eva replied as she took the menu he was offering her from his hand. She'd not been expecting a meal on the flight as it was only a short one, but then again, this was British Airways she was flying on and she guessed they had better standards than most airlines. "What would you recommend?"

"It depends how adventurous you're feeling?" the chef replied. His smile was, in Eva's opinion, definitely seductive, as was his British accent. She did her best to return the smile as she handed the menu back to him.

"Why don't you surprise me with something adventurous?" she said. "Life's too short for anything mundane."

"Isn't it just," the chef replied. "Are you stopping in London?"

"Not this time," Eva said."But I'll be traveling a lot in the next few months, so can always return to England if there's something I want there." She watched as the chef's smile broadened and wondered if the man practiced this routine on all the solo female passengers he spoke to. Eva wasn't bothered if he did. After all, practice makes perfect and if he was a high-class chef for an airline, he must be good with his hands.

"I'll leave you my card with your meal," the chef said. "Let me know if you visit and maybe I could show you some restaurants there?"

"I'd like that very much," Eva replied, enjoying the flirtatious encounter. There was something very appealing about strangers, especially ones that were as easy on the eye as this one.

She settled back into her seat, wondering what the chef was going to cook for her, and smiled with contentment. Good food was something she was going to have to get used to in her new life.

114

Caleb tried to get Maddy to move as quickly as she could as she got behind the wheel of the car. She was looking around in admiration at the plush interior of the car's cabin, her eyes widening as she took in the decoration.

"Maddy," he said a few seconds later as he placed the key he had taken from the guard on a tray in the middle of the car next to the gear stick. "We need to go. Now."

"Okay," she replied as she started the car with a press of the start button. The car rumbled into life, its engine deep and sonorous. "Wow, can you feel that?"

"Maddy, please, can we go?" Caleb replied, glancing in the mirror at the building behind them. "We don't have long." He raised his hand and pressed a button on the other key fob he had taken from the guard's hut. In front of them, the gate whirred into life and started to open.

Maddy put the Bentley into first gear and moved away slowly. Caleb looked again in the mirror, getting more concerned as the seconds ticked away. He didn't know how long they had, either until the convoy approaching reached them or until the events he had set in motion back at the institute reached their conclusion. To his relief, there was no sign of Hugo, which meant he must have decided to stay where he was. Caleb had a moment of uncertainty, wondering if he'd made his intentions clear enough for Hugo to make an informed decision about his fate, but he dismissed it straight away. He knew he had been clear enough. If Hugo thought Caleb had been speaking metaphorically, that was his problem, not Caleb's.

"Maddy, seriously, just drive it like you stole it," Caleb said, trying to inflect as much urgency into his voice as he could. To his relief, she whooped and put her foot down, sending a spray of gravel up into the air behind them as the wheels of the luxury car struggled for purchase in the courtyard.

"Yes, sir!" Maddy replied with a broad smile on her face as the car leaped into life. "Have you seen The Italian Job? The remake with Mark Wahlberg?" Maddy looked across at Caleb as she asked this, and the car narrowly avoided clipping the gate as they sped through it.

"No," Caleb replied through gritted teeth as he looked at the road in front of them. The turn off they needed was a few hundred yards away, but they would be there in no time. The engine roared briefly as Maddy shifted into second gear, prompting another spray of gravel as the car accelerated.

"Charlize Theron is awesome in it," Maddy said, looking again at Caleb. "She had to do a load of high-speed car training for the film, and she made Mark Wahlberg throw up."

"There's a turnoff coming up on the left," Caleb said, trying to redirect Maddy's attention to the road in front of them. "It leads to a dirt road that we need to take."

"She was doing a bunch of three-sixties and he made her pull over so he could hurl," Maddy replied as the car veered toward the verge briefly before she corrected it. Behind them, the institute disappeared from the rear-view mirror as Maddy steered the car round a bend, the rear end sliding out as she did so.

"We can't miss the turnoff, Maddy," Caleb said, his hand slipping to his seat belt to ensure it was properly secured. They were in third gear now and moving at speed. He looked at Maddy to see her eyes were fixed on the road ahead.

"I don't see it," she said with a frown as she pressed the accelerator even further down.

"It's coming up soon." Caleb replied, trying to work out how far away the turn off was. "You might want to ease up a bit?"

"I thought you said drive it like I stole it?" Maddy said, glancing back at him with a grin.

Caleb's eyes were fixed on the road ahead. He was looking for one of two things. The first was the turnoff, the second was the appearance of the police convoy. Suddenly, less than fifty yards in front of them, he saw a dark opening in the trees to their left.

"There!" he shouted, pointing at the opening. "That's the turnoff!"

To his surprise, Maddy pushed the accelerator down even more. When she next spoke, she was speaking in a poor British accent.

"You were only supposed to blow the bloody doors off!"

Then her foot jammed down on the clutch as she grabbed the handbrake with her right hand and pulled the steering wheel to the left in a decisive move that started the car sliding on the road. Caleb's hand flashed up to grab the handle above the passenger door as a vision of Giovanni's car rolling over and over came into his mind.

They were heading straight for the trees at the side of the road. Caleb closed his eyes and prepared for the inevitable impact.

nita tracked the black car through the scope, realizing that the convoy was about to round a bend that would put them on a direct collision course with the car. It looked as if the car Caleb and Maddy were in was traveling way too fast to make the turn when suddenly, the rear end spun out.

"You go, girl," Anita muttered as she watched the car execute a perfect handbrake turn. The rear end of the car wobbled a couple of times as it made the turn but Maddy seemed to have it under control and, a split second before the lead car of the convoy made the turn, the Bentley flew into the dirt road and disappeared from sight. By the time the convoy reached the turnoff, the black car was nowhere to be seen, but it had been a close shave.

Anita laughed as she turned her attention back to the institute. She could see no movement at the building and Hugo was still standing where the window had been. He appeared to be watching the approaching convoy, and she wondered what was going through his head. He must surely realize that it was all over?

What happened next made Anita gasp with surprise. It started at the base of the building. First, the door Caleb had used to enter the institute burst open, flying off its hinges and cartwheeling across the now empty courtyard. A jet of flame shot out of the opening as the windows on the bottom story exploded, emitting similar flames. A few milliseconds after that, the windows of the next floor up did the same thing, and then the explosion reached Hugo's floor. Her jaw dropped as she saw him disappear behind a wall of flame.

It took perhaps two or three seconds for the muffled crump of the explosion to reach Anita's position. By the time it rolled across her, thick black smoke was billowing from every shattered window in the institute, including the one Hugo had been standing at. She watched as the convoy approached the blazing building, imagining the confusion among the police officers in it. Anita wondered if the woman who'd appeared to be leading the convoy was now on her radio, summoning every fire truck in the vicinity.

The vehicles in the convoy pulled into the courtyard, avoiding the flaming debris that littered the ground, and doors opened as the police officers got out. Anita saw them gathering in small groups, watching the flames that were pouring out of what had been the Weizmann Institute. None of them made any effort to enter the building to search for survivors, and Anita wondered just how fierce the blaze was at ground zero.

"Anita?" Caleb said in her earpiece a few moments later. "Can you hear me?"

"Loud and clear," Anita replied, watching as the police officers started moving their vehicles back out of the court-yard and onto the road leading to the institute. There had been several smaller explosions as she had been watching, none on the level of the original one, but they were enough to throw more debris down onto the courtyard. "I'm watching the fireworks." There was a silence on the other end of the line. "I'm guessing you had something to do with that?"

"It's heavier than air," Caleb replied a few seconds later.

"What is?"

"Propane gas. It sinks to the lowest level, in this case the storeroom with Hugo's artifacts. Then it would have filled the building from the bottom to the top until it reached a source of ignition."

"Which was what?" Anita asked, suppressing a grin.

"I might have left a bunsen burner on in the lab," Caleb replied. "After I'd knocked the taps on the gas cylinders by accident. Who knew science could be so destructive?"

"And Hugo?"

"He had a choice," Caleb said. Anita could hear the way his voice hardened as he spoke. "I gave him a clear warning and the option to leave. I'm guessing he didn't?"

Anita closed her eyes and remembered the way Hugo had been engulfed by the fireball caused by the explosion. It could have been her imagination, but was there a look of resignation, serenity even, on his face as the flames had claimed him.

"No, Caleb," Anita replied with a sigh. "No, he didn't."

Caleb said nothing.

116

ONE WEEK LATER

Caleb sat outside the monastery, enjoying the warmth of the setting sun on his face. He smoothed the material of his robe, easing out a crease, and watched as the abbot made his way toward him. The courtyard was almost empty, with the majority of the monks having made their way into the church for evening prayers. When the abbot reached him, Caleb got to his feet and brought himself to an approximation of attention.

"Brother Caleb," the abbot said with a warm smile. "There's no need for that, not now."

"Old habits die hard," Caleb replied, returning his smile.

"I understand from Anita that you're leaving soon. I just wanted to say goodbye."

"I would have come and said farewell before leaving. Is she okay?"

"Yes, a little sad, but she understands. I will counsel her

if she requires it, but I doubt she will. The world would be much richer with more people like her in it." Caleb looked at the abbot who was still smiling. "Anita's even been in touch with her parents. I sense some form of reconciliation is on the cards."

"That's great news, but I will miss her," Caleb replied with a tinge of sadness. He liked Anita, but there was no place for him in her life. "And Maddy? Have you told her of the letter?"

A couple of days before, the abbot had received a letter with a stamp from the Cayman Islands, a small archipelago in the Caribbean, on it. It had been unsigned, but it was clear to them all just who it was from. The text of the letter was seeking forgiveness, explaining that the procedure to artificially inseminate Maddy had not gone ahead. Eva had persuaded the doctor to just sedate Maddy and then let her sleep the sedation off. When the abbot had shown Caleb the letter, they had both agreed that forgiveness was unnecessary and not theirs to give.

"No, I haven't," the abbot replied. "All will be well in the world in its own time, and Anita has said she will talk with Maddy about it before they both return to the United States. She's taken Maddy into the village to go to the pharmacy, so perhaps nature has already taken its course." He paused for a moment before continuing. "Where are you going to go?"

Caleb just smiled and raised his hand to point at the setting sun. "That way, I think."

"Very well. Thank you, Brother Caleb. Thank you for everything."

"There is nothing to thank me for," Caleb replied. "Will you return the Holy Lance to the Vatican?" Caleb was refer-ring to the blackened piece of metal, any DNA on it long since burned away, that had been retrieved from the remains of the Weizmann Institute by a fire marshal who was the brother of one of the monks at the monastery. It was now hidden in a vault beneath the monastery, its presence known only to a handful of people.

"Not for the moment," the abbot replied. "They've not done a very good job of looking after it for the last couple of thousand years, have they?"

Caleb didn't reply, but just smiled in response. "I guess not."

The abbot held out a hand for Caleb to shake. As he did so, the older man pulled Caleb into a hug, watched by a couple of bemused monks hurrying to the church.

"You'll travel safely, you'll neither tire nor trip," the abbot said. "Because God will be right there with you."

"He'll keep me safe and sound," Caleb replied with a smile as he slung his cloth bag onto his shoulder. "Proverbs, chapter three, verse twenty-six."

And with that, Caleb started walking.

Made in the USA
Las Vegas, NV
14 April 2025

20973007R00282